ON THE EDGE

THERESA SANTY

Theresa Santy

![signature]

BREATH OF FRESH AIR PRESS

On the Edge

Copyright © 2016 Theresa Santy
Published by Breath of Fresh Air Press

PO Box 12, St Clair NSW 2759
Australia
www.breathoffreshairpress.com.au

ISBN: 978-1-922135-36-0 (paperback)

National Library of Australia
Cataloguing-in-Publication Entry

Creator: Santy, Theresa, author.
Title: On the Edge / Theresa Santy.
ISBN: 9781922135360 (paperback)
Subjects: Women runners—Fiction.
Self-perception in women—Fiction.
Self-actualization (Psychology) in women—Fiction
Dewey Number: A823.4

Cover Photography: Pickrel Art & Photography, USA.
Cover Design: TLC Graphics, USA.

For all those who struggled to make it out of childhood alive
only to find that adulthood wasn't much easier.

For I am convinced that neither death nor life,
neither angels nor demons,
neither the present nor the future, nor any powers,
neither height nor depth, nor anything else in all creation,
will be able to separate us from the love of God
that is in Christ Jesus our Lord.
Romans 8:38-39

CHAPTER I

NEW YEAR'S EVE

THE OCEAN SURFACE flickers in the fading sunlight, and I glare back. The deep blue sea can taunt all it wants, but I won't walk in. I'll cut my own feet off before that happens. Go ahead, twinkle until you evaporate, you massive body of water. And keep dreaming because you will not lure me in. Not on New Year's Eve. That would make me a drama queen.

I turn my back to the water and trudge toward the crowd. This refrigerated playground is the best place to ring in the New Year, right? So why do we seem to be the only ones within miles of lifeguard tower 24? Are we the only ones who can bear the cold?

Got that right. We're true Southern Californians, for crying out loud. Mere cloud cover can't stop us from what we want to do. I mean, look at us, wearing shorts and flip-flops like it's mid-August or something.

We don't mind the chill. The real issue is whether we'll each find someone decent to cuddle up with by midnight. I'm not even fussy about the *decent* part. All I need is someone who'll laugh at my jokes and give me a reason to be here. Is that too much to ask?

Ahh, my dear friend Alana Pheasant. She tosses back her drink and continues her story-in-progress. What is that, her fifth appletini? She's a dude magnet, drawing all these men in like flies with her drunken performance. Hand gestures, exaggerated facial expressions. She's a staggering scrapbook, re-enacting our most embarrassing moments of the year.

Does she have any idea how comic she looks, that one eye remaining a slit when she widens the other one for emphasis? Should I tell her she looks like Popeye with that swelling welt?

Nah. Let her carry on. Everyone's soaking it up—laughing so hard, even the pelicans join in. Or is that barking coming from the skinny guy with freckles?

Alana pauses to chug her drink. Finally, her audience can take in a recovering breath. She tosses the bottle into a recycle bin and then turns toward me, slowly, like an automaton, her flaming red curls thrashing in the wind. I cross my arms and jam frozen toes into the sand. My smile fades. Please, dear universe, let someone else become her next mark.

"You will be spared, *ma chérie.*" Her lips curve up into that trademark devilish smile. She plows through her next martini, her fifth or sixth, and then addresses the crowd. "Kristen's disastrous year-in-review is more pathetic than amusing. So we'll let it lie."

No one laughs. Most walk away. I'd walk away from it, too — from last year, the year before, and all the years before that — if only I could. It's not all my fault. Not last year's failures, anyway. I blame Delila for those, even though she always tries to play it off as if she's just an innocent bystander.

Laughter erupts from near the three-legged food table propped up against a wooden fence. There goes the rest of the male herd, leaving Alana and me behind.

"Whatever. I get it. I mean, compared to laughter and snacks, reality bites. But this puts a snag in my man hunt."

"Just as well," laughs Alana. "My throat hurts from talking."

She grabs another drink from the cooler, presses the bottle against her welt, and bores into me with her good eye.

"What? Is it my fault I have fierce reflexes? You shouldn't have snuck up on me from behind. Come on, you saw how cramped that volleyball court was, and on a slant, too. I was having enough trouble concentrating on the game without worrying about your face getting in the way of my elbow. If it makes you feel any better, I've got a bruise, too." I lift my arm high enough for her to clearly see my injury.

"It's fine," she snaps, but her neck vein throbs. A clear indication she's annoyed.

I remove my sunglasses and buff a salty smear off the lenses. I bet she's angrier about losing the jungle ball tournament than her injury, especially since she spent most of the day bragging about her high school volleyball achievements. At least the alcohol will keep her pain at bay until morning.

"What about him?" She lifts her chin toward the skinny guy with freckles.

"Not in this life." I sip my drink and squint. "On second thought, he's not that bad. He could be my fallback if no one else comes through. He's probably the nicest one here."

"Nice, as in weak and spineless? I hope you're right, because he's my monitor."

"Say what?"

"Beach closes at ten and I didn't want a New York New Year's Eve, so I talked to Uncle Max, who knows the guy who could give me special approval. He said we can stay as late as we want, as long as we have a monitor. Enter nerdy guy. Chuck."

"Won't he report us for all this alcohol?"

"No way. He's had as much as me." She glances at her white sports watch. "It's 4:50. Gotta get that bonfire going before it's completely dark."

She jogs away while I stare at the blood-orange sunset. The fireball melts, melts, melts into the sea. I watch a few minutes longer until night falls and strings of lights pop up along the Palos Verdes Peninsula.

Did it suddenly get colder? And foggier? Half the crowd heads for the parking lot. Weaklings. The rest of us throw on sweats and furry boots and settle into our favorite spots. Camp lantern dancers mingle off to the side, jumping and writhing about, positioning themselves for opportunity. They never stop moving, as if they can't get enough music or dance, determined to try until their last breath. Definitely not *my* natural habitat. I wouldn't fit in with the stragglers, either. There they go, already starting to wander off in blanket-wrapped twos. Even Chuck has paired off with someone. He was supposed to be my failsafe. Now what am I going to do if I find myself alone at the end of the night?

Whatever.

I join the fire lovers surrounding the cemented ring and lean hard toward the scavenged wood set ablaze. Where else can I contemplate life and self while socializing and spying on other cliques? *This* is the central nervous system of the entire party. I wouldn't dream of being anywhere else.

I polish off my appletini and admire the spitting remains of my dilapidated art desk. Just look at how it glows in those giant flames. It's Alana's masterpiece, her most brazen blaze yet.

"It's a White Man fire." Andrue crosses his arms.

"Is that supposed to be a Native American voice?" Feigning shock, Alana slaps her hand to her chest. "You saying I'm wasteful, babe? I thought you liked big fires."

How adorable are they, cuddling in a loveseat camp chair? Look at them holding on to each other as if true love exists. I scan around the circle, faces of friends, acquaintances, my vet technician friend Daz, and Nate, the most talented coffee foam artist I know. If only Jenna and Danielle were here, too. They could complete nearly any gathering. I should say something about them. Something about how they would be here if not for that horrific night last January. If only Alana wasn't dominating circle time.

". . . and of course, the promotion came with a substantial raise, bigger than the last one, which means . . ."

Yeah, we get it. Now you can purchase more water toys to stuff into your triple car garage. We're all thrilled to death for you.

Andrue taps his foot in the sand. Then he jumps up and peels off toward the camp lantern dancers, spraying Alana with his wake.

"There he goes," I laugh.

Andrue Delucchi sure loves to dance with women, gyrating so close to them that they leave the dance floor wearing his musky perfume. He's a charismatic Greek-Persian-Italian mix with striking dark eyes and a body carved to perfection. Add to that his luxurious ash-brown hair, and it's no surprise he never has trouble finding a dance partner or four.

"It's all good," mutters Alana, brushing the sand off her lap. "Andrue's like an actor, and when he's on the dance floor, he's role-playing."

Her voice fades, leaving the rest of us to our own thoughts, the blasting mini speakers, and the crashing waves. How did Andrue change from the reflective gentleman Alana fell in love with to the man who bump-grind-dances with one anonymous female after the other?

Timberlake's *SexyBack* comes on next. Alana's uninjured eye opens to a full circle, her misty gray iris glowing in the firelight. One of her favorite oldies.

I raise my brow. "Are you ready?"

"Yea-uh!"

We join the camp lantern freaks, blend in, and dance like we're trying to bring sexy back. Does Andrue have any idea we're teasing him, working our hips the way we are? He tries to break into our groove and we burst out laughing. We block him and he laughs, too. He distracts himself with another dancer for a few seconds and then the cycle repeats.

Several songs pass, and I'm dying of thirst. I pull an elastic band out of my pocket and fasten my sweaty hair into a knot. On the way to the cooler, I pass the snack table and tear into a bag of Flamin' Hot Cheetos. Wait, what's that? Two silhouettes stepping onto the sand. New arrivals. Could there be hope for me after all? The shadows approach the bonfire circle.

Wow, these Cheetos are unusually spicy. My lips and throat are hotter than — oh, *no*. No, no, no. Is that Tommy? Can't be. He'd have to be an idiot to show up tonight. I step closer. Yep. He's an idiot.

Everybody says Tommy Foxx is one of the hottest up-and-rising names in L.A. Blah, blah, blah. I'm sick of hearing all the praise he gets for his outdoor living space designs. They're so expensive; they'd make a starving African child cough up his last drop of bile. How can Tommy sleep at night knowing that the money he makes off one client could feed a small nation? If only I never worked that Beverly Hills interior design job while he and his all-star crew worked outside. Then Tommy and I might never have hooked up.

If only I'd kept myself from getting sucked into his world. But he was so easy on the eyes. I never had a chance. Before I could blink twice, we were spending lunch breaks together, sitting atop piles of imported stone. Then we were spending dinners together, and then long weekends transported to faraway places by private jet. Then *poof!* He announced we were done. Said I wasn't up to his standards because I lost that contest to win my own Home and Garden show. Was it my fault Stephanie had bigger breasts and a lot more voting friends than I did?

What an ego Tommy must have to show up tonight. Give me a break. Look at him standing so wide, his chest swollen with hot air. And that shadow standing next to him. I'd recognize Barbra's purchased curves anywhere. She was evasive at the company Christmas party. That was the night Tommy disappeared for an hour to — ohh. That's why Tommy cut me loose. He was already with her.

He slides his arm around Barbra's calorie-starved waist and leans in for a kiss.

My fists clench, and I jog to the cooler. Who's the half-brain who put the drinks a mile away from the snacks? I yank out a bottled martini and run across the sand.

Alana catches my arm as I pass. "You okay? Jerk has nerve coming here."

Andrue jogs over. "Forget him, Kristen. Whatever makes Tommy so dense, he's got it nailed. I mean it, there's nothing going on between his ears." He swings his fists at the air. "You want me to go over there?"

"Down, tiger," says Alana, still gripping my arm.

"Let go," I growl.

She loosens her grip and I run from the party, along the shore and around the bend, my boots clomping through sand as I struggle to catch my breath. I run until my cheeks are raw from cold and my ankle aches like mad. Guess that old injury is going to punish me forever.

I stop and twist open the bottle, fizz oozing everywhere. Carbonated martini. What a stupid idea. What is this, my sixth? Eighth? I pace along the wet sand, my eyes flashing to the open water where the surface is blackest. That's the spot where the ocean floor drops. I'm sure of it. Waves rise and crash, the sound sharp and soothing, like punching a stucco wall but without the inconvenience of pain. The salty fog clings to my clothes, hair, and skin, and I smell like a wood chip toasted in the bonfire. But check out that whitecap foam peeking out from the darkness.

The ocean drenches the sand beneath my feet while I stand here, parched and frozen, my mouth still burning from the Flamin' Hot Cheetos. My life is one long spiral of irony. One broken relationship after another. All of my exes complaining I never let down my guard, never trusted them. All of them betraying me. I clawed my way out of a dark childhood for *this*?

The water tugs at my feet, begging me to come in. I step forward until my UGG boots are soaked. Ruined, but so what? It's only money. The urge is so strong now, I can't resist. The ocean doesn't even need to glimmer. All that matters is how many steps it will take before I'm submerged, and with my length-challenged legs, that number should be low. Last time, my thirst for air was too strong for me to stay under. Will this time be different?

I step forward, struggling to stand firm.

Vibrations erupt from my breast pocket. I pull out my cell. *Mom.* Ugh. Not a good time . . . I fumble and it slips from my fingertips, tumbling into the surf. Perfect! Soaked. Thanks, Mom. Now I need to buy a new one. Or do I? I cram it back into my pocket and hold my position against the crashing waves. The water must be freezing. I'm too numb to tell.

"Careful, child!" A voice roars from behind.

"What the . . . ?"

I spin around and face a tall, filthy stranger wearing threadbare sweats. His hair is tangled like a nest and hangs in clumps along his shoulders. He looks like Jesus. That is, if Jesus were real and living today as a transient on Bolsa Chica State Beach.

"If you go too far . . . ," he draws out his pause, "you won't be able to return."

That's the point, but whatever.

"Yeah, 'kay thanks."

"God *loves* you," he whispers, leaning in and clutching my arm.

Oh man, he reeks like a hundred thousand barnacles smothering the life out of a pier. How long has this guy been homeless? He releases his grip, turns, and walks away, his steps smooth, as if he's floating.

Whoa . . . my head sways backward. As drunk as I am, everything seems to be floating. The moon, the sand, and the large seaweed mounds undulating on the shore.

As the hobo's shadow shrinks, another silhouette crosses his path, the approaching figure growing shapely and tall. Alana. She doesn't hesitate to meet me deep inside the ice-cold water. She never would.

"What's up with Jesus?"

"I know, right?"

She tilts her head, the welt around her eye shining in the moonlight. "You okay?"

"I miss Jenna and Danielle."

She wraps her arm around my shoulder and rests her cheek on my head, holding me still in the tugging water. "I miss them too, but this isn't about them."

"Right."

"We kicked Thing One and Thing Two out of the party. It's safe to go back. Tommy'll get what's coming. Evil invites evil."

"Karma? You believe in that?"

"No, but I like to pretend it's true. Forget about Tommy, 'kay?"

"Yeah, he was the best thing that ever happened to me. I named our future children — Evan, Lily, and Felix — but sure, why don't I forget about Tommy? Great advice, thanks."

"Felix Foxx, really?"

"Not the point."

"Relax those arched brows. He's not worth it."

"I can't relax them. I was born like this. I'd trade my high arches for your perfect moon slivers any day. And while we're at it, can I have your silky red hair, too? Mousy brown is so last year."

She pulls me into a side hug. "I'd die for your brows. C'mon. If we hurry, we'll make it back before midnight."

The blasts sound off before we can pace a hundred yards. At least I won't have to endure midnight pity kisses. We stroll toward the remaining crowd, my head pounding in time with each step, as I ring in the New Year hung over and soaking wet. It has to be a good sign that we're walking away from the water and not toward it.

In another few hours, the sun will rise again. By then, maybe this overwhelming urge to walk into the ocean will disappear.

CHAPTER 2

JANUARY

GEORGINA BUROS POKES her head into the waiting area. "Hi, Kristen. Come on in."

She's the bomb. If she didn't ask me to pay every time I visited, I'd make her my best friend. As we pass the water cooler, I wave my hand before she can ask. "Nothing to drink today. Let's get straight into it."

Black and tan furniture, lemon walls, splashes of teal. The potted jasmine emitting a strong, exotic scent, the way it always does when sunshine pours in from the blinds. If a Snuggie could be a room, this would be it. I make a beeline for the loveseat, settling into the familiar notch.

Georgina slips into the wingback across from me, her glossed lips shimmering against her perfect olive skin. "What's been going on? Still having those dreams?"

"Yes."

"You didn't want to talk about them last time. Would you like to tell me about them now?"

"Fine." I take a deep breath and stare into the jasmine. "The dream's always the same. I'm running at top speed in the middle of the night, trying to escape . . . *something*. I have no idea where I am. Someplace crammed with massive buildings, like Downtown L.A., except there are palm trees everywhere. It's quiet. Too quiet. All I can hear is my own breath, and the sound of my bare feet slapping asphalt."

Georgina's mysterious eye color distracts me. Are they orange, or are they brown?

"I'm wearing this giant nightgown, but for some reason, the material doesn't affect my stride. Something's chasing me. It's a black mist — just this mass that keeps pressing me from behind, no matter how hard I run, making all the hairs on the back of my neck stand on end. Every time I

9

have this dream, I'm running all night. At least, that's how it seems. And I feel an urgency to find the ocean."

Georgina selects a fiercely sharpened pencil from a cup of many. "You're a runner," she says, scribbling in her notebook.

"*Was* a runner," I correct. That title vanished when I went by impulse rather than instinct. If only I'd made a better choice back then, I might not have broken my ankle. Could still be running today. Might even have an Olympic medal or two to show for it. But there's no chance of that now. Can't even run five blocks without limping in pain.

"Still, you have a runner's mindset. It's natural that you would dream about the tension of running a race. Could the shoreline be symbolic of some type of finish line?"

"In this dream, I'm not competing. I'm running for my life."

Georgina sits unflinching, her pencil in ready position. No way am I telling her about the lure of the water. None of this is relevant, anyway.

"The dreams only come once or twice a week." I wave my hand in dismissal. "They're not a problem, and I'd love to talk about something else. If the dreams become an issue, I'll bring them up again. Promise. Today, I'd like to talk about starting fresh."

Her brow crinkles.

"That's right. Single life rocks. Timing couldn't be more perfect. Now the field's clear. I can focus on me for a change and discover who I'm supposed to be. Tommy doesn't matter anymore."

Georgina rests back, her hands forming a power steeple, her pointers pressing against her lips. She allows a thick wedge of silence to pass before she releases the steeple. "Last year was rough for you."

I clutch the armrest and pin my eyes on my therapist. "Why keep dredging up my less than awesome past? Last year, my childhood, my Goth-stricken teen years — forget all of it. I'm ready to move forward."

"Are you saying the hurt from your breakup is gone?"

"I'm saying it no longer matters."

"So the pain you felt three weeks ago when you were crying on my floor . . . is gone?"

My eyes sting. "No, but it will be once I move forward."

Georgina sits back and cradles her large-mouthed ceramic mug inscribed, *I Can Help You Find Your Marbles.* "Does this issue with

Tommy remind you of any trauma from your past? In other words, can you identify a pattern?"

She's trying to bait me, trying to force me to relive the past, *again*. I refuse. I won't talk about my ex-stepfather. I won't have another discussion about how I blame my mother for bringing Victor into our home. None of that has anything to do with what's going on here and now. Why does Georgina always do this? She keeps pressing and I keep evading, and we play this cat-and-mouse game for most of the session.

"Yes, last year sucked," I finally concede. "As did the twenty-plus years before that, but who cares? The past is gone, and I welcome the New Year." My contrived grin widens. "This is going to be my time. Can't you see that the new me has arrived?"

I rest back and wring my hands.

Georgina sips her coffee and waits as if our time will never run out. I stare her down, but she doesn't flinch. As the seconds pass, I glance across the room to where an antique steamer trunk collects dust. Contents unknown. How long until Georgina responds? Am I supposed to answer my own question?

She sets the mug down. "Tell me about this future with the new Kristen Craemer."

What the . . . ?

"How do I know what the future looks like? Why don't we charge ahead and find out? Aren't you the one who always says I can't change the past? You're always telling me to focus on the present and consider what I'm going to do now. That's why I'm dropping my past issues like a warm sack of puke. So I can move forward."

Georgina glances at the wall behind me. The green light must've lit up. I peek at my watch to confirm. Yep, my session's over. Her next patient has arrived.

She smiles, the softness of her eyes minimizing her laugh lines. I get up to leave and smile back, certain the lines on my face remain deep.

Outside, sunshine gives way to seashore fog.

On Wednesday, rain falls hard, spilling over the curb outside the Riviera Grill. Alana needs to hurry up and get here, so I can get my mind off this horrific workweek. She and I always have fun together.

Well, *always* is a stretch, but that one time after college when she had the bright idea to form the Lonely Hearts Club — now that was fun. Who could forget Jenna and Danielle showing up at the Valentine's Day party, each dressed as cupid, wearing pink leotards and tutus, running around plastering heart stickers on everyone at the party? What a couple of weirdos those girls were. Man, I loved them.

Alana invades my booth, smiling as she knocks over my water.

"Duude . . . take it down a notch. What's the . . . whoa! What's on your hand?"

She shoves the ruby and diamond ring in my face. "Andrue proposed. We're getting married a year from Valentine's Day."

She reeks of happiness, or rather, ginger-mint body cream, her favorite scent when her mood is good. She snaps her fingers and our dear waiter Bob appears from nowhere to take our order: a pitcher of margaritas, fresh chips with fire-hot guacamole, and even hotter fish tacos.

Bob scurries away and Alana leans in. "Wait until I tell you how he proposed."

I wait.

"Bungee jumping!"

"When did you do that?"

"Yesterday." She laughs. "Andrue threw it out there. Said, 'Hey, why don't you skip work and we go do something exciting?' When have you known me to turn down a spur-of-the-moment thrill, right? So he takes me to Azusa Hills where we were supposed to hike to The Bridge to Nowhere."

"*You* hiked?"

"Hey, I'm in great shape. Ask my personal trainer. Anyway, so it's a five mile hike."

"Five?"

"Will you just let me tell the story? It was freezing cold and there was fog everywhere. But it was enchanting, because we couldn't see ten feet in front of us. Never knew what to expect next. Tangled branches. A stream. Giant rocks lying in our path. Lizards. And we saw a *snake*. Nearly scared the pee out of me. And because of the fog, everything smelled like wet earth, not usually one of my favorite scents, but it made the hike mysterious.

"When we finally got there, my jaw dropped. It's literally a bridge that goes nowhere. No roads connected to it. I loved it. I was already happy, done, ready to call it a day, you know? But we still had to jump. Andrue went first, and I figured if he could do it, so could I, but I was trying not to think about it as they strapped me up. I faced backwards because I didn't want to see the steep drop, like, seriously — was I going to smash into the rocks? Just as I was about to jump, Andrue dropped to one knee, but I didn't have a clue what he was up to, so I jumped. And as I was lifting off, he shouted, *Will you marry me?*"

I clasp my mouth.

"I know, right? And check out this ring."

I smile and nod, dazzled by the spectacle. The center oval's oppressive, like a glass of sangria trapped inside a stone, four tapered prongs clutching the life out of it. Diamond baguettes flank each side of the platinum band. I'm guessing their job is to subdue the fiery centerpiece.

"This sucker cost a fortune," Alana smirks. "The stone is Burmese, the most sought-after type of ruby in the world. Six carats."

"Congratulations." A smidgen of joy escapes from my pores. I can't help knowing that she and Andrue will be the loveliest married couple ever. My grin stretches, but then Alana directs my attention back to the ring.

"This particular color is highly esteemed. It's called *pigeon's blood red.*"

I start to grin, but then gasp, and my voice catches in my throat. No, no, not now. Any other time but now.

Too late. Hiccups of laughter escape, bursting forth. I've lost control. Curse these laughter spells, always coming at the wrong time, always exploding out of control. I mean, boasting about pigeon's blood as something esteemed . . . can she blame me for laughing? But why can't I stop? My cheeks feel like they are literally on fire. I can only imagine they're blazing bright red.

Alana's perfectly penciled brows drive into each other. People stare. I try to explain, but how can I, through slobbering laughter? Now Bob's laughing, too.

All Alana can do is throw back her drink and roll her eyes at Bob and me until we're finished. Then, after a great deal of begging, I convince Alana that I'm delighted about her engagement. And after another pitcher of margaritas, she forgives me and moves on, asking me what I was laughing at when she arrived.

"Remember that Valentine's Day party, when we played spin the bottle until midnight?"

"*Ma chérie*, how can anyone forget when you never stop talking about it?" She leans in. "You remember that time you tried to drown in less than four feet of water?"

"Yeah, yeah. In my own defense, a rip caught me. I swam so long trying to get out of it, I had no idea I'd already reached the sand bed. How many times do we need to go over this?"

Devilish curves cap her smile. "I still can't understand why you swam straight. An ounce of common sense would've told you to swim perpendicular to the current."

"Common sense escaped me for most of my teenage years. Whatever. I'm glad you saved me, Miss Junior Lifeguard Showoff. How else could we have become this close?"

She smiles. "I'm glad, too."

The windows rattle from the storm while Bob brings a new pitcher and fills our glasses. Christmas lights bedazzle the inside walls while hundreds of colorful mobiles dangle from the ceiling, each begging for attention.

"Danielle loved this gaudy place," I mumble. "Jenna liked it too, but not quite as much."

Alana nods, and then lifts her glass. "Cheers to Jenna and Danielle."

"Cheers."

"And an excruciating lifetime of misery for that creep who killed them," she adds, her neck vein throbbing.

A year ago today.

Exactly.

But I can't second Alana's motion to place a curse on the poor kid who happened to run into terrible luck on that dark night. That could've been me, texting while driving on the freeway. Not that it could happen now. I never use my phone while driving. Not anymore.

We finish our tacos while an acoustic guitarist jams to retro mixes. The night glides forward, the rain pattering against the tin roof while we chat. The intensity of our conversation increases with our level of drunkenness until neither of us cares about anything but letting the evening transform into yet another milestone memory.

Alana takes a cab home, dropping me off along the way. The rain has stopped, leaving my apartment soundless, the way it's been ever since my roommate took off. What a moody gal she was. Boiling one second, frozen solid the next. I sure don't miss having to walk around the apartment as if it were lined with rice paper. I can't believe she left because she hated my birthday gift to her. I mean, c'mon, a hand-decorated T-shirt with *Do Not Disturb* emblazoned in large black lettering. No gift could've been more perfect. She left the shirt behind and bailed out of last month's rent. And now the apartment is just empty.

I pour a glass of wine as Harley curls up next to me and purrs, then I rip into the brand-new dress I picked up at the boutique next to Georgina's office. What a beautiful garment. I can't wait to make it better — to cut, rip, and stitch, even if it takes all night. Tear here, cut here and here, and now the sleeves are gone. My arms are my best feature. Why not show them off? Pleat here, let out there — it may never end.

Why can't my friends and I stay on the same page? I love Alana. It could be the margaritas and wine talking, but I'm happy for her. Truly. So why does her engagement make me sick to my stomach?

Harley purr-rumbles as shreds of trim and thread rain over him. I pour another glass of wine and continue ripping and stitching, my movements flowing as I picture the breathtaking embroidery pattern planned for the left breast: a heart, replete with veins and pumping arteries.

I finish my glass. Other than my job, my family, the few friends I have left, and a cat, what do I have? Perhaps I should embrace my singleness like I told Georgina I would. What better way to do this than to make it my resolution to stay single for an entire year? That'll give me space to breathe and grow. Everything else should fall into place, right?

I pour another glass of wine. Georgina didn't flinch when I told her the dreams are coming once or twice a week. How would she react if I told her that every night I drink enough alcohol to pass out, in an effort to keep the dreams away?

CHAPTER 3

STILL JANUARY

FEVER, BODY ACHES, and chills smack me down hard. If this is swine flu, it had better kill me or move on because I have a lot of work to do. Debilitating illness is not an interior designer's best friend. I'll never be able to get my creative juices flowing while feeling like this. *Ugh.* And that meeting with Zahed is coming up. I haven't even started my mood board for the proposal.

Harley snuggles his warm, half-Himalayan body close, purring like a lunatic. My lids grow heavy, but I must avoid sleep. That chase dream's repeating more than ever, and I'm tired of running. I'd love to drill a hole in my skull to release the demons causing the knife-like pain radiating from my temples to my head and neck, but it seems that first I must cough up a lung.

A torrential downpour wreaks havoc outside. The wall clock reads eight fifteen. I scan the room for something to hold my attention, something to keep me awake. The framed picture on the end table — my birth father. If only I knew him. He couldn't have been more than nineteen in that photo. How old would he be now? Mom's so stingy with information. His first name's *Rick*. She says she doesn't know his last name, but that's a lie. She also says he's dead. Another lie.

Mom's own mother abandoned her, and she never knew her father. You'd think that as a long-term foster child she would understand what it's like to want to know your roots. My high cheekbones and squinty, peridot eyes come from Mom's side of the gene pool, for sure, but who gave me my unmanageable hair? Not the dude in the photo. His is rich and chocolaty. Mine's not even a color. Just a pale-ish sort of brown I have to fork out big bucks to transform into something the shade of mud.

My eyelids drop. Darkness envelops me and the fog in my brain thickens, dulling the sounds of wind and rain until it's all white noise.

Breathe, Kristen.

In, *wheeze*, out.

In, *wheeze*, out.

Harley kneads my belly with his old paws. I love you, too, Harley. Your fur's been soaked in plenty of tears ... over the last twenty years. What would I ... have done ... without you.

The wall clock ticking. Lids resting shut. Heart skipping. Crashing rain ... fading. Darkness. Growing. Now I'm running. Hard to breathe. Stride heavy. Something chasing. Beast. Keep running. Can't stop. Can't glance back. Giant buildings. Where am ... the trees. Palm trees. Beach nearby. Run faster. Must reach the water. But why? Neck hairs bristling. The *mist*. Just ... keep ... breathing. Keep running. Endless streets. Mist close. Focus ahead. Find the water ...

Crack!

What was that? Thunder. My eyes pop open as my breath chokes out in sputters. I'm awake. My hair is wet from sweat. The wall clock reads twenty minutes after eight.

Days pass, but my fever does not. Food repulses me. Even raspberry cake sounds disgusting. At least my muscles ache less.

Harley, my static cling sheet, follows me everywhere. Alana texts constantly. She won't stop, no matter how hard I try to ignore her. Whatever.

I dig into the hall closet and pull out a giant foam board. Pretty, pretty please, dear universe, send me some creative energy. The Zahed meeting is staring me in the face. This mood board has *got* to get done.

The doorbell rings.

A surprising amount of fluorescent lighting bathes my mother as she stands in the hallway. She lugs a vat of something steamy into my apartment. Sweating beneath her beige fleece pullover, she heaves the pot onto the counter and inches herself close enough to send the purply scent of her lavender hand cream up my nose.

"This will help you recover, Kristen honey."

I lift the lid. Chunks of roasted chicken breast float in a pool of aromatically intoxicating broth, heavy with garlic, rosemary, and thyme, all swirling in the midst of fresh chopped vegetables.

"Thanks," I grumble, a seed of resentment swelling inside my throat.

She presses her hand against my forehead. "It's all organic. Have you eaten? Had anything to drink? You look terrible."

"You shouldn't have bothered. I've always been able to take care of myself. Why should it be any different now?"

Mom's arched brows rise. I stumble back, dizzy, as the room spins. She catches my arm. My vision dims as she guides me to the couch, where I collapse.

She tucks me into a chunky cable knit throw. "That was a long time ago. People can change." Her voice is calm. She fingers the knitting. "You always did have trouble letting go of anger. Isn't this the blanket you started making the night Tommy broke up with you?"

Yes it is. Took forty hours, including many sleepless nights, several hand cramps, and one very rough workweek. I have trouble letting go of anger? What does she think I was doing with my needles? It's called venting. Ugh. I can't even speak without exploding. Maybe if I lie still, she'll go away.

Her breath cools my face as she wipes aside my wet bangs. After a while, her impression lifts, her footfalls shuffling through the apartment. Then it's quiet. Harley nudges himself closer, filling the space my mother left behind.

Sunshine invades my apartment early the next morning. Like a ninety-year-old woman, I shuffle toward the fridge. There's the big pot. Mom must've put it away for me. I scoop some of the organic soup into a bowl and nuke it. Then I settle in at the green and pink dining table and slurp away.

Will I ever be able to let go of my anger at my mother? She's different now that she's sober. Does that negate the times she neglected her motherly duties when I was young?

This soup goes down easy. As a child, how many times did I have to heat up the soup myself or drink it straight from the can because Mom was too drunk, too bruised, or too passed out to cook? This particular soup was painstakingly handcrafted. It's the most delicious soup ever made, and proof, as irritating as it is to admit, that my mother has indeed changed.

The doorbell rings. Please let it be someone other than Mom.

Sapphire eyes flash at me through the peephole, green and gold shadow glittering behind false lashes. Ugh. It's Delila. I grit my teeth and open the door.

"Hey there." Her voice is more throaty than usual and her tired facial lines complain of a week ridden hard. What has she been up to? And that clingy white dress . . . wouldn't it be better suited for a nightclub than work? Oh my, and those trademark purple platforms, too.

She flips her purple-tinted hair. "How *are* you?" The tone is sincere but the eyes aren't, those exotic brows rising as she glances past my shoulder, peeking into my home. She locks in on the blank foam board that's leaning against the wall. "Your client meeting's coming up soon."

I nod in the general direction of the board. "That's for a different project. My mood board's already done. I have everything ready for the meeting."

"Ahh." She wraps one arm around her waist and with the other hand she grabs her necklace, her thumb caressing the outline of the diamond star pendant. "That's good because earlier today when I passed Mr. L.A.'s office, he was throwing one of his tantrums. There were some other suits in the room with him, and there was a lot of . . . um . . . *strong* conversation about what will happen if your presentation isn't ready in time."

Mr. L.A., short for Mr. Los Angeles. Mr. Anger Management Issues is more like it. He's always throwing a fit. Who cares if he had another one today?

I set a hand on my hip and lift my chin. "Why are you here?"

She bats her lashes and smiles. "I'm offering to help, free of charge." She laughs. "But seriously, I feel bad for all the setbacks you've had. I mean, you know I had nothing to do with any of it, but since I worked on those projects, too, I can't help but feel I could have done something more. Maybe if I'd been more observant, I could've seen some of your problems before they became irreversible. I just . . . I just want to help."

Right. The wrong couches were delivered to the Henderson home three hours before their big party. Delila was in charge of following through with the order, but she said those were the couches listed on the purchase order I gave her. The paperwork had mysteriously disappeared, and I was blamed for the mistake. Same thing happened with the Menendez job.

Second coat of interior paint had dried before I noticed Delila gave the painters the wrong colors. She'd switched the paint palette with another client's, but insisted I had made the error.

"You were pretty stressed that day," she had cooed, gently rubbing my arm, feigning compassion in front of the appalled Mr. L.A. "I wondered about the choices," she continued solemnly. "I should've double-checked. I blame myself for the mess up."

It was a rough week. Tommy and I weren't getting along, and I wasn't sleeping much, and whenever I did fall asleep, I was haunted by the recurring dream. Everybody knew I was a train wreck. Sure, I *could* have made the mistake. But I doubt it. Am I the only one who sees that Delila's been involved with every one of the projects that blew up in my face? Am I imagining it?

Maybe some of last year's project fails were my fault. Who knows? There's no evidence to prove otherwise, but I still don't trust her. And the only way to ensure she can't destroy another project is to keep her off all of them. No way is she getting her claws on this one.

"Like I said, I have everything under control. Besides, you shouldn't even be here." I cough into the sleeve of my robe. "Swine flu. Highly contagious."

She scrunches her nose. "Sounds nasty, poor thing. But I've already had swine flu, so I'm immune."

"Lucky you. But really, you can go. I've got it handled."

She smiles. That *smile*. Doesn't match the frustration in her eyes. "Okay. See you back at the office, then."

She spins and swishes away.

Adrenaline jolts me off the sidelines. I haven't even started on the mood board. Mr. L.A. put me in charge of hooking Mr. Zahed, and I can't let him down. It's no big deal though, right? Mr. Zahed's a starch-collared pharmaceutical mogul bent on pleasing his wife, and *she* wants to revamp their Mediterranean-style villa. Piece of cake. So what if we're only one of four major interior design companies bidding for the project? How hard can it be to come up with the best design ideas for a sprawling twelve thousand-foot estate that sits on a Pacific Ocean bluff?

I chug my soup and take a long, quenching pull from a bottle of elderberry extract. I blast Bessie Smith from my iPod and crack open my little black sketchbook to the Zahed brainstorming pages. Using my craft knife, I trim the foam into a workable size for my mood board. Wealthy clients are swayed by emotion, which means this board will be my primary weapon. Furniture and layout are temporal, circumstantial. It's the atmosphere and tone of the home that soaks into a client's pores. Everything will ride on this board.

I open all the windows to let the coastal breeze nip its way through the apartment while I run around grabbing fabric samples, stacks of magazines, and jars of rocks, feathers, and seashells. Then I hunt, select, layer, and pin.

A swatch of fabric complements Mrs. Zahed's emerald and diamond necklace. It's perfect. Using a photo, I create a foam cutout replica of Neapolitan, Mrs. Zahed's treasured Yorkie. The mutt's striking hues of black, silver, and strawberry blond are to die for. To add tone and texture, I layer in a strip of antique flour sack, a peacock feather, and a handful of Santa Barbara pebbles mixed with coffee beans. I also include a chunk of red glass I found at the beach last summer. Probably once crimson, its color is now muted, the edges softened from months or more of churning inside the sea current.

I take a step back from the board and chew the remaining sliver of my fifth lozenge. Sweat collects on my forehead as my eyes glaze over. Good grief, the board is a total pile of trash.

Word on the street is that gray is the new brown, so I try pairing various shades of charcoal with seashore hints of moss, lavender, and aqua, but now there are too many colors competing for attention. Four years of studying at the California College of the Arts, and I can't contrive a tone. The mood needs to be calm, powerful, luxurious, and coastal. Instead, it's cold and dark. There's so much depth and shadow, it looks like nightfall and puke. Or is it just me? I step away from the board and run to the bathroom where I throw up.

Everything.

Ugh. *Everything.*

The next morning, daylight bursts into the kitchen with the might of a thousand suns. Other than a wet cough, my symptoms are gone. I've survived swine flu, assuming I had it in the first place. I dig into the fridge.

I'd die for smoked bacon and scrambled eggs smothered in Tapatío. A steaming cup of mocha would also be nice. But all my pantry offers is a freezer-burned toaster waffle washed down by stale tea. Or maybe I'll just have some more of Mom's soup.

Alana calls.

"*Ma chérie*, twenty messages and no reply — what gives?"

Well, *my darling,* I've been sick and haven't been the least bit interested in listening to your endless wedding monologues.

"How could you stand to keep me worried?" she continues. "How are you? You want me to find you some Tamiflu? Pharmacies are out, but a client of mine has a bunch of it. He said he would sell me some if you want it, but it's probably too late. You should've returned my calls."

Oh. I've underestimated Alana's intentions. She's softened over the last year, as if she's taken on some of the mothering role that Jenna used to play. Perhaps I should try to be more trusting and kind, the way Danielle used to be. But there's no time for regrets.

"Doing much better, thanks. But I'm up against a deadline and my mood board isn't working. Can you help?"

"Love to. I'm out of town, so let's collaborate online."

"My board's not digital. It's handmade."

"Really, Grandma? You listen to music on a phonograph, too? Seriously, Kristen, you need to pull yourself out of the dark ages. You have all this wonderful technology available at your fingertips and continue to chisel stone. But I don't have time for lectures, so whatever. Let's just get started. How many boards are we talking?"

"One. Something tells me Mr. Zahed prefers decisiveness."

"It's risky to pitch with a single choice, but it's your call. If you're right, the payoff will be huge."

Thank God Alana's also in design. There's a lot more wining and dining in her world than in mine, which makes her the best ally to have, given her impressive list of connections. Within minutes, we're knee deep into the Zahed project. Alana sends images and inspirational quotations, and I send back snapshots of my work in progress.

"Don't forget your power words," says Alana. "Use exotic, rich, and luxurious. Mr. Zahed will eat that up."

Yes. The magic of text and font. One of my missing elements.

"And the mutt has to go. He has no place on your board."

Little foam-board Neapolitan is adorable, but Alana's right. He's messing up the board.

Within an hour, Alana's helped me transform my darkness-and-puke mood board into a brilliant display of golden Mediterranean bliss. Yellow. Another element that was missing, and with it, everything falls into place.

After Alana hangs up, I print and paste like mad until the board is finished. Three o'clock. I still have time to spare. I call the office.

Smack is the first sound that comes from the receptionist. I tell gum-smacking Kellen about Delila's visit, but she doesn't understand.

"Today's meeting is preliminary," she says. "Trust me, *smack, smack,* nobody's worried. The yelling . . . *smack* . . . was about something else."

Somebody's lying. But is it Kellen, or is it Delila?

"You should watch your back around Delila," says Kellen in a low, secretive voice. "I'm not the one who told you this but . . . she is about to go down, and you don't want to be near her when she does, *smack.*"

"Courier the board over." Kellen's voice is suddenly back to normal. "I'll get it where it needs to go. You'll be in tomorrow?"

As if. How can I trust anyone from my office, where competition is fierce and the only thing that exceeds the fear of wrinkles and death is the fear of mediocrity? "No. I'll bring the board in myself. Tell Mr. L.A. I'll be at the meeting today."

"Suit yourself." She allows one more *smack* before hanging up the phone.

I shed my crusty pajamas and prepare to re-enter the world of the living.

I weave my way through a countless number of crazy drivers on the 405 and arrive at my downtown office in less than an hour.

Mr. L.A. steps back. "Miss Craemer, you're pale. Whatever you have, no one wants it. Go back home."

"I came for the presentation."

"Didn't Kellen tell you? Mr. and Mrs. Zahed went to Italy. The presentation has been moved to next week."

Kellen sits nearby, shrugging, stapling paper, and smacking her gum. Mr. L.A. slathers some of Kellen's sanitizer on his hands while he jokes that my brain must still be fuzzy from the flu. I play along and agree to take another day off to get well, but in my mind I'm whacking Kellen over the head with her three-hole punch.

"It's better this way," I grumble to myself in the elevator. The mood board could use a little fine-tuning, since I kind of went wild with that glue gun. With nothing left to do this afternoon, I might as well head over to Uncle Mark's birthday party.

Mom and I haven't talked since I rebuked her soup visit. Now I stand frozen on her porch, my rehearsed apology swelling inside my throat. I knock. Thank God her jacaranda tree hasn't hit its blooming season, when the dropped flowers make a horrific mess that sticks to my shoes for days.

She throws open the door and pierces me with those squinty eyes. Before words can escape my throat, she intercepts. "Come in. Uncle Mark was hoping you would show."

She's not interested in an apology. Her dismissive smile makes that clear. Once again, we're slapping a happy-face bandage over a long, deep wound. Fine with me.

"He's in the den," she adds before walking off.

Mom's husband Steve shakes my hand, thanks me for coming, says he needs to help Mom in the kitchen, and turns on his heel.

Wow. The living room never changes. Still as plain as ever. If only she'd let me get my hands on this space. An assortment of Mom's friends sit squeezed into the assemble-it-yourself furniture. Several of the women turn their heads, their conversations dwindling as they smile at me. Gotta love those women from the church-sponsored addiction recovery program. They're all so friendly. Well, most of them. Dorothy, the tallest and most oppressively dressed of them all, doesn't even try to smile. Her caked lipstick turns downward. That contemptuous sneer isn't worth any amount of warmth and comfort I might receive from the others. So I smile and wave, like a princess on a float, and dash out of sight.

Wood panels cover every inch of walled surface in the den. Dimmed lamps, outdated entertainment devices . . . all we need are mounted buck heads to complete the cheap mountain rental vibe. Mark emerges from a crowd of laughing men. As usual, his light brown hair sticks up, trimmed high and tight, his brows left untouched, wild and scary.

"There you are!" he shouts. "Get over here." He comes to me in long, thumping strides. He's tall, solid, and beaming. He wraps my shoulder in one arm and knuckles my hair.

"Enough. My hair's frizzy as it is."

Mark laughs and I drop my shoulders. My breath steadies. How easy it is to settle in to the clamor of Mark and his friends. Several fellows from the Southern California Rare Rose Society. A handful of colleagues from the city college where Mark teaches anthropology. And aren't those guys "brothers" from the End-of-the-World Survivalist Club? These men fill the den to overflowing, and yet Mark's attention remains fixed on me.

"How's life, kiddo?"

"Great." Why tell the truth? If he knew about my urge to walk into the ocean, he'd never leave my side.

"Good to hear." He slaps me on the back and then turns to gain the attention of the room.

"A toast to my favorite niece."

"Your only niece," I laugh.

I settle in, pretending the only thing that matters is the vibration of laughter coming from Mark and his friends.

CHAPTER 4

FEBRUARY

❧

A HAIR BAND, a thick cap, and more than a dozen clips — and still my hair is a mess. As usual, Alana insisted on pulling the top down on her stark white BMW 650i. It's a beautiful, sparkling February day, and we made it here alive. Can't ask for much more than that. The L.A. Fashion District, otherwise known as the hub of the apparel industry on the West Coast. It's like a slice of heaven.

As usual, Santee Alley is bloated with currents of human streams flowing in both directions, merchants shouting from their storefronts. "Fi' dolla, fi' dolla!" Alana and I dart from one shop to the next, careful to avoid the smelly puddles which seem vitalized by sunlight. We shop like mad, filling our bags with delicate skirts and tops. I'm on fire today, but Alana's well in the lead, topping off her bags with impractical winter wear.

By noon, a snack sounds fantastic, but Alana's unstoppable, and she presses me to march on while vendors keep trying to suck us in. "You want deal? I have what you want. Come back, pretty lady."

I hold on as well as I can, but midway through the one hundred and fifty or so packed vendors, I can no longer ignore the pang of my blood begging for sugar. So while Alana spies a red leather shoulder bag and veers left, I head right and follow a trail of sweet-scented churro air. Three bags of these little darlings ought to do it.

The warmth and comfort of cinnamon, sugar, and fried dough flood my system. Oh my goodness, could anything be better? It's like pure happiness surging through my veins.

I wipe the sticky crumbs from my chin and scan the crowd for witnesses to my gluttony. No one to the left. Now over to the right . . . oh no. The happy warmth vanishes. What are *they* doing here? Of all the days Tommy and Barbra could have chosen to come here, why today? *Please don't see me, please don't see me, please* . . . too late. They see me.

Why are they walking this way? Why can't they just shun me and turn around? Thank God I'm wearing my super dark shades. Are my lenses dark enough to hide my hot, wet eyes?

"Kristen." Tommy raises a brow. "I'm surprised to see you here."

Why? Because this used to be one of our favorite hangouts? Or is it because you can't imagine I'd ever leave my apartment after being dumped by you?

"Well, yeah." I paste on my best fake smile. "You know I can't live without these churros."

He sniffs. Or was that a muffled snort-laugh. Or . . . something else? Is it possible *he* has nostalgic memories of this place, too?

Barbra leans into Tommy, hooks her arm through his, and scans me head to toe. "Nice shirt, Krissy."

"Kristen," I correct. "And yes, it is a nice shirt, thank you very much. It complements my faded jeans. But my favorite part is the message, *Do Not Disturb.* So appropriate for a place like this, don't you think?"

Tommy laughs out loud, the tone falling somewhere between amusement and disgust.

Barbra glances up at him, then at her fingernails, her thumb picking at a chip on her index finger. "Babe, can we head over to the handbags now? I'm ready to move on."

"Sure," he replies, still looking at me. "We can go wherever you want. Today is *your* day."

It's like high school all over again. I'm choking the life out of a churro stub, trying to come up with a comeback — something witty but not too funny . . . something with teeth that bite — when they just turn and walk away.

"Come, *chérie.* We've got better things to do." It's Alana, clamping on my arm and leading me away. We flee Santee Alley, leaving its toxic puddles and other irritants behind. On our way over to the mother lode of textiles and notions, a single cloud blocks the sun, draping an eerie shadow over Ninth Street and sending a shiver up my spine. That feeling. Like in my chase dreams. Unseen eyes pressing on the back of my neck.

Alana, dear friend that she is, assures me I'm crazy. I scan left and right, even behind me. No one's watching. There's no mist whatsoever, and now that the cloud has passed, sunshine floods the entire block. But the chill remains. Who's watching me? Can't be Tommy. Once he walks away, he doesn't come back. And if not him, then who? Must be my imagination. Sleep deprivation is distorting my perception, allowing nighttime fears to leak into the day.

"We better get shopping," says Alana. "There's only twelve months left until the wedding, and I want my dressmaker to get started on my gown."

She takes my hand and leads me to the textiles and notions storefronts. She buys yards and yards of white silk and chooses a baby pink triple velvet for the draped outer layer of the dress. Then she grabs a bunch of gray and cream silk thread for the Celtic embroidery pattern the dressmaker will stitch on the bottom trim. She also finds some white bridal lace by Dentelle De Calais, made in France, for fifty-five dollars a yard. She picks up several yards to use for her cathedral length train. This gown will be quite an heirloom. It should fetch top dollar when Alana sells the thing on eBay once the wedding is over.

Engorged with consumption and indigestion, we shuffle toward the car. My phone rings.

"It's Delila."

"Ignore it," commands Alana.

I answer.

"Kristen, you have to help me."

"Calm down. I can't understand you when you're yelling."

"I'm not yelling! That's what they said, too. I'm upset. I've a right to be upset."

"You're still yelling."

"Sorry. It's just . . ." She breathes heavily into the phone. "They fired me."

"Fired?"

Alana smiles and shakes her head.

"Yeah, yesterday. They ambushed me. It wasn't my fault."

I roll my eyes at Alana and she shoves my shoulder. "I told you not to take the call."

"Hello? Kristen, are you there?"

"Sorry, Delila. I'm the middle of something. Can't help you right now." *Click.*

"Nice," laughs Alana.

"She's not my problem."

"Don't arch those brows at me," says Alana. "I'm on your side. That woman is toxic. You need to stay as far away from her as possible. By the way, whatever happened with the Zahed project?"

"We got the job."

"Of course you did. Thanks to me."

"Yes, you're amazing, but I worked hard on this, too. Don't scrunch your face — it's true. Fine, whatever. If not for you, I wouldn't have landed Mr. Zahed. You saved my butt again."

"You got that right."

We reach the parking lot and a fresh chill crawls up my spine. I scan the crowd. Nothing. No one watching, except for a homeless man who holds out a tin cup as he squats against a wall. He has clumpy, dark brown hair, like the hobo from the beach on New Year's Eve, except this guy's wearing a tattered gray jacket and a holey T-shirt. I pull a five-dollar bill from my purse. If only I could do more. No one should have to beg for basic human needs. And here I am with bags full of impractical clothing. I'd hand it all over to him if I thought it would do any good. Even money feels useless.

The man leans forward and opens his dry, cracked lips. I place the bill in his cup, lean closer, and await his words.

"Bless you," he says. Then he spews vomit, streaming green slime down my legs.

Lovely.

Back home, I lug my bags of purchases and quarantined clothes into the apartment building. Alana's always boasting about being prepared for anything, but her emergency water supply wasn't nearly enough to remove the slime from my jeans and tennis shoes. At least she had this super-sized zipper bag for my barfables. I'm lucky she had spare clothes in her trunk, too. The fit sucks, though. Pants are too long, too snug, and not at all flattering. And these shoes keep falling off my feet. But who am I to complain?

The lobby appears empty. So why does my flesh crawl? Why is that feeling suddenly enveloping me? There's no one here besides our fearless security guard.

"Hey, 'sup, Trent."

He slides his glasses up the bridge of his nose and gives me a half-hearted *how-do* before he sinks back into his *Golfer's Digest*. He senses nothing. I scan the premises . . . the entry . . . the lobby . . . the elevator alcove . . . the back exit. Still, I find no one. I'm crazy. That's all there is to it. I'd love to take the stairs. These eight holiday pounds aren't going to go away by themselves. But . . . that *chill*.

I rush to the elevator, bang on number five, and grip my keys, making the largest one stick out from my clenched fist. Seconds pass. The faux beryl-paneled doors start to close. Could they be any slower? And that squealing . . . like a pig on a stick. If I'd used the stairs I'd already be on my floor. For the love of Pete, how long does it take? I slam my fist into the wall. Big mistake. I blow off the pain while the doors continue to grind. Before they completely seal, a caramel-skinned woman wearing all black appears through the slit.

Delila?

The fifth floor corridor lies empty. Inside the apartment, Harley purr-snores and remains curled in a ball on the couch. I pace the floor. Why was Delila at the elevator? Was she at the Fashion District, too? I dig my fingers into my temples. Delila's not smart enough to be that psychotic.

I buzz Trent.

"Hey, there's a lunatic running through the building. She's my height with straight black hair, tinted purple, except today it's not quite straight, but snarled and ratty, and scrunched back in a hair band. She's wearing a black tracksuit, and she might be barefoot, because I don't remember seeing shoes on her feet. She looks trashed, not a stitch of makeup . . . Trent? Are you there?"

"Yeah man, got it. Barefoot lunatic running through the building."

"I'm serious."

Through his yawn, Trent promises to keep watch, but I'm sure he's rolling his eyes, as if I'm being ridiculous. Perhaps he's right. Delila would have to be whacked to have followed me all day through the Fashion District. Maybe it's something benign. If I ignore her, she might just go away. Besides, I can handle her, or anyone else stupid enough to invade my apartment.

I open my nightstand drawer and lift the false bottom to reveal a sealed pint of Jack Daniels. Ignoring the bottle, I reach below it to grab the padded case holding my loaded Ruger Security-Six. Tonight, the gun will stay beneath my pillow. But it's only a precaution. Surely, I won't have to prove the .357 Magnum's positive reputation for *stopping power*.

After a quick shower, I head to the wine cabinet, but drinking myself to sleep sounds exhausting, so I dive into bed instead.

Please, dear universe, just let me fall asleep fast, and don't make me spend the entire night running in my dreams.

I turn off the light. Settle your mind, Kristen. Just breathe.

A snap echoes through the apartment, and within seconds, in pitch-blackness, I'm sitting upright with the gun in my grip. I remove one hand to flick on the light. Harley breathes contentedly, his closed lids twitching. Chasing fireflies, I'm sure.

What's that noise? Oh, just muffled television sounds coming from Bernadine's apartment. Nothing else. So the snap was nothing . . . settling walls, adjusting to a drop in temperature . . . or perhaps only my imagination. Right?

I grab a flannel cloth. Uncle Mark would never let me place the gun back in its case without wiping it first. Even when he's not around, his voice nags, "You want that Security-Six to stain, kiddo? They don't make those anymore." Give me a break. How can stainless steel stain? "Wipe it!" he replies in my mind.

Minutes pass and the apartment remains silent. There's no one here but Harley and me. I'm going to keep saying that to myself until I fall asleep.

CHAPTER 5

STILL FEBRUARY

❧

NO HUMAN BEING should ever have to live alone. It's suffocating, and as maddening as sitting in a padded cell. I must've pulled out the Ruger a dozen times in the last week, but it's always nothing. Old pipes, clumsy neighbors. Nothing. But that feeling—of unseen eyes watching, spying, and creepily observing—is worse than ever. So either I have a stalker or I'm losing my mind.

If only Harley could either validate or calm my fears, but that's not going to happen. That old cat takes five minutes to climb onto the couch, for crying out loud. Every time a startling sound rips through the apartment, he just kneads his way into his favorite cashmere throw and curls into a ball. Harley, I love you, buddy, but I need some *human* contact.

Impetuous wind whips my hair as I stroll to the nearest coffee shop. Half a block down the path, something taps my shoulder and I jump. Just a branch snapping off a tree. Another half block down, something smacks the sidewalk and I spin around. It was a nut dropped by a careless squirrel.

Two hurried blocks later, I dash into Café Nate and take my spot in line. Ahh, people. Lots of normal, coffee-loving people . . . and there's Nate, the owner and most talented barista I know. Awesome. Can't wait to see what he comes up with this time. My shoulders relax. Nothing but caffeine happening here. No unseen eyes and no startling noises. I'm up. "Hi. Large latte with foam art, please."

I like it here. Soon I'll be settled in, watching other people while pretending to read my phone screen. These wonderful folks can be my danger gauge. If no one reacts the next time I jump, then I'll know for sure it's all in my head, that I'm simply crazy. End of story.

"Latte with foam art, for Kristen."

Nate glances over the steam machine as I step up to the counter, and I crane my neck to take in his latest design. "Holy cow, are you kidding me? Is this David Bowie?"

He blushes. "Knew you'd like it."

"I'm going to sit down and admire this masterpiece for the rest of the day. Thank you." I tuck a ten-spot into Nate's *Foam Art 4 Love* collection jar and turn away.

"No, thank *you*," he calls out after me. "And the children's hospital thanks you, too."

All the tables are taken. No way am I going to find a seat unless I squeeze between the laptop jockeys hogging the long couch. Wait, the preteens are leaving from the patio. Do their mothers know how much caffeine they're drinking?

I settle into a patio chair and gaze into my cup. How does he do that? Bowie still looks good, even after I hustled to this seat.

My phone rings.

"'Sup, Trent."

"That woman." He sighs. "I'm pretty sure it was her. Black exercise clothes . . . hair was a mess."

"She's there?"

"Was." He yawns. "Came up to my desk and started asking questions about you."

"Like what?"

"I dunno . . . like, who you live with and what's the best time of day to reach you. Stuff like that."

"What did you tell her?"

"Nothing. Told her answering questions like that wasn't part of my job, and then she left." Another sigh. "Anyway, gotta go."

"All right, thanks."

What on earth is Delila up to? Is she casing my building? Spying on me? Maybe that's where this feeling of being watched is coming from. Maybe I'm not crazy after all. If she just left the apartment building, she might still be in the neighborhood. I'd love to question her. What a relief it would be to find out that it was only Delila following me all this time. Compared to a vague black mist, the woman is as vicious as a hamster.

I snap a picture of David Bowie and reluctantly cap my cup.

Nothing happens the entire route home, but when I reach my building and open the door, a tingle runs up my spine. Those unseen eyes. Pressing on me, like at the Fashion District and inside my dreams.

Trent slouches at his desk, his nose buried inside his magazine. Otherwise, the lobby is empty. I head to the stairwell. Might as well. The elevator will be too slow, and besides, these extra pounds have to go. I dare Delila to make a move.

Second flight, ugh. Have there always been this many stairs? Should've taken the elevator. Fourth flight and, man, it's dim, but that's what you get when there's only a single light bulb for four flights of stairs. How many times do I need to report this to Trent? The guy can't take his face out of his magazine long enough to screw in a few bulbs. Fifth floor. I'm out of breath. How can I be this out of shape?

I open the door and the hinges creak. Would it kill Trent to have someone apply a little oil now and then?

The first stretch of corridor lies empty. I step swiftly right up to the corner, where I stop. The halls remain quiet. I take a deep breath and proceed. For the love of Pete, it's Delila, hunched inside the shadow of my apartment doorframe, like the cowering hamster I expected. She's wearing the same clothes I saw her in last week. Has she even washed them since then?

I march forward, and her sapphire eyes widen, tears staining her cheeks in streaks.

"Are you insane?" Sweat erupts along my hairline.

She fidgets and stuffs her hands into her pockets.

"Please tell me you weren't following me through the Fashion District last week, too. You can't be that stupid."

Her heavy brows narrow. "No!" She pulls one hand out of its pocket and twists her fingers deep into the coarse strands of her hair. What a mane. No wonder she loves the flat iron. "I—I haven't been to the Fashion District in months."

"No? But you *were* here that day, so tell me what's up with the stalking behavior . . . casing my apartment building, interrogating Trent—"

"You've got the wrong idea." She stands up straight. Her eyes are wet. "I've been trying to get hold of you. That's all."

"Really? Because it looks like you're spying on me."

"I'm not. I just want to talk to you face-to-face." Her gaze drops to the floor. "I was fired."

"Yes. You told me."

She looks up. "It wasn't my fault."

Right. It's never her fault.

"They set me up," insists Delila. "They're ruthless."

"Who are *they*?"

"There are seven of them. Kellen's one, also Ron, Dustin, Angie, Mike, Owen, and Regina. They built an alliance to steal everyone's work."

Paranoid much? "And you know this because . . ."

Tears continue to flow. "Kellen messed up my appointments on purpose. Ron asked her to do it. I overheard all of them laughing about it in the coffee room. They sabotaged me, but I can't prove it because it's only my word against theirs."

She wipes her nose with her sleeve. "And you're right. I *was* here last week, but you have to believe me. I wasn't spying on you. I only wanted to talk, that's all. These seven got me fired. I'm pretty sure they're the ones who messed up your projects last year, and I think they're going to keep doing it until you're out of their way, too."

"So . . . you're here to warn me?"

"Yes." She wipes her red, swollen eyes. "And to ask for help. Kristen, I don't have anywhere else to turn."

For the last two years, this woman has lied and manipulated to get ahead at my expense. And now she's blaming others? I rub my temples. He said, she said . . . what do I care? What's stopping me from escorting her out of the building? It's those gaping eyes sinking back into nothingness. The same questioning expression I used to find in the mirror when I was a teen. Eyes that ask, *How did I get here, and how much farther until I reach the very bottom?*

She rocks back and forth. "I don't know what to do. Can you help me find a job? I hate to beg, but I'm desperate."

I cross my arms and press my lips together tight, trying to refrain from speaking my thoughts.

She stops rocking. "*Oh* . . . you don't believe me, do you?" She sighs heavily. "It's okay, I understand. I get that a lot. I don't know how I always end up in these kinds of situations, but I do, and the blame always points to me. Well you can either believe me or not. I honestly don't know what else to say."

The smart move would be to call the police, but what if Delila's telling the truth? How can I turn her away if there's even a chance that she's the victim? With a heavy sigh, I open my door and let her in. She jumps onto my couch and pulls her arms and legs to her core. I hand her a blanket and plop into the lounger across from her. The windows rattle from the rushing wind, and Harley rubs against Delila's legs. She reaches down and pulls him onto her lap. To my horror, he settles in contentedly.

Then Delila's tears stop flat, like a salty faucet shut off, and she just starts talking. "I've always thought of myself as a survivor," she says, "but bad luck seems to follow me wherever I go." Her gaze ping-pongs around the room as she grabs her necklace pendant, caressing the diamond star outline with her thumb. "I lost my mother when I was four . . ."

Great. I nod, trying to give the appearance of interest. I mean, do we really know each other well enough for this much transparency? A small part of me pities her. That part of me needs to die. I really don't want the burden of knowing yet another sad story.

". . . and it was awful living with my dad and new step-mom." She leans forward and lifts her lashes, exposing those penetrating eyes. The lines on her forehead soften, as if she's about to reveal something big. My ears perk high.

"My dad—"

Something bangs against the window, and we both glance in that direction. A couple of feathers float away. A dove? Those birds can't ever tell the difference between glass and air.

"Never mind." Delila blows her nose. "He had issues, that's all."

She jumps ahead to when she was fourteen and ran away from home. She keeps her chin high as she describes how dangerous it was for a teenage girl to live on the street and what she had to do to survive.

Whatever happened to getting to know someone before spilling your guts? I blink and nod through it all. She says she's worked hard to make a life for herself, and would've succeeded except for all the forces that have worked against her, like the supposed "group of seven" from the firm.

"Why are you telling me all this?"

"Because we're the same."

No, we are *not* the same!

She studies my crinkled brow. "I mean, we both had rough childhoods. We're both struggling with the same kind of different thing."

My teeth clench. She doesn't have a clue about my life. She's complaining because her dad had issues? Grab another tissue, sweetheart, and get in line. Unbelievable. She's still talking. Does this woman ever shut up? "Sorry, what'd you say?"

She sighs. "I said I'm going to fix this mess. Can you help me find work?"

"Uh . . ." Really? How am I supposed to help her find work when I'm still not sure I can trust her? Sure, her story sounds *almost* believable, and her words seem sincere. But her eyes . . . the way they don't match her tone, and the way they flicker around the room whenever she's rubbing her star pendant. "I mean, I can keep an eye out, but I don't think—"

"That's fine." She lifts a hand to cut me off. "I'd be grateful if you could just do that." She forces a smile that quickly drops into a frown. "On top of everything else, I lost my apartment. Have you had any luck finding a roommate?"

Did Trent tell her I needed a roommate? I thought he said he didn't say anything.

She strokes Harley's chin and his purr intensifies. "Your cat sure likes me."

Harley's old and senile. His senses are shot. "Sorry, I already have a potential new roommate," I lie.

"It's okay. I can always sleep under the pier. It's not like I haven't done it before."

I wring my hands. For crying out loud, this woman is *not* my problem.

"Just kidding," she says. "It's not that serious. No big deal. I can sleep in my car."

This would be a good time to set some boundaries. "If you can get another job, and stop stalking me, I'll consider the roommate situation." No, wait . . . what? That's not what I wanted to say!

She bolts upright. "Really? Oh, you won't regret it."

It's time to stop the bleeding. I rise and escort my guest to the door. She's still blathering, but at least she's cooperating, following me to the exit.

"I promise to stop stalking you," she says. "Even though that's not what I was doing. Trust me. I'll find a job. You'll see."

"Goodbye, Delila. We'll talk later."

I shove her out the door, and she swishes away, her figure shrinking in the peephole. This is going to take some major damage control, but at least now I'm sure Delia's not dangerous. Well, almost sure.

I buzz Trent and tell him to keep watching for her. But it's not like I can totally count on him, so I keep my Ruger close, loaded, and ready, just in case.

Chapter 6

Beginning of March

✧

M Y THROAT HURTS from singing out loud with Billboard's Hot 100. Three hours weaving our way up one freeway after the next with the top down and the sun beating hard, and of course Alana's silky red hair is perfect, and mine's a mess. Thank God we get to stop at Mickey-D's in Mojave. We step out of the car and into the dry, desolate landscape off a windy strip of the 14—the perfect setting for a horror flick. We couldn't find a better place to stop if we tried.

Alana opens the grease-smeared doors and smiles devilishly at the sight. Piercings unfit for public consumption, grandma bikers, and oh, Thunder Woman, those jeggings aren't meant for you. What a gold mine for people watching.

While Alana orders, I head to the bathroom and straight to the mirror. Way too many knots to count. I pull out my special comb and gently work on each and every tangle, while at least a dozen other women come and go.

Finally, my hair's back to normal, relatively speaking. Alana must be wondering where I am by now. On my way out of the restroom, I pass a woman who seems to be missing quite a lot of material from her . . . um, are those supposed to be pants?

Wham! Smack into a wall of man who smells like fresh linen. We're tangled, my jacket button caught on his necklace. I gently unhook myself from his leather cord and cross pendant. *Sorry. Excuse me. Sorry.* This bearded, golden brown-haired stranger and I twirl and dance, trying to uncoil from each other, and holy cow, those are the deepest brown eyes I've ever seen. With hints of orange, like burnished bronze. The way he stares at me . . . have we met before?

"My fault." He winks, and we're unraveled. "Here, you dropped this." He bends down to grab my frosted raspberry lip gloss.

"Thanks." I bite my bottom lip, my cheeks burning. *Why?* Why on earth am I blushing?

I dash away and squeeze in next to Alana at a Formica bar where my food sits and waits, the fries half gone. She says fries are poisonous calorie sticks, and never orders them herself, which wouldn't bother me so much if she didn't always steal mine. She's still chewing the stolen fries when she narrows her penciled brows.

"Who was that?"

"Don't care."

"Right," she says. "You're panting like an animal. Go talk to him, give him your number, tap dance in front of him . . . whatever, just *do* something."

"Not interested."

"No need to scowl, *ma chérie.*" She checks him out. "You could do worse. Don't need to marry the guy, just have some fun. Kristen, you need to get back in the game."

"Why can't you just be happily engaged and leave me alone?"

"Stop acting impaired and go over there."

Where is he? Sweet mother of pearl, he's right *there.* "Shut up, Alana."

"What's that, Kristen? You want to give that guy your number?"

The bronze-eyed guy smiles as he and his friends pass our bar. I shake my head and swirl my finger around my ear, hoping the dude will get my signal: *this chick sitting next to me is out of her mind.*

"Missed your chance." Alana grabs my last three fries. "Live like a spinster for all I care, but I will *never* let you own more than three cats."

She starts talking about her wedding and I tune her out. The stranger holds the door open for a man in a wheelchair. Then he crosses the parking lot, his broad shoulders posture-perfect, and heads toward the back of a red Chevy pickup.

Alana's still talking. I'm nodding but not listening, my attention stolen by the giant tan dog bounding across the truck bed. The bronze-eyed guy grabs and hugs the dog as it licks his face, shaking the truck. That thing is huge. A mastiff. It puts its paws on the guy's shoulder . . . wait . . . that's *paw.* The dog's a tripod.

The guy secures the tether, and he and his friends climb into the truck and they take off.

An hour later, Alana and I arrive at our destination, her uncle's two-story luxury home in Mammoth Lakes. The place sprawls with so many bedrooms, pool tables, and plasma high-def televisions, my head spins.

Alana smirks. "This place cost Uncle Max a fortune."

If only I could hibernate here the entire weekend, but Alana won't allow for such a waste of time. We shuttle over to a packed Hawaiian restaurant and listen to techno music while we inhale thousands of calories of food and drink. Mostly drink. Should be a lot of fun, so why is it taxing? All that driving with the top down turned me into a slug on sleeping pills. Alana struggles to acclimate, too, both of us gasping for air on the dance floor. In this altitude, each drink soaks in like three, and with that kind of math, who can keep track?

I wake the next morning beneath fresh-pressed sheets. How did we make it back to the condo?

"They're imported." Alana towers over me. "The sheets. Egyptian cotton, hand-crafted with twenty-four karat gold thread weaved into the design."

"They're lovely."

Her brows cross hard. "You groaned all night long. I almost moved you to the floor. I'd die if you puked in Max's sheets."

"Had it again."

"What? The running dream?"

"Yeah."

"Your eyes are baggy. Didn't you get any sleep?"

"Not really. Feels like I literally ran all night, except my ankle doesn't hurt."

She shakes her head.

"Stop." I shove my palm in her face. "Don't give me that lecture again."

"It's true," she snaps. "If you grew up in a different environment, like with my papa, you would've never blown your running career the way you did. Papa would've . . ."

I cover my ears like I'm not listening, but she's right. Papa Pheasant raised all six of his daughters to be tenacious and strong, and to take life on like champions. Even overshadowed by all those Pheasant sisters, I could've reached the Olympics. Papa would've insisted on excellence.

Too bad for me, I was raised by my mother. And *she* never insisted on anything. My running career was doomed before it ever began.

I pull out a brown box. "Happy birthday."

Her lecture stops short. "Emma's Bakery?"

"Nothing but the best." The distraction succeeds.

We finish our cake-for-breakfast, and then shower. Alana plans to work me on the snowboard today, so she pushes some preventative measures on me, loading me up with ibuprofen and wrapping my ankle in athletic bandaging. We're shuttled, geared, and waiting in the lift line by nine.

From the start, birthday girl leads the way, carving the snow with her board and shredding each slope like a pro, as I, her wobbling apprentice, trail behind. I only hope she keeps her promise to avoid all the widow-maker runs. I'd die on a black diamond trail.

I exit the lifts with reasonable grace. Pat myself on the back for that. Though I'm gasping, I'm managing to keep up with my fast-riding friend. And look at the glistening runs! Fresh powder drapes the ground like a soft blanket. I let go, becoming one with mountain, gliding, letting the wind whip my cheeks raw as I'm overcome with the thrill of the ride . . . just before the board hits a bump and my face plants into the snow. I do this again and again.

In late afternoon, when the temperature drops to below exhilarating, we get in line for our final run off chair 2, a high speed quad known as Stump Alley Express.

"Next in line is a group of three," says Alana. "Let's leave that fourth spot open, so we can ride together on the next chair."

I nod in agreement.

She glances past my shoulder. "*Chérie*," she whispers, "that Mickey-D's guy is behind you."

"The one with the bronze eyes?"

"Yeah, the guy you said you couldn't care less about, and yet you remember his eye color."

She's right. I can pick up that fresh linen scent from here.

The group ahead of us shuffles toward the lift and I step forward, but Alana cuts me off, catches up to the group of three, and leaves me behind, where I stand frozen, pretending to be cool.

"Hi again," laughs Mickey-D. "Small world. Mind if my buddies and I tag with you?"

"Not at all." I stare grumpily ahead. Yes, it's a small world. Too small, if you ask me.

With one foot unstrapped, I skate into the queue and try my best not to trip over my own feet. The guy and his friends trail me right up to the lift. Within seconds, we're perched together, squashed hip to hip on the chair — these three strangers and me — the bronze-eyed one pressing against my side. Why does this freak me out? This guy's medium-easy on the eyes, not beefy, but not weak-looking, either. Rugged, close-trimmed, full beard. Nothing I haven't seen before. Except for those eyes.

What's wrong with me? It's only March. Way too soon to break my New Year's resolution. I don't need a man to be happy. Not yet.

He nudges my shoulder. "Thanks for sharing your chair. My name's Ethan Adams."

Not like I had a choice. For crying out loud, don't we already have enough physical contact? "No problem," I reply. "I'm Kristen . . . uh, Craemer." I turn away and pretend to take in the landscape. How much longer until this grueling ride ends?

He nudges me again. "These are my friends, Mario and David."

"Nice to meet you." I force a smile. How can I tell this guy I'm not interested without being rude?

"Isn't this view amazing?" He reaches across me and points past the trees. "Over there. Have you ever seen anything like it?"

"It looks a lot like the last run I was on," I reply dryly. "And the one before that."

He nods. "I guess it does start to all look the same after a while, like miles and miles of pine and snow-covered mountains. But you know what I love?" His voice is smooth and easy, a surprise coming from that stark jaw.

"What's that?"

"When I spot something different, like over there." He reaches over again and points toward the edge of the run. "You see it?"

My heart jumps and I nearly lose my breath. A glob of snow on a rock, melted into a perfect heart shape. I look up at Ethan and let my expression soften. "Yeah, I like that, too."

"So was that your friend waiting in line with you? The woman with the red hair?"

"Yeah, that was Alana. We're pretty close."

Ethan tilts his head. "I guess I'm just wondering why she left you behind."

My cheeks flush hot. "To force me to ride with you." I close my eyes and shake my head. "She's always messing with me."

Ethan chuckles. "I know what that's like." He pushes his thumb toward his friends. "These guys mess with me all the time."

Mario and David laugh smugly.

Ethan turns to point out something else. "Check out that tree over there. One in a million, right?"

"More like one *of* a million."

He laughs. "Okay, so now you know that I'm impressed by nature. What about you? What do you like; what affects *you*?"

I look away, and then back at him. "I like spicy food, but I mean . . . who doesn't? I like black glitter because nothing else in this world is as pretty and dark at the same time. And I like everything raspberry-flavored. But what *moves* me? I'd have to say the Pacific Ocean."

"Really?"

Yeah — really, Kristen? You're seriously going to bring that up?

"Because it's powerful and gentle at the same time," I continue, my voice coming out quiet and slow. "And it can make you feel so . . . small. But then you see how the waves and current and sand can transform something awful like a jagged broken bottle into a beautiful, smooth piece of sea glass, and it makes you want to be a part of that."

I can feel tears form. No, *no*. Don't say it, Kristen. Don't you dare tell him about the lure to walk in until you're over your head.

He scans my face. "I agree. The Pacific Ocean is incredible."

Silence passes. Mario and David stay quiet, too.

The ride ends. We hop off our chair and skate toward the top of our run, where the awkward silence grows like fire, melting snow and time.

Now what? Ethan has his buddies and I have Alana. Um . . . wait. Where did that no-good double-crosser go? Halfway down the hill by now, I'm sure. My foot slips and I fall onto my butt, roll backwards, and land in an unflattering position.

"Need a hand?" Ethan reaches toward me.

"I'm fine. Nothing hurt but my pride. Let me pop off my board, switch my feet around, and figure out how to remove the snow packed inside my pants."

He smiles. "Maybe you should strap your safety leash—"

Too late.

The board slides downhill, clips a passing skier, and flies.

Mario races after it, overshoots the target, shrugs, and continues downhill. David, oblivious to the crisis, trails fast after Mario.

I galumph toward the board, clomping in my gigantic plastic boots, one graceless step at a time while the board barrels downward at increasing speeds.

Ethan zips past me, speeding toward my board as he carves his way through a maze of people, rocks, and trees coming at him from every direction. He catches up to the board and curls around to block its further descent. Then he pops off his board and carries mine back to me without ever drawing an extended breath.

My eyes sting. Is it the biting mountain wind or something else? Has any man *ever* done something this nice for me? How sad that I have to ask myself that question. What about Uncle Mark always rescuing me from my mother's raging neglect? Doesn't that count?

"Thanks. You saved me quite a chase."

"No worries." He hands me the board and his snow jacket cracks open, his cross pendant beaming at me. He grins and motions toward the run. "Shall we?"

Might as well. No one else left to ride with.

With Ethan leading, we take our time, meandering down the hill and stopping at every turn to soak in the next *breathtaking* view. A quarter of the way down, Ethan rests at the edge of a turn and stares into the distance, the crisp air nipping our faces. His gaze reaches toward gigantic snow-topped trees beyond the purple-gray sky.

"Isn't it spectacular . . . all that white?" he asks.

"You've never seen snow before?"

He laughs loudly. "Yes, I've seen it. And I dig it. So pure and beautiful. Isn't it incredible to think of how many snowflakes it must take to create such a blanket of white?"

"Yeah, it's mind-blowing, and I like how the snow sparkles when the sun hits it. Shall we continue downhill? Alana's probably waiting for me by now."

"Sorry. When I see something like this, I have a hard time pulling away because it feels like I'm witnessing proof of God's existence."

I tighten the waist belt on my jacket. "Really? Because I'm standing in front of the same pristine, snow-capped mountain and I don't see God at all. I'd feel the same way if I were standing on the edge of a toxic wasteland. Beauty happens and ugliness happens, too. And sometimes friends die and innocent children are hurt. It just happens. Nothing can explain it away."

His brow wrinkles. "Sorry. I didn't mean to offend you. But can I just say—"

I turn my board and dart downhill, Ethan trailing. I'm sure he could pass me any time he wanted, but he stays behind, letting me lead. Good thing, too. It'd kill me if I had to stare at his back the whole way down. Who does he think he is, anyway? These Bible thumpers assume they have all the answers. Beauty doesn't *prove* God. It just happens, the same way awfulness happens. When Jenna and Danielle were killed, that's just the way the chips fell. It can't be explained away. There's nothing left to do but suck it up and move on.

Before reaching the bottom, I stop sharp. I'll be polite, but I am so done with this guy.

He slides in next to me. "Would you like to grab a hot cup of coffee at the lodge?"

I fake a smile and point down the hill. "Alana's right there, already waiting for me. We've got to go. It was nice meeting you."

He puts out his hand. "Nice meeting you, too. Maybe we'll meet again someday."

I shake his hand and nod as if to agree, but in my mind I'm shouting, *Not if I can help it.*

I turn and glide toward Alana, never glancing back.

"Took you long enough. Must've been a good ride." She glances past my shoulder. "Mickey-D is still watching you."

"Let's get out of here. You were wrong. I *couldn't* do worse. He's a Jesus freak. It would never work."

We return to the condo to freshen up and ice my ankle. Then we crank up the music and spill open our cosmetic bags to gear up for round two of mountain nightlife.

We shuttle over to Whiskey Creek, scarf juicy steaks, and soak our brains with potent fruity drinks. I can't down them fast enough, and neither can Alana. Later, we head upstairs where the DJ spins to a sloshed dance crowd. Wasted, partying singles mingle everywhere. The term *buzzed* has a whole new meaning in this altitude. I should be acclimated by now. So why am I wobbly? It's not bad though, having everything around me melt into a blur. But didn't we do this last night?

Alana boasts about her upcoming wedding. How expensive and luxurious it will be, and how every person alive must be dying for the event to arrive. Yep, we did this last night. If I don't do something soon, my arm is going to fall off from toasting her good fortune for the hundred-millionth time.

Oh, I know.

I run and blab to the DJ that Alana turned twenty-six years old today. He incites the crowd to sing to a slurred, non-copyrighted version of *Happy Birthday*. My dear friend's cheeks burn with embarrassment. Excellent.

Late in the evening, we're resting at the bar when Alana's phone beeps.

"What. Ever," she says after scanning the message.

"What's up?"

"It's Kira, asking if I noticed Andrue changed his Facebook status to single."

"She's joking, right?"

"Andrue and I fought before I came to pick you up. He's having one of his weeklong headache jags." She rolls her eyes. "I tried to be patient because he was — you know — in pain, but I'm sick of his annoying migraines. I yelled at him that I wasn't his nursemaid and he needed to get out of bed and get his own water. I tried to do my Yoga breathing, so I could at least fake being nice, but I couldn't stop the words from flying out of my mouth. I just kept yelling at him, bringing up a bunch of other stuff from fights we've had in the past. I can't remember everything I said, but I'm sure it was awful. I slammed the door when I left."

Speechless, I force my best comforting smile.

Alana's upper lip curls. "I suppose I should apologize."

She orders another drink and dials Andrue, but he doesn't answer. Three more attempts prove futile. Our exorbitant bar bill is unanimously declared a total waste and the celebratory evening crashes to an end.

Happy birthday, Alana.

We spend the next morning snowboarding, but nothing's the same. The clouds are thick and gray and the snow's dull-looking—not one sparkle in sight. It's just a big, cold blanket of ice, freezing the life out of the mountain. My ankle aches. No sign of Ethan anywhere on the hill. Why do I care?

My phone rings during our drive home.

"Ugh. I don't want to talk to anyone."

"Let it ring," says Alana. "I'll bet my best bra the call is from that dreadful Delila. If it's not her, it's your mother. And to be honest, I'm not in the mood to listen to you talking to either one of them."

The phone stops ringing. Good. If it *was* Delila, I'm glad I missed the call. She never did come back to my apartment after that day I found her crumpled at my front door. But she won't stop calling. She tries to convince me she's not psychotic, but I'm not buying it. She keeps reminding me she's homeless and asks if I've found a roommate.

That word. *Homeless.* Why does it irritate the life out of me when she says that? It's like an incessant, nagging ache, suggesting that maybe this time I do have the ability to help someone get off the streets.

The phone rings again. I jam my hand into my bag and grab it. After a long sigh, I answer. "Yeah, Mom."

At first, her words don't soak in. Something about an old lady in a green beater truck sideswiping Uncle Mark's car. A hit-and-run. Air bag didn't engage . . . severe head trauma . . . unconscious . . . "Unable to be roused even with the most painful stimuli," Mom sobs into the phone.

Then it hits me. Uncle Mark has been in a brutal accident.

Alana leaves the top up for the ride home. She sets the station to NPR news. Never-ending coverage of Middle Eastern conflict provides comforting white noise against Alana's relentless griping about Andrue.

"Who does he think he is, breaking up with *me*? He can't even dress himself. *I'm* the one who buys all his clothes. *I'm* the one who got him the marketing manager position at Greenspace Technologies. He would be nothing without . . ."

Alana's voice floats in and out of the fog that fills my brain as I rub the blank screen on my phone. All I hear is a blurred version of her complaints mixed in with NPR headlines. How many miles does this go on? I seem to have lost all sense of time and distance.

Suddenly, she clears her throat. "I've lost you, haven't I?"

I set my phone down and stare blankly ahead.

"Look at me," she says, "ranting at a time like this. Sorry, *chérie*. I can't imagine how you feel. But Mark's so strong and stubborn, I'm sure he's going to pull out of this."

We both remain silent as the long miles home stretch toward eternity.

Chapter 7

STILL THE BEGINNING OF MARCH

❧

WITH MY HAIR wadded into a cap and NPR commentary still ringing in my ears, I dash into the hospital lobby. Mom grabs my arm and rushes me up to room 505, while bystanders watch with pinched expressions. What? They don't like my road trip aroma or something?

I burst through the door, half expecting Uncle Mark to startle. Instead, he lies on the bed with his lids shut, his mouth open, and his chest rhythmically rising and falling. I could believe he's just sleeping, if not for the lacerations covering his arms and face. And the miles of gauze wrapped around his head.

This can't be happening.

The last time I saw Mark, we laughed until our sides ached. The doctors must be mistaken when they say he has an eighty-five percent chance of either dying or remaining in a permanent vegetative state. So what if they performed neurological tests? I don't care how thorough they were. They *have* to be wrong.

"Those are projections from men." Mom picks at the sleeve of her fleece pullover and flicks a tuft of lint to the floor.

From what I've been told, two of the doctors from Mark's team are women, but who's in the mood to argue?

Mom adjusts her gold cross pendant until it rests inside the hollow of her throat. "Only God knows what will happen in the future. Man can only summarize history and experience, and then *guess* what the future will bring."

So many chaotic thoughts race through my mind, I'm unable to form a single word. Doctors tell us it's a miracle he's breathing on his own. They also say it's good for Mark to hear our voices. Mom whips out her Bible and reads until her voice goes dry. When it's my turn, I read from an outdated magazine I find lying around.

"I'm meeting Steve at that little restaurant across the street." Mom glances at her watch. "You want to come?"

"No, thanks. Can you bring me some Raspberry Zingers on your way back, if the snack machine has them?"

She nods and then leaves. I scoot close to Mark and take his hand. Laughter rolls in from the nurses' station down the hall. Machines beep. Mark breathes.

I pull my sketchbook out of my handbag and crack it open. "Not sure why I brought this. Wanted to show you some design ideas I sketched in the car, but it's not like you're going to open your eyes just because I have something to share."

I close the book. "Do you remember how much I used to love sitting in your lap? Man, I had a lot to talk about back then. And you were patient. *Are* patient. You're still here, so it's are. You saved me, Mark. I wouldn't have survived without you. Remember when you found me alone in the bath when Mom had passed out from drinking? Eleven months old. Of course, I don't remember the actual event. I only know because you told me. If only it was like that for everything . . . not being able to remember. I still need you, Mark. Who's going to keep saving me from myself?"

I glance around and lower my voice. "I'm still having those dreams. I think I'm losing my mind, but maybe I'm making too much out of it.

"Speaking of crazy, I met this guy in Mammoth. His name's Ethan. I'm not interested in him as a boyfriend or anything like that. I'm pretty sure he's a Jesus nut, so it would never work — not that we'll *ever* run into each other again. But for some reason, he keeps popping into my head. He rescued my runaway snowboard. Stupid, right? Why am I making such a big deal about something so small? Because it was nice, that's why. Another reason it wouldn't work. I'm more of a narcissistic-worthless-fellow kind of gal. How else can I succeed in my plan for ultimate self-destruction?

"Um, can you hear me? If you can, for the record, I'm totally kidding."

I lean back and shrug. "Whatever. Life goes on. As usual, I'm struggling to stay above water at work.

"Tell me, Mark. Who am I supposed to be? And how on earth am I going to keep myself from walking into the ocean? Haven't told you about that one yet. If you wake up, maybe I will."

Anonymous people shuffle past Mark's room. Machines keep beeping. Hours blend into days and days stretch into weeks. I drag myself to the hospital, through the corridors, and into the suffocating stench of disinfectant and death. How many of these lives hang in the balance?

Mom and I wear our voices thin reading and talking to Mark. He has the appearance of function, but he never responds. Regardless of how many times I check in, day after enduring day, nothing happens. I hate it here, but I miss my uncle's smile, so I keep coming, forcing my presence on him, hoping one day I'll see that smile again.

The worst part is the abundance of Zingers at the hospital. My extra eight pounds have grown to ten. Mom enjoys these raspberry flavored cream cakes, too, and we often buy a pile of them and eat until we're sick. When was the last time she and I had bonded over anything? I guess that's something good that's come from this. We're both devastated by Mark's condition. Finally, we have something big in common. Is that cruel irony, or what? This morning, it actually felt like we were getting along as we sat side-by-side in Mark's room.

"You should take a break," Mom had said, gathering up our Zinger wrappers. "I'll call if anything happens."

What could I possibly do to keep myself busy outside of Memorial Hospital? I'd tackle something from work, if the Zahed project hadn't been taken from me. If only I had known it was a bad idea to ask for some time off. Mr. L.A. was gracious enough to allow it, but how was I to know his patience would only last five days, and that on day six he'd hand the project to Owen?

Owen. According to Delila, he's one of the "seven." And now I'm a floater, barely pulling in thirty-five hours a week.

I took Mom's advice anyway, and left the hospital. And now I'm alone in my empty apartment, wandering from one chilly room to the next with absolutely nothing to do. A nap sounds good, but instead I reach into my nightstand drawer, lift the false bottom, and caress the sealed pint of Jack Daniels. The bottle is supposed to be a reminder of the whiskey's potential for evil. Give me a break. Why would I need a reminder to recall the night I kissed my best friend's boyfriend and almost killed a little boy from behind my drunken wheel? Three years have passed, and I can still hear that kid yelling at me in angry Spanglish.

I grab the whiskey and head for the beach, a mere two hundred feet from my apartment complex. My legs are on autopilot, moving me out of the building, down the walkway, and into the sand before I realize what I'm doing. But I know. *Oh, I know.*

Salty wind thrashes my hair, turning me into a raging Medusa, snaked strands writhing on top of my head as I march up to the water. Fog smothers the horizon. My heart pounds at the sight of the water. So intense. So deeply charcoal-blue. My pulse slows at the roaring sounds of the crashing waves, the rhythm pressing me to step close. Instead, I step back and plant myself on a ridge of sand above the lapping water, where I pick at the bottle's seal.

What are you doing? I ask myself.

I'm thirsty. And I want to be numb. It'll be easier this way.

Do you really want this?

Yes, I do. I want to submerge myself inside a liquid cocoon and forget the world.

Is it that bad?

I wipe my eyes. No, I suppose not. Good grief, where are all these tears coming from? I didn't shed one drop when Mom told me about the accident, and not one during all the visits when I sat for hours staring at Mark . . . so why now?

Because you cannot lose Mark. He's the only solid foundation in your life.

Why does everything have to be so hard? Haven't I suffered enough?

Waves roar and the ocean laughs, drawing me in with its repetitive pull. I set the bottle down and step forward, ankle, knee, and then hip deep, the water numbing my legs. It'll be easy. I won't even need the JD. And this time, I won't struggle.

My phone rings, zapping me out of my trance-like state. Unknown caller. Curiosity compels me to answer.

"Hey there, it's Delila. This a bad time?"

"Um . . ."

"I'll be quick. Promise. I've been going to the library, working on my graphics design business. Everything's going my way. Reconnected with an old friend who's letting me crash on her couch for a few days. It's been nice not having to sleep in my car. By the way, have you found a roommate to replace the old one? Because I think my friend is anxious to get her couch back."

Waves crash against my thighs.

"Hello, Kristen? You at the beach?"

"Yeah, listen, I can't take you in if you can't pay rent."

Where are these words coming from?

"I *can* pay," she insists. "I've got five clients and I'll have three more by next week. Already have enough cash to pay first and last month's rent. My business is growing. Can you believe it?"

"Fine," I blurt, the words rushing from my throat before I can stop them. "You can move in May 1st, assuming you're still earning enough money to pay rent."

She squeals and my stomach churns. But I don't care. I'm sick of living alone. Delila can't be any worse than my last roommate. I hang up while she's still celebrating. I leave the water, grab the whiskey, and return home. Today's not a good day to walk into the ocean. Mark could wake up tomorrow.

CHAPTER 8

LATE APRIL

❧

I   T'S ALREADY THE end of April, and Mark remains still. Wind rushes
by outside the window, tugging on branches, forcing the trees to bend
farther than they seem to like. I hate this coma, this beast that forces us to
exist in separate worlds. "Open your eyes, Mark! Open them! Why won't
you open your eyes?"

Nothing.

I rest my head on his chest and give up. I just . . . give up.

"Kristen, are you awake?"

I lift my head and wipe my eyes. "Yeah, Mom. Just tired. Of all of this,
you know?"

"Yes, I do." She takes a seat across from me and places her hand on
Mark's arm.

"Have you called your parents?" I ask. "Do they know about Mark's
coma?"

She shifts in her seat and averts her gaze. "I don't talk to them. And
neither does Mark."

"I know they were *only* your foster parents, but they're also the only
parents you ever really knew. Haven't you had *any* desire to contact them
since the day you and Mark ran away? I mean, I know they were upset
over your teenage pregnancy, but they can't hate me so much that they
would still be mad at you."

"Kristen, honey, it's not you. They . . ." her mouth opens and her chin
quivers. Then she stands up and walks away. Just like that.

So we're done bonding over Mark? No more conversations where
we're actually listening to each other?

I should give her a break. When they were growing up, Mark took his
job as older foster brother seriously. He protected her and took care of
her. I guess now it's Mom's turn to watch out for Mark.

55

Dude remains in a persistent vegetative state. Still alive, still breathing on his own, and still not doing anything. Once he drew a high fever, which excited the hospital staff, but only once. Mom plans to move him to a long-term care facility and she has to fill out a ton of paperwork from attorneys and insurance agents. The bureaucracy has manifested itself as an invisible weight pressing on her shoulders. Exhaustion seems to be pulling her away from me.

A week later, I let go. I give Mom space to breathe and she uses it to spend time alone with her comatose brother. I head downstairs and find Mom's recovery friends fluttering in the lobby, weaving themselves into a human nest, where they feed on prayer and support. They're like hungry little birds, mouths open, waiting for whatever comes next. Reminds me of the time Robyn's son went through chemo, and the time Molly lost her newborn grandchild. And again, two years ago, when Dorothy had a mental breakdown.

There's Dorothy now, standing at the outer edge of the recovery flock, praying like the others, except *her* expression is frosted over. As usual, the climate surrounding Dorothy is arid, a good twenty degrees cooler than the rest of the planet. I'd better veer toward the other end of the nest.

Robyn breaks away from the prayer circle to wrap her bingo-winged arm around my shoulder. "How you doing, sugar?"

"Good, except money's been tight since my roommate left."

She gives me a squeeze.

"I have a new roommate moving in soon. Delila. Something's off about her. Can't pinpoint it exactly. I mean, I have a hard time believing everything she says. But she doesn't have anywhere else to go, and I'm a sucker for the homeless."

"I'm always praying for you, sugar. I'll add Delila to the list."

"Thanks." I smile, and then slip out from Robyn's hold. "Delila's harmless. Has a strange sense of style — she'll probably turn my apartment into a Hindu lounge, smothered in red and purple — but I'm not in any physical danger."

Robyn nods and then moves back into the group. The women, no longer praying, stay huddled together, chattering among themselves. I take a step toward the convenience store, but freeze when a familiar profile comes into view.

No way . . . it can't be, can it? Broad, posture-perfect shoulders. And that jaw . . . beard's gone, but I'm sure it's him. Alana's going to flip. Ethan's *here*, in the same building as me, bee-lining toward our group. But I'm not his target. His focus is on someone else, his grin expanding as he approaches. The next few seconds tick past fast, his steps moving him closer to the group and right up to Dorothy.

"Hi, Mom." He leans in and kisses her forehead.

What?

Dorothy asks him about his flight. Have I ever seen her expression so soft? I duck behind Robyn's generous frame, my heart pounding in my ears. As I hunch down, Robyn turns to me, her brow crinkling. She's concentrating, calculating. She throws a hand in the air. "Ethan, sugar! Have you met Mary's daughter, Kristen?"

Dorothy whips her head around, her eyes growing as large as saucers.

"Kristen?" Ethan's pitch is high, as if he swallowed a flute. "Is that really you?" He glides over, approaching so close I have to step back.

"Ethan. Wow. Imagine the chances of us meeting again."

"Yeah, imagine that." His stretching smile gleams.

Dorothy jabs a knobby arthritic finger into our conversation. "You two are familiar with each other?"

"We met in Mammoth several weeks ago," explains Ethan.

"Wasn't that a *men's* retreat?"

"Yep. We're still on for dinner?"

"I was hoping we could catch up now."

"I want to visit with you, too, Mom, but I have just enough time before my meeting to catch up with Kristen. We'll have plenty of time to spend together at home. All right?"

She scowls, but Ethan doesn't seem to notice. He smiles at me. "You have time for a quick cup of coffee?"

Are you kidding? I'd do anything to keep that steam blowing out of Dorothy's ears. Her reaction is priceless.

"Sure."

Ethan kisses his mother's forehead again and we're off.

Before we reach the cafeteria, Ethan stops at a vending machine. "I wonder if they have Barbeque Corn Nuts."

"They do, and Raspberry Zingers, too."

He feeds change into the machine, then presses K7 and J11, releasing a three-pack of Zingers and a bag of Corn Nuts from their spiraled yokes. The nuts and cake crash into each other in the bottom tray. Ethan hands me the Zingers and we move on, his ever-present smile beginning to creep me out.

Inside the cafeteria, I lean back into my chair, gripping my cup of coffee like the horn of a saddle. What's wrong with me? I sip the pungent sludge as I stare at his cup. Neither of us bothered to add milk or sugar to our liquid ooze. I scan him over. He sure cleans up nice. Slate cotton trousers and gray boat shoes. White, lightweight button-up shirt. Not a runway look, but a clean, friendly one.

"Fresh haircut?"

"Yeah." He blushes, raking back what's left.

"That's a great style for wiry hair." No, that sounded like an insult. "You might try using some product to give the front a little swoop to the side. Highlights would look good, too." Shut up, Kristen. You're making it worse.

He nods. If only he'd stop grinning. His shirt's unbuttoned on top. That pendant — a cross made from real nails bound with copper wire. *Aack!* He sees me gawking.

"So Dorothy's your mom?"

"Yes," he says. "I grew up with my dad in Colorado, though. My parents divorced when I was seven."

"Your mother didn't fight for you?" Nice one, Kristen. What? You couldn't think of something even more stupid to say?

Ethan's smile fades. "Mom visited when she could. I came out here a few times, too. It was complicated."

I nod. *Complicated.* Yep. Been there. "Dorothy's not happy that we know each other. She's never liked me, you know."

He doesn't respond. Is he afraid I'll jump all over him if he speaks, like I did on the mountain?

I sip my sludge. "To be fair, when Mom joined the recovery group, I was an angry pre-teen. Goth. You know, dressed like death all the time. And I had a horrible attitude. Anyway, I must've made a strong first impression, because no matter how much I've changed, Dorothy's attitude toward me never has."

"I'm sorry my mother makes you uncomfortable."

My cheeks flush. "No, I'm sorry. That's no way to begin our conversation. I mean, how small is this world? I can't believe we met again."

He smiles knowingly, but about what, I have no idea. He peels open his bag and chews a single Corn Nut. Then he pins his eyes on mine. "Mom told me her friend's brother was here, but I had no idea Mary was your mother." He leans close and places his hand on my arm. "I'm sorry about your uncle's condition. I'm praying for him."

"Thanks." Another prayer warrior. Wonderful. "Are you here visiting Dorothy?"

He finishes crunching a couple more nuts. "I have an internship in physical therapy at this hospital. I'll be living in the area for the next nine months." He lifts and rocks his empty cup. "I'm going to grab a refill. Can I get you one, too?"

"I'm good."

While he's gone, I use my tongue to scrape a chunk of Zinger from the roof of my mouth. How is it that my snack is gone, when his bag's still full? So this guy's going to be around for the next nine months. Interesting.

He returns with a full cup of sludge.

"You'll like California," I say cheerfully.

That smile again. "I'm sure I will, but I already miss Colorado. My dad, the mountains, fishing the big lakes."

"Boat fishing? You can do that here."

"Yeah, I'm looking forward to taking my buddy's yacht out on the ocean. And shooting, I can do that here, too."

"You shoot? Me, too." I shake crumbs from my blouse.

"Really?" He tucks the half-eaten bag of Corn Nuts into his pants pocket. His eyes keep sweeping over my face, as the dead silence grows more awkward with each passing second.

"What's with the face?"

"Sorry." He rubs his forehead. "You seem familiar, like I've met you before Mammoth. It's your eyes."

"Squinty and green? What about them?"

"They're unusual, but I've seen them before. You could be Milla Jovovich's sister."

"You mean I could be the sibling that was short-changed on gene-pool allocation day?"

"No, not at all."

"Oh, well . . . thanks, but how about a change of subject?"

"Do you work nearby?"

"I work for an interior design firm in L.A." I roll my eyes.

"You don't enjoy your job?"

"I love it. At least, the creative side. It's the people I can't stand."

"Difficult clients?"

"Yeah, and sometimes my co-workers are even worse." I pick at the lip of my cup. "Design was my second career choice. I used to be a runner. Was a track and field all-star in high school. Coach said I was Olympic material, but I never believed it. I loved running, though, getting into that mind-body zone and escaping from everything else. And I was good at it. My times earned me a scholarship and a spot on a decent college team."

"You raced in college?"

"No. I broke my ankle before the first major race. That ended my running career, so I transferred to art school."

"How'd you break your ankle?"

"You ask a lot of questions." I cross my arms. "I was co-dependent back then, okay? I let an abusive ex-boyfriend suck me back into his world — don't look at me like that — I don't need pity."

He polishes off his coffee, leans back, and rests his hands in his lap.

"I never let the guy run me over. Whenever he came at me, I flared my nostrils and charged him right back.

"Anyway, after we broke up, suddenly he was this nice guy, trying to win me back. Like an idiot, I let him talk me into smoking a joint three days before the first big race of the season. I hoped the weed would calm our nerves, help us work through our issues. I still loved him. Or at least I thought I did. But as soon as we started talking about our relationship, he got angry and shoved me into the side of a building."

I lift my cup to my lips, but the edge is jagged from being picked at, and the sludge is gone. Ethan sits and waits to listen for more, as if this is the most everyday story he's ever heard.

"I shoved him back at first," I continue, "but then all I wanted to do was get away from him, so I turned and ran. I wasn't far from my dorm and I knew . . . I *knew* he wouldn't follow. But I kept running as fast as I could. I could hardly see from all the tears streaming down my cheeks and didn't even notice the plastic bag lying on the cement. All I knew was that my right foot slipped and I heard a loud snap. Broke my ankle in two places. Even after surgery and rehabilitation, I was never able to run competitively again."

Holy blabbermouth, where's your filter, Kristen? And why is Ethan's face deadpan? Not even a flinch. Seriously?

"Wow, that's . . ."

"Sucks, right?"

"Yeah." He glances at his watch and then at me. "I'd love to talk about this some more, but I have to go. I have a meeting with the Department of Rehabilitation. Would it be okay if we exchange phone numbers? Maybe even meet at the shooting range sometime?"

He's asking for my phone number after that? I'm going to have to work harder to shake this guy off. He pulls out an old-school flip phone. Probably doesn't even have a camera on it. I scribble my number down on a napkin and slide it toward him, then stand and walk away. Zinger crumbs drop from my lap to the floor as I leave him and his creepy grin behind.

On my way home, I drive up next to a homeless man begging from the center divider. Decked out in fatigues and combat boots, the man shivers against the determined wind. I search for cash, as if money will make any difference. No amount of cash could ever shake my survivor's guilt. Even though it was Mom, not me, who sold our souls to Victor so we wouldn't have to live on the streets.

I flick through my wallet, fumble in my pockets, and rattle the change tray — all empty. Lucky for this guy, I have fresh-purchased groceries in the car. I call him over. He approaches my open window, his long tangled curls bouncing in chunks. Same wild hair and demeanor as the hobo from the beach on New Year's Eve, and the one who barfed on me at the Fashion District. That's silly, though. How can these three men possibly be the same?

Good grief, he smells like a garbage can full of rotting food.

"I have a baguette," I offer.

"Not sure what I'd do with bread." His words come out slow, as if the light signal will never change.

I raise my brow. "You could *eat* it."

"I ain't got no teeth. Lost 'em in Vietnam."

And then I see it . . . the empty space that fills his mouth. The guy has three teeth at the most.

"Oh." I glance to the floor of the car, next to my handbag, where a clear plastic box glistens. The container protects a slice of red velvet cake, a moist, sugary treat I've been drooling over for more than an hour. I hesitate for about five seconds before grabbing it.

"I have cake. Would you like it?"

He nods, and I eye the mouthwatering delicacy one more time before I hand it over.

"They dang near killed me in that Vietnam war."

The light turns green.

"I'll bet they did," I reply before taking off.

I'm going to really miss that piece of cake.

CHAPTER 9

MAY

∝∽○

DELILA STRIDES AHEAD, toward the sand, while Alana meets me in the parking lot, her lip curling back as if she smells something bad.

"I hate you for making me come to this stupid *Welcome Delila* party. Who throws their own celebration, anyway?"

"My new roommate, that's who."

"Don't get me started," she grumbles. "You're an idiot for letting that woman into your home."

"You're a fool for getting back together with Andrue."

"Andrue and I are made for each other. Nothing can keep us apart, so stop trying to change the subject. How could you let Delila manipulate you?"

"She was living on and off the street."

"If Charles Manson was homeless, would you take him in, too?"

"It's going to be fine."

"Why are you acting like such a doorknob?"

"She's harmless."

Alana raises her penciled brows.

"Sure, she's a little sketchy," I respond. "I mean, her eyes creep me out. They never seem to match the words that come out of her mouth. So yeah, I don't believe everything she says. And I still think it's strange that every time something went wrong last year, I found her standing in the middle of it."

"And you invited her into your home because . . ."

"Because something about her draws me in and tells me that deep down, way beneath that erratic exterior, is a person with a real beating heart who is only trying to survive. Just like the rest of us. Besides, no matter what Delila is or what her intentions are, I can handle myself. I'm not worried. C'mon, let's join her and get this party over with."

63

We walk up to Delila, who stands arm-in-arm with a tall, brawny man near the fire pit.

"This is my man, Legion," she announces.

"Hey," he grunts, reaching a hand out to Alana, then to me, deep creases running across his forehead. Dude seems too young to look that old. Ink covers his arms, neck, and legs. The sheer number of tattoos is astounding. So many intertwined that I can't appreciate, let alone distinguish, any single image. Nice-looking fellow, though — shaved head, amber eyes, bursting muscles.

"Pleased to meet you," Alana says, and I do the same.

"I brought a case of Deschutes Black Butte Porter." He reaches into the cooler, uncaps a few bottles, and fills four red plastic cups. He passes out the drinks and raises his cup. "To Delila's new home." In a single swig, the drink vanishes.

Delila giggles.

Alana and I sip along, raising our brows at each other.

"*Mmmm*," I moan after a long sip. "Um . . . was that out loud? Good stuff."

Legion laughs and tops off our cups.

"What do you do?" asks Alana.

"Ex-Marine." His throat catches on the words as if they've summoned a flood of memories packed with emotion. He narrows his eyes, hard lines forming along his jaw.

After a few awkward moments of silence, Alana smiles. "For work, I mean."

"Construction, but I'm out of work."

She rolls her eyes. "Yep. This economy sucks for contractors."

The four of us nod in unison.

Ethan arrives next. If he could handle one of my *real Kristen* stories without flinching, then I suppose I won't mind hanging out with him. Besides, I didn't want to be the only one at this party who came alone, so why not invite him here? He's wearing jeans, a faded blue tee, and that blasted cross pendant. I hope he doesn't feel out of place. He's sure to be the only one wearing long pants at this beach party. He embraces me in a strong hug. It's quick, definitely in the friend zone, but long enough for me to catch that fresh linen scent.

As Ethan's getting acquainted with Delila and Legion, Andrue approaches from the parking lot. I whisper in Alana's ear. "When did he start wearing wife beaters?"

"Tell me about it. He says I'm too controlling. Moron wants to be independent. Wants to dress himself. So I'm out of it. And *this*," both hands thrust forward, "is what we end up with."

"Moron? You understand he's your fiancé, right?"

"Don't remind me."

My phone rings and I step away to answer.

"Kristen, honey," Mom says breathlessly. "Can we meet? We need to talk."

"Can it wait? Delila's bonfire party, remember?"

"Bolsa Chica?"

"No, Dockweiler. Why?"

"Are you near the parking lot?"

"Kind of . . . why? Mom, pleeeease don't crash the party. We'll talk tomorrow."

I hang up. *Party* is a stretch. No one else has arrived.

Mom won't come here. God, please don't let her come. Every time she wants to "have a talk," I'm the one who comes out mangled on the other end.

"Where is everybody?" Alana's eyes are wide and mocking.

Delila pecks at her phone. "I invited a bunch of people. Got some messages saying they can't make it. No answer from the rest."

Alana leans over Delila's shoulder. "Your screen is blank."

Delila slowly lifts her eyes to Alana. "I just turned it off."

"Well, flip it back on. Let's see all these friends you have."

"Alana!" I glare at her. She knows the look.

"Fine." She claps her hands. "Let's get this ghetto party started. Kristen and I will set up the net."

I yank on her arm as we walk away.

She feigns innocence. "What? That's the nickname for this place, *the ghetto people's beach*. I'm not bashing the location. Hey, I can ghetto like the best of them, but wouldn't it be better to party somewhere not overrun by gang-bangers?" She nods toward a large group setting up two fire pits away.

"You're stereotyping. And you know that's not what I'm talking about. Do you think you can get through the next few hours without pummeling Delila into the sand?"

She secures the net to the first pole, cinching it tight. "Her screen was blank, and she didn't just turn it off."

"Why do you care?"

"She said she invited a bunch of friends. Where did all these friends come from? And if she's got a bunch of them, why are *you* the only one who can offer her a place to live?"

"Maybe she doesn't have any friends. Maybe we're it, and maybe she lied about it because she was embarrassed."

"Aren't you curious to know for sure?"

"No. It's a beautiful day and we're at the beach. How about we just focus on that?"

"It's foggy, sixty-five degrees, and we're setting up camp beneath LAX flight traffic, next to the Hyperion sewage treatment plant. Yeah, I'll savor the moment."

Our neighbors crank up their speakers, and thumping booty call beats waft past. Alana stomps to the second pole, snatches the rope from my hands and pulls hard, overextending the net. She scowls at the source of the music and then turns away. "Help me scan the sand for nails and broken glass. I've cut my feet at this beach way too many times."

We toss our collected sharp objects into the trash and head back to the others. "No one else is coming," huffs Alana. "Let's start the volleyball tournament."

She assigns the teams: Delila and Legion, me and Andrue, and Alana and Ethan. She must've checked Ethan out when he rallied with Andrue while we set up the net. That's why she put Ethan on her team and not mine. She wants to win. Fine with me.

By a draw of sticks, Alana and Ethan are chosen to play Delila and Legion. They'll play best of five while Andrue and I wait on the sideline.

"This sucks," gripes Andrue. "I want to play now. How about we rally while we wait?"

"No, thanks. I wanna watch the games."

"Oh yeah? Who you want to watch? Ethan?"

"Shut up. It's not like that."

"Sure it isn't."

"What are you, twelve? Ethan's just a friend."

"Uh-huh."

"He's never made a pass and that's fine with me because he's not my type. We have fun talking on the phone, but it's all stupid stuff, like how girls talk. Maybe he's not into girls. Maybe he's gay. Either way, we're just friends and I want to watch the game, so leave me alone."

"Somebody's defensive. I'm getting another drink. Want something?"

"Sure. Another beer sounds good."

Alana serves first, the ball slicing past Legion's reach. He catches the next one, Delila sets, and he slams it over the net. Ethan dives to catch it. Alana sets and Ethan slams, but Legion blocks it. They have the ball.

All four play hard, sweating and diving like mad. Delila's quick and consistent. Legion and Alana are power hitters, wearing game faces that could frighten timid children and small pets. Ethan's swift, even in those restrictive jeans, and he never stops smiling. Never misses a ball, either. It's like he knows where they're going before they get there. It must suck for Alana, knowing every point they've lost has been because of her.

The teams are a close match, each earning two wins by the end of game four. No one wants to take a break. They're all hungry for the win.

Game five is rough. Legion's not missing any of Alana's serves and her neck vein throbs nonstop. Delila steps up her game, trading consistency for risks with big payoffs. Alana and Ethan have kept up, but now it's game point for Legion and Delila.

I've never seen Delila so lit up. She jump serves and pounds the ball to the far corner of Alana's side of the court, but Alana dives for it and gets the ball up. Ethan lunges for the ball, but trips.

Seriously . . . on what? How did he fall?

The ball drops to the sand.

Legion and Delila win.

Alana storms off.

Andrue and I are up against Legion and Delila. Best of five takes all. They decline the offer to take a break, even though they've sweated through five games in a row already. Andrue's been drinking like a fish today, so I'm grateful for the handicap. In spite of the weather, the four of us remain stripped down to minimal clothing.

Delila and I face each other from across the net. I crouch in ready position and marvel at all the tattoos I never knew she had. The images are different from Legion's, but they have a similar blend of mysticism and fantasy.

We play hard. If only I wasn't such a grunter, animalistic sounds coming out of my body every time I touch the ball. But my spikes are killing it, so who cares? I'm in the zone. Andrue's on fire, too. Drunk or not, he's got game. He's a little testy, though, snapping at me every time I miss, even when the fault is his.

Andrue and I take the first game. Barely. Legion and Delila take the second. With Andrue wasted and Legion and Delila exhausted, we're an equal match. Andrue and I take game three. They take game four. The fifth game runs long, all of us diving like lunatics, coating ourselves in thick layers of sand and sweat.

It's thirty to twenty-nine, Legion and Delila's game point, Ethan watching from the sidelines while sweat rolls down my back. I squat into position at the net, face-to-face with Delila. Her mouth curves into a surprisingly sinister grin.

Legion serves short and I block. Delila returns my block and Andrue digs deep into the sand. I set, and Andrue slams it over the net for an impossible return. Legion leaps across the court in time to get the ball. By the time Delila sets, Legion's at the net and he drives the ball hard into the husband-and-wife spot — that ominous space between Andrue and me where communication has evaporated.

"That was yours," snaps Andrue.

"Or it was yours. Chill, man. It's just a game."

He blows out his heated breath.

We walk over to salute the champions. Who knew those two could play? I guess they don't spend all their free time soaking their brains in booze.

I grip Delila's hand. "Congratulations. You two deserved the win. Too bad we don't have a real prize. All you'll have to take home is recognition."

Delila bats her false lashes. "Recognition is all I ever wanted."

Our eyes lock. Does she want to say something?

A plane passes overhead and the booty call beats get louder. The moment fades.

Ethan congratulates the winners and Alana follows his example, not an ounce of bitterness escaping her pores. Her walk must have cooled her off. "You guys are good," she says. "Where did you pick up those skills?"

"High school." Delila blushes.

Turns out she led her state championship girls' volleyball team in serving aces, like Alana. Legion says he learned to play "on the streets."

Wait — didn't Delila tell me she ran away at fourteen? Is she lying to impress Alana?

Andrue jogs over to the cooler and I find myself alone with Ethan, who smiles maniacally at me. "You take this game seriously."

My knees, elbows, and face burn from abrasion, and I've got sand caked in places I don't want to talk about. Why don't Olympic volleyball players ever walk off the court looking like they've been tied to the back of a speeding truck?

I brush sand off my arms. "You don't take it seriously enough. You threw that game. If Alana figures that out, you're dead."

He laughs. "What? I tripped."

"Uh-huh. Why'd you do it?"

"I'm not admitting anything, but let's just say that sometimes it's not about winning."

"You understand you're playing with fire, right?"

He glances over at Alana, Legion, and Delila huddled deep in volleyball conversation. "Looks to me like she's already gotten over it."

He pulls out a film camera. Holy cow, what else does he have in his backpack, a Walkman?

"Smile."

"No, I'm a wreck."

"You look great. I'm sending a bunch of pictures of "California life" to my dad."

"Really? Sand-coated sweaty girl, who's trashed from volleyball, represents California life? Whatever . . . *cheeeeeeeese.*"

The sun sets, but the party carries on. We settle into camp chairs and huddle around the cement ring stamped with large red lettering, CAUTION — HOT COALS. We chat about nothing special. Legion and Alana throw in a few crude jokes. Ethan pulls out a giant thermos and an entire set of stackable ceramic mugs from his tiny backpack, like he's David Copperfield. He offers coffee all around, but gets no takers. We're all holding red cups full of beer, for crying out loud. But I guess I'm done. I mean, haven't we checked off all the boxes yet? Isn't it getting close to when we can call it a day?

"I'll have a cup." I set down my beer, and cradle the delicate mug while Ethan fills it. I watch the others roast hot dogs and marshmallows over the bonfire while I take long, slow draws of some of the strongest coffee I've ever tasted.

An hour later, Alana and Andrue get into a heated argument, their tempers reaching the sky. Alana jumps up and turns her head toward the water. I bet she'd run and dive into the fifty-seven degree ocean if it was any other beach, but the water here is disgusting. Fear of tetanus, or worse, one of those freaky flesh-eating viruses, keeps her at bay.

She faces Andrue and continues scolding: *you never listen, you're a stubborn blockhead, and what exactly is your problem?*

He yells back: *you never make sense, you're a control freak, and you don't get me.*

Alana shoves his shoulder and he shoves back, hard enough to knock her down. Ethan and Legion jump up and step between the fighting couple. I offer to help Alana up out of the sand, but she brushes me away. Planes keep flying past, whistling like overworked vacuum cleaners, as our neighbors' music blares on.

Legion's had way too much to drink, and he's in Andrue's face. "That's no way to treat your girlfriend, man!"

Andrue pushes back hard. "Step away, Marine."

Ethan wedges himself between them. "It's okay. Relax. Put your fists down. Both of you take it easy."

They keep yelling, but Ethan keeps himself wedged between them repeating his mantra . . . *it's okay . . . relax . . . it's okay . . .*

Legion and Andrue are beefy men, but Ethan's got them beat in presence. Something about his confidence and the soothing tone of his voice. Tempers cool. Andrue apologizes to Alana and they hug, promising they'll never fight again. We settle back into our chairs, all of us trying to act unruffled. Delila yammers on about her new graphics design business, but Ethan's the only one who's listening. I'm grateful for the white noise.

My phone rings. It's my mother, fifth time since I got here. I turn it off. What does she want to talk about this time? The last time we "needed to talk," she guilted me into signing up for anger management classes. That went over well. Spent the next day patching a hole in my wall from where I threw a marble candleholder. No, we don't need to talk. Not tonight, anyway. I stand up and head toward the water, with zero intention of walking in. I just need to put some space between the chaos and me.

Ethan follows me and catches up. "You're not going to leave me alone with a bunch of strangers, are you?"

"You're kidding, right? Mister Social? Besides, you've been around them all day. You know them as well as I do now."

"Actually, I'd like to talk."

"You too, huh?"

We stroll right up to the wet sand and stop. That long pause before a person gets something off his or her chest is always the worst. Why can't people spit out what they need to say?

"That day we had coffee together at the hospital," his voice comes out cracked, as if he's forcing himself to speak, "you mentioned that my mother never liked you."

"Yeah . . ."

"It's not personal. My mother has a lot of issues."

"Ethan, when someone attacks you, it's personal."

"Okay, maybe you're right. But she's trying. You should've seen what she was like before recovery. She's changed since I was a little boy."

"I'm sorry. The divorce must've been hard."

"It was. But it was worse before the divorce. She was still drinking then, and she was *not* a happy drunk. She's much nicer than she used to be. And she's still trying to improve."

An image of a young Ethan cowering beneath an even-worse Dorothy enters my head.

"Okay. This is the new, improved version of Dorothy. I'll try to remember that the next time she attacks me. But it won't be easy. She's been awful to me for a long time. And I don't think that's going to change any time soon."

"I know."

"You agree?"

"Yeah . . . sometimes forgiving feels like we're making ourselves vulnerable."

"That's not what I said, but I guess you sort of get it."

The moonlight flickers against the ocean like thousands of diamonds floating on the surface. Unceasing flight traffic drowns out the sound of crashing waves, but at least that horrid music is muted from here.

"So . . ." he says, "why'd you leave the bonfire?"

"Because of *my* mother." My upper lip curls back. "She won't stop calling me. Has something she wants to talk about. And whatever it is, I'm not in the mood."

Ethan just stands there, all awkward and silent.

"Um, you've got that wild look again."

"Sorry," he says. "It's those eyes."

"The eyes again, really? They're nothing special."

He steps closer. "They're unusual, and yet . . ." His breath grows heavy. Is he leaning in? No. He steps back and rakes his fingers through his hair. "Can I ask you a personal question?"

"Can I stop you?"

"Back on the mountain, you mentioned some of the ugliness in this world, like how friends die for no reason and innocent children get hurt. Were you speaking from personal experience?"

I narrow my eyes. "Yes. I lost my friends Jenna and Danielle. Alana, these two, and I were supposed to be best friends forever. We did everything together, even formed our own exclusive, sisterhood club. After college, Jenna and Danielle went to some revival camp, only because they were bored. They never expected anything to happen. But they came back 'saved,' as they put it. Two weeks later, a texting driver killed them. And then they were gone. *Gone.* Some good being *saved* did them, huh?"

"Wow. That must've been awful. I can see how it would be hard to imagine there's a God when something like that happens."

"Yeah, it sure is." I cross my arms and press my lips together.

"Listen," he says. "Sometimes I get caught up in my faith, but I know how bothered I get when other people try to push their agenda on me when they haven't even gotten to know me first. So will you please let me know when I go overboard?"

"Uh, yeah. I mean, I'm actually surprised to hear you say that . . ."

A horrifying noise pierces my ears. "Kristen, honey!"

"Are you serious right now? She actually *drove* down here?"

"Your mother?"

"The one and only."

She's running in the sand, stumbling and flapping her arms.

"I'm going to head back," says Ethan, "so you can talk to your mother. And I'm truly sorry about your friends."

He turns away and I exhale. As his frame gets smaller, Mom's gets larger. My shoulders stiffen, sending a sharp pain up and through my neck.

Mom reaches me. Gasping, she bends over and plants her palms onto her thighs.

"Sorry . . . to interrupt . . . your party," she says, still short of breath. "I couldn't wait . . . any longer."

"How'd you find me?"

"Steve helped." She points to a shadow in the distance. "We've been up and down this beach—"

"This isn't a good time."

"Kristen, honey, let's sit."

I start to turn away, but she grabs my hand and eases me down with her onto a mound of sand near the water. She takes my face in her hands, re-directing my attention from Ethan and the bonfire to whatever holy mess she plans to unleash.

"You don't need to do anything," she says, laying her words down one at a time. "Just listen."

Her wisps of hair lift in the breeze. Has it always been so thin?

She draws a deep breath. "Do you remember the steps I went through when I first joined the recovery program?"

"Sorry, Mom. I was an idiot back then. I didn't pay attention to anything."

She closes her eyes and breathes in, then opens them and breathes out. "As part of my journey to recovery from alcoholism and . . . domestic violence, I had to go through a set of twelve steps. It's the same twelve steps used at Alcoholics Anonymous. Are you familiar—?"

"Mom, how long is this going to take?"

"This is important and I want it to come out right."

"Fine. Sorry. Go on."

"I made it through all the steps, and by the grace of God I haven't had a drink since." She smiles. "Thirteen years."

I can't help but smile, too. "That's great, Mom."

"I've grown and healed since then. I'm no longer the little girl tormented by her mother's abandonment and her foster father's hatred. I'm not the weak alcoholic that let her husband throw her around. And I'm not the useless mother . . ." she chokes back tears, "who failed to take care of her own daughter. Kristen, I'm not who I used to be."

Her quivering voice gets to me. "Mom, I—"

She puts up her hand. "I'm not asking for forgiveness or validation. I just need to get this out. What I'm trying to say is that even though I've healed, I still have pain. I'm still holding on to part of my past, and I think it's because I mishandled number nine."

"What's that?"

"From the twelve steps. I was supposed to make amends with the people I had hurt, unless I couldn't do it without injuring that person or someone else. I had a hard time figuring that one out. You see . . . I kept a secret from you." She gazes at her hands. "I knew if I told you, it would've hurt you, but I also knew that by not telling you, I was still hurting you. I didn't like either choice."

She lifts her head. "Out of fear, I kept the secret to myself. Kristen, *honey!* I should've told you a long time ago."

"Fine, tell me now. But please, do it fast. I'd like to get back to the party before the bonfire goes out."

"Kristen, my foster parents were never angry about my teenage pregnancy because they never knew about it."

"Wait—didn't you run away because they found out you were pregnant?"

She hugs her stomach. "No. Mark and I ran away from home because of our foster father." She shakes her head. "He used to make us call him John Junior. We weren't allowed to call him Dad. He abused us, beat us violently, and no one seemed to care."

My teeth clench.

"Mark and I had our reasons for keeping this from you, Kristen. Victor was awful, but John Junior was worse. His brain wasn't right."

"Victor was evil. Do you have any idea what it was like to be a little girl, cowering beneath Victor's rage?"

"Yes. John Junior hated me with such a violent loathing that he hurt me whenever he could." She sighs and tucks her wispy hair behind her ears. "My foster mother was weak and powerless. She just stood by and watched."

That sounds familiar.

She wipes her tears. "John Junior rarely touched Mark, which gave Mark survivor's guilt. He went out of his way to protect me. He became my hero, distracting our foster dad from coming after me, or scraping me off the floor afterwards when he couldn't."

Her chin quivers. "You've got to understand that our world was upside down. We lived inside a nightmare. I know you suffered in childhood, too, and I'm not discounting that. But you're much stronger than I am. If I had your resolve, maybe I wouldn't have let the abuse destroy me the way it did."

She gazes into the night and draws two deep breaths. "Through it all, Mark comforted me," she says. "He made me feel safe. He was my strength."

"Yeah," I reply. "He makes me feel the same way. And I get it. You two are close. I'm aware."

Please get to the point.

"On my fifteenth birthday, right after my foster mother set down my cake, John Junior yanked me off my chair and started hitting me, for no reason at all. Mark jumped out of his seat. He was tall by then, but thin, and no match for John Junior, so he ran into his room and came back with a bat. He hit our foster dad on the head and knocked him down, grabbed my hand, and shouted, 'Let's go!' And we ran."

"Why didn't either of you ever tell anyone about the abuse? Why did you let it go on for so long?"

Her mouth freezes open, her head tilted sideways.

Why is she looking at me like that . . . *oh*. I grew up in an intolerable environment, too. Why didn't *I* ever tell anyone?

"By then, we were both messed up," she finally replies. "We lived in a remote area, miles from our nearest neighbor. We grew up isolated. Our foster parents worked hard to keep us out of public view. I was never able to make any friends because I was always too busy with some giant list of chores.

"We were inundated with physical and psychological abuse, and that was our reality. There was a high turnover of caseworkers coming to our house, and they were always distracted and overworked. No one reached out to us, or even noticed anything was wrong. And we didn't know any better." Her eyes slant sadly. "Or maybe we didn't believe we deserved better."

"*That's* the big secret? A family history of abuse? This shocker couldn't wait until tomorrow?"

She takes a deep breath. "Mark and I were terrified the night we ran away. If John Junior found us, he would have killed us both. We didn't think it through. Mark told me to run, so I ran. We ran until our house was out of sight. Then we walked until we came to an abandoned barn, and we collapsed, both of us crying."

She pauses and wrings her hands. "We were exhausted and emotionally spent," she continues. "We lay on the floor and held on to each other, neither of us able to let go."

My eyes flash open and my stomach lurches. "Mom, what are you saying?"

She rests her hands on her lap, a deep sadness spreading across her face. "Your Uncle Mark . . ."

"My *Uncle* Mark what? What are you saying?"

She's shaking. I'm shaking too, quivering from head to toe.

"Mom, you said my real father died. And what about that picture on my nightstand? Who's in that picture?"

She squeezes her lids shut, and then opens them. "He's no one. A clothing model."

I turn away from her. I need to scream, cry, run, or do anything other than face her horrid expression.

Then, in a crystal clear voice, Mom finishes what she came to say. "Kristen honey, Mark is your father."

CHAPTER 10

STILL MAY

⁂

GEORGINA GREETS ME at the door and her forehead wrinkles. She peers into my sunglasses, and then glances at my clenched fists. Can she tell that my eyes are trashed from tears and my stomach is twisted in knots?

"Would you like some water?" she asks, and I accept. "Still having your chase dream?"

"Yes." I gulp the water, crunch my cup, and dive into the loveseat.

"Still once or twice a week?"

I rub my temples. Georgina's Grecian nose smells trouble, but she's nowhere near the source.

"Can we talk about something else? Like that major oil spill in the news? Hundreds of thousands of gallons flowing into the Gulf every day, and everybody's chasing their tails. All that wildlife soaked in oil. Livelihoods ruined. *Nothing* will be the same."

Georgina tilts her head, her shih tzu mop of hair swooshing.

"This morning, the Pacific Ocean flashed at me from outside my window. I swear it was mocking, the way the water rolled and curled, acting carefree. How could it be so happy when its sister waters are suffering? What about the pelicans and turtles, and the poor little dragonfly whose entire universe is now uninhabitable . . . doesn't anybody care?"

"Kristen, it's your dollar, but I can't help you if you don't tell me what's going on."

I blow out my breath and glance across the room. What could be inside that annoyingly mysterious steamer trunk?

I face Georgina. "I came across a photo online, a stunning close-up of a dragonfly perched on a bush at the site of the spill. Oil smothered everything—the branches, the base, the ground. The dragonfly sat on a tiny section of bush that happened to be oil-free, but there was a black smudge on the tip of the little bug's wing. That smudge killed me. It was insignificant compared to the size of the bush, and invisible compared to the universe. But it was monumental to the insect."

Georgina blinks and swallows.

"I'm the dragonfly. My universe has been contaminated and it's no longer habitable."

"Okay," says Georgina, snatching up a fresh pencil. "Let's start from the beginning."

I laugh bitterly. "My mother's been keeping a secret from me. She couldn't hold it in any longer, and like that faulty tanker, she burst at the seams. She crashed Delila's party at the beach to tell me my Uncle Mark is also my biological father. Yeah, that's right. Talk about a toxic spill. Now I can't get it off me, and it's choking me. All that time I used to imagine my real father was as cool as my uncle was — it just makes me sick."

"The man in the photo on your nightstand is not your father?"

"No!"

I stand and let my hands and arms flail. "All those years I spent staring into that picture, and that man had nothing to do with me. And all along, my real father stood right next to me . . . and now he's in a coma . . . and he's my mother's brother. Mom says her foster father was abusive, and by the time she and Mark were teens they were messed up in the head." I roll my eyes. "Sound familiar?"

Georgina sets her notepad down, her expression flat as she clasps her hands into her classic power steeple. I sit back down, struggling to catch my breath. I want to grab Georgina's steepled fingers and pull them away from her face. Instead, I pin my hands beneath my thighs.

She releases the steeple. "Mark and Mary were foster children from different birth parents, right?"

"Yeah, why? They grew up together as brother and sister. They treat each other like brother and sister. So how does a lack of blood connection make it any better?

"Remember that startling moment in Star Wars, after Darth Vader cuts off Luke's hand and says, 'I am your fa-ther, *kshhhhhh?*' Yeah, I'm Luke. Except I'm not an invincible warrior, and Mark's not an evil lord of the dark side. I suspect *my mother* could play that role. I pity her. That's right, *pity.*

"I guess I should be thrilled that Mark is my father. All I ever wanted was a dad, but it would've been nice to learn this earlier. My life could've been different. There must've been an occasion or two during the last twenty-four years when I could've been informed of this relevant information.

"I can't put all the blame on Mom. Mark kept this from me too, but how can I hate him when he's in a coma? Whatever. I've had a billion cups of coffee today. Can someone die from too much caffeine? Because my heart is racing and I'd love to have a glass of milk, or some bread, or maybe just water. That'll dilute it, right?"

Georgina walks to her desk drawer and grabs a snack pack and a water bottle.

"My life is built on sand," I continue, peanut butter cracker bits flying everywhere. "And I'm sinking. Alana knows I'm hiding something, but it makes me sick to my stomach to think about it, and I can't bring myself to tell her.

"Then there's Ethan. I'm sure he's dying to find out what Mom wanted to talk to me about. I bet he'd flinch at this one. Maybe he already knows. I'm sure Mom told all her friends, one of which happens to be Ethan's mother. I told Delila and asked her not to tell anyone else. I may as well have tweeted it."

Georgina's eyes narrow.

"Yeah, that Delila." I shake my head. "She's my roommate now. Don't ask how that happened. I'm not really sure. I'm not sure why I told her Mom's secret, either. Maybe because she was there, right in front of me at the kitchen table the next morning, as I was rubbing the skin off my face and trying to figure out if what happened was really real. I guess I just needed to tell *someone* right then."

Georgina remains silent.

"I should give Delila credit. She didn't freak out when I told her about Mark. She said I'd gained a father who loves me, and dysfunctional or not, he's better than no father at all. She seemed sincere."

Georgina cradles her coffee mug. This one reads, *And how does that make you feel?*

"Okay," she says, "you just found out Mark is your dad."

Yes, Georgina. Good girl. You caught up.

"I understand why you would be upset," she continues. "Finding this out after all these years."

Yes. I want to jump up and clap. She gets it. I would scream for joy if Georgina would only stop talking.

"You can't go back," she says. "You can't change anything, so we need to figure out what you're going to do now."

Oh, good job, Georgina. You've earned your paycheck. I've done all the talking, but you isolated the issue with only a few words. I want to go back. More than anything, I want to prevent my mother and uncle from having sex. I can't do that, and if I did, I wouldn't exist. I also want to prevent them from making a pact to keep their secret. I can't do that, either.

If I'd known earlier, I could have lived with Mark. Why didn't he tell me he was my father? He could've taken custody and saved me from my mother. He could've saved me from Victor. He could've prevented everything. I could've had the chance to make better decisions, and I wouldn't have to keep stuffing childhood memories back down my throat. If only I could go back and change it all, but I can't change any of it. So where do I go from here?

We fill my calendar with future therapy appointments. Georgina instructs me to journal as often as possible. She tells me to talk to friends and loved ones about Mom's confession.

"Those who love you will understand," she insists.

She glances at the wall behind me. Green light. My time's up.

CHAPTER II

JUNE

❦

CHIPPED PAINT AND gun smoke invade my senses. Adrenaline rushes blood to my brain. What a dingy, cement cavern of a place. Seems like it was only yesterday Mark introduced me to this shooting range for the first time. I shivered at that first feel of cold metal in my hands. The air hung thick with anticipation that day, with a dozen men peppering their targets—not one of them noticing that a little girl in pink sweatpants had taken her lane for the first time.

Ethan arrives with a toothpaste ad grin. He gives me a friendly hug, sincere and brief, before flashing those eyes at me and leading me to the check-in desk. A crotchety old man pries himself away from his mini television screen just long enough to sign us in. Then Ethan and I slip into the last available lane. Thankfully, the place is packed. We'll have little chance to talk. Alana didn't freak out when I told *her*. But she was preoccupied, since she and Andrue are fighting again.

Ethan lets me shoot first. So I take my stance, settling the Ruger into my palm as I lean in. I take a long, deep breath while lining up the sights. I fix the gun on the target, click the safety off and cock the hammer back into firing position. Concentrating, I move my finger into the trigger and upon exhale, I squeeze, smooth and firm — *POW!*

That was terrible, Kristen.

I'm off to the right. Too much finger on the trigger. I re-grip the gun, lean in, and fire again, paying closer attention. Dead center. The remaining shots are grouped close to the second.

"Not bad." Ethan admires my target as I empty the shells from my barrel. "You're a steady shot." He sets his target farther back, and then slides the first clip into the chamber and aims his weapon, a Colt .45 M1911.

"That's one of Mark's favorite semi-automatics."

"Mine too," replies Ethan.

Streaks of his hair glisten beneath the fluorescent lighting. Ha. He went for the highlights I suggested. He takes his stance, his muscles flexing as he lines up the sights. He fires all seven rounds back-to-back, his hands hardly jumping at the recoil. He pulls in the target. All of the shots are grouped close together, dead center.

"Only six holes. You shot two bullets through the same hole?"

"Yep. In the center of the bull's-eye. See how big that hole is?" He winks.

We shoot three more targets each, his remaining consistent, and mine beginning to stray. When we're finished, we lock up our guns and ammo, tuck them into our cars, and walk toward a nearby Japanese restaurant. I press my chin into the warmth of my hoodie to escape from the unseasonal chill. Ethan wraps his arm around my back and squeezes my shoulder. This "hands on" friendship is starting to drive me crazy. He's trying to sneak a peek at my face. Why does he do that?

"Mark bought me my first gun when I was ten," I blurt.

Ethan stuffs his hands into his pockets and keeps his eyes on the path ahead.

"He taught me how to shoot," I continue. "He was always teaching me how to take care of myself. He also spent a lot of time saving me. Didn't matter what it was, he would find something to rescue me from."

"Sounds like Mark's love for you is pretty strong."

I stop walking and Ethan stops, too. I look directly into his eyes. "Once, when I was eleven months old, Mark came over in the afternoon to check on us. When there was no answer, Mark broke through the door. He found Mom passed out on the couch with an empty bottle at her side. He heard me squealing in the back of the apartment, where he found me belly deep in bathtub water. He said I laughed when he came in — said that I was filling little cups with water and pouring it all over the floor. He pulled me out, took me to his place, and left Mom on the couch. She came for me two days later and promised it would never happen again. And he gave me back." I shake my head. "He always gave me back."

Ethan squints, and a line forms across his forehead. "That must've been hard for him to do."

"You already know about Mark, don't you?"

"My mother called." He studies my expression. "I'm not sure I understand the whole story. She was hysterical."

"Dorothy already hated me. I can't imagine what she thinks of me now."

"My mother is strong-tempered and opinionated. She has issues, but I love her," he says. "She's my mother, you know?"

"Yeah, I know."

"That doesn't mean I'm always going to agree with her. I can form my own opinions."

"Want to hear my side of the story?"

"I'd love to."

I clutch my stomach as I tell Ethan everything my mother said to me that night at the beach. Ethan listens carefully.

"Mom and Mark aren't blood related, but they lived together as brother and sister, and I'm having a hard time getting through that. But then, like what you said earlier, they're my parents, and I can't hate them for very long. They were messed up. They were weak. They're only human, right?"

"Right. But still, it must be painful. How are you dealing with all of this?"

"Not very well. I'm spinning in circles. First I feel sick. Then I meditate on it and I start to hate them less, and I start to feel less guilty for not recognizing Mark as my father . . . and how I took him for granted . . . and how now it might be too late. I can't understand how both Mom and Mark could keep this from me, and I'm not sure which one of them irritates me the most. And then I start to feel sick about the whole thing all over again."

"It sounds like you've spent a lot of time thinking about this, and you're right — this is so huge and so complex, that it's easy to get confused about how to feel. I mean, how can you *not* feel personally affected by something like this?"

"I know, right?"

He nods, glances down at his feet and then back up at me. "You know, I've faced some painful, humiliating situations in my life, too, and you know what helped me?"

"What's that?"

"Realizing that my identity comes less from what my parents have done than who I am in God."

"Yeah? How does that work when someone doesn't have an identity in God?"

"What I'm trying to say is that you're beautiful in God's eyes, no matter what has happened."

My cheeks burn. How could Ethan know what his God thinks of me?

His head whips around. "Over there."

"What?"

"C'mon." He leads me into an alley. "See the dog hiding behind the trash can?"

"He's so skinny. Poor thing."

"Wait here. I'm running to my car to grab a few things."

"Wait — what?" But Ethan's already running, leaving me alone in the dark alley with the mangy German shepherd. Distant lights brighten the mutt's eyes as he growls, his lips curling and teeth bared. I hold my ground, and so does the dog. After a few seconds, I concede. "Fine. I'm backing up. I'll stand over here. Happy now?"

He stops growling, but keeps those ferocious eyes pinned on me.

"You can save the attitude for the other guy when he gets back. This isn't my idea. I'd be happy to let you be."

We stare each other down, neither one of us moving an inch as the noise of passing traffic *whooshes* in from the street. The dog's ribs jut out and fur is missing in large patches . . . one ear half gone, jagged at the top, as if it was torn off. *What* have you had to endure, boy?

"I'm back. Can you hold this?" Ethan hands me a leash. His jacket is off, rolled up and tucked under his arm. He approaches the dog. "It's okay, girl. It's okay."

"Girl? Ethan, what's the plan here?"

"I'm going to try to rescue her." Ethan steps closer and the dog backs up into a corner, growling loud, teeth exposed, body shaking.

"She's not happy you're here."

"Yeah. This one has had more than she can take."

"She doesn't *want* to be rescued. Can we proceed to the restaurant?"

Ethan backs up a few steps and faces me. "I want to try. That is, if you can handle it. This might take a while. Are you going to be okay?"

"*If* I can handle it? I'll be fine. Do what you've got to do."

He pulls a baggie of bacon out of his pocket and breaks a piece off. Then he tosses it toward the frightened dog. She eyes Ethan's hand, eyes his face, and then sniffs the bacon.

"Go ahead, girl. You're okay. Try it."

She steps forward, snatches it with her teeth, and chomps it down. Then she scoots back into her corner and growls. Ethan throws another piece, and after a few seconds she eats that one, too.

He backs off and stands next to me. "She's starving."

"This is a thing you do? You carry bacon in your pocket in case you find a dog to rescue?"

He chuckles. "The bacon was dumb luck. But yeah, I rescue dogs on a regular basis. Been doing it since I was a boy."

"That three-legged mastiff in the back of your truck in Mammoth?"

"That's Tank. A rescue from an abusive owner back in Colorado. I fostered Tank until I could find a good home for him. He was the hardest one I ever let go. I still miss that big ol' dog. But he's with a family that's crazy in love with him. The kids sent me some pictures and a five page letter telling me how much fun they're having with him. I know he's going to be fine."

Ethan nods toward the dog in the alley. "You ready, girl? I'm coming in." He takes the leash and moves closer to the dog, but she bares her teeth again. Poor thing doesn't have an ounce of trust in humans. Who can blame her? Ethan keeps at it, the three of us shivering in the dark, while he offers treats and moves in closer and closer. When he runs out of bacon, he pulls out a baggie of commercial dog treats.

After twenty minutes, my hands are frozen numb, but Ethan has made his way up to her. He leans in and reaches the leash noose close. The dog barks and nips it.

"It's okay. Go ahead and bite it." She chomps on it — hard.

Ethan pulls the noose back and then forward again, and over her head as she growls at it, but he gets it over. She's still shaking, but she's calmer now, and her snarl is less fierce.

Traffic noise continues to echo through the alley as Ethan grabs his rolled-up jacket and reaches toward her with it. She barks at it and latches on, then lets go. He does it again, and she snarls at it. He pushes the roll forward and pets her with it. She's still growling, but she's not biting the roll anymore.

Eventually, Ethan's able to place the roll on the dog's neck and reach behind it to pet her with his hand. Ten more minutes of this and Ethan's able to pet her without the protection of his jacket. He stands and takes a step and tugs on the leash. "Come on, girl."

She takes a step to follow. She's shaking, but she's not resisting the leash.

"That's incredible. What're you going to do now?"

"I know a vet," he says. "We'll get her medical needs taken care of first. Then we'll try to get her placed in a foster home while we attempt to find her previous owners."

"You think you'll find them?"

"No. This girl's been on the streets for a long time. I doubt anyone is looking for her. It's more likely that we'll need to find her a new forever home."

A forever home. Why do I well up at the sound of that?

"How are you going to get her to the vet? Aren't you worried she'll attack you in the car?"

"I'll tether her up in the back, but she doesn't want to hurt me. She's scared. I've done enough of these rescues that I can tell the difference." He winces. "All right if we skip dinner tonight? Reschedule for next week?"

"Yeah, sure. No problem. Let me know how it goes with her."

"Will do."

In the middle of June, I storm Georgina's office, not bothering to wait for her to invite me in.

She whips open her notebook. "Have you seen Mark yet?"

"No. I've been avoiding him since I found out he's my father. He's still in a coma, so does it matter? And why aren't you asking me about my recurring dream? Because they come almost every night now, with me running from that cold mist, and it's driving me insane."

She tilts her head and opens her mouth to speak, but I interrupt.

"Work's crazy again, too. No matter what I do, it's never enough. I work so many hours I don't have enough time to go to the gym. The only exercise I get is from hoofing the five flights of stairs to and from my apartment. And I keep running into Tommy. He's everywhere, and I—"

"What else is going on?" Georgina sighs and glances at her watch.

"Harley's sick. The vet says he's got diabetes, so now I have to give him insulin shots."

Georgina sets her pencil and notebook down and grabs her mug of the day. *Do not make me use my therapist voice.*

She pins me with a dead stare. "It's been more than a month since you found out Mark is your father. Do you have plans to visit him?"

I growl like an animal and roll my eyes. "Yes. On Sunday. Father's Day."

"How do you feel about that?"

Ugh. "Take a guess. How would you feel? I want to hit him over the head with a baseball bat. How could he have been so stupid? Then again, how could I have been such an idiot for all these years?"

"Okay. If you learned long ago about Mark, how would that have changed your relationship?"

Sunshine blasts through Georgina's blinds, igniting the lemon walls. I clutch the life out of the arm of the loveseat as I race through memories of Mark. One of him teaching me how to catch grunions at midnight. Another of him standing in front of me like a shield when Victor was throwing a fit. And how Mark used to tell me stories and make me laugh. Summer nights on his back porch, when he would lift me up high while I grabbed at stars. And teenaged Friday nights gone bad, when he had to pull me out of the gutter. Mark was always there, saving me from the horrors of childhood. And he was there to show me how to become an adult. He always loved me. How could I have missed who he was to me?

Tears race down my cheeks while Georgina waits for a response. I've ached for a father my entire life, and he was in front of me the whole time. Georgina wants to know what I would do if I could go back in time, but isn't it too late for that?

"I would've been grateful," I respond. "I wouldn't have let Mark's love spill to the ground. I would've taken it and used it to fill the hole in my heart."

Georgina leans in. "You can be grateful now."

"I am. Doesn't it show? But what if Mark never recovers? He'll never know how I feel."

On Father's Day, I find myself standing in front of the Ocean View Medical Center. Mark's new home. I tread through the long-term care facility, passing a long line of faded beach prints as prevalent scents of urine, baked ham, and ammonia envelop the heavy stillness.

At Mark's room, my pulse throbs in the palm of my hand as I grab the doorknob. Inside, a pair of TOMS black canvas slip-ons, attached to scrawny ankles, stick out from beneath his bed.

"*What* are you doing, Mom?"

"Al-most fi-nished," she sings.

A nurse appears in the doorway. Her giant nametag reads, *Mabel*.

"You must be Kristen. Your mama prays over your uncle like this all the time."

I suppose Nurse Mabel's unaware that Mark is my father. How would she react if she knew? Her eyes are tired, but strong, as if she's lived hard and hasn't always preferred sensible shoes. Something tells me she'd understand.

"If Mom's praying *over* Mark," I ask, "why is she *under* the bed?"

Mabel's smile softens her hardened face. "She holds her Bible near your uncle, one section at a time — his head, stomach, arms, and feet — and reads Scripture." She drops her chin and peers up at me, as if over imaginary reading glasses. "We worry about your mother."

"How's Mark doing?" I ask, avoiding familial titles.

"No change," she replies, and then she slips away.

Mom wriggles out from beneath Mark's bed.

"Kristen honey, I'm glad you're here. We need to talk."

Good grief. What does she want to slam me with now? I lower myself to the very edge of Mark's bed, ready to run if necessary.

Mom dusts herself off and sits in the hard plastic chair in front of me. "My birthmother was extremely poor. Before she dumped me, we were in and out of shelters, and often we slept on the streets. My mother was very proud. She refused to 'sell out' in order to provide for us. She would never steal or give herself away for food and shelter. But she also hated seeing me shiver and starve.

"One day when I was eight, she left me at a park in a wealthy neighborhood. She promised everything would be all right, that someone would come and help, and find me a home. She promised she would visit me every week."

Mom wrings her hands in her lap and looks deep into my eyes. "My mother came to the foster home about a month later and had a long conversation with my caseworker about making plans for reunification, but then she blew off her next scheduled visit. I kept waiting for her to return, but she never did. Her disappearance was worse than the beatings from my foster dad.

"When you were born, I promised myself I would *never* abandon you no matter what I had to do. But in the end, that's exactly what I did. I escaped through drugs and alcohol and left you to fend for yourself. I was a terrible mother. I cheated you out of the childhood you deserved, and on top of that I lied to you. I'm not proud of myself," she sighs. "But I can't change the past."

Sounds familiar.

She takes my hands in hers. "I hope you'll succeed in life. Every day, I pray that you'll find joy and thrive, regardless of my failures."

Her eyes are wet, and mine are, too. She glances at the wall clock.

"I have to go, so Mark is all yours."

She kisses my forehead and walks off, leaving me stunned, and marked by her cherry Chapstick. My whole life I've wanted to hear her say those words. Oh, how I've craved for her to admit she messed up, and that she ruined my life. So why am I so sad?

I stand over Mark and scan his lifeless frame. Mom's been trimming his hair, keeping it high and tight. She even groomed his brows. He's breathing on his own, but nobody dares to guess about his chances of waking up, and if he does wake up, whether or not he will recover at all. I sit on the bed, curl up my legs, and place my head on his chest. I can't do anything but lie here and listen to the steady beat of his heart.

Happy Father's Day, Uncle Mark.

CHAPTER 12

MY PEN SCRAWLS across the page. *Smoke escapes the industrial-sized ovens of Bayou Barbeque while racks of rubbed and sauced meat churn through their slow rotation to perfection. Patches of mortared brick peek through the restaurant's crumbling stucco walls, revealing a contrived corrosion that imitates a true Deep South barbeque hole-in-the-wall. The affluent section of Los Angeles can afford such a luxurious illusion. At least the music is authentic, not one synthesizer in sight. Just a few old souls called The Bourbon Creek Four, telling their stories through lyrics and filling our ears with that deep, southern jazz push and pull that mimics those common afflictions of the human condition: joy and sorrow, life and death . . ."*

Ethan peeks at my sketchbook from across the table. "What're you writing?"

I scrape a diagonal line across my paragraph. "Garbage. My therapist wants me to journal, but I'm not doing it right." I flip back one page to a rough sketch of the band. "I should stick with sketching, no?"

He nods slowly. I've already told him I have a therapist, right?

"This bluesy jazz reminds me of my mother's *good* days. She loved Bessie Smith, but Victor hated jazz. Had a noise sensitivity to it or something. Made him crazy-mad. Lucky for us, Victor traveled a lot."

"For work?"

"Yeah. Sales rep for a company that specializes in wastewater treatment technology. Anyway, sometimes he'd be gone for weeks, and when he was, Mom played Bessie nonstop. She drank her way through most of my childhood, but whenever Victor was away, she was a happy drunk, singing along with Bessie and dancing around the house." I wince. "It was the best of the worst of times."

That grin. Why does he smile so much? I mean, no one's *that* happy all the time.

I miss the beard. There's so much jaw now. His bangs are great, though. Finally tried the swoop thing I suggested.

Alana leans close. "If your friends don't stop kissing and touching each other, I'm going to have to do something."

Legion and Delila really should get a room. Ethan's sitting right next to them, but he doesn't seem to notice. He leans forward to engage Alana. "Where's your fiancé?"

"We're not together anymore," she huffs, then glances at me.

Once a Lonely Hearts Club Member, always one, I suppose. The four of us — well, the two of us who remain — are destined for singleness.

"He's insane," Alana continues. "He explodes over the stupidest things. He's got a lot of stress from work, and I get that, but I can't live my life walking on eggshells. I moved out and blocked his number."

"Has Andrue been violent?"

"No, nothing like that. That night at the beach, he shoved me hard, but he didn't mean to do that. He'd had a lot to drink. I just don't want to deal with him right now. He's too stubborn. Won't let anything go. He'll pick a fight and then he won't stop going on and on about it. He was calling me at work to rehash arguments we had days before."

Ethan glances at her hand. "You're still wearing the engagement ring."

"Are you kidding? This thing's too expensive to return." She flashes her eyes and a wide, bright smile, but as he stares back without responding, her smile dims. "Maybe when Andrue's work calms down, we can start talking again." She glances down at her hands and twists the ring around her finger for a few seconds, then looks up and slams her hands flat on the table. "Forget Andrue. Let's talk about your girlfriend Kristen here, how she nearly drowned in four feet of water."

Ethan and I are just *friends*. And is she really going to tell that story again?

"It was a typical summer day at the beach — Death Valley hot, like tonight, but without the A/C. Like every other teenager there, I was minding my own business, trying to act cool, listening to music, you know, working on my tan . . ."

Wow. What a talent for deflecting and maintaining attention at the same time. If Jenna and Danielle were here, they'd find a way to tone Alana down. Does she miss them as much as I do?

Ethan ate so many of my smoked wings, I can't believe I still have some left on my plate. Mint julep's not bad. I've had better. Alana's still bragging about how she saved me from my own stupidity, how I would've drowned if she hadn't come along and told me my feet could touch the ground. I refuse to listen. But that laughter's hard to ignore, especially Legion's. He's so entertained he's not even fondling Delila anymore. Alana should take her act on tour.

Ethan winks at me. "You never know where that drop-off is going to be."

"Exactly. How could I have known I reached the ledge?"

Alana carries on, her voice fading into the background.

What a motley crew we have at this table. A handful of misfits disguised as friends, celebrating life on a hot, jazzy summer night. What am I doing hanging out with Legion and Delila? And what *is* Ethan to me? Why does he keep calling me, and why do I love talking to him so much? And what's up with the winking thing? He's such a cheese ball, how can I stand it?

Whoa. This is only my second mint julep, but my brain feels heavy, as if it was soaked with bourbon.

The A/C fights against the heat while our crew grows more animated. Ethan's got a lot of energy. Is that his third or fourth cup of coffee? He's singing ancient television theme songs. He starts out humming, and then he sings out loud — he can't carry a tune, but he sings anyway — while the others try to guess the show. Everyone laughs, guessing one show after the next. Except me. I can't guess any. I can't remember watching a stitch of television from that period. In fact, at this moment, I can't recall a single event from the age of six to sixteen. The entire decade escapes me.

Our waitress brings over a tray of tequila shots, sets one down in front of each of us, nods at Legion, and walks away.

Legion lifts his glass. "Friends, a toast to my beautiful girl, soon to be my wife."

Delila laughs. "Yep," she says, her voice as throaty as ever. "Legion and I are engaged." She flashes a ring-less hand. "Ring's on layaway, but I'll get it next week." Her grin stretches.

Stunned, we clink shot glasses and coffee mug, and down our drinks.

"Congratulations." Ethan shakes Legion's hand, then Delila's.

I force my congratulations. Alana lip-syncs hers, her brows rising high. Legion and Delila hug and make out for a bit, applauding themselves at our expense. I smile despite the nausea filling my stomach.

Delila grabs her necklace and fingers the diamond star pendant. She glances at me and then sweeps her gaze across the table. "Speaking of weddings, have you guys heard about Tommy?"

The room drops silent. I swear, even the Bourbon Creek Four stop singing as my heart falls into my stomach and Ethan's expression goes blank.

"Yeah, Tommy and Barbra are getting married." Delila wipes her purple lipstick off Legion's neck. "Crazy, right?"

I gasp uncontrollably, as if a safe just dropped on my chest. Ethan glances at me, but I turn away. My cheeks get hot as tears pool in my eyes. No, *no*. Don't let it get to you, Kristen. Little Felix and Lily Foxx were never meant to exist, and you and Tommy were never meant to be. If only you'd known that before you fell so hard for him.

Alana tosses her wadded napkin across the table. "What's wrong with you, Delila? Are you impaired?"

Delila flips up her palms, "What? It's no big deal. Tommy's a worthless creep. Barbra can have him. I mean, c'mon, harassing an ex-girlfriend at the Fashion District — who does that?"

What did she say?

Alana stands and jabs her finger in Delila's face. "Shut. Up."

Legion jumps to his feet and leans across the table, towering over my hot-tempered friend, but Ethan jumps up, too, slipping his arm between them. "Sit," he says, and they obey. Ethan, the freakin' dog whisperer. What is it about him that makes creatures and people respond? Except that Legion and Alana are still snarling.

Don't disrespect my girl!

Stay out of it!

Ethan keeps his arm between them. "It's okay. Let's all calm down. Relax. It's okay."

While Legion and Alana keep repeating the same insults, my head swirls. How could Delila have known about the Fashion District encounter? I press my palms onto the table, and lift myself from my chair. I lean over the pitch of Legion and Alana's argument to confront Delila.

"Were *you* at the Fashion District the day I found you sneaking around the apartment building?"

Legion and Alana shut down, waiting for Delila's response.

"What? No! I already told you I wasn't there. Why would I lie?"

"I never told you I saw Tommy there that day, so how did you know?"

Delila rakes back her stiff, flat bangs, revealing a widow's peak of wild and crazy hairs before the bangs snap back in place. "I heard it from somebody in the business. I mean, most *everybody's* heard it by now. Kristen, you know gossip travels like wildfire in our circles."

Yes, but if she's telling the truth, then who lit the match on this one? Tommy? Barbra?

Delila glances past my shoulders. She jumps up and points at the entrance. "No way, it's Andrue." There he is, standing outside the double glass doors with rumpled clothes and a crazed expression.

"How did he find out I was here?" Alana reaches inside her designer handbag for her phone.

"You didn't tell him?"

"No. And I won't talk to him. Somebody get rid of him."

Ethan shoves back his chair and nods at Legion. "We got this."

Legion follows Ethan as they make a beeline for Andrue. The live band takes a break while *Kneeling Drunkard's Plea* by Johnny Cash plays through the speakers. The men talk outside, Andrue shifting from side to side, his hands and arms jerking wildly.

"I'm not putting up with this anymore," says Alana. "I'm calling my cousin, he's a cop." Phone to her ear, she glances at Delila and curls her upper lip. "How *did* he find me?"

Delila rubs her forehead. "Who knows? I'm just glad the band's taking a break. They're giving me a headache."

Alana reports Andrue, while I drain the rest of my drink.

An LAPD squad car arrives within four point six minutes, well above the average response time. While the officers talk with Andrue he acts anxious, shifty, like a restless jumping bean. A few minutes later, the officers shove Andrue into their car.

When the men return, Ethan places a hand on Alana's shoulder. "He wanted to see you. We told him it wasn't going to happen today. The police tried to calm him down. At first, they considered letting him go."

"Yeah, but then he annoyed the lady cop," butts in Legion. "He shoved his hands in his pockets and she asked him to take them out. He said *no*, and she threw him against the car. You should have seen it . . . a chick that small, throwing Andrue around."

"They found a knife in his pocket," says Ethan.

Legion removes a toothpick from his mouth and laughs. "That thing? Hardly bigger than this stick. A harmless little penknife."

"He always carries that," says Alana. "Legion's right. It's nothing."

"I don't know Andrue very well," says Ethan. "But from what I've seen, he seemed uncharacteristically agitated. He might be more dangerous than you think."

A week later, Alana's got a restraining order on Andrue and I'm still drowning at the office.

I get home late from work, bloated and craving Raspberry Zingers, even though I'd inhaled six of them at my hospital stop. I take the stairs to burn a few Zinger calories. Man, the last three flights are still dim. What do I have to do to get Trent to fix the lighting?

The moment I step into the apartment, giggling erupts from the shower. Delila and Legion are in there together. Gross.

I nuke a freezer-burned dinner and pop open a beer. The shower stops, the dryer starts, and then there's laughing. They're getting ready to leave. Good. I'll drown them out with my iPod until they're gone, and then I can finally have the place to myself. Except I left my ear buds in the car. Back down the stairs I go.

Apartment sounds flow into the empty stairwell, muted, sounding like an underwater party. I can take the darkness, but what on earth is that stench? The muffled noises grow louder, now sounding like a mansion abandoned by the living and infested with the dead. A chill crawls across my skin. Did it suddenly get darker?

I step faster, but when I turn the corner, I bump into a wall of musk-scented flesh.

"Andrue."

The absence of light exaggerates his unkempt features, as he twitches and shifts from side to side. I reach to pat his shoulder and he flinches, his nostrils flaring as he speaks through his teeth. "Don't. Touch. Me."

His bloodshot eyes dart behind me, to the left and then to the right. Dude's altered.

"I'm heading to the car to get my earbuds. Wanna come?" Casually, I point over his shoulder. Dear God, don't let him see how fast my heart is beating. I track his eyes, as black as onyx. Will he take the bait and let me pass?

He continues to shift from side to side, his gaze ping-ponging around the stairwell. "Look," he snorts. Then he grabs a clump of his hair. "I don't . . . I don't want any trouble. Tell me where I can find Alana. She's not at home and she's not with her sisters."

"Sorry, can't."

He rubs his face. "I just want to *talk* to her. Tell me where she is . . . and I'll leave."

I step to the side and so does he. He blocks each time I try to pass. His chest heaves as he waits for me to make the next move. He can stand there all day for all I care. I'm not saying a word.

But maybe I should run.

I step back and Andrue lunges, clutching my shoulder with both of his hands. I thrust up my pressed palms and break free. *Holy cow*, that rocket move works!

I slip past him, kick off my heels, and run—barreling downward toward the lobby, where I'll find witnesses and bright open spaces. I fly down the steps in gaps of three, like a gazelle running from a predator.

Andrue stays on my tail, yelling, "I'll *kill* you, Kristen!"

I fly ahead. Fourth floor, *whoosh*. Third floor, *whoosh*.

Andrue catches up on the second floor, the weight of his frame slamming me hard against the wall. Pain explodes through my skull, and then a cool, electric *zing*. Was that glass shattering? The broken fire extinguisher case . . . pain in my hand . . . blood dripping from cuts.

The room spins. I'm still standing. I must be. Yes, I'm standing. Andrue holds me from behind, an arm wrapped across my chest, the other waving that stupid little penknife in front of my face.

"Tell me where she *is*," he grunts, gripping me tighter.

Breathe, Kristen. Remember what that self-defense instructor once said. *Your attacker will be larger and stronger than you, and in order to stop him, you must drive through him as if you are breaking through a brick wall. These techniques are not meant to slow your attacker down. They are meant to stop him.*

"Tell me. Where. She. Is." He grips me hard.

Who is this madman? Not the likable, smooth-talking Andrue I've known for years. Only a degenerated version of him. And this version is psycho.

"Where *is* she?"

If only I could remember the move our instructor taught us for this kind of hold. Oh, right. I lock in on a focal point and release my breath, then slip my hand beneath Andrue's grip and stomp wide to get leverage, but he grips harder, drawing me in tighter, his wet breath on my neck. This move is useless.

"Tell me!"

Assess the situation, Kristen. What's exposed? His head, his ribs, and his flip-flopped feet. I could do some damage with a head-butt, and elbow and heel jabs . . . right *NOW!*

He grunts and his grip loosens. I jump toward the landing wall and grab the fire extinguisher. With Andrue leaping toward me I swing the canister with everything I've got, swinging *through* the brick wall. Swinging *through* his face.

He screams and falls to the ground, and I run — no longer like a gazelle, but like a drunken sailor, staggering all the way to the bottom floor where I enter the shocking normality of the lobby.

I wobble, disoriented. "Help," I mumble. "He's in the stairwell."

A mother yanks her child away from the barefoot woman who's dripping with blood. The elevator opens, and half a dozen people gape, but none of them do anything.

I stumble toward Trent, who pulls his nose out of his magazine long enough to understand that something is wrong. He dials the police lethargically, as if nothing could be more annoying than doing his job.

A crowd gathers while I tell my story. Legion and Delila emerge from the elevator in their party clothes — Legion in a crisp, white collared shirt unbuttoned to his navel, and Delila in her purple lipstick and matching platforms.

I rattle on, trying to explain what happened, but all anyone does is blink and nod. My fumbling speech betrays my utter lucidity. I urge Trent to check the stairwell, but he insists on waiting for the police to arrive. The crowd labels me insane with their silent rebuke.

Legion shifts from side to side, flexing his fingers and balling them into fists, over and over. "I'm going after him."

"No, babe." Delila places her hand on his arm. "Wait for the police."

She believes me. She understands the severity of Andrue's psychosis. If only she would stop that incessant petting of my hair.

The police arrive.

Two patrolmen stay to take a crime report, while two others search for Andrue. They lock down the bottom floor and search the stairwell as I'm being interviewed. One patrolman puts out a broadcast while the other listens, his tape recorder rolling as I blather on.

"His name is Andrue Delucchi, that's A-n-d-r-u-e D-e-l-u-c-c-h-i. He's my best friend's ex-fiancé . . ."

They find my heels in the stairwell, but Andrue's nowhere in sight. They canvass the building, knocking door to door, trying to get people to open up. One woman on the second floor reports that Andrue ran down the hall toward the stairwell on the other side of the building. "He's got to be long gone by now," she says.

I'm telling my story, everything that happened from the time Andrue knocked Alana over — the restraining order, Andrue's erratic behavior, the penknife. How he smashed me into the wall . . . and his words, *I'll kill you, Kristen*, echoing through the stairwell. I tell them I hit Andrue hard with the fire extinguisher, so I imagine he's messed up in the face. They scan the gash in my head and the cuts on my hand. Following their eyes down, for the first time I notice my feet are cut, too.

They find the broken glass, the fire extinguisher on the ground, splatters of blood on the wall and the landing, and drips leading to the lobby. Mine. They find drips leading down the corridor of the second floor. Andrue's.

Andrue disappeared. The police are pretty sure he's gone. They put a "want" on his plate, notifying every other police officer in the area to keep their eyes open for it. He won't get far. Any officer who sees his car will pull him over.

The building's no longer locked down, and everyone is free to go. Legion and Delila head out to the Comedy and Magic Club. They've already paid for their tickets, they explain. Otherwise, they'd follow the medics who take me to the hospital.

I waste the next several hours racking up a fortune in tests so intern newbies can tell me what's already clear, that I'm fine. I'm achy, bruised, and annoyed, but nothing's wrong with me except for a few stitches on my forehead. I hope it doesn't scar. I'd hate to have to wear bangs for the rest of my life.

Detectives show up at the hospital to get a more detailed statement, but how much more specific can I be? I give them my story. It's the same as the first time I gave it. They tell me they found Andrue's abandoned car three blocks from my apartment. They're going to interview Alana next.

Hours later, I'm home. Trent tells me the stairwell lighting is now fixed. Great. Thanks, Trent. That's *super* helpful.

CHAPTER 13

JULY

❦

I KEEP CHECKING MY perimeter, like a paranoid schizophrenic, as I approach Mark's room. Every stranger — every shadow — looks like Andrue. Like the man with the baseball cap ahead of me in the hall. This guy's got his head tucked down, his hands stuffed in the pockets of his black windbreaker. Did he come from Mark's room? He's moving fast, but with a limp. My stomach muscles tense and my pulse races. *Could* that be Andrue? No way. Too stocky, and Andrue's back is not quite as broad.

I enter Mark's room, practicing controlled, deep breathing as I ease myself onto the edge of his bed. I lay down a dozen packs of Raspberry Zingers, and my heart flutters more than ever at the sight of the pile. I emptied the vending machine of them. I've got a serious problem with these things.

Mark's lids rest closed. His breath remains steady and his expression vacant. I wolf down the first pack of Zingers in ten seconds flat. Mark breathes. Open your eyes and say something. Twitch. Cough. Just *do* something.

I peer out the sliding glass door that leads from Mark's room into a shared patio. My eyes follow the winding garden bursting in yellows, blues, and bright orange-reds. A breeze drags fallen leaves across the flag-stone path. Mark continues to do nothing.

The wall clock ticks.

I scarf down the second pack of Zingers.

"You had a visitor today? I didn't recognize him. Is he a new club member?"

Nothing.

"Rose Society? Or is he a guns and grain survivalist type?"

Still silent. I'm already exhausted from his lack of participation. This visit is going to kill me.

I open a third pack. "Fine, I'll do all the talking. It's been two weeks, and Andrue's still missing. His home appears abandoned and he hasn't shown up for work. Alana's hired a private investigator to find him. She's crazy, right? It's like she doesn't care that Andrue held me at knifepoint. She's got a restraining order on him, but she still wears the engagement ring. And now she's hired this guy — P.I. Brock. He claims he used to hunt down the top ten most wanted terrorists, but now the government is after him, so he lives underground. Literally, like inside some elaborate burrow system constructed by cannibalistic underground dwellers five thousand years ago. Yeah, I know, whatever — right?

"If you asked me, I'd say Brock is a few fries short of a Happy Meal, but that's Alana. He's expensive, and he's popular with the rich and famous, so she loves him."

My eyes roll over Mark's motionless body. I chug my bottled water, and rip open a fourth pack of Zingers.

"I hit Andrue hard with that fire extinguisher." I rub my forehead. "I'll bet his head gash is worse than mine. Man, the way I was able to break free from him, you would've been proud, Mark. Dad. Vegetable. Uncle-father."

More water. A fifth pack of Zingers.

"We're quite the dysfunctional family, aren't we?"

No response.

I scoot closer. "I can't wrap my brain around all this. You know — you and Mom, together. Still makes my stomach churn. Unless that's just the Zingers I'm trying to digest."

Mark doesn't respond, not even when I laugh and slap his arm.

I wipe the raspberry-frosting smear off him and sigh. "How would you expect me to react?"

More awful silence. For the love of all that is good and decent in this world, why doesn't he wake up already? I stand and move toward the patio door. The leaves dance and whirl outside the glass. Most of the debris is greenish brown, except for a tiny red petal flapping in the dead center of the swirl, like a beating heart.

I return to the bed, finish my sixth pack of Zingers, and take Mark's hand. "That's all in the past. We're here now, and there's one thing I know for sure about this present we've found ourselves in—"

My lips clamp shut. Then, a voice . . . *Tell him.*

The voice doesn't have any describable attribute, except that it's undeniable.

"Tell him what?"

The answer fills me, like a long deep breath. "Mark, I have a lot of unanswered questions, but one thing I know for sure. I love you, and I'm glad you're my father. I love you, Dad."

I kiss his forehead a zillion times, leaving one of my tears on his cheek. Wait, is that mine or his? Then another one, coming right from the corner of his eye. The pretty little drop rolls down Mark's face and plops into his pillow.

A tear.

I jump up, check for witnesses, glance at Mark, sit . . . and then jump up again, still holding Mark's hand. "Are you crying? Mark, can you hear me?"

I say his name again and again, and after the third time, he presses my hand.

"You heard me."

I yank my hand from his, dart through the hall, and scream, "He's waking up!"

No one appears, so I run faster, screaming louder. By the time I find Nurse Mabel, I'm ranting like a lunatic. She keeps stacking charts while she listens. I grab her arm and drag her and several other staffers into Mark's room, where he lies as motionless and unresponsive as ever.

I shout my story, re-enacting the event, running around and squeezing everybody's hand so they can feel what I felt. I run to the pillow and jab at the spot where the tear fell, but by this time, it has dried. The staffers seem more shocked by all the empty Zinger wrappers than by my reports of Mark's condition.

"Eh, we've seen tears in coma patients before," the shortest one says. "Doesn't necessarily indicate perceptivity."

What's wrong with these people?

"No, no, no, this is different. The timing . . . he *was* perceptive. He squeezed my hand. And what about the voice? It was crystal clear."

Mentioning "the voice" was a mistake. I can't explain this voice in a way they can understand. I can't hold my own voice down to a reasonable volume. They're all sure I'm nuts. They tell me to calm down, perhaps step outside and take a break, since it can be wearing to watch a loved one in this condition.

It's because they weren't there when it happened. They can't understand without having seen. I should let it go and move on, but I can't. Somehow, I must get them to understand. I keep trying to force them to appreciate the situation until I've exploded into a full-blown rage, screaming and ranting as I slam my fists against expensive medical equipment. I start shoving the staffers, one by one, until a beefy intern named Josh comes in and herds me into a corner, one step at a time. I have no way out.

"I just want someone to understand. Why won't anyone listen?"

I'm shaking and my heart is about to pound outside of my chest. Josh keeps me pinned in the corner and the nurse patiently stares at me, pity pouring out of her eyes.

"Fine. If giant Josh will step aside, then I'll leave and simmer down somewhere else."

Josh raises his hands and backs off.

I rake back my hair, blow out my breath, and glance at Mark. He's as annoyingly comatose as ever, so I leave, knowing I'm the sole witness to his failed attempt to climb back into our reality. Mom will believe me, but everyone at Ocean View thinks Mom's a lunatic, so how does that help me? I don't care anymore. The moment was fleeting, and now it's gone. Just like every other good thing that's happened in my life.

My twenty-fifth birthday. Twenty-five on July twenty-fifth. Can't believe I've survived this long. Dinner would've been nice, but the drive to Summerland will be more interesting. Besides, how could I say no to Ethan after he got that call about the stray? Poor beagle's been sitting on top of a sand dune, crying, for the last week.

"You sure?" Ethan asked. "It's your birthday."

"Totally sure," I said. "Count me in."

Ethan arrives with bed head. If I were a man, I'd probably give up sometimes, too. Taking care of wiry hair is a lot of work.

To clear a spot inside Ethan's truck, I have to shove aside a half-eaten bag of Barbeque Corn Nuts, two empty travel mugs, a couple of leashes, and a clump of poop bags. My feet kick over a stack of paperbacks.

"John Grisham fan, huh? This one's different . . . *Works of Love?*"

"Great book. Take it. There are a lot of scriptural references," he warns, "but the way Kierkegaard reflects on love, I'm sure you'll like it."

"Is it about God or is it about love?"

"Read it, and you tell me. Trust me. You'll enjoy it."

"Fine. I'll give it a try. What've I got to lose?"

He takes Pacific Coast Highway most of the way, so we can take in the scenery. The view is breathtaking, except for the sections recently charred by wildfires.

And then there's Ethan's profile. Has he *seen* his hair today?

"I still can't believe the constant perfect weather here," he says. "Clear skies. Seventy-five degrees. You don't get this in Colorado. The skies are always changing. Here, it's always bright and sunny, or if it's not, it will be soon. Colorado's amazing though, awe-inspiring. God's everywhere there, in the mountains, streams, trees—"

"You can't see God here?"

He glances over, right as he speeds into a turn. "Yeah, I can," he replies. "But the view is often obstructed."

He hugs the turn, and then accelerates out of it. Then he moves on to another subject, speed talking to keep up with his miles per hour, while I'm clutching my seat.

In less than two hours, we reach Summerland, where we stop at Sandy's Café for lunch. Ethan orders three cheeseburgers to my one. We order cokes and a side of fries to share.

My eyes roll back. "I forgot to eat breakfast, and this burger tastes fan-tastic."

He smiles. "Best birthday meal ever?"

"You kidding? Cheeseburgers are one of my favorite foods." I glance at the plastic baskets in front of him. "And yours, too, apparently."

"Yeah, I dig them, but only one is for me." He winks. "These others are for doggie bribes."

My heart jumps. Why am I so excited about this rescue?

"Any news on Andrue?" Ethan lifts his brow.

"Nothing."

"I'm praying for him every day."

"While you're at it, pray for Alana. I don't know why she's trying to find him, why she freezes every time I mention his name, and why she still bothers to wear that obnoxious ring. We had dinner together to celebrate my birthday, but it was an epic fail. All she talked about was Andrue."

"Sure. I'll pray for her, too."

Our waiter brings our bill and Ethan asks for doggie bags, but only he and I get the joke.

"I'm worried about my mother's mental health," says Ethan out of the blue.

"Yeah? Mom says Dorothy hasn't showed up for recovery meetings, and hasn't returned anyone's calls."

"When did that start?"

"The day Mom told the group about her and Mark. Maybe Dorothy can't get past it. Maybe she sees it as an unforgivable sin or something."

"No way," says Ethan. Then he rubs his face. "Maybe you're right. Except something bigger is going on with her."

"Like when she had her breakdown?" I ask, scraping out every single fry crumb from the bottom of the basket.

Ethan blushes. Didn't he know that I knew?

He leans forward with clasped hands, his muscled forearms resting on the table. "Yes, it's exactly like when she had her breakdown. She has past issues that she hasn't dealt with. Serious stuff. Painful memories that she refuses to grieve. She believes her issues are under control, but they're not. They're eating her from the inside out, and I'm not really sure what to do about it."

Ethan's talking about his mother, so why is he staring at *me*?

My stomach churns and I shove the baskets away. There's nothing left anyway.

We're within walking distance to where the beagle was spotted. What a beautifully layered section of coastline. A thin strip of brush lining the highway, then a thin, rocky strip of sand, then another layer of brush, and then a final, shallow strip of soft sand that butts up to the shore.

We grab our supplies out of the truck and break through the layers. As soon as we pass the second layer of brush, it appears. A little brown and white ball resting on top of a sand dune. We try to sneak up, but it spots us right away.

"How about you go past the brush to the rocky strip of sand and follow us from there?" says Ethan. "You'll need to block her if she runs through that first strip of brush. We don't want her reaching the street."

Her? Can he really tell from this distance?

I take my position and observe Ethan and the dog, my head flipping back and forth as if I'm watching a tennis match.

Ethan steps forward and the dog jumps up. He tries to go around the dune to approach from behind, but the little beagle runs, taking off like her tail's on fire. She darts across the sand, Ethan running close behind. I'm running, too, trying to peek through the brush along the way. If she turns and tries to dash through the brush, I'll catch the little stinker. I won't let her pass.

We're all running fast. How long can my ankle hold out at this pace? Doesn't matter. I won't stop, no matter what. My stride remains smooth and swift. A quarter of a century old, a permanent ankle injury, and uneven ground — and I'm still a phenomenal runner.

The beagle stops short. Ethan and I do, too. Ethan pins his eyes to her as he catches his breath from running on the soft sand. He should try running on sand and rock. The beagle stares him down, both of them frozen. Then she runs, darting toward the brush.

I duck low, hiding behind a dense section of leaves, readying myself to snatch her if she tries to break through. She crawls into a small opening of the thicket, not ten feet away from me, but she's too focused on Ethan to have a clue that I'm here.

Ethan approaches the brush. "Hi, good girl. That's a good girl." He inches his way closer and she holds her position. "It's okay. You're all right. It's okay."

Poor thing must be tired. She doesn't even attempt to run. She just widens her eyes at Ethan as he draws even closer. He raises his gentle snare, that contraption made with a pole and a noose, and he reaches it toward her head. She raises her chin, but doesn't growl or bite. On his next try, Ethan gets the snare over her head. "Yeah, you're a good girl. Aren't you?" Ethan rubs the top of her head and then he tries to lead her out of the brush, but she tugs back hard.

"Kristen? Why don't you come in here and try to give her some hamburger."

I'm on it. But the opening is so low that I have to slide in on my back, feet first. How did Ethan squeeze into here?

The beagle doesn't budge as I slide in. As soon as I'm near her, I reach into my bag and pull out some cheeseburger crumbles. She sniffs at them and then eats right out of my hand. I pull out some more and she plops down, right next to my legs. She eats more cheeseburger and then licks the death out of my palm. This is, without question, the sweetest dog in the world.

Once her tummy's full, Ethan and I spend a few minutes petting her like crazy. After a few minutes more, she willingly follows us out of the brush and lets me lead her all the way to the car. Then this impossibly precious creature curls up into my lap for the ride home.

"I could do this every day forever," I tell Ethan as we're driving away.

"It's addicting, isn't it? But many rescues aren't this easy."

"What happened to the German shepherd we found in the alley? Did she find a forever home?"

Ethan shakes his head no, keeping his eyes on the road. "She was too sick. Never made it out of the vet's office."

Tears well up. "*Oh.* That's awful." I pet the fur ball in my lap. "This one seems pretty healthy."

"Yeah." Ethan smiles. "She's going to be fine."

"Where will she go?"

"We'll drop her off at an organization nearby. And if they can't locate the owners, the woman who called in the rescue will take her."

"She's not riding home with us?"

"Afraid not."

Silence fills the car. That is, except for fluttering beagle's breath barely breaking through the roar of the truck.

The ride lasts only ten minutes. Ethan pries the beagle from my arms, and I stay in the car while he goes inside. Twenty minutes later, he comes back without the dog. On second thought, I couldn't do this every day.

We're back on the road, coastline rolling past my window.

Ethan pulls out a thermos from the center compartment. "Coffee?"

"No thanks."

"Would you mind pouring me a cup?"

"Sure." I grab one of the travel mugs and pour.

"Thanks." He takes a long pull, then sets the mug down. "Mind if I ask you a question?"

I turn away so he can't see my eyes rolling into the back of my head. "Something tells me you're going to ask the question whether I mind or not."

We fly along the highway a good ten miles per hour above the speed limit. He clears his throat. "What do you believe about spirituality, and . . . uh . . . the universe?"

"What do you mean?"

He glances at me, and then returns his focus to the asphalt whipping past our tires. "Do you believe in a Creator?"

I lower the window, hoping to cool my burning cheeks. What an impossible question. The roadside blurs past while Ethan waits, like a patient bomb waiting to go off.

"I don't believe in God."

Silence.

"Scratch that. Sounds too final. I'm not sure what I believe. I suppose it's possible that *something* is out there, some sort of God or creator. But what that something is, I can't be sure. If I have to put a label on myself, I'd say I'm undeclared."

More silence.

"What, no response? I know you've got something on the tip of your tongue."

"I'm just wondering how that's working out for you. I mean, do you ever have the urge to search for something more?"

"Not really, no. Why? Is that surprising?"

"To be honest, yes."

"Ethan, I'm glad you believe in something that works for you — I mean it. But I'm not into any of that. So I'm afraid I'll be heading straight down after this life. And I'm okay with that. Really."

Ethan steps on the gas. "Kristen, I'm not judging you. I'm curious, that's all."

Seconds of silence pass.

"And you know what I think?" He clears his throat. "Deep in my heart I know that when I go to heaven, you'll be there."

He winks at me and then sets his eyes back on the road.

"Because if you weren't there, well, then it wouldn't be heaven."

Wow. Patronize much? "Wait. You're saying *I'm* going to die first?"

Ethan laughs out loud. I roll my window back up, and we spend the rest of our journey in near silence, while I try to visualize the thought bubbles above Ethan's head.

CHAPTER 14

AUGUST

⟶❧⟵

I SETTLE INTO THE familiar indentation of Georgina's loveseat and breathe deeply as exotic jasmine calms my nerves. Sunshine reflects off Georgina's glossed lips. She grabs her pencil and notebook. "Happy birthday. You just had one, right?"

"Yeah, my twenty-fifth, thanks. Can we talk about my dreams?"

"Okay, talk."

"This one's new, but also recurring. It starts with Ethan and me standing together in a garden. Then he takes my hand and leads me down a path."

I rub my neck and fan my shirt. Am I the only one sweating like a dog?

"Then we're inside a building and he hands me a little white jewelry box. When I open it, a light comes out and blinds me. I assume there's a ring inside, but when I reach for it, nothing's there. Only the dazzling light. Then Ethan walks ahead, and I close the box and follow him. Then a ton of people surround us and we're all walking in the same direction, toward a gigantic banquet room filled with long benches."

Georgina grabs a fresher pencil and continues scribbling.

"Everyone's smiling like they're drugged or brainwashed or something, and they're freaking me out. It's like everyone on the planet's been taken over by some *thing* and I'm the only normal human left.

"Then we're all seated and I see Alana standing on the opposite side of the room in her wedding gown, holding a bouquet of white orchids. She's beautiful, the typical radiant bride, except her neck vein is throbbing. Then a stranger walks to the front of the room. He's wearing jeans and a white T-shirt, and he has long wavy hair. He looks like the homeless man who took my red velvet cake, except this guy's got a full set of teeth. Sunlight pours through the stained glass windows, and all these bright

110

colors scatter throughout the room. There's a plain metal cross hanging on the wall behind the jeans guy, and that's when it hits me that I'm inside a church. A *church*, of all places."

Georgina clamps her lips together.

"I feel trapped and I scan for exits but the room starts to spin. The only way I can get it to stop is to focus on the stupid box. Then the guy with the jeans and the perfect teeth explains that everyone has received one of these little white boxes. They're initiation gifts, or something like that. Ethan's staring straight ahead this whole time, smiling and bouncing in his seat like a little boy on Christmas morning.

"I want to leave, but that would be rude. So I sit and wait for the ordeal to end, so I can hand back the box and run away as far as possible. Then I wake up."

Georgina chews her lip and glances at the steamer trunk. She taps her pencil on her notebook, and then sets them both aside. "Have you considered the possibility that *God* is trying to speak to you?"

I throw my head back, inadvertently knocking it against the wall.

"Ouch. Um . . . yeah, no way. He and I aren't on speaking terms. It's more like a representation of my own fear, like my fear of God, or my fear of Ethan sucking me into a cult. He and I had a conversation about heaven and God. Maybe this dream is an aftershock of that."

Have I become the therapist? Why do I keep paying this woman?

"Do you *fear* God?" she asks.

"I'm not sure I *believe* in God."

"Well," she says, "There's a God-like signature written all over this dream sequence. The light, the cross, the bride, the symbolism of marriage. I'm wondering if God is trying to hint about something in your future."

"Marriage to Ethan?"

"Marriage with Jesus." Her eyes are shining.

"You're Christian?" I hold my cheeks, which must be flaming red. If smoke could physically come out of my ears, it would.

"Yes. Greek Orthodox, to be specific." Then she lowers her tone. "Kristen, I'm careful about when and how I bring faith into a therapy session. I wouldn't have mentioned God to you without first giving it serious consideration. If you find it offensive, I'll pull back."

"I don't mind you talking about God, as long as you understand I'm not buying into it. No matter what you say or do, I won't drink the Kool-Aid."

"Deal," she says, clutching her mug. *Trust me, I'm a therapist.*

"And what about the first dream?" I ask.

"You'd like my interpretation?"

I nod slowly.

"In your chase dream, you're running away from something. That likely represents your past. Perhaps you're trying to run away from the trauma you experienced as a little girl."

"Trauma? I mean, yeah, my childhood sucked. My mother was a fall down drunk and I had to watch Victor beat her senseless. Sure, he came after me, but he never beat me, not *really*. He preferred verbal abuse with me."

Georgina shakes her head. "Verbal abuse is as destructive as physical abuse, if not more."

"I get that words can hurt, but I doubt Victor's verbal abuse is the reason for my screwed-up life. I did more harm to myself as a teenager than he could have ever done."

She cocks her head to the side. "Could there have been more to your relationship with Victor than the verbal abuse?"

My cheeks flush. "I've told you *everything*. He shoved me into a wall a few times. Gave me a few minor bruises and told me I was a waste of space. Maybe threw in a few nasty nicknames. That's it."

She nods. "For now, let's concentrate on your dreams. You say that in the chase dream, you have an urge to find the ocean, but you never reach it. You haven't reached the finish line. Perhaps once you do, the dreams will stop. Pay careful attention to these dreams. Look for something new, some small detail you may have missed in the past. Off the record, my gut tells me both of your recurring dreams are related."

She glances at the wall behind me. Session's over.

The same two dreams haunt me for the next two weeks. Most nights, I'm running through the chase sequence until I wake up, exhausted. On other nights, I wake from having the dream with Ethan, the one with the eerie, cult-like congregation and the strange white boxes. I see no connection between these two dreams, like Georgina suggested, except that in both scenarios, the urge to run overwhelms me.

One August morning, while the air is still cool and fresh, I take off on a run for real. A pod of dolphins escorts me northbound as I run barefoot along the wet sand, soaking in the water, sky, and the breathtaking dawn. It's been a long time since I've run in the daytime. I forgot what it's like to run with a purpose other than to escape, and to move forward with intention, at perfect peace with what I leave behind.

Before long, the pain in my ankle forces me to walk. What was that, five minutes? Am I going to have to pay for *that* mistake for the rest of my life? Still, it's good to be on the beach with the cool sand beneath my feet.

Georgina is nuts. My dreams can't be messages from God. The physics alone are incomprehensible. No, I need to focus on what is tangible, like Mark. Will he ever wake? Will he still be here a year from now?

I grunt out an eleven-hour workday. Then, like the day before, and like the day before that, I visit Mark, and he's as dull as ever.

Across the hall, the cancer patient's room bustles with visitors, noise spilling into Mark's room. Sometimes, she and her cancer-fighting friends sneak off to the garden to smoke their medical marijuana. Is that her secret? According to the rumors buzzing around at the nurse's station, this patient has shattered everyone's predictions of her expected death.

Bored by my own company, I text Ethan and ask if he's free to meet for coffee. I'm sure he will, because he's always in the mood for caffeine. To my surprise, he responds: *Patient load too full today. Catch you next time* ;)

I shiver. I've been doing this ever since that blasted beagle rescue. Every time I think of Ethan and that cheese ball wink of his, I shiver. Why do I do that? Not only that, but I keep imagining new rescue scenarios — Ethan and I saving dogs from unimaginable circumstances. In one fantasy, his cross pendant snags on a tree limb, breaks off, and plummets over a cliff. And he doesn't care. He just lets it go as we continue our rescue mission.

What's wrong with me? We're just friends. It can't work any other way. Guess I'll have to settle for coffee by myself.

I enter the visitor's lounge for the billionth time and after filling my cup, I scan the Wall of Inspiration, a section of the room plastered with notes written by staff, patients, and family members. I step closer to read one of the tear-stained papers when something black passes by. I turn my head. It's him, the stocky one, heading down the hall, limping, and wearing the same windbreaker and baseball cap. I follow.

He makes all the turns necessary to reach Mark's room, but then he slows his pace and cocks his head a quarter turn. I stop dead.

He walks faster, but I'm on his tail.

As we approach the final stretch, a commotion brews. It's a swarm of activity as people migrate toward Mark's room. The stranger surprises me by veering away from the crowd. It can't be possible that Mark has a close friend that I've never met, but my curiosity about the stranger is no match for the growing excitement.

I tread carefully while doctors pile into Mark's room. My mind races, but time moves underwater. I'll claw through this dense crowd if I have to, but wait . . . it's parting, like a human Red Sea, a dozen stunned eyes fixed on me as I pass through.

My view of Mark's bed is clear. A grinning physician flanks each side, and there is Mark, with his head turned toward me, his eyes wide open.

What a lovely face!

The crowd closes in, watching in silence, waiting for my reaction. But I have none. After five months, he's awake, and I stand frozen in awe.

Mark pins his eyes on mine and I pin mine on him. His cheeks are wet with joy. So are mine. His lips twitch and his breath catches. I run forward and embrace him. His right hand trembles, both arms remaining at his side. The crowd begins to murmur, and then life whips into a frenzy.

Over the next couple of days, Mark's room swells with visitors, more than the cancer patient has ever seen. Many of Mark's friends come, but never the stranger I followed through the halls. When I ask Mom if she knows the man, she shrugs.

Whatever. My priorities lie elsewhere. Mom's out of control. She prays like a madwoman, praising God every second of the day. She's certain Mark will have a full recovery. The doctors, though excited, remain conservative. They remind us of all the possible limitations of Mark's progression. They use lots of fancy words backed up by scientific studies. They advise us to set our expectations low, so we won't be disappointed if the worst should happen. But that *never* works. I've set my expectations low my entire life, and not once have I avoided disappointment.

Alana must be swamped with work, because she still hasn't answered my frantic call. While Mark naps, I try her number again, and she finally answers.

"Mark came out of his coma," I choke through tears.

"Wow, Kristen."

I ramble like a lunatic. "It's a miracle, or at least it will force the number crunchers to reconsider their statistics, right? But his recovery will be excruciating. He's making slow progress. I'm glad he woke, but it's not at all how I hoped it would be. He wears a diaper. He can't eat, walk, or talk. He's like a newborn, only much larger, so I can't even hold him. He'll have to re-learn everything. Assuming he can re-learn anything. It's terrifying to watch such a strong man struggle—"

"I'm happy for you," Alana interrupts. "Listen, work is crazy busy. I'll call you back later. 'Kay?"

Really? If Jenna and Danielle were still alive, they'd have been here within minutes of my first call. But whatever, Alana.

On the third day after Mark's awakening, Harley's gait changes. His head droops and his feet move as if every step is excruciating.

I call Daz. She's adored Harley since the first time I brought him into her animal hospital eight years ago, and once she hears the news, she rushes over.

She examines him briefly. "He's on his way out." Her expression remains soft. "Would you like me to take him in?"

"No. Not now. Maybe in the morning."

I can't. Not when morning arrives. Not ever. Harley's been my anchor since I was four. How can I let go of him now, at a time like this?

I keep him home, all to myself, and we cuddle on the couch and watch black and white movies all day while he eats and drinks nothing. I play Bessie Smith from my iPod. Visions of childhood pop in my head. My mother blasting Bessie to celebrate Victor's absence, and tugging on my arm to get me to slow dance with her. Then she would get tired, and I'd pick Harley up and we'd spin and twirl to the music that played on and on as if Victor would never return.

I scoop up my withered kitty and place him into the fold of my arm, and I sway the way I used to when we were both small. Faded memories play like a tribute in my mind, vague recollections racking my brain. If Harley leaves, who'll soak up my tears for the next twenty years?

We continue to listen to Bessie, over and over, as we sway to the raspy sounds of her soulful, jazzy blue sweetness.

Late at night, I tuck Harley into bed next to me, and I fall asleep to his quiet purr. By morning, he is gone.

Outside, joggers and walkers travel the crowded beach paths, carrying on with their lives. I suppose I'll carry on with life too, only with a Harley-shaped hole in mine.

Weeks later, Mark still struggles to interact with the world. Day after day, he loses this battle. Every visit begins the same. The moment he sees me, he stiffens as he tries to speak. He arches his back, pushing his chest out. His lips move, releasing pathetic gurgling noises. After a time, he falls back and turns away. He's learned how to say many words, but for the life of him, he cannot say my name.

I kiss him and hug him, but he shoves me away. If only he could fall back into his coma. Maybe then, we could all get some peace.

Mark's recovery team insists that support from family members will improve his progress. Too bad Mark's family tree is little more than a stump.

As usual, Mom's husband Steve is apathetic. What on earth is that man's value, other than *not* being a violent alcoholic like Victor? I try to help as much as I can, but overall, Mom is alone in her efforts. She works hard, while she prays over Mark every day, using one hand to hold her Bible near him and her other hand to reach the sky. She's too exhausted to care that everybody still thinks she's nuts. The woman is positively fatigued. Her eye sockets have gone dusky and her shoulders are always slumped. Her skin hangs more than it used to. Has she lost weight?

CHAPTER 15

STILL AUGUST

⌒⨯⌒

W E RUSH THROUGH the corridors of a luxurious Downtown rental
structure. Mr. L.A. leads the pack, followed by Ron, Mike, and then
Regina. As usual, I'm dead last. When will I learn that high heels are a
stumbling block in this fast paced job? My cell phone buzzes at my hip,
and I glance at the caller ID. Of course. Who else would call at the worst
possible time?

"Yeah, Mom." My breath comes out heavy.

"Kristen, honey?"

"Can't talk now. Work crisis."

"Is it that bad? I need a break and I don't want to leave Mark alone."

"Yes, it's that bad." I scramble to keep up with the pack. "Go home
and rest. Mark will be fine alone for a few hours. I'll come by later this
afternoon."

"I'll wait until you get here." She sighs and hangs up.

Mr. L.A. pounds on the door to suite 540A. Regina steps back, crossing and re-crossing her arms. Ron and Mike adjust their hundred-dollar
ties. I clutch my little black sketchbook and hook the other thumb in the
pocket of my knockoff slacks, while my heart pounds like mad.

At six feet, Mrs. Crogg towers over Mr. L.A., peering down at him over
her high-collared blouse. "You're one minute late. Come in."

"Wow," gasps Regina.

Rich exotic tones, overstuffed furniture, and subdued backdrops fill
the open space. If animal prints were my thing, I'd die for this place.

Mr. L.A. steps forward. "Mrs. Crogg, we have designed and furnished
more than two hundred and fifty of these lofts, and Kristen has managed
over half of them."

"Don't patronize me. Most of your referrals came from *me*."

"My point is that we haven't had a single complaint."

"You have one now. This . . ." she sweeps her arm across the loft, "is not what I requested."

"What, specifically, is wrong?"

"Everything. The couches, the patterns, the ghastly pillows. And the walls. I hate the walls. I wanted greenish-whitish-green. This is whitish-greenish-white. I hate it."

Ron steps in. "Is there any time of the day when you do like the color?"

"For heaven's sake, young man, if you're going to speak, try to make some sense."

Yeah, Ron. Get to the point.

"Sunlight affects the wall color." He approaches the floor-to-ceiling windows. "So the shade and tone of your wall will change throughout the day as the sun rises and falls."

Mrs. Crogg crosses her arms and curls her upper lip. "I suppose I do like the color better in the evenings."

Brilliant, Ron. But why are you helping me when this would be the perfect opportunity to throw me under the bus? Is Delila wrong about you and your involvement in the "group of seven?"

"We can adjust the daytime color with something as simple as altering your indoor lighting and finding the right shade of sheers." Ron steps back, pretending to appraise the panels.

"Fine," replies Crogg, a hint of a smile peeking through her foundation. "What about the rest of this chaos?"

Mike steps in and puts his hand on Crogg's shoulder. He's the only one here who can do that without reaching up. "Do you remember our meeting, when you signed some papers?"

She glances at the portfolio in Mike's hands and her posture stiffens, her cheeks flushing. *Does* she remember? Or is this another one of those "senior moments" where her memories seem to escape her?

Mike retrieves the proposal agreement and flips the pages of specification sheets, purchase orders, and invoices — each individual sheet imprinted with Crogg's unmistakable signature — that obnoxious "C" and the ringlet tail from the second "g." Then Mike shows her a photo of the mood board. She cried the first time we showed her the board. Now, she scrunches her face. It's as if she's never seen it before. "I . . . I don't remember signing any of those papers."

Mike slips the paperwork back into the portfolio. "But *we* do. Ron, Kristen, me—"

"Me, too," chimes Regina.

Mike and Regina are part of the supposed conniving group, too, yet they're all supporting me. Could Delila be wrong about all of them? Or is it possible she made the whole thing up?

Crogg flashes angry eyes at Regina and then at Mr. L.A. "That's it, then? You brought all of them here to gang up on me?"

Mr. L.A. opens his mouth, but Crogg waves him off. "I don't want you to say another word." She sits on the couch. "Kristen's been silent this entire time. I want her to speak."

Yes, I've been silent. Per instruction. It's Mr. L.A.'s favorite tactic: good cop/bad cop.

I sit next to Crogg, my hands folded atop the sketchbook on my lap. "I'm sorry you're disappointed with our work. At Hamilton Design, we believe home should be a place of rejuvenation, a place of comfort and rest. So tell me, what can we do to transform your home from a source of disappointment into an oasis?" I open my sketchbook, ready to take notes.

Slouching, she rubs her forehead. "I like Ron's idea of switching out the lighting and the drapes."

"And the pillows?"

"No. I . . . suppose I like the pillows."

Of course she does. She picked them out.

Broken, Mrs. Crogg concedes in writing that she is once again happy with our work. She also signs new forms agreeing to pay for the purchase and installation of the agreed-upon adjustments.

The second we return to our office building on the other side of town, I leave the others behind so I can hunt down a sizeable slab of chocolate. Perhaps that will soothe my aching brain. I press my palms hard against the revolving glass door.

For the love of Pete, is that Tommy in front of me? The tall blond veers left. Nope, not Tommy. Somebody else who dresses and walks as if the entire planet worships him. If only I could get my mind off him. Tommy's impending wedding is all anyone talks about. Can't get away from it, no matter which way I turn. I'm sure it's trending on social media, which is why I prefer the nostalgia of water cooler conversations. Of course, those conversations would be a lot livelier if I wasn't the only one there. On Tommy's wedding day, everyone else will be at the wedding, and I'll be at the water cooler, sipping water from a paper cup, mumbling nonsense to myself.

I smack my forehead, trying to knock Tommy out of my head as I trudge through the cement jungle of Downtown L.A. Stay focused, Kristen. Giant bars of dark chocolate beckon you from inside the coffeehouse a mere three blocks away.

Vagrants gather near restaurants, while faceless, well-dressed people pass by. Can't anyone see the unsheltered? They're everywhere, sleeping in the alleys, standing on street corners. Dozens of them, hard to miss, with that same weariness pasted on their faces, and . . . hey, isn't that the guy who ate my red velvet cake? Same fatigues. Same clumpy, dark brown hair. Same. Toothless. Grin.

We stare at each other, frozen in time as countless strangers stream past. What is so captivating about this guy? I step forward, and the toothless smile fades. I nearly fall over backwards at the sight of his eyes. Deep, burnished bronze, like Ethan's.

"Not yet," the vagrant says, and then he turns and walks away.

What the . . . ?

I take off after him, and he runs. I run as fast as I can in my heels, *click, click, clicking* along the sidewalk and past towering buildings. *Click, click, clicking* through, between, and around somber businessmen and women. *Click, click, clicking* as the man slips into an alley, where my heel snags on a crack and snaps off. I trip, sprawling across the filth-stained asphalt.

The faceless crowd shows no interest in the fact that I'm lying flat. The bronze-eyed hobo disappears.

I pull myself up and limp back to the office, *click, thump, clicking* for more than half a mile before sinking into my chair. My slacks are ripped at the knees, my arms are swelling with scrapes, and my hands are empty of chocolate.

I'm rubbing my aching ankle when Ethan calls. "I only have a short break, but I wanted to tell you that my internship at Memorial ends in January."

"I guess you'll need to start job hunting."

"Yeah, that's what I wanted to tell you. I've got two offers."

"Fantastic. Where are they?"

"One's at UCLA Medical Center."

"Perfect. We could meet for lunch when I'm working out of the office."

"The other offer is at Sky Ridge Medical Center."

"Oh, where's that?"

"Denver."

"Are you considering that one?"

"I'm considering both. It's going to be a tough decision, but I'm praying about it."

UCLA versus Colorado — is it really a tough decision? What about the life he's established here? Can he really leave everything behind? Who's going to rescue all the stray dogs in Southern California if he leaves?

"Okay . . . well, thanks for telling me, but I gotta go. It's been a horrific day at the office, and now I have to visit Mark."

I hang up, grab my purse and keys, and head home. There's no way I'm going to visit Mark today.

The next day, I'm walking through Downtown again, this time in flats. I spy more than a dozen homeless people. None of them is the guy I chased yesterday. If only I had more time, but Alana sounded anxious on the phone. It's been too long since we had lunch together, and I don't want to be late. I stand outside the restaurant and scan the sidewalk in both directions. What would five minutes of searching hurt?

Alana bursts through the door. "Good, you're here. We've already got a table."

"We?"

She rests her hand on my shoulder and looks down at me. "Yes, *chérie*. We. Follow me." She clicks through the restaurant and I shuffle behind. "I have a surprise for you, but you have to keep an open mind. 'Kay?"

No, this is not okay. I hate surprises.

Throughout the restaurant, well-dressed customers chat and sip wine at one in the afternoon. No surprise here. She leads me past tables reserved for regulars, and in the farthest reaches of the restaurant, in the most private, premier booth, I find my surprise in a crisp, pink polo. His hair is well-groomed, thick waves flowing to the side. He certainly cleans up well. Except for that scar, a two-inch line dividing his cheekbone.

He smiles, looking a lot like the charming Andrue I used to know, but I'm not buying it. The stairwell memories are too fresh. I turn to leave, and Alana grabs my shoulders. "Trust me," she whispers. She gestures toward the woman sitting next to Andrue. "Kristen, this is Karen. Andrue's mother."

Alana slides into the booth, across from Andrue. I take Karen's hand and make contact with her brilliant green eyes. She reminds me of the youngish moms I find at Trader Joe's, wearing yoga pants and ponytails, shopping for organic foods and giant blocks of raw goat cheese. Everything on this woman appears natural. Except for those colored contacts. Nobody's eyes are the color of a radioactive Granny Smith apple. She smiles. If only I could close my mouth — then at least I could fake a smile back.

I slide in next to Alana, across from Karen. Andrue stares at me, boring a hole through my forehead. The *nerve*. Last time we were together, he waved his knife in my face.

"Quite a swing you've got." He rubs his scar.

The young, attentive waiter takes our order. Karen asks for a gluten-free, cage-free, chicken avocado sandwich and a shot of espresso. The rest of us order bacon-jalapeño cheeseburgers and Diet Cokes. I ask for a side of fries for me and another side for Alana, who I assume is still in denial over her obsession with them.

Karen sighs and flashes those colored contacts at me. "Andrue loves Alana."

"Love?" I laugh out loud.

Karen clears her throat and nudges Andrue. He reaches across the table, placing his hand on top of mine. I gasp and try to jerk my hand back, but Alana slaps hers on top of the pile. What? Andrue washed his hair, so now we're all going to act like nothing happened? Has everyone lost their minds?

"Kristen," pleads Andrue, "I have bipolar disorder."

"Oh." He's more of a whack-job than I presumed. But wait . . . "How does that justify you jumping me in the stairwell?"

"It doesn't," he whispers. "I'm sorry."

I yank my hand away. "No. You're not going to do this to me. I can't pretend nothing happened. You need help, Andrue."

"I know."

Alana bores into me with those giant eyes of hers. They all watch me while I sit speechless. I hate being on the spot like this. If only I could just disappear. Finally, I find my voice. "What do you guys want from me? Forgiveness? Fine, I *forgive* Andrue, but I can't go back to the way things were."

"I should never have agreed to keep Andrue's psychiatric disability hidden," says Karen. "But he convinced me he had it under control. I had no idea he went off his medications."

"You went *off* your meds?"

"I'm back on them. And I'm going to stay on them."

I turn to Alana. "You didn't know?"

She shakes her head.

"When did you find Andrue?"

"Couple of weeks ago. Brock found him at Lincoln Park, hanging out with three other homeless men."

I turn to Andrue. "You lived in the park?"

"No," says Alana. "He couldn't sleep there because the cops sweep the park too often, so he had to find someplace else, like an alley or an unlit section of a parking lot. He never stayed in the same place very long. He had to keep moving, so he wouldn't draw too much attention to himself."

Alana keeps glancing at her fingernails and sighing, trying to act casual as she fills me in on Andrue's homeless experience, but I'm not stupid. She's pushing my buttons, trying to soften me up. When she's finished, I raise my brows at Andrue. "I'm sorry you have a mental illness, but to be honest, I don't feel safe around you anymore."

"I made a mistake," he says. "I should never have gone off my meds. Kristen, you have to understand . . . this disease makes me do things I don't want to do. It turns me into a person that is *not* me."

"You threatened to kill me. How am I supposed to assimilate that?"

"I'm going to take responsibility for what I've done. After lunch, I'm turning myself in."

"Assault with a deadly weapon's a felony," says Alana. "He has to face the prosecutor, and he's got to go through the process of the law. If he doesn't, they're going to drag him in the next time he gets pulled over for a traffic violation or anything else. We're hoping you'll come to the hearing and tell them you forgive Andrue, that you know he didn't mean to scare you . . . that you know he wouldn't have hurt—"

"Are you joking?"

"If you tell the prosecutor you understand Andrue wasn't in his right mind and that you forgive him, they'll be more lenient on him."

"I'm sorry I scared you," says Andrue. "I would never hurt you. You have to believe that."

"No, Andrue. I don't *have* to believe that. And I'm not sure that I do."

They all look at me. Sad-puppy-faced. It's a *Twilight Zone* freak party and I'm way outnumbered. Our food arrives and I try to eat my lunch, but even the jalapeños are bland.

He seems normal, sitting there in his pink polo. Why am I the only one who doesn't trust him anymore? He would've killed me in that stairwell if I'd let him.

My hands clench tight. "*Urgh*, just . . . whatever. Fine, I'll come down to tell the prosecutor I'm not mad at Andrue. But nothing is the same." I turn toward him. "Things are *not* the same."

Alana pats my hand. "It'll take time."

It's going to take more than that. I rake back my hair and try to digest my lunch. Then I bolt upright. "Wait — is the wedding still on?"

Alana smiles devilishly.

CHAPTER 16

SEPTEMBER

❧

I CLUTCH A TEAL throw pillow as I marvel at the strands of sunshine blasting through Georgina's blinds, variegating everything in the room. Georgina rests back, cradling her mug that reads, *I see crazy people.* If only she could see her own striped face. I drop my head into my palms to restrain a giggle.

"How are you?" she asks.

I lift my head, the urge to laugh gone. "Sometimes... I can't stand to visit Mark. That's bad, right? But it's hard. Do you have any idea how exhausting it is to watch someone you love struggle?"

Georgina nods slowly. "Tell me about his progress."

"He can move his legs and he's regained full use of his arms, but fine motor skills are an effort. He has aphasia. You know, trouble speaking. He can say some words and short sentences, but sometimes he forgets really basic words. He gets confused when there's more than one person in the room."

I wrap my hair into a knot, securing the wad with one of Georgina's pencils. Perhaps now my neck sweat will dry.

"The speech pathologist told us to read to Mark to help him re-learn language, so I read whatever I can get my hands on, whatever's lying around. Mom always reads from her Bible."

Georgina scribbles into her notebook.

"Yesterday, Mark yawned through an article on *How to Train Your Cat to Use the Toilet*, so I tossed the magazine aside and pulled out some photo flash cards designed to trigger parts of the brain that should help Mark re-learn how to speak."

"Where did these cards come from?"

"Mark's occupational therapist made them using a bunch of photos Mom and I gave him. The first card I showed Mark was a photo of me, from the day of Delila's beach party. It was a picture Ethan took after our volleyball tournament. I was covered in sand and sweat, but it was just a headshot and surprisingly, I didn't look half-bad.

"Anyway, Mark welled up when I showed him the picture. He recognized the image, but couldn't say my name. He pressed his lips together and his eyes darted around the room. I was sure he was trying to find something within reach that he could throw, so I flipped to the next card. But then he calmed down and it happened. He said *Kristen* for the first time since he woke."

"That's great," says Georgina.

"Yeah, it was. One of those memory-making moments, but then Mom walked in, and she got excited, and the three of us were beaming at each other about it — and that part was still great — but then I got this overwhelming urge to tell Mark that Mom revealed their secret. Mom and I had already agreed to wait until Mark got better, and he *was* better. It was the right time, but when I pulled her out of the room to suggest it, she yelled at me. She *never* yelled at me like that before. She was so angry about it that I dropped the subject."

"You're keeping it a secret?" Georgina lifts her eyes from her notebook.

"Yeah, can you believe it?"

She smiles, her pink lips glistening.

"Oh, and Andrue's back."

She lowers her chin.

"I know, right? Brock found him at a park, hanging out with some homeless men. He has bipolar disorder. Nobody knew, except his mother. He went off his meds. That's why he went berserk. Alana ambushed me. Had me meet her for lunch, and Andrue and his mother were there, too. They all pressured me to forgive Andrue. *He's sick*, they said. *He didn't mean to scare you. He's very sorry.*"

"Did you forgive him?"

"That's a good question. I told him I did, but I'm still freaked out by the whole thing. I know he's trying to do what's right. He even turned himself in and sat in jail for an entire week."

"He's out now?"

"Yeah. Alana hired an expensive attorney and there was a lot of legal maneuvering. She even talked me into coming to the hearing so I could tell the judge and the prosecutor that I forgive Andrue. I agreed to do it because even though my overall feeling was that I couldn't trust him anymore, part of me wanted to believe that everything would be okay.

So there I was, testifying that *I know Andrue's sick and he didn't mean to do it.* Karen, Alana, and a couple of doctors spoke on Andrue's behalf, explaining that Andrue was psychologically impaired because he was off his meds and went wacko. So now he's free."

"They dropped the case?"

"They came to a plea bargain, ordering Andrue to enter a six-month mental health program and go on probation for three years. They were going to issue a restraining order telling Andrue he had to stay away from me during his probation, but his attorney talked them out of it."

Georgina's brow crinkles.

"Whatever. If it were up to me, I'd never go near Andrue again. He has a nasty scar on his cheek where I hit him with the fire extinguisher, and I can't look at him without reliving the stairwell incident. I mean, how can I be sure he won't wig out again? But Alana's my best friend, and she and Andrue are getting married in a few months. How can I *not* go to her wedding?"

Georgina smiles. "There are lots of options for rehabilitation for a person who has bipolar disorder. There is no reason that person cannot have a rich and meaningful life."

"I get that. But I can't go back to being buddies with him when I can still see his penknife flashing in front of my face. Karen and Alana want me to commit to becoming one of Andrue's *accountability* partners. No way. It's too weird." I rub my forehead. "I've got my own problems to deal with. Work sucks. I have no idea where Ethan and I stand, or whether or not I can trust Delila. I miss my cat. When I sleep it's horrible, and my dreams are growing more bizarre every night. I'm stuck in an endless loop of exhaustion, coffee, and insomnia."

"Tell me about your dreams."

I draw a deep breath. "Last night, I woke up drenched with sweat and out of breath as if I'd been running a marathon. The chase dream had started like usual, with me barefoot, and all that mindless running. I still can't see how any of this can be a message from God, by the way, but you were right about watching for something to change."

Georgina's ears perk up.

I roll my eyes. "Try to stay calm, and you can keep your *I told you so* to yourself."

"Go on."

"In this chase dream, after running for a long time, a light appeared in the distance."

Georgina grins wide. I hate when she does that.

"This light was glowing like the sun, but it was something else. I stared at it and stopped running, as if I hit a wall and couldn't take another step. The mist kept clinging to my neck, but it never consumed me. It stopped moving forward the moment I did. I didn't dare turn around. I kept facing the strange glob of light and then a noise erupted, like a crowd gathering in the distance. For the first time in the chase dream, I wasn't alone."

"Your chase dream has merged with the one with the dazzling light coming from the white box?" asks Georgina, rhetorically.

"Yeah. You were right. The dreams are related."

She nods.

After the session, I head straight to my mother's house to celebrate her birthday, even though there are a hundred other things I'd rather do than spend an evening with Mom and Steve.

I saunter through the open door and into the kitchen, where Steve labors over a steaming pot of his famous spaghetti sauce, the comforting aroma of garlic washing over me. Mom works near Steve, chopping lettuce, tomato, and cilantro, then whisks white balsamic vinegar, lemon juice, olive oil, salt and pepper. She tastes, adds more salt, and then tosses everything together. Steve pours more wine into the sauce while I stand across from Mom, like a third wheel. Or more like a weathered dinghy, moored to the edge of the island.

We sit for dinner. I could eat this spaghetti every day. It has a bit of a kick. Is it the white pepper? The mealtime conversation could use a little seasoning, though. Mother, daughter, stepfather. Are we even compatible? As soon as Steve serves the cake, I'm out of here.

Mom clutches her stomach. "I'm going to skip dessert tonight, if that's okay with you. Kristen honey, I . . . I need to lie down. Probably the flu." She glances at Steve, who gazes deep into his plate.

"You sure? It's a Lady Baltimore, your favorite."

She winces.

"Never mind. You should rest."

I labored over the cake during my limited time between work and therapy. But it's fine if she wants to blow it off. No big deal. It's her birthday. She has the right to act as rude and anti-social as she wants.

Whatever.

Except now I'm alone with Steve. "Can you pass the garlic bread, and may I please have another glass of wine?"

He passes the bread and fills my glass. "Your mother has some photos." He fills his own glass and takes it to the hearth, where a storage box lies open. I grab my wine and leave my bread behind.

"Wow, these must be ancient. Before digital cameras, yeah?"

"Mary said you should take all the pictures you want."

"She's getting rid of them?"

"They're copies. She's got a full set of originals in another box."

Why the sudden urge to clean house?

Steve rifles through the box, flames from the fireplace kindling his eyes. They're glittery golden brown. Why does this feel like the first time I've ever looked at them?

Steve watches me gulp my wine. "I'm sorry I couldn't be the father you needed. I should have tried harder."

"Stop. I'm the one who pushed you away."

We sift through pictures. I was too far gone by the time he came into my life, and he was too cautious. But that's all in the past, so why don't we push it back under the rug, like we always do in this family?

Steve lifts his head out of the box. "Would you like to come to church with your mother and me this weekend?"

My pulse races. "You're ... I mean ... I didn't know you went to church with Mom."

Steve smiles, but doesn't respond.

"I'll think about it."

We both know I won't.

"You've got to be kidding," I blurt.

It's a photo of Victor standing next to Mom. Victor with his usual fresh cut and shave, a light, eerie smile, and those cold black eyes. And Mom squished into a tight black dress. Wow, look at the platinum bleached hair, false lashes, and bright red lipstick. When was this? Victor made her dress like that, but what for? Some sort of business dinner? I recognize the picture, but I can't quite remember the night.

"You can have any picture you want," says Steve.

"I don't want this one. Why does she keep it?"

Steve shakes his head. Then he takes the photo from my hands and tosses it into the fire.

I dig some more and find a picture of Mom and me. I remember this one! Was I four or five? It was one of Mom's good days, when she was sober enough in the daytime for us to take a walk. She asked the ice cream truck driver to take our picture. He gave us free snow cones. I toss the photo into my keep pile and dig some more.

Here's one of Mom holding me when I was just a baby. Dark bags hang from her eyes, but her smile is bright. The photo goes into my pile and I dig again, finding a picture of Mom and Steve on their wedding day. Worst day ever. Would it be rude if I didn't take this one? I put it in my pile and dig again. Here's a picture of two kids dressed as clowns. They're at that awkward stage where they're too old to trick-or-treat, but too young-at-heart to skip it.

"This clown looks angry. Is it me?"

"Yes," says Steve. "Your mother and I had recently started dating and she asked me to come along for trick-or-treating. What a night. All the recovery moms came too, with all their kids."

I must have been twelve when the picture was taken. Memories slowly filter back.

It was right after Mom joined the recovery group, the first year she was sober enough to take me trick-or-treating. It was also the first year I did not want to go. My friend Lilly was having a sleepover party. Mom said Lilly was a bad influence on me and I couldn't go, and that I shouldn't hang out with her anymore.

I was livid. Lilly and the other girls would be sneaking sips of brandy from the cupboard as soon as her mother passed out. And while my best friends laughed and drank, I would be holding a stupid pillowcase in my hands as I begged for candy. I complained that I was the only one of my friends missing out.

I examine the picture. Both clowns suffer from fierce red-eye. Mom never could use a camera. Why does the makeup-caked clown standing next to me seem familiar?

"Who's the boy?"

"You don't recognize him?" Steve grins. "That's Ethan, on one of his visits from Colorado. Your mother put you two together for the photo."

"Are you kidding?" I vaguely remember that Halloween night. There was a large group of kids there, but I ignored them all. I don't even remember this picture being taken. Why would Mom want this? Even the heavy makeup doesn't hide my scowl. I can't believe Ethan and I met before Mammoth.

The picture goes into my pile.

I take a cab home, where I'm blessed with the delightful absence of Delila and Legion. They must've gone out for the night. I grab a bottle of wine and a glass, wrap myself inside fluffy layers of bedding, and then peel open *Works of Love*, by Søren Kierkegaard.

"There are a lot of scriptural references," Ethan had warned when he insisted I take the book. "But the way the author writes, the way he reflects on love . . . I'm sure you'll like it."

But. As if scriptural references are some sort of repellent to me. So what if it's true? Why did he have to say it like that?

I scan the book, snuggling deeper into my bedding as I pay special attention to Ethan's markings and notations that blanket every other page. I down my glass and refill it. I draw the book close, inhaling heady scents of confidence and cleaned linen, essence of Ethan leaping off the pages. Please, *no*. I can't be falling for this guy.

Wait, what's this highlighted nugget? It's about when the heart is full . . . you shouldn't keep quiet. You should speak. I shiver. Why did he set apart this section? And what's up with all the question marks and exclamation points in the margin?

I flip pages, reading Ethan's highlights one after another. This Kierkegaard writes so deep, he makes my brain ache, but I like what he says about love. A sort of love that lies hidden, but out of need expresses itself naturally. It *blooms* out of need!

How can I have this?

Tell me, Søren, how can I make my heart so full it has no choice but to bloom? Is this anything more than a profound thinker's fantasy? How can I love all people when I'm raw from the friction of humanity? How can I love life without exception when the pressure from living makes me insane?

Søren, your thoughts are gorgeous, but I'm afraid I'm far more likely to crack than I am to bloom.

That's enough depth for one night. I use the picture of Ethan and me dressed as clowns as a bookmark, and turn off the light.

CHAPTER 17

OCTOBER

∽○

I LEAN AGAINST THE wall at the back of the conference room, clutching my sketchbook into the fold of my arms. All the heavies have taken the mesh-back chairs. Delila's *seven* found seats, too. Commotion circles the racetrack table as our newest client enters the room.

The woman slams down a stack of paper and nods at Regina. "Dear, would you pass these out?" She eyes the crowd. "These are privacy agreements. Everyone here will sign one. Whether you know my real name or not, you will call me Eddi. You will not reveal one detail about this project, me, or my personal life to anyone — not to your best friend, your mother, or your dog. Got it? And if I see one tweet, or one comment in any form of media, it will cost your jobs." Her voice cuts through the sounds of shuffling paper and clicking pens. "And thank you, Ralph, for letting me run this meeting."

Mr. L.A.'s phony smile distorts his face.

"Ralph and I go way back," Eddi continues. "I trust him, and I trust Hamilton Design to provide the services I need. Today I'm searching for the right person to lead this project. The purpose of this meeting is to sift out the bottom feeders and find someone I can tolerate for the next six to eight months."

Around the table, chests widen and smiles gleam, as I slink deeper into the shadows. Eddi explains her plans for an extensive remodel and design of her twenty million dollar beachfront Malibu estate. The chick's a tank, plowing a path of discussion few can keep up with.

Poor, slow-witted Regina opens her mouth. "What about Tommy Foxx? We can subcontract him for the outside space."

Mr. L.A. shakes his head at Regina and curls his upper lip.

"No way," laughs Eddi. "I work with egocentrics all day. The last thing I want is to come home and find Foxx's big head blocking my ocean view."

133

A short laugh bursts through my mouth. Eddi places her hands on her hips and raises her brow. "You have something to add?"

"I do." I step out of the shadow, one thumb hooked inside my trouser pocket, the other hand loosely holding my sketchbook at my side. "You want comfort and luxury," I continue, projecting my voice to imply I'm more confident than I really am.

"You also want to break free from the traditional Malibu home themes. *Charming* is not your style and you don't want to live in a sand castle. Think *nature meets technology*, pairing these two realms by combining natural, carbon-neutral materials with the finest industrial materials technology has to offer. Picture a variety of exotic woods, recycled steel, and sustainable finishes, along with a generous use of glass panes to bring the Pacific Ocean landscape into your home. Inside, we'll repeat the theme of metal, glass, and wood throughout — quartz and limestone countertops... natural wool carpeting . . . and custom furniture and fixtures."

Snickers erupt from my peers, but Eddi's smiling, and her opinion is the only one that matters.

"What's your name, dear?"

"Kristen," blurts Mr. L.A.

"Kristen, come sit next to me."

I saunter over, my heart thumping a million beats a minute. Eddi kicks poor Regina out of her seat. Then she places her hand on Mr. L.A.'s wrist. "This is the one. Everyone else can leave."

Chairs slide out, as more than a dozen pairs of eyes stab me in the back.

Eddi grins at me. "Give yourself a pat, dear. You've landed lead position on what is likely your largest project to date."

She's right, it *is*. Largest single project, anyway. Why am I smiling? I'll never be able to handle a project of this scale. I have no idea what I was talking about. Most of that baloney came from a conversation Delila had with one of her clients this morning. If only Eddi knew that I just remembered a few key words that came out of Delila's mouth, and then spit them out.

She asks to see my sketchbook. The top five pages are sketches I made, based on my eavesdropping. Sure, I added my own flair, but they're little more than *doodles*. Thank God, Eddi likes them. In one fantastic blur,

I'm put in charge of selecting the design team and consultants, as well as directing the architects and planners, hiring from outside when necessary. Holy smokes!

We set a date for an in-home consultation. Just me and Eddi. Mr. L.A insists there's no need to worry about this meeting. All I need to do is make a stellar second impression. Yeah, sure. All I have to do is convince Eddi she's certain she likes me, and we can solidify the deal. I could stand to gain or lose everything from this next encounter, but no need to worry.

The night before my big meeting with Eddi, I'm desperately searching for hidden details in my recurring dream. Again, the two different dreams collide. That overwhelming orb of light appears in the distance and I stop running. The cold mist stops moving, too, and it clings to my neck. As I regulate my breath, the mist stays behind, refusing to make a move.

Then I force myself to turn around, and for the first time, I stand face-to-face with the thing that has been chasing me for all these months. My breath catches in my throat. Just as I imagined, it's an immense, formless mist.

I poke at it and it slips back. Then the mass of vapor swirls in a fast and violent rotation, kicking up dirt and increasing speed. I jump back and watch the thick, churning blackness. The mist swirls and shrinks, the particles drawing together, taking shape. The formless mass grows more and more defined until I recognize the image.

No. *No*, it can't be!

I turn back to the streets and run like mad, my bare feet slapping asphalt as I ignore my peripheral vision. All that matters is the light in the distance, and I'm running toward it as fast as I can.

I wake exhausted and starving. I grab a cup of instant coffee, but skip breakfast. The 405 is paved with molasses, a hundred thousand drivers trying to get to the same place at the same time. An old, hard-rock hit with brooding lyrics and an enraged guitar riff blasts through the car speakers as my palms sweat all over the steering wheel.

Miles later, as I merge onto the 10, some idiot tries to cut me off. No way, dude, I'm already running late. He flashes a jazz hand at me, purses his lips, and points to the back of my car.

Smoke fills my rearview mirror. That's coming from *me*? What the . . . what's that noise? This engine's never run this rough.

I cut off a teenager in a Prius and rumble toward the nearest exit, the engine groaning as I leave a wave of smoke. Then, *bang!* The Mustang dies a hundred yards from the corner gas station, and a blue Dodge Ram skids to a stop, tapping my bumper.

I draw a deep breath as I scan the bundle of testosterone stomping toward me — a six-foot-seven Marlboro Man. It's a good day for me to be wearing a silk blouse and snug-fit skirt. His razor-stubble face softens the closer he approaches, but he throws his hands up. "What kind of stop was that?"

I shrug. "The car just died."

He spits out the accumulated juice from his chewing tobacco, and then looks up. "To be clear, I'm *not* at fault."

California traffic law is on my side, but I don't have time to split hairs. "There's no damage, so let's not bother exchanging information. But if you don't mind, I could use a hand pushing the car to that station on the corner."

Marlboro Man obliges, and then he presses to get my number, "in case something comes up." I escape to the ladies room, where I call Eddi's personal assistant, warning her I'll be late. Then I whip out the Executive Hertz Gold card Mr. L.A. gave me when I landed Eddi's project and order a rental.

I wait in the restroom until I'm sure Marlboro has left. Then I call Alana. My regular car guy went out of business, but she'll know who to recommend. She's *got a guy* for everything.

"Your Mustang died? For no reason? Have you checked for grease beneath Delila's fingernails?"

"Delila isn't behind everything bad that happens."

"I'd bet my best bra she's behind everything bad that happens to you."

"Why would she mess with my car? You think she's trying to kill me?"

"I don't know, *chérie*. But I do know you take good care of that car . . . whatever. Give me your location and I'll send Robby over. He's the best in Mustang repair."

"Thanks. Love ya."

"You're a fool to let her live in your apartment."

"Fine," I say. "But I'm not the only fool here. Are you seriously going to marry Andrue, knowing he's bipolar?"

"If he was physically disabled from a car accident, would I abandon him? Of course not. I know what it's like to be abandoned, and I wouldn't do that to anyone."

"Your mother?"

"Don't analyze me. The point is, I'm loyal."

"I know you are. 'Kay, I gotta go. My rental pulled up. A shiny silver Lincoln ls."

"Gross."

"Tell me about it."

The friendly voice of the Lincoln's GPS guides me toward my destination until finally I arrive at Eddi's place. It's an hour past our appointment time, but Eddi greets me with an enormous hug, and then wipes her hands on her jeans. Next time, I'll opt for a blouse made of breathable fabric. I'm sweating like a pig in this one.

Eddi and I settle onto her couch and slip into the comfortable, animated conversation of old friends. Twenty minutes in, Eddi surprises me by getting into project details. Wasn't this supposed to be friendly chatter? Specifications fly left and right as my legs and back stick to the leather cushions.

Uh-oh, I left my pen and notebook in the Lincoln. "Do you mind if I record this?" I ask, pulling out my digital recorder.

"Knock yourself out."

I press the power button and nothing happens. I'd bet Alana's best bra these batteries are brand new. I'm screwed. I smile and carry on, pretending the thing is working. Eddi smiles back and continues to list, in excruciating detail, everything she wants to happen with this project.

She talks fast, while I struggle to store the details to memory. I try all sorts of tricks, like association and mnemonics. I repeat key words in Eddi's sentences, both to absorb what she's saying and to give the impression that I'm paying attention. After a while, I begin to sound like Rain Man. "Thirty-six. Yes, thirty-six. Definitely thirty-six."

My stomach growls.

Eddi's brow rises. "Would you like something to eat?"

"No thanks, I'm fine."

Then my cell phone goes off. Forgot to put it on silent. Of course I did. Eddi laughs.

Ugh.

By the time I leave Eddi's estate, my head's ready to explode from information overload. I drive around the block, park, and scribble down everything I can remember — *yes, that was thirty-six, definitely thirty-six* — while a lady and her purse-sized shih-poo growl at me from a nearby sidewalk.

Mr. L.A. yanks me into his office the moment I return, his eyes wide and bright. Somehow, Eddi still likes me and I've solidified lead position on this project.

I leave work and head straight for the beach, where I carve a sand angel in the shape of a height-challenged woman wearing a sticky silk blouse and a tight-fitting Armani skirt.

Once I'm done making the impression, I sit on a ridge in the sand. The Pacific Ocean churns and glistens beneath unobstructed crystal blue skies. Amazing. I have no desire to walk into the water. An army of waves crashes before me. Over and again, the water creeps up the mound and tries to drench me. But it can't even reach me. I'm as safe as the pelicans flying overhead.

Alana was right. I *do* take good care of my car. At least I did until my mechanic closed shop, and I've never had trouble with it before. But Alana's suspicions of Delila fade against the glow of my triumph, my biggest accomplishment to date. I've finally arrived. Things are going to change for me. For sure.

Several minutes later, a cavalry of black clouds rides in from the north to assault the tranquil blue skies. The birds scatter. Lightning cracks the darkening sky, marking the beginnings of a Southern California storm. It's nothing more than a hearty sprinkle, but it seems nature found a way to get me wet after all.

I duck into the safety of the oppressive rental car and head to Ocean View Medical Center. Drenched, I dash through the double doors and dart through the lifeless corridors.

Before I reach Mark, I pass another patient who sits up, alone in his room. My pace slows. The old man stares at me, hunched as he sucks air from the gigantic oxygen mask strapped to his face. His withering hand clasps the mask as if he's holding on to the only thing he has left. Hope, perhaps, for holding on a little longer. Or for suffering a little less. The dying man nods in my direction. Had this exchange happened any other time, I might've walked into his room and sat for a while. Instead, I nod back and walk on, increasing my pace.

I skip into Mark's room. "Hey, how's it going?"

Mom and Mark smile back.

"Kristen!" bellows Mark, showing off his newfound skill.

We embrace and then I bounce over to give Mom a big squeeze. She jerks back, but I keep squeezing as her purply fresh lavender scent envelops me.

"You're early," says Mom, adjusting her crumpled beige cardigan.

"Got the rest of the day off. I landed a new client, Mom. A big one."

Tommy will be jealous for sure.

Mom's eyes narrow, but she hasn't stopped smiling. "That's great, Kristen honey."

I rattle on about my meeting with Eddi, recklessly ignoring the privacy agreement I signed earlier. I provide every amusing detail. I mean, how would Eddi ever find out, anyway? And isn't it worth the risk just to hear Mom and Mark laughing so loud?

Soon, we're reminiscing about some of our best moments together, like the time Mark fell into a stranger's lap when he tried to get a decent shot of me accepting my college diploma. None of the bad memories come up, just the good ones, and Mark keeps up with the conversation brilliantly. When was the last time he suffered from confusion? It's like he's almost back to normal. He talks about wanting to go home, and makes us write down all the things he's going to do when he returns. How can it be possible that he's come this far?

Tears roll down Mom's cheeks as she laughs. And I'm floating, like an untethered helium balloon. Wait — don't balloons pop when they float too high? In a minute, I'll dial it back. Right now, I'm stuck inside that laughter. It's like I'm seeing Mom for the first time. She's constantly exhausted, but mentally strong. Not the powerless alcoholic I grew up with. Has she really changed, or has my perspective?

She catches me staring, and she gazes back. A grandfather clock chimes in the distance. That's what I love about this place. It smells like disinfectant, but hardwood furniture strategically placed in the lobby and halls give it a homey vibe.

At the end of the chiming, the mood of the room tenses. Without speaking, Mom and I agree. We can no longer avoid the inevitable. I grab and squeeze her hand, and she squeezes back. "Let's do this," she says.

I nod and turn to Mark. I watch from a distance, as if I'm beyond myself. My future sits before me. A father to know and to hold, waiting.

Mom drops my hand and takes Mark's. "We need to talk."

Finally, I'm on the sending end of this statement. Ten million butterflies flap in the pit of my stomach. Mark's chin quivers while a large bead of sweat meanders down the side of his face. I jump in. "Mark—"

"No," interrupts Mom. "Let me start."

"You can both wait," demands Mark. "I'm going first."

Mom and I eye each other, a silent question passing between us.

"Kristen," Mark says, his chin firm and high. "I . . . I'm your . . . father."

"I know!" I throw myself onto his chest. "And I love you. I love you, I love you, I love you."

Mom places one trembling hand on my back and another on Mark's shoulder.

Mark loses it. "Oh, God forgive me," he cries. "Please forgive what I've done. I never should have—"

"May God forgive us all," interrupts Mom.

"It's going to be okay," I say, sniffling. "You can't go back in time, none of us can." I'm starting to sound like Georgina. "Sure, it was a mistake. Brother and sister should never . . . not that you were actual . . ."

I can't finish, but I don't need to say it. Everyone in the room knows what happened. "It's not all bad," I say, trying to move beyond the awkwardness. "I mean, come on. Look at me."

Mom and Mark laugh through their tears. We're a frightful lot, but somewhere deep inside the mess, hope flickers. Somehow, our lives make sense, even if only for this fleeting moment. We try, unsuccessfully, to wipe our faces dry.

Mom sinks into a chair and sighs.

"You should go home and rest, Mom. You look beat."

"I will," she says. "But first, we need to talk."

CHAPTER 18

OCTOBER/NOVEMBER

⌒◯◯⌒

THE ENTIRE RIDE home from my visit with Mark, it feels as though I'm fighting a gale force wind. Every inch of the five-mile drive is excruciating. Where did all these cars come from, anyway?

Nothing's going to be the same. I should never have stayed after Mom said we needed to talk. I should've run away when I had the chance.

I drop my purse and keys on the floor and shuffle into my room, where I collapse on the bed, sand-caked outfit and all. So that's why Mom's been exhausted. If only I didn't know, but it's too late for that. It's too late for a lot of things.

The phone rings.

"Hi, Ethan."

"Hey there. I hate to do this . . . but I'm not going to be able to make it to the Halloween party."

"Okay."

"What's wrong? You sound down."

"It's my mother."

"What happened?"

"She has breast cancer — stage four. Six months to two years with surgery and treatment. That's how it was presented to me an hour ago."

"Oh, I'm sorry."

"So am I. This is what happens when I let my guard down. I mean, so what if I just landed a major client, right?"

"You did? Today?"

"Yeah, and it was awesome, but I wish I hadn't let myself get so excited. For a few hours, I actually believed things were going to change for me. I believed it was okay to be happy. And I just stood there like a numbskull, sharing my recent success with Mom and Mark, while this giant target sat on my forehead. And now—"

"Kristen, I'm so sorry to hear about your mother. How long has she known?"

"Two weeks."

"I'll pray for a miracle. I don't know what else to say."

"Thanks. A miracle would be nice."

"I'll pray for two. I'm going to need one of my own."

"Why? What's up?"

"The reason I called . . . it's my father." Ethan sighs. "He's had a stroke."

"Oh, Ethan. I can't believe all of this is happening at once. How is he?"

"Not good. I'm flying to Colorado tonight, which is why I can't make the party."

"No worries. You need to go. I'd offer to pray for your dad, but it wouldn't mean anything."

"It would mean something to me."

I squeeze my lids shut tight. "That's not my thing. How about I send positive vibes your way instead?"

"I'll take it."

In the late afternoon of October 31, hypothetical futures race through my mind, different scenarios, all with the same outcome. A funeral, the loss, the void, my regret . . . stop it! She's not gone yet. Anything could happen. My fists clench. I'm unfit for public consumption, unprepared for the masquerade that lies ahead. But nobody misses a party hosted by my boss. *Nobody.* So I may as well make the best of it.

I take a final look in the mirror. Towering wig cascading down the sides of my powdered face. Check. Enormous dress dripping in layers. Check. It's Marie Antoinette in the flesh. What a perfect costume — expensively authentic and equally obnoxious. Leave it to Alana to find such a treasure.

Legion's dressed as the Mad Hatter. At first, I didn't get it — the checkerboard pants and sleeveless tuxedo jacket, revealing decades of tattoo addiction. But then I realized he meant the Batman super-villain version of Mad Hatter, not the one from *Alice in Wonderland*. Delila wears white from head to toe, a curve-accentuating silk dress, sheer lace covering her arms and face, and a wired boa crowning her head. Lady Gaga, space-age vintage-glam edition.

"You sure you want to be mixed back into that crowd?"

Delila laughs as we head out the door. "Memories are short in our circles."

There she goes again with the "our circles" thing. Whatever. At least I have a ride.

With some assistance from Gaga and Hatter, I stuff my towering wig into Delila's purple Volkswagen Bug, and off we go.

Once at the party, my chin held high, I trip over the raised threshold, but I remain calm and carry on, entering as if I'm walking the red carpet, except there's no one snapping pictures and not one soul acknowledges I've arrived.

Oh hey, a muscular young man in a shirtless French waiter suit walks past carrying a tray of hors d'oeuvres. I trail right and race after the spicy crab puffs, leaving Gaga and Hatter in the dust of my cascading rippled skirt.

Between bites, I chase after a well-endowed young French maid, who carries little blue cups filled to the brim with Malibu Bay Breeze. Coconut rum mixed with pineapple and cranberry juice. I'll take four, thank you.

Giant glass doors open to a backyard that would incite envy even among the rich. Yep, a Tommy Foxx design. A personal oasis, with rolling landscape, an outdoor kitchen, lighted waterfalls cascading into the pool, modern sculptures—oh, and there he is. Tommy, dressed as Batman. What a dork, even if he does look good in tights.

Barbra's standing next to him, dressed as Catwoman, her spandex unisuit split generously at the top, as if we need a reminder of the fullness of her purchased breasts.

Ah, and there's Mr. L.A. standing at the far end of the yard, dressed as Count Dracula and sipping something red, engaging a group of important-looking men with what I can only assume is mindless chatter.

I down two more Bay Breezes and stroll on, passing the dynamic duo with great air, the girth of my skirt coming within inches of sweeping Catwoman into the shallow end of the pool.

Mr. L.A. greet-slaps me on the back, then turns to his audience. "Meet Kristen Craemer. Remember her name. She's our newest rising star."

I smile and shake hands and they tell me their names, but their words go right through me as I peek over their shoulders to spy on Tommy. Is that a dark cloud forming above his head?

"Kristen landed a big project," continues Mr. L.A. "We can't wait to see what she brings to this one."

Ralph goes on and on, but what he fails to mention is his propensity for micromanaging. The man can't keep his hands out of the finest detail. He's made every important decision to date. But fine, I'll play along. Sure, why not? I'll smile and nod and keep my expression dignified as I drink in the sweet nectar of praise, taking full credit where none is due.

After ten minutes — not that I'm counting every second — I figure I've put in my time. I excuse myself to the ladies' room, but head straight for the closest roving tray of hors d'oeuvres. I swoosh into the front room, where I find Gaga and Hatter making out on the sofa. Delila was right. No one notices or cares that she came.

Gasps erupt from the entryway. In walks an angel-in-black, tall, with wings towering above her head. Her medieval velvet dress is snug to mid-thigh, where sheer black lace sprays to the floor. Alana. She floats across the room, clearing a path as feathers shed in her wake. She reaches me and leans in, whispering through flaming-red lips. "What are *those* two doing here?"

"Gaga and Hatter? They wanted to come. I needed a ride. What's the big deal?"

"How about the fact that she's trying to kill you?"

"Dramatic much?"

"What did Robby say about your car?"

"He said the spark plug wires were switched around, and that led to *catastrophic* failure."

"Uh-huh. And you don't think that's a big deal?"

"Of course I do. The entire bottom end needs to be rebuilt, the block, crankshaft, cam . . . I can't remember all the damaged parts. It's going to cost me a fortune."

"You're missing the point. The wires didn't switch themselves. Some-body tampered with your car."

"You think I'm an idiot? Of course I know somebody switched the wires."

"Delila did it."

"No way."

"Who, then?

"Someone from work, jealous that I landed a big project? Punk teenagers wandering the streets late at night? There have been cars broken into in the neighborhood recently. Oh, and what about those twin teens who live around the corner? They just got back from juvie. Who knows?"

"Have you called the police?"

"What good will that do? I'll just have to fill out a bunch of paperwork. Besides, I'm sure it was nothing more than someone else's idea of a harmless prank. No one's trying to hurt me. I'm not that important."

"You are so thick, Kristen. But I have better things to do than argue with a brick wall. Where can I get something to drink?"

"There's a full bar out back. Let's go."

We storm toward the bar, black feathers flying off Alana's wings.

"I see Dumb and Dumber are here," she says as we pass Tommy and Barbra. We reach our destination, and I introduce my angel to Jared.

"The mojitos are pretty good," he suggests.

"Nah. I want a shot of that." She points a devilish finger at a large bottle of Jack Daniels. "Two please. One for me, and one for Marie Antoinette."

"Pass. Don't you remember the last time I touched that stuff? Your wings are fantastic, by the way. Real feathers, right?"

I caress the grainy fluff as I try to ignore the glow of the bottle of my old friend JD. Nothing good ever happens when I drink whiskey. Sure, it always starts well—the searing rush of fire running down my throat, comforting me like a warm blanket. But then I always wake up in a pool of regret and vomit.

Alana drains her shot and slams down the glass, winking at Jared in plea for another. "Yes, real feathers, hand set. These wings are a high-end, one-of-a-kind prop, made for a demons versus angels film that never made it to the big screen. Andrue hates them. He says they're a waste of time and money." Her neck vein throbs.

"Trouble in paradise?"

She shrugs. "We're struggling to get back to the way things were before he had his meltdown."

"That's what we're calling it now? A meltdown?"

She ignores my question. "Can you believe this is already our second Halloween without Jenna and Danielle? I bet they'd have come up with fantastic costumes."

"Yeah." I glance around the party and my upper lip curls. "But they're not missing much."

Alana makes a goofy grin and then launches into the wedding plans — the painstaking details and the sheer expense. She carries on for more than twenty minutes, while my untouched shot of whiskey sits on the bar, glaring at me. Then Andrue calls and Alana's eyes grow cold. She takes the call and walks away, leaving me alone with Jared and that blasted shot of whiskey.

Jenna and Danielle might not be missing much, but I am. When we were four strong, I was never left alone. There was always someone to remain at my side and protect me from myself.

My phone beeps. A text message from Ethan. *I'm taking the job here in Colorado. We'll talk soon. E.*

Really? Wow. I guess the decision wasn't a difficult one after all.

The sky darkens, igniting the lighted waterfalls that spill like liquid jewels in deep shades of red, purple, and gold.

"Miss," interrupts Jared. "Your drink?"

My eyes lock on the whiskey as it screams at me, demanding my attention.

"You should stay away from that." It's Tommy, with Barbra at his side.

I lift my chin, wink at Tommy, then down the liquid amber.

The sweet, strong shot bursts into flames, warms my throat, and conjures memories of all those nights gone wrong. But this is different. This time, I'm not running away from anything. I just need to take the edge off — from work, Mom, Mark, Batman and breast-woman . . . all of it. I'm smart enough to know when to stop. I slam down the glass and nod at Jared for another. And after I drain the second shot, I swish away.

A couple more Bay Breezes and several shots of JD later, I'm shoving an untold number of mini chèvre and bacon paninis into my mouth. I talk about anything to anyone who's standing nearby. I can't remember the last time I laughed this much. More drinks, more food, and every speck of pain fades.

Sometime later, the room sways, smooth and floaty, as if under water. Suddenly, everyone ignores me. Can anybody see me? Am I really here? I remove my shoes and climb atop a mirrored cocktail table. I yell at the crowd, stabbing the air with a spiked heel, trying to get anyone's attention.

The room sways more violently. Lady Gaga, the Mad Hatter, and an angry dark angel try to lure me off the table.

"Time to go home," says the angel, "before you do something we'll all regret."

"No one cares," I whine. "Of course not. Why should they? They're all too busy caring about themselves. You're all selfish and phony!"

My diatribe carries on, words flying out of my mouth unfiltered.

Sometime later, everything goes black.

I wake the next morning sprawled across the couch, my ankle bruised and swollen. How did I get here? And who replaced my costume with fuzzy pajamas? Apparently, there *is* an amount of alcohol that will render my brain incapable of recalling dreams, and that is exactly the amount I consumed last night.

My stomach lurches and I run to the bathroom. All those snacks were far more tantalizing sitting on sparkling platters than they are floating in the toilet.

I crawl back to the couch. My head throbs, pounding out clips from the previous night, a merciless stream of memory reel — of me as Marie Antoinette, tripping over furniture and into people, ranting as I dribble caviar down the delicate bodice of my dress.

Everyone who was anyone was at that party. Co-workers, peers, possible future clients. Eddi too, watching as I blathered on, telling the world how alone I was. *Poor me, poor me, poor me,* I kept ranting, carrying on about how everyone who meant anything to me was either gone or heading out. How long did the spectacle last? Everyone tried to ignore me while I kept throwing out insults.

The memories trail past, some clearer than others, like the one of Tommy standing in a corner and smirking. If he had any doubts about breaking up with me before, they're gone now.

What have I done? Have I lost my job? This must be the same terror that went through Marie Antoinette's mind as the guillotine blade raced toward her perfect, young neck.

Delila walks in and sets down a glass of tomato juice and a plate of dry toast. She curls into a neighboring chair while I grab the offerings.

"Aack! What's in this?"

"Jalapeño vodka with tomato juice. Good for hangovers."

"I'll stick to the toast."

Delila squints. "How long has your mother known?"

I rub my face and scrape my hair into a knot, using a dull pencil to secure the wad. "Little over two weeks."

"She had no idea before that?"

"Yeah, she did." I wipe my lips. "She noticed a lump back in January."

Delila's exotic brows rise.

"When the breast scan came back negative, my mother, the Queen of Denial, wrote it off." I gaze at my hands. If only they could latch on to Harley's thick fur coat. "The lump never went away, but Mom never pursued it. Then Mark's accident happened and Mom put all her energy there."

"That stinks. I wish I could tell you I knew for sure your mom will come out of this okay." Delila grabs her diamond star pendant and rubs it as she gazes into space. "I miss my mom so much. It's awful."

Wait . . . what was that feeling? Warmth? A hint of connection squeezing my heart?

I rake back my hair and sigh. "Mom kept telling herself the lump was shrinking. Then when the exhaustion came, she blamed the flu. Steve begged her to get checked out again, and after wading through a mile of doctors and paperwork . . ."

"How bad is it?"

"Doctors say six months to two years, but Mom doesn't buy it. She keeps telling us to stop throwing dirt on her grave because she's still breathing."

"She's got her boxing gloves on."

"She's survived much worse than this."

"Cancer sucks." Delila rises from her chair, takes a few steps, and then stops to turn back. "That's what took my mom. Four years old, and I was stuck with my dad and a stepmother. Hated them both."

She twirls a strand of hair. "It's strange, though. As much as Dad hurt me, I kept trying to get his attention, but he never saw me. He traveled a lot, but when he *was* around, he never paid attention to me. Even while he was hitting me, he looked straight through me. To him, I've been invisible since the day my mother died."

She flips her purple-black hair and starts a pot of Ethiopian brew. "You're lucky to have a father like Mark."

Seriously? Is there not one normal family tree in the world?

Hours later, Alana stops by and wakes me up. "*Chérie,* you're a hot mess."

"It's my I-just-destroyed-my-career-in-one-night look. You like?"

"It's those psychotic dreams. That's what's messing you up. Here, take this."

I scrunch my nose. "A Dior gift bag? How will this help?"

She raises her brows. "Open it."

Inside, there's a sample sized Dior De-Puffer and a bottle of 30mg Temazepam tablets, prescribed to "Alana Pheasant."

"O-kay. Thanks?"

In the evening, Ethan calls. Thank God he's in Colorado, far away from all the Halloween party-from-hell gossip.

"Got a minute?" he asks.

"Sure."

Whatever.

"I want to apologize."

My heart pounding, I head to my bedroom, away from the noise of Legion, Delila, and the blasting television.

"I shouldn't have texted that last message. I should've called you."

"It's fine."

At least, it is now that he recognizes how awful that was.

"Moving back to Colorado was a difficult decision to make, but it's the right one."

Ouch.

"I'm happy things are working out for you," I snap back.

"Hold on, I didn't say that right. What I mean is this was a huge deal. It was so significant that I wanted to tell the person who was most important to me. I was at the hospital with my dad and couldn't have a phone conversation then, so I sent the text."

If this lunatic doesn't stop sending mixed signals, I'm going to explode.

"You have no idea how much I've prayed about this," Ethan continues. "With Dad so sick, the Colorado job offer was the only reasonable choice.

A lot has happened — things I can't describe without sounding crazy — but I'm sure I'm supposed to be here. Does this make sense?"

I shake my head no.

"I hate that we'll be apart," he says. "But you can call me anytime, and if you ever need me — for any reason — just ask me to come, and if there's any way I can, I will. I promise."

Why does my chest hurt like this? We're *just* friends.

"There's a reason for all of this," he continues. "I don't know what it is yet, but there's a future for us. For some reason we need to be apart right now. You have no idea how much I care about you, but this break will be good for us."

Wait — what? He's talking in circles.

"Ethan, I don't understand what you're saying."

"You're right. I'm not making sense, but I have to go. My father needs me. I'll call you soon."

Ten minutes later, I'm still clutching the phone. I'm exhausted from being awake, but I don't have the energy to run all night. Hang on … the Dior bag. Where did I put it? Maybe Alana's on to something. I find the bottle, pop one of the sleeping pills, and beg the entire universe to please, please, *please* let me get a peaceful night's rest.

CHAPTER 19

DECEMBER

∽∾○

TEMAZEPAM ROCKS. I'VE been sleeping like a baby since the first night I took this stuff. Five beautiful, dream-free weeks. Maybe I'm still having the dreams, maybe I'm not, but I can't remember having even one. I've almost forgotten what it's like to have to run for my life every night.

Each morning, I wake up strong. Sure, I'm sluggish at first, a little hung over perhaps, but it's nothing compared to waking up after trying to drown my dreams in alcohol. A few fantastic weeks of sleep and I'm a new woman, able to take on anything. Good thing too, since life is squeezing me like a vice.

Eddi's fickle, can't make up her mind, and I've got Mr. L.A. tying my hands with his incessant meddling, but I continue to make progress. I even survived Tommy's wedding, not that I was there, but I had to suffer all the chatter that continued for days after.

And now this with Mom. I can't believe her surgery failed. They opened her up and just stood there, dumbfounded. Were her insides really too messed up for the surgeon to do any good?

When Mom was admitted to the cancer center's back wing for palliative care, I asked a nurse if that was good or bad. "The goal of palliative care is not to cure," she said. "The goal is to comfort, providing supportive care and symptom management."

So the plan is to keep her comfortable until she dies?

Mom insists it's not as bad as it seems. She's cheerfully convinced all her friends that she'll be coming home soon, but I'm not satisfied. Late evenings, partial weekends, and shared visits aren't enough. I need a full day with my mother.

Besides, it's pouring rain out there. I'd have to be insane to drive to Malibu today. Chaos reigns over Eddi's project, but so what? My co-workers are professionals, perfectly capable of navigating mayhem for a bit. Mr. L.A. makes all the decisions anyway, so how hard can it be? Calling in sick for *one* day is not going to be the end of the world.

I pull a stack of gossip magazines out of my bag and hand them to Mom's roommate, who accepts them with trembling hands. Ruth is too young to be so frail and hard of hearing. But I guess that's what can happen from aggressive cancer treatments.

Mom sits straight up in bed and bursts with conversation. "I like it here. I've said that before, but it's true. The staff is amazing — one of the nurses likes to sing while he works and he has the most beautiful voice. I have lots of visitors every day. Everybody comes. Except Dorothy. I'm praying for her. Oh, and the food isn't all that bad."

"I'm glad, Mom. You look good. Really, really good."

"Come again?" interrupts Ruth.

I raise my voice. "I was telling my mom how good she looks."

"Oh," says Ruth. "You weren't talking to me?"

Sweet, sweet Ruth — the mother of all distractions. She's the most fragile little thing. Eighty-five pounds soaking wet. Merciless, though, often stealing Mom's guests because she never gets any of her own. She interrupts every time Mom or I speak, until I give in and drag my visitor's chair back far enough to include her in the conversation.

Over time, Ruth relaxes to the rise and fall of our voices. Inclusion in the conversation is enough, and soon she falls asleep.

Mom and I laugh, cry, eat, and then do it all over again. Other visitors weave in and out of the day, and in the early evening, just when Mom looks like she's about to nod off, she bolts upright. "I'm going to die from this cancer."

Slam!

Why does that hurt so much? It's like I believed I could get through an entire day without facing this monster.

"The only mystery . . . is when," she continues. "The doctors say weeks. Pfsht! I never listen to doctors."

I wipe my face. I'm *not* going to cry.

Mom catches her breath. She tugs my hand and draws me closer. "Right now, I feel great, and I can't imagine anything happening anytime soon. But eventually, it will happen. My heart aches when I think about leaving you and Steve, but one thing is certain — are you listening?" She draws two deep breaths. "When I leave this place, I *will* go to heaven and it *will* be dazzling."

Dazzling?

Her smile reaches her peridot eyes. Squinty, like mine, and sleepy. "All this craziness on earth pales in comparison to what awaits. Do you understand, Kristen honey?"

I smile and nod as if I do, but I don't. She's drifting off. Medication must be kicking in.

I return home on stiff legs and drag myself past Delila. She's too busy on her laptop to notice me.

Alana calls, and I take it in my room.

"Did you get your car back yet?"

"Yep, yesterday."

"Great. How about we ditch work tomorrow and you pick me up for a joy ride?"

"Already missed today. Can't take two days off in a row."

"You're kidding, right? After how hard you've worked? Kristen, it's New Year's Eve tomorrow. We *have* to get together."

"What about an evening thing?"

"Can't. Heading out for that conference back east, remember?"

"Right. But this project is insane. Everybody's on edge and I don't want to set anybody off.

"You're about to set me off right now. What about a long lunch — can you at least do that?"

"Fine. I'll pick you up at one."

"Great, and how about we do a digital fast, leave our cells behind, so we can have quality time? Everybody's doing it these days."

"Really? With my mom's life hanging in the balance?"

"Give the hospital the restaurant phone number before you leave the office. If something happens, they'll reach you."

"Fine."

"How is your mom, by the way?"

"She's great. Except for, you know, the *cancer*."

"I'm sorry."

"Yeah. Me, too."

The next morning, I wake sweaty and out of breath. I don't remember dreaming, but my limbs act as if I did. Please don't tell me my body's acclimating to the sleeping pills so much that they'll eventually stop working and I'll have to face my nightmares again. Tell me anything but that.

At lunch, the headache from my morning Temazepam hangover persists. But Alana and I are celebrating, so I order the works — a spicy Cuban sandwich with porchetta, gruyere, mustard, and pickles. And a *double* order of fries.

"I'll have the same," says Alana. "Except no fries. That stuff'll kill you. And bring us each a glass of your best Cabernet from the *brooding and intense* section of your wine list."

I order banana cream pie for dessert and request that it arrive first.

Alana shakes her head at me as the waiter dashes off.

"What? An earthquake could strike at any minute. It would suck if I missed dessert. We're celebrating, right?"

"This is why your blood sugar is so messed up. You eat like an un-supervised child."

"Whatever. How's it going with you and Andrue?"

"Great." She averts her gaze, and then brings it back. "How are those sleeping pills working?"

"Perfectly. Until this morning . . ."

The waiter returns with our wine. That was fast.

"Happy New Year's Eve," cheers Alana, clinking my glass and then gulping away.

"Ditto," I reply. "Mmmm, good stuff."

"At twenty-five dollars a glass, it should be. By the way, I still believe Delila messed with your car."

"Why don't you hire your paranoid P.I. to investigate, then?"

"Maybe I already have."

Her cell phone vibrates from inside a designer clutch.

"What happened to digital fasting?"

"About that," she says, pulling out her phone. "Took me five minutes to figure out I don't have time for that nonsense. I've got a wedding coming up, remember? And hey, look who it is now." She holds up her long index finger, pressing an imaginary pause button on me.

I wave approval, but she's already knee deep in conversation. "I booked my reservation eleven months ago. If there's a mix-up with the reception hall, it's on your end. I have the signed contract, so what's the problem?"

Alana drains her glass and lifts it to the passing waiter so he'll know she's empty.

"No, Mr. Phipps," she continues. "I won't accept a different time slot. And listen — I'm well connected, so trust me when I say failure is not an option. You cannot afford to mishandle this."

Click.

She grabs at my fries and then peeks at me over her glass of dark red wine. "I don't want to talk about it."

Fine with me.

Her phone rings again.

"It's Andrue." She declines the call.

"Doing *great*, huh?"

"We do better when we talk less."

"You're getting *married* in a few weeks."

"I know, right?"

She crams more fries into her mouth, washes them down with wine, and orders a third glass. By the time we pay our bill, it's four o'clock, and I've asked our waiter ten times if anyone has tried to call me from the hospital. Ten times, he answered no. Alana has eaten most of the fries and finished four glasses of wine to the one I nursed all through lunch. Being the designated driver stinks. My head throbs the entire trip back.

The second I reach my office, I grab my phone. A million missed messages, most of them from Mr. L.A. His voice is hoarse and low, a clear indication that the liquid inside his veins is as molten as the earth's core. He left thirteen messages, all of them colorful. Beneath the thick layers of slowly-spoken obscenities, the same message repeats: "Where the *bleep* are you? And why aren't you answering your *bleeping* phone!"

I dash into the lobby, where the gum-smacking receptionist paints her nails.

"What happened, Kellen?"

She looks down at me, despite the fact that I tower over her.

Smack! "Why don't you ask Mr. L.A.? He's waiting for you in his office."

Smack!

The twenty yards of hall leading to Mr. L.A.'s office stretch to the length of a football field. My stomach churns. I wasn't even hungry. Why did I eat so much? By the time I reach the penthouse office, my boss's face burns red, his hands gripping the armrests of his high-back chair.

I cross the Oriental rug and stop a few feet short of his black lacquered desk. He motions toward the small, frail visitor's chair. I remain standing, my fists on my hips. No thanks. The last thing I need right now is to put myself into a submissive position.

He shakes his head and presses his lips tight.

"What? Did something happen?"

"You shouldn't have to ask that question. You should already know."

"I took a long lunch. I'm back now. Can you please fill me in?"

"Eddi needed you and you weren't available."

"That's it?"

"That would be enough, Miss Craemer, but Eddi is also unhappy with the custom furniture designer you selected."

I rub my temples. "Wait — that was *your* decision."

"You are the lead. You are the one responsible for this project."

"*You* overrode my decision. I wanted to go with the guy from Santa Barbara."

"And that's another thing, your lack of leadership on this project."

"You're joking, right?" I fan my shirt. "Is it hot in here?"

"You're becoming a liability to the firm."

"Excuse me? A few weeks ago I was your rising star."

"The Halloween party incident, taking days off, not answering your phone, your inability to take charge of this project . . ." He squints. "Eddi says most of the time you're half asleep."

"But that's only in the mornings . . . please don't take this project from me."

"I'm sorry, we're letting you go."

"Wait — I'm *fired?*"

The room spins and my legs wobble. I take the small, stupid chair and lift my eyes up to him.

He rests back and the heat drains from him, leaving his face pale and eerie. Suddenly, I'm six years old again, watching Victor's expression fade from violent to calm after he'd knocked my mother out cold. I'm little and

Mr. L.A. is big, insisting this is all my fault. That if I had behaved, none of this would've happened.

"Eddi won't stay on with us otherwise," grunts Mr. L.A. "It's better this way. You've been an intern long enough. Think of this as a boost to help you fly from the nest. Nothing personal."

"Oh, um . . . okay."

"Frankly, Kristen," he says with that sandpaper tone of his, "I'm surprised you're not fighting harder to keep your job. Good luck. You know the way out."

Brain fog fills the next twenty-four hours.

Why *didn't* I fight harder to keep my job? Why did I freeze up like that? I could've done better, not only in my last conversation with Mr. L.A., but during the job, running Eddi's project. I could've poured more into it. Or was that my best?

At least my headache is gone. Doubling the sleeping pill dose did the trick. Brain's a little sluggish, but no headache of any kind, and more importantly, no memories of any dreams.

After visiting my mother, I return home and shuffle past Delila, who's working from the dining table.

"It's not your fault," she says, banging away on her keyboard. "I'd bet a million bucks the group of seven set you up, like they did to me." She stops typing and meets my eyes. "If you're looking for work, I've got tons. My client list keeps growing, and at this rate I'll need to start hiring soon."

Graphics design would be fun. Set my own hours, work from home, and create stuff all day. But I will *never* work for Delila. Not as long as McDonald's is still hiring.

"No thanks. I can dip into my savings until I find something else."

I fix myself dinner. Veggie chips and jalapeño hummus. "Where's Legion? He hasn't been around."

"He's in Vegas."

"Oh?"

"Yeah. He's got a short-term construction job opportunity out there." She keeps clicking away. "How about you? What will you do for work?"

"Thinking of starting my own interior design business, pick up one client at a time, and go from there."

"Like me," she says, and I cringe. She stops typing to look at me. "Hey, have you opened Ethan's Christmas present yet?"

No.

The note on the outer box read *Do Not Open until December 24. Merry Christmas. Love, Ethan.* That date's passed. And what's up with the *Love, Ethan?*

Since our "break," we haven't talked much. Sure, we've texted and chatted a bit, all surface level stuff.

How are you doing?

Fine and you?

Blah, blah, blah.

Then he sends a Christmas gift with a note signed, *Love, Ethan.*

"What're you waiting for?" asks Delila. "Open it."

Why not? I've got nothing else to do.

Inside the box, a wrapped gift rests in a bed of packing peanuts. I grab the gift and sink into my overstuffed couch, then caress the pink silk ribbon.

"For goodness sake, rip that paper off!" pipes Delila.

I slip off the ribbon and set it on the coffee table, remove the taped edges, and unpeel the chocolate paper as if disarming a bomb. The wrapping slips to the floor as I hold the gift. A book, bound in pink and brown leather, with my name inscribed in silver on the front bottom edge.

"A Bible."

Delila stops clicking and lifts her head out of her laptop.

"Good Lord," she whispers, and then she dives back into work.

It presses into my hands, heavy, like a small animal. The first Bible I've ever held. I cradle it as if it were Harley in his old man years, carry it across the room, shuffle down the hall, and place it on the tall dresser across from my bed. I stroke the leather. Soft, cool, comforting. I finger the silver engraving, *Kristen Addison Craemer.* Glittery.

I fan the thin pages, unfamiliar words rippling past. My stomach clenches. I raise my hands and back away. Back, back, back, until I'm on the bed, sitting against the headboard.

I click on the television and settle on New Year's Rockin' Eve. Love the giant, bedazzled ball. *Dazzling.* Why had Mom chosen that word to describe heaven?

A quick internet search from my phone tells me the Times Square New Year's Eve Ball spans twelve feet and weighs nearly twelve thousand pounds. Covered with 2,688 sparkling Waterford crystals. Lit with 32,256 LED lights. What a spectacle. Before I die, I must be a part of the team that creates this monstrous jewel.

What a year it's been. My uncle falling into a coma, turning out to be my father, and then miraculously waking. My dreams hunting me down. Opening up to my mother, then finding out she's dying. Wrestling with my best friend's fiancé, and becoming roommates with my adversary. Losing Harley, and still missing Jenna and Danielle like crazy. Climbing the ladder of success, only to slip off the top rung and hit the bottom hard. Meeting Ethan . . . and not knowing what box to put him in.

I still can't get Tommy out of my head, and the urge to walk into the ocean keeps growing stronger.

The Bible stands out on the dresser top, pulsating, as if alive. Why did Ethan send it to me? It's beautiful, but I will never, ever open it.

Never.

The countdown flashes. It's one minute to midnight. Here we go. What will the New Year bring?

Ten . . . nine . . . eight . . . seven . . . six . . .

Chapter 20

February 14

I**T'S ALANA'S BIG** day, and it'll be a miracle if I can stay awake through the entire ceremony. Two Temazepam aren't enough to keep the dreams away anymore, and I'd rather die than wake up the Pheasant sisters with the moaning and tossing that comes with my dreams. But why did I take three pills? What was I thinking? I'll never be able to keep my eyes open.

I shouldn't have agreed to spend the night at Papa Pheasant's house. So what if I'm in the wedding party? But it's too late now. I'm the walking dead, having only a vague recollection of this morning's activity. Something about Alana cramming bagels and coffee down my throat and rushing all of us to the salon. They tell me I've been scrubbed, masked, massaged, and mani-pedi'd. I'm sure it's all been fabulous, if only I was lucid enough to notice.

I swivel in my chair and wait for my updo, while fluttering Pheasant laughter rattles through the studio. Why shouldn't they be happy? They've all got dates for this Valentine's Day wedding. Except Milana, but she'll have one by the end of the night, no doubt.

How can I stand it? Seven of them surrounding me with their big, beautiful, magnificence. Compared to them, I'm a child. It's no surprise my position at the altar is last in the line of bridesmaids. Aesthetics are everything to Alana, and I'd look ridiculous standing between Alana and her sisters. So I'll stand last, as an end cap, paired with Andrue's short, hulking, older brother Matthew, who will round off the other end.

"I love Pheasant hair," squeals Tiffany as she caresses Alana's silken wonder. "It's so rich and smooth. Gorgeous, natural highlights. It's always a pleasure to work on you and your sisters."

Angelo adjusts my chair to face the mirror. We tilt our heads as he tries to rake his fingers through my unruly mane. One of his many rings catch.

"Rough night," I joke. "Be kind. You can leave the dog brush in the drawer — 'kay?"

He laughs, his thin mustache expanding. "Chin up, doll, your eyes make up for your hair."

A bold-faced lie, but not a bad save.

"You girls need to be sure that Andrue and I don't see each other before the wedding," says Alana. "Don't want to jinx it."

Jinx what? Their dysfunctional relationship?

"Is it hot in here?" I mop the sweat off my forehead and pant. "Are we going to eat soon? I'm shaking."

Alana's perfectly penciled brows cross. "Her blood sugar's crashing. Angelo, get something!"

Angelo jogs to the back room and returns with a little carton of milk and three homemade granola bars. "You diabetic?"

"Hypoglycemic." I snatch the food.

Alana rolls her eyes. "She'd be fine if she ate like a real human being."

I cross my brows at her as I gulp and munch. I can't get the granola into my mouth fast enough.

"I bake them myself," boasts Angelo. "Aren't they swell?"

Head nodding, crumbs dropping. "Mm-hmmm."

Fifteen minutes pass. Ahhh, the food's hitting my bloodstream. My pulse is slowing, my muscles relaxing. Angelo's still trying to smooth out my dull brown hair. How long until he has it fixed into a suitable style for my choppy cut? Enough already. Let's get to the brow shaping and makeup.

Hours slur past. The shaking disappears, but my brain remains in a fog. Did I fall asleep during the car ride over? I vaguely recall Pheasant sisters dressing me, dousing me with designer perfume, and placing me in my queue — why is everyone looking this way?

Oh! It's my turn. Here I go, step-tap-stepping up the aisle at The Neighborhood Church. If only I could escape long enough to explore this quaint architectural gem. I'd love to wander the grounds and creep along the jagged edge of the cliff on which this place rests.

My hand keeps slipping. Don't know how I'm supposed to keep hold of Matthew's enormous forearm. Dude's way pumped. He could curl me if he wanted, but he'd better not dare.

We reach Andrue and he's positively beaming. Such a stunning groom, except for that scar on his cheekbone. My pulse accelerates — the stairwell, his penknife flickering in the dim light . . . stop it! That's in the past. Time to move on.

Andrue smiles and dabs the sweat off his neck, razor stubble swelling in a line along the side of his jaw.

Matthew and I separate and shuffle to opposite ends of the long line of gorgeous men and women. I settle into my position. Please, whatever God is presiding over this wedding, let Andrue be well-medicated.

Heady fragrance rises from my bouquet, drawing my eyes to the dark red roses in my grasp. These were Danielle's favorite. The white calla lilies were Jenna's. What a great way to honor our dear friends without depressing the wedding guests. After all, this is a celebration, not a memorial.

Beneath my dress hides a garter with a silk heart and the letters LHC sewn on. Alana has one, too. Does anyone else realize that half of the members from the Lonely Hearts Club are missing? That Alana's bridesmaid line is too short . . . and that even now, hearts are aching?

Good grief, how long are we to wait? An eternity has already passed. Guests begin to whisper, spreading a wave of gossip across every bench in every row. Alana's poor little niece has thrown up all over her expensive flower girl dress and will not make her debut. Kira sighs. At five foot ten, Kira is the shortest of the sisters, which places her one step above me in the lineup. After this unfortunate incident with her daughter, her ranking might slip.

I pat her shoulder. "No worries. It could be worse."

Violinists ready their bows. The crowd rustles. An instrumental rendition of *Bittersweet Symphony* wafts through the sanctuary, quietly at first, then picking up steam, like a train that's lost its brakes. I whisper the lyrics not sung, until at last, here comes the bride.

She's positively radiant, her expensive smile gleaming. Papa walks tall and proud at her side. He couldn't possibly smile any wider. But wait — Alana's dress drags more than it should. And if I'm not mistaken, her neck vein is throbbing.

Whoa, where did that dizziness come from? Pull yourself together, Kristen. If you drop at Alana's wedding, you'll never hear the end of it.

Papa weeps as he gives his daughter away. The maid of honor adjusts the train — oh, that's the problem. Alana's barefoot. What happened to her Jimmy Choos?

The ceremony begins, the officiant's voice silky and hypnotic. How long will this go on? I need to sit down. But why am I in a hurry? I've got nothing to look forward to but a long, drunken reception where I'll be the only single person for miles.

On Valentine's Day.

Again.

At least Tommy won't be there to rub it in.

Beyond the bride and groom, and past the line of groomsmen, glass-paned windows drape the entire west wall, inviting the Pacific Ocean into the ceremony. Defused sunlight shimmers off the surface, dancing its path toward the horizon. Nothing on earth could be more beautiful. Nothing would please me more than to march right up to the water and nap in the sand.

Something flashes at the entrance. Someone trying to sneak in. What a loser, can't arrive on time to a wedding — wait a second. Is that Ethan? Glowing smile, brighter than the midday sun. Why yes, yes it is. Fresh cut and highlights, shaved beard, stark chin . . .

The room spins.

Stupid Temazepam. Are the dreams worse than this?

What's Ethan doing here? He said he wouldn't be able to make it. If only I'd known he was coming, I could have . . . what am I saying? I look fabulous. Smell great, too. Seriously, I'm stunning. How can I not be, in this bridesmaid dress? Draped crimson chiffon, empire waist, one-shoulder, floor length — positively flattering on this imperfect, height-challenged frame.

He came to see me.

Stop. This isn't about you.

But it could be.

Idiot! There's nothing going on between you and him.

Maybe that's true, and maybe it's not.

Stop it.

Laughter erupts. What did I miss? The bride and groom are kneeling, the words "HELP ME!" screaming from the soles of Andrue's shoes.

Matthew snickers. Sure, it's funny, but if anyone's in danger, it's Alana. And why are they kneeling for a non-denominational service?

Now they're standing, the bride and groom speaking their vows, both sobbing like idiots. When was the last time Alana cried? Is she overcome from the ceremony, or does she miss her crystallized suede and mesh heels?

I face the bride and groom while Ethan's eyes burn a hole into the side of my head. Or is it my imagination?

Suddenly, Andrue collapses and lies crumpled on the floor. Fainted. Everyone stares at him and a brief burst of laughter escapes from my lips.

Uh-oh.

I slap my hand to my mouth, trying to hold back a volcanic eruption. No, no, *no* — not now, please. I drop my bouquet and press both hands against my mouth, and still the laughter slips out.

Kira draws near and latches onto my arm, her slanted brow warning me to stop.

I'm trying . . . *I'm trying.*

Thankfully, Andrue's causing the main distraction. Matthew tries to lean over him, but his thick muscles resist. "Bro," he grunts, kicking the unconscious groom. "Not cool, man. Wake up."

Kira scoops up my bouquet. "Will you pull yourself together," she snarl-whispers.

One more burst of giggles slips through my lips and then — nothing. It's over.

Kira smiles, tight-lipped, then settles back into her position, and I do the same.

Andrue stands. He's back in the game.

I recovered fast. How lucky is that? Did Ethan notice? I turn my head and he winks. I shiver. For the love of all things bright and beautiful, are we about done here? Not sure how much more of this I can take.

They're saying *I do.* Beautiful. If only I had my camera.

They kiss.

We cheer.

They walk.

We walk.

Hallelujah.

Photographers corral the wedding party and shove us toward the edge of the cliff where we're told to stand on a pink marble, eight-circuit labyrinth. It's a giant memorial plaque that reads, *For the journey of life to help you find your way.*

The photo session lasts forever. Guess my reunion with Ethan will have to wait.

The two-mile drive to the golf course and country club feels like ten. Is Ethan already inside? Dial it back, Kristen. He might not be as excited about this reunion as you are.

I jump out of the parked limo and walk fast, smiling, *click, click, clicking* — *ouch!* What'd I kick? An active hive . . . lying on the ground!

Bees swarm, blackening the air, buzzing and circling our heads, sending me and the Pheasant sisters screaming. What a scene — six giant, beautiful Pheasants flailing and a short oddball raving like mad. If only someone could catch this on video.

By the time we reach the far side of the lot, the bees have receded. Returned to their queen, I'm sure, to report fourteen hits on the brides-maids, five on the shortest one alone. A glob of bee guts throbs at the end of a stinger sticking out from my bicep. Kira gasps for breath.

"You allergic?"

She nods, whips out an inhaler from her garter and a credit card from her bra, then sucks on the inhaler while scraping the stinger and guts from my arm.

Club employees storm the scene, hastily securing yellow caution tape around the agitated hive. If only they had done that ten minutes earlier. Two scrawny college kids whisk Kira and me to a first aid station while the remaining sisters join the newlyweds en route to the reception.

The lankiest guy scans my swelling, throbbing welts. "Are you allergic to bee stings?"

"Not that I'm aware."

"Have you ever been stung before?"

"I . . . don't think so."

Have I? Wouldn't I know if I had or hadn't been stung? It's not like it's something I'd forget. Why am I not sure? Did I get stung during that gap in my childhood, that period when I can hardly remember a thing?

They give Kira and me Benadryl and hold us for observation. Twenty minutes later, they release us. Kira's breathing is back to normal, my welts have stopped swelling, and we've missed the grand entrance.

Kira runs off to find her little girl, and I pan the room. Where *is* he? Red, pink, and gray everywhere. Splashes of black, tons of glimmer, and *oh*, the ice sculpture . . . two massive overlaying hearts. How are they standing up without support?

"Hey."

Chills run up my spine.

"Ethan!" I fling my arms around his neck. Way to look both ways before crossing the street, Kristen.

He slides his arms around my waist. *This* is new. More firm and intimate than usual. I bury my head in his shirt and inhale the fresh linen scent. Then we both jerk back.

Awk. Ward.

He looks fantastic in that stylish suit. And can it be possible I'm growing attached to that jaw of his?

"I saved you a seat." He grins.

Can I do that? Sit with common folk? The tables flanking the pedestaled bride and groom are meant for the wedding party, but it's obvious the system has already been subverted. Pheasants and their guests mix with abandon. Based on Alana's laughter, I'd say she's already a couple of drinks under and couldn't care less.

"Lead the way."

Ethan's table is in the back and off to the side. Three Pheasant sisters sit with us, including Kira, along with her daughter and husband. Next to me sits a loud, gray-haired couple.

"We only got invited so Alana can keep parking her boat in front of our house," says the old man.

"Consider yourselves lucky," I reply with a smile. "They went way over their budget and had to reduce their original invite list by half. Both my fathers have known Alana since she was a teen and neither one of them made the final cut."

"Two fathers? One of those kind of families, huh?"

"Not exactly. One's a stepdad and the other is my mother's . . . um . . . yeah. One of those kind of families."

Matthew squeezes in an extra chair next to Milana, the oldest, tallest, and most beautiful Pheasant sister.

"Dude, are you kidding me? She's got a foot and a half on you. Besides, she's the maid of honor and you're merely an end cap." Oops, did I say that out loud?

Matthew laughs as he fills every wine glass but one. Ethan's the only one with a teeny tiny white mug of coffee sitting in front of his place setting. He's asked for so many refills, he's now got a little white pitcher in front of him, too.

"Ethan, I don't mean to judge, but you drink a lot of coffee. I'm thinking it might be healthier for you to just have a glass or two of wine instead."

He flashes a smile that dims quickly. "After seeing what alcohol did to my mother, and how that affected our entire family, I can't even bring myself to try it."

"Ah. I get that. I mean, I saw what alcohol did to my mother and my family, too. But I'm not like my mother. My drinking habits are *nothing* like hers."

He sighs but doesn't respond.

I turn to Matthew and the Pheasants who are drinking wine like it's cool water in the desert, but it's the old couple that surprise me most. I lose count with them. The waiters can't clear the bottles fast enough, so Matthew hides some beneath the table. I've had one glass . . . maybe four. It's hard to keep track when my glass gets topped off after every sip. Probably shouldn't have any, what with the Benadryl, the sleeping pill hangover, and hypoglycemia on board, and that reminds me — where's the food? Oh, there it is. Prime rib with whipped horseradish. Fan-tastic.

Ethan glances at my welts. "Should I call you the girl who kicked the beehive?"

He laughs way too hard. Maybe he should slow down on the coffee. He asks a waiter to bring us some ice, then wraps the cubes in his linen napkin and presses it against the wounds on my arms, my collarbone, and my neck.

"Why didn't you tell me you were coming?"

"What can I say?" He shrugs. "I love the expression on your face when you're surprised. The way your forehead widens. It's adorable."

"Whatever. You're strange."

As the night progresses, Ethan and I carry on as if he still lives in California and nothing has changed. We act as if we're the most deeply affectionate platonic friend couple that ever existed.

That's normal, right?

The newlyweds present their first dance . . . oh good, Alana found some shoes. Man, look at the way she holds on to Andrue as if she'll never let go.

"You okay?" asks Ethan.

"Yeah, I'm fine." Just lost my breath for a second.

The newlyweds tour the banquet room, enchanting each guest in turn. Matthew gets Milana to follow him to the dance floor. Ethan and I go, too. Anything to avoid a face-to-face encounter with Andrue. We reach the floor in time for the next song — *Forever* by Chris Brown.

Looks like the DJ's playing classics tonight, but uh-oh, this isn't a song for posers. I'll be fine, but what about Ethan? Whoa. Seriously? The same man who can't carry a tune has moves like this? He's moving and I'm grooving, and we're together, synchronized, connecting through each hard and soft beat. The music, the lights, the crowd, his legs, my hips — all coming together, beat after beat after beat.

He's goofing off now, a little freestyle, a little hip-hop, and I'm right with him. Oh, we're freeze-framing now? Yeah, I got that. Now Matthew and Milana are doing it, too, except Matthew's muscles are too pumped to budge. He's a hobbit next to Milana, and she's not even wearing shoes. Ah. That's where Alana got them.

When was the last time I had this much fun?

Ethan and I dance together perfectly. The party-pleaser ends and a drastically slower song begins. Ethan pulls me close. He slides his arms around my waist and holds me tight. I could learn to enjoy this, but will he stay this time?

My arms wrap around his neck. Glide step glide — be *careful*. His eyes on my face, and mine on his, glide step glide — don't *fall for it*. He pulls me closer as we continue to drift across the floor. Have we ever been this close for this long? Can he feel my heart beating so hard? Because I can sure feel his.

"Kristen!" Kira rushes up. "Your cell is blowing up with text messages. It's your mom. Says it's urgent, you've got to rush to the hospital."

Dizziness sweeps in. No. *No.* Her health is improving. Last week, the doctors talked about letting her leave, setting up in-home hospice care. This can't be happening.

Ethan drives us to the hospital in my car. For the entire fifteen minute ride, he white-knuckles the wheel and keeps his jaw set tight.

"It could be nothing," I say. "My mother can be dramatic."

"I hope you're right and that's all it is."

"I hate leaving the reception."

"I know, but I'm sure Alana will understand."

At the hospital, my heels click rapidly through the halls as the draped chiffon of my dress flutters behind me. Ethan keeps up, remaining at my side through every turn and stride, and then into the room.

"You're here." Mom's sitting up in bed, smiling. "What are all those welts from?"

"Long story, what's up? You said it was urgent."

"It *is* urgent. Ruth's dying."

"Why didn't you tell me that in your messages?"

"You wouldn't have come." Mom turns toward the frail, evaporating woman. "Doctors say she has another day, but I'm sure it's only hours. No one is coming. I didn't want her to be alone."

Of course. If Mom were in serious trouble, it would have been a nurse who called. I can't believe I freaked out like that. And she's right. If I'd known it was only Ruth, I wouldn't have come. Now I can't leave.

Mom settles into a lounger next to Ruth. Ethan and I sit on the other side. Ruth's breath crackles. Is she sleeping or unconscious?

I text Alana an update and then sit and wait. Alana sends back an image of her and Andrue cutting the cake with the caption, "Wishing you were here."

Yeah, me too. That cake looks divine.

"We're all staring at Ruth," I text to Alana. "Her eyes are closed. We're holding her hands and petting her. I hope she doesn't hate it. Remember how Jenna used to pet my hair whenever I was sick? I couldn't stand it."

Alana sends an image of the drunken crowd attempting the Chicken Dance. Matthew, Milana, Kira and her daughter, and the frail old couple — arms and knees jutted out, their mouths opened wide in mid-laughter.

The minute hand races around the wall clock.

"No change," I text. "Except Ruth's breathing's getting worse. Mom and Ethan are praying and we're all crying, even Ethan."

Kira sends twenty-five images of the newlyweds' goodbye wave. How can Alana's hair still be perfect after partying so hard?

"Ruth's awake," I text to both Alana and Kira. "She doesn't recognize us. The chaplain is here."

Midnight. I send another message. "You're probably on the plane by now. Congratulations. I'm happy for you and Andrue. Ruth's still awake. She recognizes us. She's talking to her lap, saying it's her dog Trixie, who Mom says died twenty-five years ago. She's all smiles."

If only I could be like that on my deathbed. All smiles.

CHAPTER 21

FEBRUARY TO APRIL

⁓

ONE IN THE morning. Ethan rests his hand on Ruth's shoulder and prays, while Mom accompanies him with whispered *amens*.

I pet Ruth's cold arms. "A/C running on full blast or something?"

Still praying, Ethan removes his jacket and places it on my shoulders. What is this, wool? There go my welts, all itchy and throbbing again. I lift my arm to my nose and inhale. This coat smells like heaven. And coffee.

Four-thirty in the morning. I send Alana another message. "Are you there yet, or still sleeping on the plane? Wanted to announce that Ruth's gone. Have a fantastic honeymoon. I'm happy for the two of you. For a while, I wasn't sure, but I am now. You guys are meant for each other and I love you both to pieces. Sorry if this message sounds silly. Benadryl, wine, sleep deprivation, and watching someone die, all catching up to me."

Ethan and I stagger out of the medical center and into the parking lot, where thick, dewy trees burst with vibrant song. Not even the birds will pause to notice the world has lost someone precious.

In the car, Ethan checks his phone messages before we take off and on our way out of the lot, he sighs heavily. "My flight leaves at noon. I'd stay longer if I could, but Dad isn't doing well."

"I get it. You need to be with him." I smile at Ethan, then slump deep into my seat.

He smiles back. "Wanna grab some coffee and sit on the beach during sunrise?"

"You realize this is the west coast and the sun rises in the east, right?"

"Just thought it would be nice to watch the beach wake up. How about it, you in?"

"Sure."

You bet your cross pendant I'm in.

At six in the morning, Ethan and I sit on a ledge in the sand, a thin blanket shielding us from the icy coastline winds. We sip our supersized coffees and snuggle as the sky above the water transforms from murky gray to a misty cobalt blue. If only we'd made a stop at my apartment before coming here. I'd give anything to be able to throw on some sweats and wash my face.

I rub my ankle and Ethan glances over. "You want me to take a look at that?"

"Nah. It's just sore from being in heels all night."

"You realize that's my job . . . physical therapy? I treat ankle injuries every day."

"I've got it handled, but thanks."

I rest my head on Ethan's shoulder. "It's too bad about Ruth, dying so young. And *alone*. I can't believe no one else was there."

"Yeah. Makes me wish I knew her story. What was her childhood like? And whatever happened to her family? But I'm glad, at least, that the three of us could be there for her."

"Right. I'm glad we were there, too. But I can't get over how sad I am. I mean, that was the end of her life? What was the point?"

His posture stiffens and I lift my eyes to him. "What?"

"Nothing. I didn't say anything."

"You want to, though. I can tell you have something to say."

"I just don't think that was the end for Ruth."

"Huh? Oh, right. *Heaven*." Immediately, my blood boils over. Why am I getting so hot over this? I toss the blanket off my shoulders, pin my eyes to the shore, and mentally slap each crashing wave.

"How do you *know*, Ethan? How can you be sure Ruth went to heaven?"

"Well, you heard the chaplain talking to your mom, right? Ruth was saved."

Bam! Slammed again by the elephant that keeps wedging himself between us. I jump up and throw my arms in the air. "Saved by whose standards, Ethan? I've been saved by Mark a dozen times, so am I saved, too?"

"I mean in a spiritual sense. Ruth believed in Jesus, so—"

"What about *me*, Ethan?" I jam my fists into my hips. "Am I going to heaven?"

He sighs. Then he scans my face, searching for words between the hard lines.

"Unbelievable. You're certain I'm going to hell, aren't you?"

He squints and sighs. He says nothing, but that's my answer.

"Doesn't that bother you, Ethan? Don't you care?"

"The Bible says it's God's desire that *no one* be lost and die without . . . you know . . . salvation." He looks up at me with wet eyes. "That's my desire, too, but to be honest, at this very moment, there's something that concerns me more — that so many people choose to live here on earth, separate from God, and miss out on all He has to offer right now, at this very moment."

Oh, so it's *my* fault I'm separate from God. But wait — if I don't believe in him, then why do I care? I turn and storm away, the wind whipping up my blood-red dress as I approach the unceasing incoming waves.

Minutes pass without words. I step into the water, my toes stinging from the piercing cold. Don't I have enough mental debris to sift through without having to process all this? If Ruth hadn't drained all my tears, I could add volumes to the ocean depth. My head throbs with heat, but my feet are frozen numb.

Is Ethan behind me, or still sitting? I refuse to turn around. If only I could run, but where would I go?

Ethan approaches, takes my right hand and stands at my side, both of us calf-deep in the water. We stare out over the ocean through several cycles of frothing, crashing waves. Then Ethan turns his head to look back over his shoulder, pauses, and faces me. "Sunrise is my favorite time of day," he says. "It's like a new beginning."

I glance back over my shoulder to see what has put that gleam in his eye. It's a beautiful baby blue canvas, with shredded pink cloud fluffs stretching for miles. A cotton candy sky.

He clears his throat. "Would you *like* to be saved?"

I yank my hand from his. "Even if I did believe in God, I'd never buy that He'd waste his time on me."

"God loves you."

"He doesn't even know me."

"I don't believe that."

"I do."

I rip all the pins from my hair and run my fingers through the wind-blown disaster that was once an Angelo masterpiece. A God who would let me go through the childhood I had? *Impossible.* A God who would love me after what I've done since? *No way.* Such a God can't exist.

I face Ethan. "In your mind, you're sending me to hell. How can you do that without even flinching?"

His massive jaw clenches. "*I'm* not sending you anywhere. I'm just trying to be honest about what I believe."

"What if I died today? What then?"

He holds me with those eyes, burnished bronze, red and wet. "If you died today, I don't think I could bear it."

He faces the ocean, tears rolling down his cheeks. His lips move without the merest hint of sound escaping. Then he kneels, his face planted in his palms.

There is nothing like watching a grown man cry. I drop down next to him and wrap my arms around his shoulders, and he returns the hug, holding me firm as water splashes past. A chill envelops me. Did Ethan shiver, too?

He pushes me back and breathes heavily. My stomach flutters, ten million butterflies trying to escape at once.

Guard your heart, Kristen!

Waves keep crashing, but for me, nothing else exists beyond Ethan's expression.

It's too late. I can't turn away.

He jumps up, pulls me with him, and draws me in. He wraps my waist with his right arm, his left hand sliding behind my head. Then he pulls me closer, our wet bodies pressing together, nothing but thin layers of soaked wedding clothing between us. His mouth meets mine, gently at first, until our lips part. Then restraint gives in to desire.

You're on your own, dear heart.

The kiss runs long, sweet — and maddening. We're both crying. Why are we crying during our first kiss? Minutes pass like this . . . or was it just one? He leans back and we gawk at each other. He tucks a clump of hair behind my ear.

I tilt my head and squint. "You just kissed a lost soul."

"You kissed an unworthy sinner, so we're even."

And there we stand, while sunlight pushes up from the east and lifts the darkness from the ocean's surface. Our toes sink deeper and deeper into the wet sand, and we just keep beaming at each other while waves continue their destruction of the shore.

Then Ethan flies back home.

I can't believe Mom gets to live at home again. Goodbye, Oncology Institute of Hope & Grace. How awesome is it that her cancer stopped growing? The tumors aren't shrinking, but at least they're not expanding. She's doing great — insisted I take her to the South Coast Botanical Garden, *The Jewel of the Peninsula*. And why wouldn't I, on such a bright and beautiful day?

I push her wheelchair through the entrance and she perks up. "Look at the bottlebrush blooms, so pretty. Run over there so I can take your picture."

I shuffle toward the assigned spot and smile. Then my mouth sags as she fumbles with the camera.

I run to her side. "Ah, yes. These gadgets usually work better when you turn them on."

She continues to struggle. By the time the *click* snaps, I'm laughing madly. "Beautiful," she sighs.

This morning broke in overcast, but that's gone now. What an obnoxiously sunny day. Golden rays shining from above, igniting row upon row of vibrant, dancing blooms.

"Lovely," says Mom. "We should come back next week."

"Your second round of treatments starts next week. You'll be tired."

No response.

"Treatments start next week, right?"

She tracks a turkey vulture's determined flight. "I'm not doing them."

"What do you mean?"

"It won't cure me. It'll make me weak and sick, and I still won't outlive this cancer."

I keep pushing the wheelchair, panting as the grade of the hill steepens.

She reaches her hand back to touch mine. "Kristen honey, I left the hospital to live out my remaining days at home. You understand that, right?"

I struggle to breathe. This incline is unbearable.

She rests her hands in her lap, the breeze lifting her wisps of hair. "I need assurance you'll be around for Steve," she blurts.

I park her chair at the Mediterranean Garden. "What does Steve have to do with this?"

"He's my husband. And *your* stepfather. After I'm gone, you'll be his only family."

But he's not my father, not my real one. Do I even have a *real* father?

"Why are you talking like this? We still have time. You're doing so well. Every week, you're getting stronger."

"Promise me," she insists.

Pushing and panting again, I reach my sight to the distant sky. Trumpet trees stand tall and blurry, dripping through my tear-soaked eyes. I don't deserve a real mother. That's why she's leaving when we're finally getting along.

"Fine. Yeah, of course I will, Mom."

"This is important," she says.

"Okay. I promise."

A little girl sits inside the Banyan Forest and flaps her inconceivably long lashes while gigantic topsoil roots swallow her entire body. I help Mom out of her chair and we hobble into the shade near the little girl.

"It's a shame the jacarandas haven't begun to bloom," Mom says.

All this botanical wonderment before us, and she misses the blooming jacarandas?

"The treatments would only give me a few extra months. What good is that if I'm a wreck the entire time?"

I stare a hole into her squinty green eyes. We've already missed out on too much. A few extra months would make all the difference.

"This isn't easy." Her voice quivers. "But I love you so much; I want to be present in every minute I have left with you."

Fine. Whatever.

"Oh, and I want some of my ashes sprinkled into the ocean."

"Really?" I smile, wiping my cheeks. "I've always pictured you as an ashes-in-the-garden-where-the-flowers-grow kind of gal."

"And where dogs and cats take their business?" She laughs, then stops short. "The ocean is important to you, and I want to be a part of that."

My lungs collapse as my heart drops to the ground. How much does she know? She couldn't possibly understand the pull the ocean has on my soul. Could she?

"Sure, Mom. I'll do it."

I squeeze her hand and help her back into her chair. Leaves rustle, birds soar, and a mouse scampers into a thicket. The girl with the lashes skips away to chase a monarch butterfly with her camera. We follow the little girl, her breathless grandparents, and the elusive butterfly all the way to the Garden of the Senses. The fragrant plants sit tall in their high planters, as if waiting for us to sniff them. *Mmmm.* Chocolate mint geraniums, rosemary, and thyme.

Together, we move on, rolling through the rest of the afternoon, collecting memories canopied by trees and illuminated by the vibrancy of quivering beauty.

CHAPTER 22

MAY

⌒⌒◯

I STROLL THROUGH the Riviera Village, my hair thrashing in the wind. I haven't had a session since I lost my job. Why did I wait this long?

So many thoughts crash through my mind — regrets, worries, and unaddressed issues that seem to multiply, like an army of demons gathering, arming, and preparing for war. It probably wasn't a good idea to withdraw four hundred dollars from my savings account. I *had* to visit Georgina, but why did I take out so much?

"Ethan's striking my last nerve," I blurt while rushing to Georgina's loveseat. I sink into the cushions, throw back my water, and crush the little paper cup.

Her smile glistens. "Nice to see you, too."

I wrap my hair and fasten it with three sharpened pencils, stupid tears already flowing. "When Ethan moved to Colorado, I wrote him off. But then he showed up at Alana's wedding."

Georgina settles into her wingback. "How would you describe your relationship with Ethan now?"

"One word? Psychotic. We started out just friends, but somewhere along the way, everything changed. Must've been that dog rescue at the beach. Something about seeing Ethan earn the trust of that beagle, and then how he pulled me into the process. I can't explain it with words, but I've looked at him differently since then.

"Then his dad had a stroke, and he took the Colorado job. Moved away without thinking twice. *Left me behind.* So whatever, I moved on. We were still just friends. I accepted my new, Ethan-less normal, and then he popped in for Alana's wedding. Why is he messing with my mind? Why did he do that?"

Georgina keeps nodding away as I tell her how much fun we had at the wedding and then how we left early to go watch Ruth die. Her brows rise when I tell her how we went to the beach during sunrise, right before he had to leave again.

"I know, right? Sounds like the makings of an amazing ending to his visit. And it would've been, if *God* hadn't gotten into the middle of it."

She tilts her head, but keeps her lips sealed.

"I'm still trying to figure out what happened." I rub my temples with my forefingers. "One minute, we're arguing about heaven, and the next minute we're knee-deep in water, kissing, like we're starring in some sappy romance novel."

I scowl at Georgina. "If I had the choice, I'd keep our dysfunctional relationship the way it was before that horrible, double-edged kiss. Right after that, he left and flew back to Colorado, to go hide inside his shell. He hasn't brought up the kiss, and neither have I. He keeps telling me he's praying for me, but other than that, our conversations are paper-thin. He talks like he's sad or depressed or something. He says he's going through a dark period in his faith, but I have absolutely no idea what that's supposed to mean."

Georgina leans in. "What's stopping you from talking to Ethan about the kiss?"

"My debilitating fear of confrontation."

"What exactly are you afraid of?"

"That he'll say he regrets the kiss and that he's never liked me."

Georgina hands me a box of tissues so I can wipe the snot from my lip.

"*Every* time Ethan and I have a conversation with any amount of depth, God gets into the middle of it. And it never ends well when God comes up. When I talk to you, I can mention God without the subject slamming back in my face. But with him, it's different. I get defensive, but only because he's so irritating about it.

"That morning on the beach, I asked Ethan if he believed I was going to hell, and he didn't respond. I wanted to smack him. He could've lied, or changed the subject, or done *something*. But no, he sat there with that dumb look on his face, like *yeah; you're pretty much doomed to spend eternity inside the fiery pit.*"

"You wanted him to lie about his convictions?"

"It would've been nice if he tried to assure me that someone like me could never end up in hell."

"Many biblical documents indicate that those who trust and rely on Jesus are not saved by whether they're *good* or *bad*. They're saved by their faith. Given that perspective, can you understand why Ethan couldn't give you the answer you wanted?"

"I suppose, on a logical basis, I get it. But why couldn't Ethan explain it to me like that? He just stood there. He couldn't answer because he believed my fate was set, end of story. It's like he sentenced me without a trial. It was insulting."

"You've said you don't believe in God or heaven. Do you believe in hell?"

"No."

"So why do you think you felt insulted by Ethan indicating you're going to a place that isn't real for you?"

More tissues. More nose blowing. "Part of me wants to believe, not so much in hell, but in heaven. Especially now, with Mom so sick. She's sure she's going there, and man, I'd love for that to be true. But I can't bring myself to embrace heaven as more than just a marvelous concept. Even supposing heaven was real, how can I buy the possibility they'd let me in?

"I've never told Ethan, but I often wonder about God. I have lots of questions, but every time I search for answers, all I find are more questions. Who wrote the Bible, and who's to say they're right? And what about all the other religions — how can so many people be wrong? Why are so many *saved* people stupid and mean? And who is Jesus, anyway? Can he really be who he says he is? I could go on and on with unanswered questions, but Ethan acts like he has all the answers. It makes my blood boil."

Georgina glances at the steamer trunk and says nothing. She cradles her mug — *Emotionally Liable* — and squirms in her seat. Then she stands, bends over the mysterious trunk and opens the lid. The thing is a virtual library, *full* of books. She riffles through them until she finds the one she wants.

"Here," she says, handing me a red and blue paperback. "This book won't answer all of your questions. But it will tell you who Jesus is."

The title flashes in my eyes, *The Experience of God: Orthodox Dogmatic Theology, Volume Three, The Person of Jesus Christ as God and Savior.*

Holy cow, that's an eyeful.

I pan the room. No one at the door. No one visible through the window. No witnesses. I snatch the book and shove it into my handbag, my hands sweaty and shaking. "Uh . . . thanks."

"You're welcome. Now, tell me about your dreams. Still having them?"

"No. They're gone."

She pins her eyes on me, hard.

"Almost gone. I . . . um . . . started taking sleeping pills, to keep the dreams at bay."

She whips out her notebook. "What are you taking?"

"Temazepam. They work. I'm finally getting sleep."

"When did you start the pills?"

"October."

"Regular dose?"

"Yep."

A pause. She can smoke a fat one if she's waiting for me to admit to taking more.

"Before you started taking the pills, did you follow my suggestion? Did you try to find more details inside your dreams?"

"That's the problem. On your suggestion, I dove deeper into the dream, searching for hidden details. When the two dreams collided, I stopped running. So far, nothing new, right? But when I stood and stared at the light, I noticed that even though the mist clung to my back, it never enveloped me. So I tried something different."

Georgina's eyes widen. "What did you do?"

"I turned around."

She scribbles fast.

"I faced the *thing* that I've been running from all this time. I don't know what I expected, like maybe it was going to swallow me whole or something, but when I spun around, it just hung there. Just a big glob of mist. Then it started swirling and I jumped back. The black vapor kept spinning faster and faster, and then it shrank." I narrow my eyes. "Then it took shape."

"What shape did the mist form?"

I mop the sweat off the back of my neck. *Urgh*, is this the same wad of tissues I used on my nose? Gross.

Georgina sighs. Fine. Here goes . . .

"It was a man."

"Did you recognize him?"

How can she not already know the answer? I yank the pencils out of my hair and scruff it up. "It was Vic-tor," I groan, barely able to get his name out.

Georgina gasps. She never, *ever* does that.

"I know, right? I never want to have his face that close to me again. That's why I started taking the pills. They've got to be better than the gallons of alcohol I used to drink to drown the dreams."

Georgina's brows rise. Have I failed to mention the gallons of alcohol before? With her head back in her notebook, she asks, "Do you see the connection?"

"I don't want to see the connection."

She sets her pencil and notebook down. "You see it, then? Victor is the black mist. All this time, you've been running from your past."

I rub holes into my temples. Georgina and her endless obsession with my past. The past is past. It's over. Victor's abuse wasn't severe enough to cause as much pain as I have suffered. The source of my problems has to be something else.

She glances past me. The green light. Thank God.

Or whomever.

I escape her office and head home. Salty coastline air sticks to my skin while an army of dark clouds assembles overhead. Please, weak brain of mine, wipe Ethan from my mind. Stop playing that blasted kissing scene over and over. But you're not going to do it, are you? You're going to keep torturing me with thoughts of that stark-chinned, fantastic-smelling, bronze-eyed Jesus Freak until I do something about it, aren't you?

I dial Ethan the moment I return home.

He answers quietly. His father's had another stroke.

"Oh, Ethan! I'm sorry." The timing can't be any worse.

"Thanks," he replies.

"So hey, about that morning on the beach . . ."

"The kiss?" His voice squeaks.

"Yeah."

"I know."

"You know?"

"Yeah."

"Wait — what?" My heart races through the distance between us.

"Yeah, I'm sorry about that," he mutters.

"Huh?"

"I shouldn't have. Not that I didn't want to . . ."

Blood rushes to my head, draining my senses. Ethan says something about having wanted to kiss me ever since the first time we bumped into each other in Mojave. Then he muddles on — making crunching sounds — continuing to say that just because someone *wants* to do a thing, does not mean that person *should* do the thing.

I scowl, but Ethan carries on, something about how it wasn't fair of him to give in to temptation at my expense. He crunches in my ear some more and then concludes that it was selfish for him to have led me on.

"The way things look," he says, "I don't think this relationship can move forward."

Wow. Such astounding multi-tasking skills. Grieving his ailing father, slicing me to pieces, and filling his stomach with . . . what? Corn Nuts?

He's still muttering, but I'm not listening.

"Goodbye," I say, my voice mechanical, flat lining until the *click*.

Not one tear forms. Not one. Thunder cracks. Rain patters against the windows. And numbness envelops.

Click. Gates locking.

Chck-ch. Weapons engaging.

Swoosh. An impenetrable sheath, encasing my heart.

Twice in a row is too often to be crushed. I'm done. From this point forward, I will do everything within my power to make sure this never happens again.

Friday morning. A surprise guest startles me in my living room.

"Legion!" I shuffle back two steps.

"Nice to see you, too."

He pulls Delila closer to him on the couch and she giggles. "Isn't it wonderful?"

They lock lips and I pretend to straighten up the coffee table. Good grief, how long are they going to do this?

"Legion landed the job he was going for," says Delila, wiping the extra saliva off her mouth. "He's guaranteed work for an entire year."

"Nice. But won't it be difficult for you guys to be apart for that long?"

"We'd never do that," says Legion.

Delila squints at me. "I'm moving to Vegas to live with Legion."

"Oh. When are you leaving?"

"Tomorrow. Sorry for the short notice, but I've already missed him too much."

"We're going out tonight," says Legion. "Come with us. Our last blast, before we leave town."

"Sure. Why not?"

Yeah, why not? If anybody could use a night out, it's me. I still have cash in my purse, and I wouldn't mind having a drink or four. Maybe Alana will come, too.

"Sorry, *chérie*," responds Alana. "Andrue and I are having dinner with his mother."

Sure they are. Maybe Alana's telling the truth, or maybe I no longer fit into Alana's white picket fenced world, now that she's married and I've become CEO and sole member of the Lonely Hearts Club.

Delila chooses O'Sullivan's, a pub across town that's overflowing with wasted revelers. It's perfect.

We grab a table in the back of the room.

"Bar matron," announces Legion, "bring us some drinks. Whiskey, straight up."

We press ourselves into our dark corner and throw back the glasses of liquid fire. Thank you, sir. May I have another? Man, am I thirsty. The rounds keep coming and I keep tossing them back. Delila and Legion crack jokes, and I burst with gut-splitting laughter. Have they ever been this funny? Music and slurred conversations stuff the bar like blown-in insulation. Everything becomes pleasant and dull.

"I'll cover the tab, 'kay?"

Legion nods, but Delila gazes into space, her left hand rubbing her star pendant.

"Hello . . . Delila? You with us?"

"Huh?" She shakes her head and releases the pendant. "Sorry, I was thinking about . . . one of my jobs."

"So what's the deal with that necklace? Do you realize you're always grabbing it?"

"Oh, yeah. It was a special gift. From Legion." She glances at him and he raises a brow. "He gave it to me when I landed the job at Hamilton Design. After I'd struggled for so long, it was a huge deal, but I guess since I lost that job, the necklace doesn't mean so much anymore."

Legion downs the rest of his drink and slams his glass on the table. "You don't need to wear that thing anymore," he says. "You've got a whole new thing going now, and you don't need to be reminded of your past."

Her phone rings. She glances at the screen and her face pales. "I've got to take this."

She steps away from the table and Legion follows her. They return after ten minutes, both of them sniffling. And those jaws . . . the way they grind back and forth. Cocaine? Was that call from a dealer or something? Whatever. All that matters is that I'm out. Sooooo weightless and unchained. If this isn't heaven, I don't know what is.

Another round of drinks later, they take off again. As I sit and twiddle my thumbs, I get a long text from Ethan. Pfsht! He's high if he thinks I'm gonna read whatever absurd message he's trying to send. Does he think we can still be *friends?* What a joke.

Some bar jockey gawks at me. I set my phone down and grin back. The guy saunters over, takes a seat, and looks me over. I lean to the side and scan him head to toe. He laughs.

"Name's Rocko."

"Yikes. Your parents hate you?"

"It's a nickname, 'cause my muscles are solid, like rocks."

"I'm Kristen. That an east coast accent?"

"Grew up in Boston, but I been all over. Don't like to let my roots grow too thick, know what I mean?"

"Not unless you meant *deep* . . . but whatever. I'm tired of sitting by myself."

I laugh, he flirts. I flirt, and he laughs. Nothing wrong with that. We're having the time of our lives. Dude seems to be missing a few marbles, but he's not hard to look at, and besides, he will *never* mean anything to me.

Several drinks under, and I'm saturated with numbness. No more sharp edges. Could not care less about anything. Ever.

I get a text from Delila. They went outside to get some fresh air. Fine. Me 'n' Rocko can keep entertaining each other — playing, teasing, and drinking, while the night keeps slurring along.

We dance and laugh through several songs. Then nausea strikes. I drop into the nearest chair and my head transforms into a balloon stuffed with fog. Man, I'm an idiot. When was the last time I ate, anyway? And *how* many drinks have I had?

"You okay?" Rocko leans close and places his hand on my arm.

I lift my eyes up at him, my head swaying back as I let his face come into focus: bent nose . . . eyes too close together . . . thick, coarse brows . . .

I lean in and squint. Is this the same guy? Ugh! What was I thinking?

"I'm fine." I yank my arm away. The room spins and my stomach lurches. My blood sugar's crashing. What would Ethan say? Why do I care? I owe him nothing. He made it clear we're not together.

But I'm done with Rocko.

I force a grin and stand, wobbling like a baby giraffe on my go-get-em heels. "I'm gonna look for my friends, 'kay?"

"Need some help?"

Eww. That moist, slithery voice. Dude grabs my elbow to steady my stance, his fingers scratching my skin like strips of sandpaper. A bent smile sweeps across his face. I pull away and stumble off, mumbling that I'm fine. I wipe drool off my chin as I trip through the blur of music and drunken fools.

Ahh, outside. Refreshing, except for the heavy, wet air. And the dimness. They could use some more lampposts out here.

I stumble along the side of the building, closer to Delila's purple vw Bug, looking for steam dripping from the windows. Nothing. No sign of Delila or Legion. I should call . . . wait. Pocket's empty. Must've left my phone inside.

I turn back to get it, and Rockwood blocks me, that bent nose sticking in my face. "Lose something?" he hisses.

"Go. Away."

The ground sways, the alcohol hitting me harder than ever.

"Settle down, Krissy. No need to get worked up."

"It's Kristen, Rockhead." Even his voice makes me sick. "Dude, it'ss binfun," I slur. "But iss over now, ssoo step off."

His smile stretches. And twists. He steps forward, as if he could get any closer.

I stumble back against the building. "You 'ave problem with yer ears? I ssaid step offf. Means go. A-way."

He leans close and whispers, "I'm not going anywhere."

He presses his lips against mine. I turn my head to the side and try to shove him away. The man's chest is made of stone. Rocks. Rocky . . . that's the name. Eww, his sticky wet mouth on my neck. Repulsive. And that breath! The contents of my stomach rise up my throat, but I swallow it down. I try to jam my knee to his groin, but my tight skirt prevents the impact. I stab my pointy heel into his foot, but the heel is useless against his thick boot.

"Stop squirming, you little—" *Wham!* His fist slams my temple, the sickening crunch of my skull bouncing off the side of the building.

A familiar shouting voice enters the scene. A shock rips through my spine as I'm hit again. I try to move but can't. A blur of tattoo-covered flesh sweeps in front of my face, and I fall to the ground.

I wake up alone inside a cold, white room, sunlight boring through the window. Nurses buzz the hallways. My brain revives, throbbing with images from the night before. The pub. The whiskey. Delila, Legion . . . and Rock-something, morphing into a beast. The slithering hisses. The hits to my head. The tattooed arm flashing in front of me, the images familiar. Legion, in living color, saving me from Rocko-psycho. What happened after that?

A nurse walks in. A full-framed gal with a weak smile and a tight salt-and-pepper bun. "You're awake."

"Where are my friends?"

"Who would that be, hon?" She keeps her eyes pinned to mine while adjusting the sheets. Her nametag reads, *Dottie*.

"The ones who brought me here."

"I'm afraid you were dumped, hon. Left in the ambulance driveway. Good spot, though. Lots of foot traffic there."

The nauseating scent of soap-like sanitizer pours out of Dottie. Every time she moves, I get another whiff. My head spins and I moan. Would it be rude to ask her to leave?

She asks if there's anyone I'd like her to call. I give her Alana's number.

A doctor enters the room and asks me what happened.

"I was hoping you'd tell *me.*" I smile at him, but his expression remains flat. Can I trust my own memories? Better give him a short version — I went out, drank too much, and got beat up.

Doc confirms my name. Says I have a mild concussion, no broken bones, and should be released after he runs some more tests.

The tests come and go, but I'm held captive. For *observation,* I'm told. I scan the ceiling, my head pounding as I count the passing seconds.

Alana rushes into the room. How much time has passed? Did I fall asleep?

"I would've come sooner," she says, urgency ringing in her voice. "Some jackass big rig tipped over on the 405 and clogged it up for miles. What on earth happened to you? You look like you were tied to the back of a speeding truck."

I reach my hand to the cut on the side of my head. "Looks like I hooked up with the wrong guy this time."

She paces the floor, raking her silky red hair over and over. "I talked to the cops."

"What cops?"

"Investigators. They want to talk to you."

"Well, I don't know anything about the guy who hit me, and I only want to rest. Can you just tell them to go away?"

"No, they're not leaving. The young one tried to drill me, but I told him I don't know anything. I don't know anything about this, right?"

"What're you talking about?"

She impales me with her fierce eyes. "You have no idea?"

"No. I really don't know why everyone's freaking out. I'm going to be fine."

Alana sits on my bed and pets my hand. She might as well dig her claws into my skin. "They found a dead guy in the trash dump behind the pub."

"Are you kidding?"

"*Ma chérie,*" she whispers, leaning over me. "They found your ID and cell phone in his jacket pocket."

"He's *dead?*" Is it even the same guy?

Wait . . . my cell phone and ID? It has to be him, but how? Legion couldn't possibly have . . . no, he couldn't. I rub my forehead. "What am I going to do?"

Alana stands and throws her hands up. "How do you always get yourself stuck in messes like this?"

"Wait a minute. That guy attacked *me*. He was alive when I passed out. And by the way, this is my first involvement in a murder."

"It's not just this. It's *everything*, Kristen. You're like a black hole, attracting chaos from every direction. Which reminds me, I'm not refilling your Temazepam anymore. You're taking too much and that's part of your problem."

"But I'm all out. I was hoping you'd bring me some today. Besides, you're the one who gave me the pills, and they have nothing to do with this."

"Don't you get it? It's not about *this*." Her hands swirl like a furious conductor. "It's about everything—your troubled past, all the drama, your never-ending well of need—and I'm sick of it."

"You mean like my mother getting cancer? That's my fault?"

"See what I mean? It's always about *you*. I liked it better when it was the four of us. When Jenna, Danielle, and I could take turns dealing with all your mess. It's just too much for one person to take."

"Where is this coming from? I'm in the hospital, if you haven't noticed. You're freaking me out. For the record, I miss Jenna and Danielle, too. They were both far less mean than you."

"There's something bigger happening here than your personal suffering. The man who attacked you is *dead*, but you don't get it, do you? It's still all about *you*, and how it's going to affect *you*. It's time for you to grow up, Kristen. Put someone else first for a change. You're not the only person in the world who has a problem."

"What are you talk—"

She jabs her finger at me. "No. Not one word. I'm not dealing with this right now." Then she storms away.

Nausea swells in my stomach. Unable to bear it, I roll over and vomit onto the floor. Nurses are still scrambling to clean up after me, when the police investigators walk into the room.

CHAPTER 23

STILL MAY

⟨∿⟩

THE YOUNGER DETECTIVE turns back to the door and cranes his neck to look down the hall. "I'm running downstairs for a minute," he says to his partner. "I need coffee." And then he's gone.

The other one scrapes a chair across the floor and sits next to me. "Hi, I'm Sergeant Hygleson. I work investigations here in Redondo Beach." He points his head toward the empty doorway. "And that was Detective Sharman."

He faces me and narrows his eyes, his brows pulling down in concentration. "How're you feeling, Miss Craemer?"

Soothing voice. Fresh, pepperminty breath.

"My head hurts. Do you have an extra stick of gum?"

He smiles and hands me a stick, then pulls out a notepad and pen. "We got a call from the hospital that you were here and that you were the victim of a beating. Can you tell me what happened?"

My pulse accelerates, sending too much blood to my head. What did happen last night?

"I . . . went to a bar with a couple of friends, and we had some drinks. Then my friends left me, and this guy came on to me. Next thing I knew, I was fighting the guy off outside. Then I woke up here."

"Okay. Let's go back to the beginning. Who did you go out with?"

"My friends, Legion and Delila." And I'm using the term *friends* loosely.

"Can you tell me their full names and spell them out?"

"Legion Reigns, that's R-e-i-g-n-s, and Delila Twynn, T-w-y-n-n."

"And how did you decide to go out? Whose idea was it?"

"Legion suggested it. He wanted to party. And Delila picked the place, O'Sullivan's Pub."

My stomach clenches. *They* picked the time and place. Is it possible they orchestrated the entire evening?

Hygleson jots down one-word notes.

"Were you just planning to go out with Legion and Delila, or were you going to meet anyone there?"

"No, just us. I asked my friend Alana to come, but she couldn't."

Legion and Delila couldn't have planned what happened because they couldn't have known Alana wouldn't come. Could they?

With his questions, Hygleson walks me through the night, step by step, wanting to know who, what, where, when. Asking for excruciating details, like the time we left, whose car we took, the make, model, and color of the car, where we parked, when we arrived, how many people were at the bar, where we sat, what happened next, and what happened next, and what happened next . . . all while my head throbs violently. Some questions I answer completely, but for others I remain vague.

Hygleson looks up from his notepad and addresses me squarely. "How much were you drinking last night?"

I rake back my tangled mess of hair. "A lot."

"What's a lot? Can you give me a number? Was it more than five drinks?"

"I don't know the number, but it was definitely more than five."

"Were you drunk?"

My eyes pop open wide.

"It's not against the law to be drunk," he assures me. "I just want to know what happened."

"Yeah. I was drunk."

"Okay, so tell me what happened after your friends left you alone at the table."

"This guy who called himself Rocko came over and started flirting with me."

Hygleson digs in and the questions continue. Can you guess his height? Did he give you any other name besides Rocko? What was he wearing? Did he tell you anything about his personal life, like where he lives or works or what he does with his free time?

The questions pound on and on. No, I can't guess his height and he didn't tell me *anything*. I spent the evening with a man I knew nothing about and I didn't even bother to know. How much more stupid could I have been?

"So yeah, besides the clothes and general description I gave you, I don't remember much about him. I can't even think of what we talked about. I remember laughing at lot, you know — at first. We even danced. Dude seemed friendly. I had a blast, until every ounce of alcohol I drank slammed me all at once. Nausea, dizziness, difficulty walking, and then all of a sudden, we were outside and he was shoving me against the side of the building."

More questions. Is this when he started attacking you? Where exactly did this occur? What hand did he hit you with? Was anyone else out there? Was it dark or light? Did you notice any cameras?

My head spins. It's getting harder to filter my answers, to omit where necessary, and to keep track of what I've left out, like my suspicion of Legion and Delila doing cocaine, that I saw Legion's tattoo-covered arm come between Rocko and me before I passed out, the fact that Delila was my roommate, and that I know they were planning to move to Las Vegas.

Hygleson stares at me, the way Georgina does when she's waiting for more. But he can't possibly know there's more to tell if he wasn't there, right?

Ugh. Bile's creeping up my throat. I think I'm going to be sick again. That had to be Legion who came onto the scene before I passed out, but he couldn't have killed Rocko. Could he? My brain fogs over, but I'm sure Legion saved my life. I'm not going to throw him and Delila under the bus. I'm going to insist I never saw them after they left the table, and I have no idea where they went.

Agent Sharman steps back into the room, no coffee in hand.

Hygleson sighs, gives him a funny look, and then flips through his notes.

"My head hurts and I don't feel well," I complain. "Can I rest now?"

"One last thing," says Hygleson, and then he pauses.

Sharman stuffs his fists in his pockets and gazes out the window.

I grab my stomach. "Well, what is it?"

"Is there any possibility you were sexually assaulted while you were unconscious?"

"No."

Hygleson clears his throat. "Okay. Most women would know if they had, but to be absolutely sure, are you interested in checking? We have a procedure called a rape kit, and the doctors would come in to do the examination, not us—"

"No thanks. I wasn't raped."

"You're sure?"

"Of course I'm sure. I'd know if I was raped."

"Fair enough. I think we're finished with questions for today. Oh, wait, one last thing. Do you mind if I take a look at your ID? Do you have it with you?"

My brows cross together hard and my head tilts far to the side. "Why are you asking me that when you already found my ID?"

"Excuse me?" says Hygleson, his face burning with sudden anger.

"Alana told me you guys talked to her earlier and told her you found my cell phone and ID on Rocko's body."

A phony smile spreads across Hygleson's face. "Okay then, that's it for now. We'll likely be in touch for a follow-up interview."

And then he storms out. Sharman drops his chin and shuffles behind. As soon as they're outside the door, Hygleson's angry voice trails behind them. "How many times do I have to tell you, Sharman? *Never* let them know what you know. You may have seriously jeopardized this case. If this happens again . . ."

The next morning, Hygleson catches me as I'm checking out of the hospital. Says he wants to ask me a few more questions.

"I've told you everything I remember."

"Yes, Miss Craemer, but we just need to ask you some more questions about Legion and Delila, and clarify some of the facts about that night."

He knows. I'm sure he knows I've lied. I drop my head in my palms. "This is a bad time for me to talk. My cab's waiting downstairs and I have a horrific headache. Can we make an appointment for another time?"

"Sure. I'll be in touch."

At home, I rub my fingers along the old farm table, slip into my usual fuzzy pajamas, and sink back into my favorite worn-in spot on the couch. But nothing is the same. Thanks to Alana, I have no more Temazepam, and the dreams have returned with a vengeance. When I call Alana to beg for more drugs, she changes the subject, confessing that when she talked to Detective Sharman before she came into my hospital room, she told him that Delila was my roommate and that she and Legion moved to Vegas. So thanks to my dear friend, Hygleson knows I was lying during the interview.

Fourteen new messages blink on my home phone. Mom, Mom, Mom, Mom, Ethan. Whatever. Mom, Mom, Steve . . . ugh. I'd better call her before she sends Steve out to hunt me down.

"Hi, Kristen." Her voice is breathless, but cheery. "I'm glad you called me back, I was beginning to worry."

"Mom, I wasn't avoiding you. I was . . . wait, are you okay? Is something wrong?"

"No. I just wanted to talk. Are *you* okay? Why weren't you returning my calls?"

I tell her everything. Sort of. Best to give her a condensed version of the story I gave to Hygleson. When I get to the attack, Mom's breath pours fast and thick into the phone, so I breeze quickly past the worst of the scene, and when I'm finished, I wait. And wait . . .

"I'm coming over." Her tone is adamant.

"No, don't. I'll come to your place. How about tomorrow?"

"I'm coming today," she insists. "You're exhausted, and I have too much energy. I want to see you, and I need to get out of this house."

"No."

"Really, I feel great. Steve can drive me. Be there in an hour."

Three hours later, Steve calls.

"We were stepping off the curb, on the way to the car so we could come see you, and this truck came from nowhere, driving way too fast and way too close to the sidewalk—"

"Mom was *hit* by a car?"

"No. It didn't touch her, but it came so close it blew wind in our faces, and you know how weak she is these days. Well, that's all it took to knock her over, and she fell. So that's all it was. A fall. She's okay. Has some bruises, but nothing serious. Our in-home nurse says she doesn't need to go to the hospital unless something changes."

"Wow, was the driver drunk or what?"

Steve blows into the phone. "The truck never stopped."

"What? Did you get the license plate?"

"No. Just saw that it was an old green truck, that's it."

My heart races. "Are you serious?"

"Yes, why?"

"That's the same type of vehicle that swiped Mark. Don't tell me the driver was an old lady."

"You're right, that was an old green truck, too. I'd forgotten about that. But no, this driver wasn't an old lady. It was a young guy — long blond hair and wearing a white T-shirt."

"Don't you think it's strange that both Mom and Mark were hit by old green trucks?"

"I think it's just a coincidence. What are you thinking? Conspiracy?"

"Yeah. Sounds crazy, I know, but there's a lot of strange stuff going on. Back when Mark was still in a coma, this guy in the halls gave me the creeps. I didn't catch his face because he was turned the other way, but it looked like he'd just come out of Mark's room. Then I saw him again the day Mark woke up. He was heading toward Mark's room until he saw the crowd. Then he went a different direction."

And then there's my car sabotage, but I won't tell Mom or Steve about that one.

"I'm not sure why, but he made my skin crawl. It's probably nothing. I mean, seriously, how can that guy be related to the old lady and the blond guy? I'm sleep-deprived. My brain's glitching. There's nothing to these crazy thoughts I'm having. I'm just glad Mom's okay."

"Don't worry about it. We're all strained. We'll get through this. I've already filed a police report. I'll keep you updated."

It's 10 p.m. when Steve calls again. Mom's back at the Oncology Institute. She can't stop throwing up.

I take a cab to the hospital and join Mark, who's already there, along with Steve, several of Mom's friends, and all the recovery women, except Dorothy.

Tests reveal nothing, leaving the good doctors scratching their heads. Helplessly, we wait while night fades into morning.

When it's my turn to visit Mom, I watch her rest in her little, sterile bed. Sometimes, she opens her eyes and smiles. Most of the time, she sleeps.

Dear God, please let her live. You probably hate me because I'm awful and I don't believe in you, but my mother loves you, so why not let her live? Please don't let me be the cause of her death.

The vomiting stops after three days. So does Mom's desire to eat. Exploratory surgery reveals a length of intestine that had disintegrated. This fragile strip ripped apart because of the impact of her fall. The doctors say they might be able to repair the damage, as soon as Mom's fever and blood pressure drop.

Mark, some of Mom's friends, and I wait silently, while Steve, Robyn, and the rest of the recovery women fill the lobby with prayers. Mark balances his laptop on his knees. "Check this out, kiddo," he says. "There are all kinds of stories on the internet about people surviving for long periods without food."

"Can we talk about something less stressful? Like puppies?"

"There are lots of cases here where patients survived four to six weeks without food."

"So that's a no on the puppies?"

"And check this out," he continues. "It says that ten political prisoners in Ireland lived seventy-three days without food before succumbing."

"Are you saying Mom could go on like this for months?"

"Hey, I didn't post this stuff, but a man has to hang his hope on something."

A doctor saunters in, a short, pleasant fellow with a meaty baritone voice. He tells us Mom's fever and blood pressure have dropped and he's scheduled the surgery for early tomorrow morning. Then the good doctor leaves.

Murmured prayers rise in the background.

CHAPTER 24

STILL MAY

⟡

THE HOSPITAL LOBBY bustles with loved ones. Steve paces, Mark taps his cane, and the recovery women keep sharing stories about Mom. Alana's already come and gone. She says her work's keeping her too busy to sit at the hospital for hours on end. She also said she was sure Mom will be fine, but she didn't say much more than that. Whatever's eating her, I hope it passes soon.

I should be grateful Alana left, since Andrue left with her. When he was here, he just kept staring at me and rubbing his scar. I've had enough of the silent accusations. *He* attacked *me*. I had to defend myself.

What time is it, anyway? I tap my pockets, and then start digging into my bag in search for my phone. Oh yeah, I don't have it. Hygleson's holding it hostage for the investigation. So I lean a bit to get a peek at the obsessively over engineered, apocalypse-proof watch strapped to Mark's thick wrist. The room temperature and air pressure are nearly perfect, and in our present time zone, it's 9 a.m. How much longer will the surgery last?

The recovery women gather and link hands. Time for another circuit of prayer-go-round, their pleas ranging from soft meditations, to deafening supplications. Layer after layer of prayers rise like vapor, billowing throughout the room.

"They did the same thing for you," I whisper to Mark. "Every stinkin' day. All those weeks and months that you lay in a coma. Day after day, nothing changed, but they kept coming, praying like mighty warriors. They never wavered. They expected a miracle — and look at you now."

"Will prayers be enough this time?" He crosses his arms and tries to squeeze back tears.

Will the prayers be enough? I rub his shoulder and pan the room. Where did all these people come from? There's the group of recovery women. I recognize a couple of others that Mom used to work with. And that quiet group taking up the good couches, holding a private prayer circle of their own — they must be from Mom's church. What about the rest of them? Doesn't that lady with the ponytail work at Mom's grocery store? There must be more than fifty people crammed into this small space. Half of them unfamiliar to me.

I should call Ethan.

No. I shouldn't. We haven't talked since that awful phone call. How many days has it been? Seven? Eight? If only I could read the last text message he sent when I was at the pub that night. Has Hygleson hacked into my phone and read all my messages, including that one from Ethan? Has Ethan sent more?

"Be right back, Mark."

He grunts.

I dash into the gift shop and scan the racks. Candy, gum, magazines, deodorant, teddy bears . . . prepaid phones. Excellent.

"Got anything besides black?"

"You can always bedazzle it," quips the clerk.

Funny girl.

After my purchase, she helps me activate the phone, and then I step outside to search for privacy. I pull out Hygleson's card. What're the chances he'll read me all my missed messages?

I punch in Ethan's number instead. Something is seriously wrong with me. What am I going to say? It's the machine. Maybe I should hang — *beeeep.*

"Hey. Wanted to tell you I don't have my phone. I . . . uh . . . lost it. Long story. Tell you about it later. So yeah, if you sent any messages the last few days, I haven't received them. I'm using a prepaid phone now. The number should show up on your phone.

"Anyway, hate to tell you this on voice message but I'm sure you'd want to know. I mean, why wouldn't you, right? It's my mother. She's back in the hospital — The Oncology Institute of Hope & Grace — not from the cancer, not specifically. A hit-and-run driver clipped her. Crazy, right? What is it about my family and hospitals? Mom's in surgery right now. There's a ton of people here. I gotta go. Hope your dad's okay. Call you later. Bye."

Lame message, but whatever. Can't undo it now.

I return to the lobby. Why is Mark standing with his backpack on and cane in hand?

"My legs ache from sitting," he says. "Let's take a break from this vigil and walk through the patio. There's a rose garden out there."

"Sure."

We shuffle toward the garden in measured steps. Mark's limp is worse than when we arrived.

"You have got to be kidding me," he shouts as we enter the patio. "Doesn't anybody maintain this place?"

Spoken like a true rose enthusiast. With his free hand, he deadheads the expired blooms and peels off the rotting leaves from the rest.

"These bushes look like hell . . . everything's dead or dying." He squints at the thin streak of sunshine getting through. "They aren't getting enough light. Who's the genius who picked this place for a rose garden? Building structures block the sun on three sides. Any fool could see that."

"Maybe that's my problem," I reply. "Planted in the wrong place. Not enough light."

No response. Was that not as funny out loud as it was in my head? I join Mark in the picking and peeling, and prodding and deadheading—and pretend I didn't say anything, as we continue pruning the bushes in silence.

Half an hour later, after we finish accosting all the roses, we return to the lobby.

Something's changed. Everyone's standing. The room's cold. As we reach the crowd, murmurs rise and someone gasps. We find Steve with his head buried in his palms, the surgeon standing in front of him.

As time thrashes by, it becomes clear that the doctor is explaining how he lost my mother. But his words are nonsense. They're phrases from a storybook, a tale of something terrible that happened to someone else. Because I talked to my mother a few hours ago, and there's no way she could be gone. She smiled at me and said she would see me on the other side. Her friends have prayed like lunatics, for crying out loud. Is this doctor sure he's talking about the right patient? Charts get mixed up all the time. There's no way Mary Craemer has died. Not this soon.

Steve and Mark cry out loud, and their naked grief slaps me awake.

It's true.

And it's my fault.

I killed my mother.

If only I hadn't gone to the pub that night. If only I hadn't been so stupid, Mom wouldn't have insisted on visiting, and she would still be alive.

I should be crying, but all I am is numb. I back away from the crowd, turn, and head for the exit, passing two older men in scrubs who are laughing about something irrelevant.

I have to get out of here. I burst through the doors, keys in hand. The ocean. I need to get to the beach.

It's because I don't deserve to be happy, isn't it? After all I've done, how could I have expected more? Why have I struggled so hard to make this life work? No more. I'm done fighting.

I hoof up the parking garage stairs and scan level four. Where on earth did I park my car? The pull is so strong, there's no way I can fail. I just need to get to the water. Then I won't have to suffer anymore. There's no other way. I can't stay here and face my mother's death.

But what if Mom was telling the truth?

No. Heaven can't be for real . . . but that *has* to be where she's gone. Otherwise, she's gone forever. God *can't* be real, but just in case . . .

"Dear God, if you're really there . . ." my voice cries out in an anguished whisper, "can you hear the sound of my heart breaking . . . from wherever you are?"

"I can."

I spin around and my jaw drops. "Ethan! Where'd you come from?"

"I just parked and saw you here. Alana called me yesterday." He sighs deeply, his expression tense. "I came as soon as I could. How's your mother?"

I bite my lip and shake my head, but my eyes are still dry. "She's gone."

"Oh . . . *no.*" He steps close and wraps his arms around me. "I'm so sorry," he whispers. "So, so sorry."

He holds me in this warm hug that seems to have come from nowhere and everywhere, his cheek resting softly on the top of my head while he rocks side to side. Many, many seconds pass like this, with both of us standing together in the middle of the parking garage, his arms bracing me, keeping me from slipping into nothingness. I cling to him, not wanting to let go, not wanting to fall.

My keys slip from my hands and clatter to the ground. He reaches for them. "Were you heading somewhere?"

My eyes bug out wide and I grab a clump of hair. If only I could yank out the entire chunk. "I *have* to get out of here."

"There's a park across the street. How about we go and sit for a while? It's nice out, and the jacarandas are starting to bloom."

There's no way I can sneak off to the beach now. Ethan would only follow me. I concede, letting him lead me away from the parking structure. Lucidity flows in and out as we search for a bench on the shady side of the park.

We sit and stare at the jacaranda trees. Some minutes linger and others pass in a flash. As if inside a dream, I sense the essence of dogs off their leashes, babies in swings, and toddlers in the sand. I glimpse a gray-haired couple walking hand in hand along the concrete path.

A breeze blows and my mouth opens. "How much do you know about what's happened over the last few days?"

"Alana said you were in trouble, and that your mother was at the hospital in critical condition." He watches the old couple pass by. "She didn't tell me much more than that."

I gaze into space and start speaking, words pouring out as if someone has opened a valve. I tell Ethan everything. How I drank too much at the pub . . . how I flirted with Rocko. My tone is flat, monotonous. My filter is nonexistent. I tell Ethan about my attack and every detail about that night — the cocaine, Legion saving my life, how I woke up in the hospital, and how Rocko ended up dead. I tell him about Hygleson's investigation, how I lied to protect Legion, and how I have to go in for further questioning.

If ever Ethan had a reason to judge me, now would be the time. But he doesn't. He simply sits and listens.

Then I remember our last conversation. "Why did you bother to come, Ethan?"

"I deserve that." He rakes back his hair. "I've been an ass. I'm sorry. I'm going through some issues myself, but I don't want to talk about me right now. I'm sorry I hurt you. I hope you can forgive me."

Ass? This is a new flavor of vocabulary for him. I smile weakly. Then I glance at the giant, lush umbrella of purply flowers hanging over his head and it hits me . . . like a *truck.* "These are Mom's favorite trees, and she's missing the blooming season."

"Kristen, I can't tell you how sorry I am," he says. "I know how much you wanted to have more time with her."

I nod, slowly, struggling to breathe and still unable to cry. "Mom wanted to visit me when I returned home from the hospital. She was hit when she was on her way to see *me.* How can I live with my mother's death hanging over my head?" I pin my eyes to Ethan's. "When you found me in the parking garage, I was on my way to the beach. I was planning to . . ."

I ball my hair up with a rubber band and blow out my breath. My biggest secret is about to be revealed, and I have no ability to stop it from coming out.

"I'm afraid to go to sleep at night because the nightmares are getting worse, and there's not enough alcohol in the world to drown out the feeling that I'm entirely alone. In the daytime, I fight to succeed, but I only make one mistake after another.

"I haven't told anyone this . . . I don't know why I'm telling you now. For the last couple of years, I've had this intense draw to the ocean. I've had this pull, this . . . irresistible urge to walk into the water and never return."

He nods, his eyes getting red and wet.

"I've tried to do it several times. This time, if I'd made it to the beach, I wouldn't have failed."

His eyes widen. "I know you're hurting right now, but you're *not* alone."

My heart jumps into my throat. If only I could believe that was true.

He leans back and rubs his jaw, where peaks of new beard growth emerged through his skin. Then he points to a young woman pushing a toddler on a swing, both of them laughing. "My guess is *that* wasn't your childhood. It wasn't mine, either. My mother's alcoholism tore our family apart. She was an abusive drunk. Her attacks were always verbal, but her words cut deep. I would've preferred that she smacked me around now and then instead. Friends and relatives avoided our house. Dad was a wreck. By the time I entered first grade, I made it my job to keep the peace. I used to think if I could only be good enough . . . if I could only keep everyone happy . . . then everything would be okay.

"The divorce was devastating because it meant I'd failed, and I went through a serious bout of depression. I never made any plans to kill myself, but I spent a lot of time wishing I'd never been born.

"One day when I was feeling pretty bad, Dad came into my room and said, 'Son, when we find ourselves at the bottom of the deepest, darkest pit, we have no choice but to look up.' I was young then, but I got it. It was like my mind cleared and I understood exactly what he said. From that moment on, I knew that no matter how bad things got, or how isolated I felt, I always had someone with me."

Ethan wipes his eyes, and then takes my hand, his gaze resting on me softly. "I know you're not ready to buy into . . . well, a lot of this stuff, but what if it was true? What if you *can* find peace through a relationship with Jesus? And what if nothing else could even come close?"

"I can't go there right now. I wouldn't even know where to begin."

"What about having conversations with God, even if you don't believe in him? Address the four walls if that feels more comfortable, but just start a dialogue. You can say something like, 'God, I don't know if you're real or not, but I want to know. If you're real, will you reveal yourself to me?'"

I stare at Ethan blankly. He wants me to talk to myself? Sounds so silly. But isn't that what I was doing in the parking garage?

Three purple petals fall to my lap. Three little petals from Mom's favorite type of tree, and finally I'm able to cry.

CHAPTER 25

JUNE

⚬✦⚬

THE GRAY SKY makes a striking canvas for the jacaranda blooms. They're so pretty, bursting in purply waves overhead, beyond the cemetery and through the residential streets that led me here. I still can't believe you're gone. If only you could see this, too. Can you? Is this why you wanted your service held graveside, instead of at your church? So these trees would surround us?

How ironic that you filled your life with beige cardigans and white walls, but wanted us all vibrant and colorful after you were gone. Do you like my raspberry floral dress? It's the liveliest piece from my closet. Can you see how everyone complied with your request? Alana and Andrue wearing coral, and the recovery women in yellows, reds, and blues. We must be a sight. A colorful scoop of rainbow sprinkles distributed across the grassy mound.

"You okay?"

Tears pool. "No, Mark. I'm talking to Mom in my mind. Crazy, right?"

"Not at all." He shrugs, gazing at the table. A potted orchid, a simple photo arrangement, and a small mahogany box holding half of Mom's ashes, saving the other half to be scattered in the ocean. "Steve did okay."

"Yeah, the table looks good, but why did he drape it with a white cloth when Mom asked for color?"

"It's what Mary would've wanted. For *us* to stand out, not her."

I tried to get Steve to let me help plan for the service, but he insisted on doing everything. If only I could've decorated the house for the reception. That's my thing. I would've painted, changed out the fixtures, and rearranged the furniture. Maybe that's why he held me back.

I should've at least tried to contact Mom's foster parents. They have no idea she's gone.

Who knows if *they're* even alive?

Pastor Carl climbs to the top of the mound and stands near the table, his yellow button-down, curly red ponytail and matching goatee poised before us. Middle aged. Ex-tough-guy look. Short sleeves revealing his ink-covered arms, fat-lettered designs, like an inner city wall tagged over, and over, and over again. How did this guy end up a pastor? Are they recruiting from Harley conventions now?

"Today we are gathered together for the graveside service for Mary Craemer."

He pans the crowd and flashes his teeth, the smile way too big, like a newscaster hamming it up for the camera. How are we to expect a shred of sincerity?

"On behalf of the family, I'd like to thank all of you for coming. First, Mary's husband Steve will read a verse from the Bible."

Steve approaches the table, sweat shining off his forehead despite the overcast day. He shifts from left to right. "I'd like to . . . uh . . . read . . ." He fumbles through pages and clears his throat. "Romans, chapter 8, verses 38 to 39. Mary's favorite Scripture."

He dabs his eyes, then pins them to Mom's Bible held open in his shaking hands. "For I am convinced that neither death nor life . . ." He chokes, rubs his face, and begins again. "For I am convinced that neither death nor life, neither angels nor demons, neither the present nor the future, nor any powers, neither height nor depth, nor anything else in all creation, will be able to separate us from the love of God that is in Christ Jesus our Lord."

I gasp, my lungs expanding in an instant. How is it possible that every word pierced my brain? I *never* listen to Scripture. Why did time stop while those words soaked in? And why am I offended? You say the love of God can never be separate from me? How can that be true? How can the love of God place me here, in this dreadful place, next to my mother's ashes?

But those words . . . the reckless claim they make. Nothing can separate me from the love of God? Not my anger, my disbelief, my utter worthlessness? Can this be true even if I am irredeemable?

My pulse races as Steve returns to the crowd and pastor Carl hits *play* on his iPod, the attached mini speakers sending Bessie Smith's *Muddy Waters* through the graveyard.

Bessie's song strikes us all as it undulates with the breeze. Silently, I stand in my vibrant attire, my heart pounding against my chest. I sway to the trumpets and trombones, and the jazzy moans and groans, while fluted jacaranda petals rain upon my head. Mom must have played this song a hundred thousand times, singing out loud, drunk and happy in Victor's absence. *Oh Mom*, my heart cries out for the muddy waters, too.

I shiver. Childhood memories rushing up my spine, or something else? Someone watching me? I scan the crowd. Nothing but a sea of colorful guests bowing their heads. Wait a minute — who's the large woman dressed in black, standing out like a mole on the other side of the crowd? *No.* That scowl beneath the veil . . . could that really be her?

I whisper into Steve's ear. "Dorothy's here?"

Steve glances at the mole, raises his brow, and shrugs. That explains the chill. What possessed her to crash the funeral? She hasn't talked to Mom in more than a year. God, please make her go away.

The song ends. Soft-spoken Carl moves to the front. "1 Corinthians 15, verses 51 to 55. Behold, I show you a mystery; We shall not all sleep; but we shall all be changed, in a moment, in the twinkling of an eye, at the last trump: for the trumpet shall sound, and the dead shall be raised incorruptible, and we shall be changed."

The dead shall be raised incorruptible? What the—?

"So when this corruptible shall have put on incorruption, and this mortal shall have put on immortality, then shall be brought to pass . . ."

Am I the only one who thinks this sounds like gibberish?

"O death where is thy sting? O grave, where is thy victory?"

Where's the sting? It's in the box filled with ashes. Somebody, bring me a drink!

"Mary Craemer is not here. She stands in the presence of the Lord, the same Jesus who said to the dying man on a cross, 'Today you shall be with me in Paradise.' The ashes that lie before us are the remains of Mary's earthly tabernacle . . ."

How long is this going to go on? Mom wanted it short and simple, but Carl keeps rambling.

". . . and the body shall again be united at the coming of the Lord."

Silence.

That's it? Uh oh, there's going to be a ton of hugs and tears.

"Mark, I've got to run to my car."

"What?"

But I'm already heading to the parking lot, leaving the rest of the tear-soaked rainbow sprinkles behind. Can't let my makeup run yet. We can all cry at Steve's house.

"You!" sneers a familiar voice.

I spin and fall back against my car, a fake smile spreading across my face. "Dorothy. How are you?"

"We need to talk."

Fantastic. And why on earth is she wearing wool? This is California, where only two days out of the year are cold enough for that oppressive suit, and today isn't one of them.

"Ethan tells me you still keep in touch." She scowls.

"Um, yeah . . . kind of."

We're back to being dysfunctional friends, if that's what she means.

Her eyes frost over. "That needs to stop."

"Um, I'm sorry you feel that way, but—"

"I don't blame you for chasing him."

No, she did *not* just say that.

"He's a catch," she continues, "but even you can understand that Ethan deserves better. He needs a woman who's strong, someone with values."

Come again?

"Besides, you don't want to waste your entire life chasing something you'll never have, do you?" She spins on her heel.

I rub my forehead and stare at my feet. No. I don't want to spend my entire life chasing something I'll never have. I look up and she's gone. Vanished, like the shadow of a ghost on this gloomy lot.

And still, invisible eyes press against the back of my neck.

At Steve's house, the dining table is crammed with assorted breads, deli meats, cheeses, and fresh seasonal fruits. Cookies, coffee, punch, and Zingers sit on the kitchen counter. There are plenty of vegetables, but nothing spicy, and not one ounce of alcohol. The mourners saunter, mingle, and laugh. They share stories of Mom while licking their platters clean. Their shoulders hang low, but only a few tears stream. What did I expect?

A mourn-fest, that's what.

Andrue sits alone on the sofa, rubbing his scar while stabbing me with his eyes. I pretend to laugh with a group of strangers, but that awful stare . . . I've had it. I won't put up with it. Not today. I storm toward Andrue and stop in front of him, fists on my hips. He sinks into the couch as I tower over him like Wonder Woman. "What's your problem?" I dare him to blame me for what happened.

He drops his gaze and I stand at ease, weighted on one foot, arms crossed. He peeks at Alana who's making new connections. Working the crowd near the kitchen, she slips a business card into her handbag. He looks back at me and smiles. "Every time I look in the mirror, I'm reminded of that night in the stairwell." He winces. "This scar is *my* fault."

I stand in front of him with my mouth hanging open.

"Alana wants me to see her plastic surgeon," he chuckles. "You know how she is about appearance."

I do. I smile because I know.

"I don't want to fix it," he says. "It's a reminder of how easily I can deceive myself, how quickly my life can fall apart." He sits up and leans forward. "That was an awful thing for one friend to do to another. I'm sorry for scaring you. I hope you can forgive me. That man you fought in the stairwell was *not* me. That is not who I am deep inside."

I lose my breath for a few seconds. It's him — the old Andrue. Same fantastic hair, same charming smile. More subdued, not quite as effervescent, but it's him. I wipe the corners of my eyes. "Of course I forgive you."

This time, I mean it.

By evening, only Steve and I remain. I should go. If only I hadn't made that promise to Mom. Good grief, how does she expect Steve and me to build a relationship after all this time?

Steve smiles cautiously. "You're welcome to take home all the leftovers you want."

He saunters toward the dishes. Without a word, I collect abandoned plates, half-filled cups, and wadded napkins. Steve washes each dish separately, tons of soap and water slipping down the drain.

"Strange that Dorothy crashed the funeral, yeah?"

"Not really." His voice is barely audible above the running water. "Not when you consider everything she and your mother went through together."

"Yeah, but she hates Mom now."

Steve turns off the water and faces me. He dries his hands on an old apron of Mom's, white with bold letters, *Kiss the Cook*. "Maybe she doesn't hate your mother as much as she acts like she does."

My eyes widen. "Maybe." And maybe that's what I did for all those years. Only pretended to hate my mother. I cross my arms and lean back against the counter. "Did you hear all those Christian women bashing Dorothy today? Was that crazy, or what?"

"They were surprised."

"They called her a nut case and laughed behind her back. Aren't they supposed to be Dorothy's friends? Aren't Christians supposed to be nice?"

"We're all fallible, Christian or not," he says.

"So it's okay for Christians to put other people down?"

"Is it okay for anyone to put another person down? The women reacted from pain. Dorothy disowned them. She tore down bridges in the process. And just because these women are Christian, doesn't mean they're bulletproof. I'm not saying it's right, but that there's a cause."

"Dorothy came up to me after the funeral."

"Really? What did she say?"

"To stay away from her son."

"You and Ethan dating again?"

"No. As if we *ever* dated. To be honest, I don't know what we're doing."

He places his hand on my shoulder. "I'm sorry your relationship with Ethan is difficult. And I'm sorry Dorothy is mean to you. Would you like to talk about it? We could sit in the living room—"

"No . . . thanks." I wince. I've already said too much. "One baby step at a time."

He smiles.

Without Delila or Legion around to annoy me, the walls press in, squeezing all the oxygen out of my apartment. I head straight for the bedroom where the pink and brown leather-bound book beams at me from the dresser top — the Bible Ethan gave me for Christmas. Why can't

I stop looking at it? What is the big deal with the Holy Bible, anyway? Am I the only person alive who can't understand its significance?

I haven't cracked it open yet, and I doubt I'll have the desire anytime soon, so I snatch it, dash to the side yard, and toss it into the trash bin. I cringe at the sight of the Bible nestled against common household trash, my name glittering in silver inscription, screaming from inside the bin. *Ugh!* How can I leave you there like that?

I fish it out, lug it into the house, and toss it onto a plastic bag on the kitchen counter. It lands open-faced next to the treat bag I brought home from Steve's house. I grab a handful of cookies and cram them into my mouth.

The book remains open, begging for my attention. Persistent little sucker. I wipe my mouth and draw near, sliding the thing closer. "Ecclesiastes. Hmmm." Certain words rise above the others.

"'Meaningless! Meaningless!' says the teacher. 'Utterly meaningless! Everything is meaningless.'"

Ha! I mean, rock on dude. I hear ya, but these are the last words I would've expected to read from the Bible. What was that thing Mom used to say, that when Scripture jumps at your face, you were meant to read it? Nonsense. The book could've fallen open at any page.

I grab a few more cookies and dare to read more.

"I said to myself, 'Come now, I will test you with pleasure to find out what is good.' But that also proved to be meaningless. 'Laughter,' I said, 'is madness. And what does pleasure accomplish?' I tried cheering myself with wine, and embracing folly — my mind still guiding me with wisdom. I wanted to see what was good for people to do under the heavens during the few days of their lives."

Laughter is foolish? Seriously?

"Yet when I surveyed all that my hands had done, and what I had toiled to achieve, everything was meaningless, a chasing after the wind; nothing was gained under the sun."

A chasing after the wind? Pfsht! Sounds about right.

But what does it mean?

CHAPTER 26

STILL JUNE

⁓

I SETTLE BACK into the couch as I place the phone to my ear. "Hey."

"How are you?" Ethan's tone is soft, velvety.

"Not bad for a drizzly June day."

"Maaan," he groans. "I've missed that voice."

If that's true, why does he always text rather than call?

"What's up?" I feign politeness.

"It's Dad. He's gone."

A stroke. At least it was quick. Ethan must be in shock, because he's laying out the details surrounding his father's death mechanically, as if he were reading tax codes.

Since the day we met, our relationship has been anything but normal. And now his father has died. How am I supposed to absorb this news without breaking from the weight of everything that's going on?

"Ethan, I'm sorry about your father."

"Thanks. It's rough. Bittersweet. Dad's in a better place, no doubt. He's perfect and complete. Nothing's more beautiful than that." He draws a deep, tear-crackled breath. "I'm stuck here, though, missing him like crazy."

"How about I come out for the funeral?"

"Not a good idea."

"No?"

"It's my mother," he explains. "She's coming. Insists she needs to say goodbye to him, even though they haven't been on good terms for more than a decade."

"She enjoys crashing funerals, doesn't she?"

"She's not well," explains Ethan.

"No kidding. Did she tell you she confronted me at my mother's funeral?"

"Yeah. I tried to talk her out of going, but she's stubborn. I prayed something good would come of it. She called me when she returned from the service. She was hysterical and said some awful things."

"Like what?"

"I really don't want to repeat it. She had no right to speak the way she did. Mom's in a bad place. Kristen, I would fly you out in a heartbeat. Man, I would love to see you, but this is a bad time for you and my mother to be together."

"I get it."

I do.

The next day, I meet Mark at Café Nate.

"I ordered a new .357 Magnum," Mark blurts out the moment we sit.

He's always talking about his guns, the weight of them, the scent of them, and the way they glimmer in the slightest streak of light. The man already has an arsenal, but he always needs to add *just one more.*

"Gotta love the stopping power of the .357." His eyes twinkle, his brows poking out as wildly as ever. If only his rose club buddies could see him now. I like guns, too, but can we please talk about something else?

"So anyway," I interject. "Alana sent me a card and an expensive potted orchid."

He nods. Good. Maybe he'll take the bait.

"She left the nametag on the plant. It's called *God Only Knows.* I bet she didn't notice that. She'd only care about the price. She left that tag on it, too."

Mark stares into his cup filled to the brim with black, foam-free coffee.

"It was a nice gesture. Orchids are my favorite. But otherwise, Alana has been avoiding me. She barely talked to me at the funeral. I guess I no longer fit into her perfect world where people don't get fired, land in the middle of murder cases, and cause their mother's death."

Mark shakes his finger at me. "Mary's death was not your fault."

"Yeah, I get it. The cancer would have killed her anyway. But if she wasn't trying to visit me—"

"Don't talk like that. It's nonsense."

"I just want her back."

"Me too, kiddo." He sips his coffee.

I glance at a chip on the edge of the table. "Hygleson's come to the apartment three times to 'clarify my facts.' He keeps asking the same questions. I think he's trying to trip me up and catch me in a lie."

Mark glances at my shaking hand and his brows rise. Even Mark doesn't know the whole truth. What version of the story did I give *him*, anyway?

"Hygleson's very tight-lipped about the case, but every now and then he slips me a tidbit of information. It's incentive, I think, to get me to talk more. Last week, he told me Legion and Delila were living off the grid — even Delila's website was down. He asked me if I'd heard from them and I said no, which was true.

"Then yesterday, Hygleson told me Legion and Delila got married in Vegas, so now he has a lead. Hygleson and Sharman are driving out there today to find them and see if they can get them to voluntarily come in for questioning. After he told me this, he asked if I'd like to come in and clarify my statement. I said no, I already told him everything." I rub my forehead. "I just hope this doesn't blow up in my face."

Mark stares at me like he's thinking of what to say next.

I squirm in my patio chair, searching for a new subject. "I'm stuck, Mark. The investigation aside, my life is a mess. It's like I'm standing at an intersection with a dozen paths leading from it. The choices are paralyzing."

He leans in. "Let's talk about these choices."

"If I stay at the apartment, I'll have to commit to another year-long lease. Meanwhile, the bills keep coming. I'd rather get my teeth drilled by toddlers than search for another roommate, but at this rate, I'll drain my savings in the next few months. I need to find a source of income. I could start my own home design business, but finding new clients will be tough."

"Life is tough," says Mark.

"No kidding." I roll my eyes. "I could try to land another nine-to-five job, or I could file for unemployment, but those are my least favorite choices."

"Why would you bother with your least favorite choices?"

"Because then I'd be less likely to fail."

"Failure is the mother of all successes."

"You get that out of a cookie?"

He grins and pulls a little white strip out of his pocket and I laugh out loud. He tosses the fortune cookie wisdom onto the table. "Forget about failure. Assume a net will break your fall. No risk. What would you most like to do? Where's your heart, kiddo?"

I sit up straight. "I love arts and crafts, and design." My hands and arms join the dialogue, flailing left and right. "Especially anything and everything to do with home design. Conceptualizing, planning, coordinating . . . I love it all. I have thousands of ideas already sketched out in my journals. So yeah, home design. That's my zone. I could do it every day forever. I'd love to be able to make a living in that field."

"Tell me — what's stopping you from doing this?"

"Confidence, I suppose."

"Confidence is a matter of the mind," says Mark. "And no, that wasn't a fortune cookie. That was all me."

I smile and lean back. If only confidence was that easy to master. How can I work on my future, when I'm still running from my past?

He tries to sip his coffee, but it's empty. "If you need a place to stay until you get back on your feet, I've got a spare room. And I'd love to have your company."

CHAPTER 27

JULY

W HAT A HEAP of junk I've collected. Outdated design magazines. Glass, rags, metal. Wait, what's this pretty red envelope? Valentine's Day party photos. That time Jenna and Danielle dressed as cupids. What a couple of adorable goofballs.

I sigh, dig some more, and find a frilly toothpick from Sandy's café, from that day Ethan and I rescued that beagle. I toss it into the box and cram in a few other loose items, like Ethan's copy of *Works of Love*, and my Bible.

More photos. These are of Tommy and me, his image embellished with mustache and horns. I press my lips together as I toss it all into the trash, but my eyes remain fixed on these pictures. Just look at the joy in my face. I couldn't have had any idea it would all end soon.

Stop it. Don't go there, Kristen. I press my palm toward the trash bin and turn my head away. Had I known that packing all my junk would become such an emotional chore, I'd have hired someone else to do it.

Then, as if being controlled against my will, I shuffle back to the trash bin and pull out the only photo that hasn't been vandalized. What's the harm in keeping this one? I looked good in that dress. I can always crop Tommy out later. I toss in the photo and seal the box, the screeching of the tape echoing through the apartment. I write "Miscellaneous" on all sides. More like *motley*.

Living with Mark will be fine, I'm sure. It's not like I have a choice.

I shake open a contractor-sized trash bag and head to Delila's room. Man, she left half her possessions here—bed, gossip magazines, and a ton of clothes heaped on her closet floor. I dig into the clothes pile, carefully examining each article before stuffing it into the bag. This one's too long. That one's too sheer. They're all too fancy, too colorful, and just too much. I can't use any of these in my wardrobe rotation. I'll put it all in storage until the first of the year. If she hasn't returned for it by then, it's going to Goodwill. Hey, she left a pair of her purple platforms. These look new. A half-size too small, but I can squeeze.

I dig again and strike something. What's this? I yank it out from beneath the pile. A manila envelope addressed to Delila Twynn, already opened. No return address, postal stamp dated October.

It would be wrong for me to peek inside.

But who would know?

I unwind the string, round and around and around until the fastener is free. Deep breath. Do I dare? It's probably benign, an old client contract or something like that . . . right?

Right. Go for it.

A knock rattles though the hall. By the time I reach the living room, Agents Hygleson and Sharman have already stepped through the open door.

"Going somewhere?" asks Hygleson.

He's a sharp pencil, that detective, picking up on subtle clues like empty shelves and boxes stacked high. Sharman leans against the wall by the door, his lips pressed together as if sealed by invisible tape.

"Lease is up," I reply. "Moving in with my dad. So how'd it go in Vegas?"

Hygleson saunters along the stacks, tapping on boxes as he passes them. "Very well." He glances at Sharman, who leaves the wall and starts roaming the room. Great. Now I've got two of them snooping, roving like human-shaped robot vacuums.

And what, exactly, did Hygleson mean by *very well*? Did he find Legion? If so, what did Legion say? Was he arrested?

"The case is moving along, but we seem to be missing a few pieces to the puzzle," says Hygleson. "Is there anything else you can think of that you haven't told us yet? Maybe another memory jogged from that night at the pub, or something Delila might've left behind?"

I shake my head. "Nope. Can't think of anything I haven't already told you."

That fake smile. "Okay, but I'd still like you to come in for another interview, if you don't mind."

Hygleson leans over to read the label on one of the boxes. *My Little Black Sketchbooks.* He takes his time scanning the box.

Yes, that's right, Mr. Investigator. The entire box is stuffed with my little black sketchbooks, and every page in every journal has been drawn on. An uncountable number of ideas. Only a tiny fraction of them used.

Sharman continues to wander aimlessly around the apartment until he stops at the hallway entry. *No.* He's not going to walk into the bedrooms, is he?

I fake busyness, dusting, wiping, and straightening anything I can reach. "Fine, yes," I blurt. "I'll come in. Just say when." Whatever. Just leave before Sharman starts walking down the hall.

Hygleson smiles, summons Sharman, and they leave.

I bolt the door behind them and rush into Delila's room. I open the envelope and drop to my knees as I empty the contents onto the floor. Two sheets of paper stapled together. The first sheet is some kind of internet printout. It's a car engine diagram. *Not* a client contract. My heart pounds. Above the diagram, the caption reads, "Classic '65 Mustang Sabotage."

That's *my car.*

Beneath the diagram is a list of instructions. The papers shake in my hands. I toss them to the floor and rub my forehead repeatedly. No. *No way.* Delila couldn't have messed with my car. But . . . the evidence.

I grab the papers again. On the second sheet, a typed letter. "By switching the spark plugs, as instructed on the first page, the oil will wash off the cylinder wall. This will cause a loss of compression and then fuel will leak past the rings into the oil pan. If, by some miracle, you manage to do it correctly, the bottom end will eventually fail."

Blood rushes to my head as I continue reading out loud. "Her tailpipe will start to smoke, but she won't have any warning until she hears the bang. And this is the best part: the car will still run, so she'll probably try to drive it farther than she should. And before long, the car will stop abruptly. I want maximum impact from this, so be sure to switch the spark plugs before she plans to drive the freeway. Call me when it's done. Don't fail me this time."

Cold panic sweeps across my skin, raising the hair on my arms. Who *is* this psycho? And how long has this been going on? Could Delila really go along with a plan like this? I can't even wrap my brain around the possibility. The postmark reads "Redondo Beach." My city. So all those times it seemed like someone was watching me . . .

The following morning, regretting not bringing the envelope with me, I hesitantly slide my butt onto the metal chair across from Hygleson's desk. I made the right call. He would've only run off and arrested Delila without giving her a chance to explain. And given the chance, I know she'd be able to explain.

There's got to be something I'm missing. How could Delila have dared to mess with my car? I just can't see it. Maybe someone set her up. Could it be one of the seven, after all this time? Maybe one of them has some sort of hold on her. Or maybe Alana planted the envelope, as a joke or something. She does have a key . . .

Hygleson sits there, waiting. This meeting isn't about the envelope. It's about the inconsistencies in my story about that night at the Pub, like how he asked me if I knew where Legion and Delila could be and I said I had no idea. But then he found out that Delila was my roommate and I knew full well where she was planning to go. He knows I'm trying to hide something.

My mouth opens, but only breath escapes.

Hygleson rests back in his chair. Still staring, he says nothing as he swivels. He rocks. He swivels. He clasps his hands in his lap as he rocks and swivels. Then he leans forward and says, "Do you know what aiding and abetting is?"

"Huh?"

"It means you helped a suspect after the fact. It means you've helped in such a way that you've lied to the police. I believe you've been lying to me all along. I think you know more than you're saying. I'm telling you this for your benefit because I don't want you to get in trouble, but if I find out down the line that you've been lying to me . . . well, that's a felony."

I gasp and slap my mouth with my hand. Then I sigh. "Fine. I give up. There is more. Probably. I mean, I have so many versions of that night playing in my head, I'm not sure I know what really happened."

"We could try doing another recorded interview. Start from scratch, going through the night step by step."

I rake back my hair. "I'd be willing to do that, but I'm just not sure how well I can recall every little detail after all this time."

Hygleson jolts upright. "We could try something else."

"Yeah? What's that?"

"Hypnosis," he says. "It's unconventional. The guys around here will probably tease me about it, and I wouldn't be able to use the results officially. But I used it on a recent case, and it actually resulted in a new lead."

I shiver like a mouse trapped in a corner. Under hypnosis, I'd have no control over the words that fly out of my mouth. If I say no, I'll still be in the hot seat. Either way, I can't win. If only I'd brought the envelope to use as a distraction.

"How about we do it after you're settled into your father's place, say one week from today?"

"Fine," I grumble, and he gives me that fake smile again.

Maybe I can still get out of it.

Maybe a bus will hit me before then.

During the week, Mark helps me prepare my bedroom and bathroom. I paint the walls teal to compliment the linens and furniture. Mark buys me a sparkling chandelier that I hang from the ceiling. I install French doors, that I score cheap at a flea market, to replace the outdated sliding door that opens to Mark's garden. And I have a reading nook. That is, if I can call an eight by ten alcove with a stone hearth fireplace and wall-to-wall bookshelves a *nook*. A long hall separates my living space from the rest of the house. It's like I've got my own wing of a castle. My enchanted ever after.

Yeah, right. I used to be one of those little girls who pined for Prince Charming to scoop me up and gallop away to my happily-ever-after. Except instead of a prince, I waited for the father I'd never known. I imagined my real father longing for me to find him, and this hope made Victor irrelevant.

Thirteen months have passed since I found out Mark is my father, so why can't I shake the nagging suspicion that he's not what I was looking for? What else could I possibly need?

"Ready, kiddo?" Mark's voice echoes through the hall.

"Coming."

I lift the false bottom of my nightstand drawer and reach for my gun case. There's the envelope. I should show it to Mark, but that would make it all too real. I just can't accept that someone is trying to hurt me. But there's no other explanation, is there? I need to get in touch with Delila. I want her to explain to me how this envelope ended up in her closet.

Showing the envelope to Mark would be a bad idea. He'd only freak out. He's so volatile these days. Sometimes he acts fine, the same old cheerful Mark. Other times he's gloomy, obsessing over his guns and roses. When he's in the worst of it, he plants himself in his library, pouring over Mom's old Bible, reading it through the night, and then greeting the next day like a man who has crawled out of a cave. If only Steve would've kept that Bible to himself. It's not helping anyone.

No, I won't show the envelope to Mark. If I can't reach Delila soon, I'll show it to Hygleson.

I close the drawer and join Mark in the hall.

He lifts a painting off the wall and presses a hidden button. The fake wall slides away and reveals the pyro-block safe that houses his arsenal. He examines the collection, his eyes lighting up like one of Alana's bonfires. "Wanna shoot with something wild today?"

"I'll stick with my Ruger."

"I'll bring my new .357 then," he replies, but he's still searching the safe, hesitating.

"Pick something, so we can get there already. I need a distraction from thinking about tomorrow's hypnosis."

He scans my face. "It won't be fun, kiddo. But aren't you ready to find the truth?"

"That's rhetorical, right?"

He doesn't respond and neither do I. He grabs the .357, and we head to the shooting range.

CHAPTER 28

STILL JULY

⸎

WHEN I ENTER my old apartment building, Trent pulls his head out of his *Golfers Digest* without me prompting him. I reward him with a giant smile. "Hey there, buddy. You have my security deposit?"

He hands me the envelope, avoiding eye contact. "A mean lady came by this morning, asking about you. I told her you went to live with your father, and she said Satan was your father and then she left."

"What did she look like?"

He looks up at me and clears his throat. "Tall, overdressed. Had on a hat, like she was going to an Easter parade. And she looked real mad."

"Trent, that was no lady," I assure him.

Once home, I dial Ethan so I can yell at him. "Dorothy's hunting me down."

"My mother has lost it," he mumbles. "Ever since Dad passed away, she's been out of control — more stubborn and opinionated than ever. I've tried reasoning with her, but she won't listen to common sense. I've prayed my throat hoarse over her."

"You have to *do* something," I snap. "I can't have her chasing me through town. Seriously, Ethan, what happens if she shows up at my front door?"

"I'm sorry she's doing that. Ignore her, if you can. She's harmless."

Silence blasts from my end of the phone to his.

"*Physically* harmless," he concedes.

"Aren't you the one who said you'd rather she smacked you around than lash at you with verbal abuse? I haven't done anything to deserve this. You and I aren't even dating. We're *just* friends."

"You're right. She's awful, and you don't deserve it, but I haven't given up on her. I'm coming out to California a week from now."

I take in a truckload of air.

221

"I have a plan," he continues. "Mom's active at her church, volunteers a lot, maintains a high profile. I contacted some of the church leaders, and we're going to have an intervention. We'll use the prayer and worship team as a net to trap her."

"Fine." The words *net* and *trap* are in the plan, and that's all I need to hear.

"Sooo," he sings, "I'll be in town for your birthday."

"Yeah, I guess you will."

"Would it be okay if we got together? I'd like to celebrate with you, and talk face-to-face."

It's like ocean waves, how they keep coming and crashing. Sometimes there's a lull between the moments of destruction, and just when it seems safe to step forward, another wave comes from nowhere. Can't we continue with the way things are now, keeping all that's unsaid between us tucked away? Why do people always want to talk?

"Okay. Whatever, but I've got to go. That hypnosis thing's today."

"Now?"

"Soon."

"Oh. Would you mind if I prayed with you about it, right now over the phone?"

"Um . . . sure."

"Lord, thank you for this opportunity for Kristen to go have her memory jogged about what happened the night she was attacked . . ."

And I've tuned out. I don't have time for this.

After hanging up, I log onto my laptop. Delila's old phone number still doesn't work and I can't find any new listings. But her business website is back up.

I click on her contact page and my fingers hover over the keyboard. Keep it short, Kristen. And don't show all your cards.

I dive in, typing fast. "Wanted you to know I put all the stuff you left behind in storage. Also, I found an envelope in your closet — we need to talk." I include my current cell phone number and ask her to call me as soon as possible.

Before the hypnosis, I'm instructed to write down my recollection of that night at the pub. I scribble down the sketchy details.

Agent Hygleson sits quietly as I'm told to lie next to Jerry the hypnotist, or as he introduced himself, *the mind expert*. White button-up, a red pin-striped tie, and charcoal dress pants creased just-so, his outfit screaming *clean cut*, until my eye meets his espresso hair pulled back into a braid, and forearms bearing the markings of tattoo removal. I can only imagine the image that could have been more regrettable than those scars.

"Let's begin," he says, his words pouring out like warm honey. "Concentrate on the sound of my voice. Relax. Close your eyes. Place your hands at your side. Listen to the sound of my voice. Concentrate on your breath. Your breath should be slow and steady, deep and soothing. You should have no unnecessary fear. You should have no unnecessary anxiety. All you have to do is listen to the sound of my voice . . ."

His words drift, but remain clear. My own voice detaches from my body, as if belonging to someone else, someone who likes to ramble. "Yes, I remember that night at O'Sullivan's. We got a table right away. Nice little one in the corner, tucked away from everyone else — perfect for people watching. We ordered drinks. I had whiskey, straight up. Six or seven of them, maybe a few more."

Jerry redirects my attention. Am I awake, or asleep? I'm sure I can open my eyes and stand whenever I want, but for some reason, the desire isn't there. Or maybe I can't move at all. Jerry pulls on the reins.

"Yes, I can sense everything . . . like I'm inside a movie reel. That awful red glow coming from the bar sconces . . . the hideous abstract wall paintings . . . B.O. pouring out of the dude at the next table . . . and an inscription carved into our wooden table. *Bruno was here. Now he's gone. Your loss.*

"What else do you see?"

"A woman wearing red lipstick and a tight black dress. She's flirting with the bartender. Delila and Legion leave."

Jerry leads me deeper.

"This guy sits next to me. He's got a horrid bent nose, close-set eyes, and thick brows. We're flirting . . ."

My mind blanks. Jerry redirects me.

"Now I'm standing outside the bar. I'm drunk and dizzy, and I'm searching for Delila and Legion. My hair's wet from the mist. I can't see them anywhere.

"Now this guy, Rocko, is standing in front of me and I feel sick to my stomach. My heart's racing. Every moment is dragging. Now I'm fighting with the guy, choking. It's like the air is made of cotton. Or is that from his hands around my neck? I'm trying to make a plan to get free, but my brain isn't working. Wait . . . someone's approaching. The woman with red lipstick. My vision's blurred, but it's definitely her. That red lipstick pierces through the darkness."

"What is she doing?" asks Jerry.

"Standing in the open, staring at us."

"Do you know this woman?"

"No. Rocko sees her. He grins and keeps attacking me. The woman just stands there, watching, not doing *anything*. Why doesn't she do something?"

"Relax," says Jerry. "Listen to the sound of my voice. You're safe. Look around. What else do you see?"

"It's not clear. Brain's fogged and — oh, somebody *help* me."

"What is it, Kristen? What's happening?"

"It's *Victor*. He's the one attacking me."

"Kristen, who's Victor?"

"Victor. *Please* God, no. It's Victor. I can't go through this again. I need to get out of here. Take me out of here! I want out now. Get me out!"

Jerry pulls me out of the hypnosis, he and Agent Hygleson standing at my side. I'm shaking, and my face is hot and swollen, as if I've been sobbing. Jerry calms me with that warm honey voice. He asks for a post-hypnosis report, so I write everything down, this time in excruciating detail.

I remember everything, including a cross hanging on the wall next to a memorial plaque for a fallen officer who used to frequent the pub. I record the sounds of the crowded bar — laughter, flirting, witless banter, and a jilted lover's revenge song whining from the jukebox. I describe the nauseating scents of nightlife — sweat, fruity e-cig vapor, and God only knows what. Everything's in this report, like how I suspected Delila and Legion of snorting cocaine because they returned to the table with red, running noses. I include a description of the woman who wore red lipstick, her straight platinum blonde hair, her sharp cheekbones, and her giant fake lashes. I write about her tattoo — a snake coiled several times around her ankle, extending its head at the center of her calf, mouth open and fangs dripping with blood.

I keep writing. When I get to the part where I'm wrestling with Rocko, while that woman who wore red lipstick stands there like an idiot and does nothing, it happens again. The hideous image of Victor replaces the image of Rocko in my head, and it's as if it *was* Victor. It wasn't him that night at the pub. Couldn't have been. So why does he keep popping up in my mind as I cry and sweat and write?

Jerry's soothing voice calms me down, and I write the part that didn't show up in the hypnosis. This is the piece I have held back from the beginning — the piece that will place Legion at the crime scene. I write how, before I passed out, a tattooed arm flashed before me. Someone trying to help me. The tattoo was clear — blue, yellow, black, red, and orange. A dragon breaking through chains, breathing fire at everyone. A Legion-original design.

I write that the next thing I remembered was waking up in the hospital. Then I set my pen down and explain to Jerry and Hygleson that Victor Dragon is my mother's ex-husband and that I haven't seen him in more than ten years. Victor was not at the pub that night, and I don't know why he showed up in the hypnosis. "Could it be possible that the dragon image on Legion's arm reminded me of Victor?"

"Hmmm," replies Jerry. "Except the tattoo comes after the attack. It's more plausible that the attack triggered a memory from your past. Perhaps it awoke from your subconscious the memory of an event that likely involved Victor, something traumatic that your mind chose to repress."

Jerry and Hygleson stare at me, waiting for me to confirm or deny Jerry's analysis. I do neither.

"Am I finished here? I'm wiped out. I want to go home."

I head straight to Georgina's office. The black and tan furniture and the potted jasmine are as I remember them, but it's like I'm far away from anything familiar. How long has it been since my last visit?

Georgina white-knuckles today's mug, *Psycho Therapist*. Her lips flatten. "Why didn't you tell me you were going under hypnosis? I would have come to support you through it, if only I'd known."

I squint against the sun-lit lemon walls as Georgina chews me out, insisting I contact her next time something this big comes up. But aren't we both hoping something this big *won't* happen again? Georgina's also disappointed that I haven't discovered anything new inside my dreams. My ninety-five bucks would've been better spent on my hair than on therapy. Nothing was accomplished here.

Less than a minute before my session's up. The green light will flick on any second. Delila's mysterious envelope sits on the tip of my tongue, trying to come out. But I can't do it. Georgina would just get mad at me for keeping that from her, too. So I fill the last few seconds with random thoughts, mindlessly strung together.

I'll give Delila a few days to respond, and if she doesn't, I'll have no choice but to tell somebody else.

CHAPTER 29

STILL JULY

⁓✺○

I F ONLY I had never agreed to go under hypnosis. I haven't been able to get Victor off my mind since. He's like a clump of gum stuck to the bottom of my shoe, thick and sticky, mercilessly clinging. I scrape at him with rocks and razor blades, and the persistent clot will not go away.

Victor's anger rumbled through the apartment whenever he and Mom fought. Every now and then, he threw household objects across the room. Dishes, chairs . . . my mother. I can still feel her screams slicing through my skull.

At the first sign of trouble, I'd run down the hall and into my little room on the right. Harley and I hid beneath the bed covers and waited, hoping that when Victor was finished with my mother, he was done for the night.

By the time I was five and a half, I learned how to angle a chair against the doorknob to hold the door shut. Sometimes it worked. Sometimes it didn't, and he came into my room. Why can't I remember anything after that?

During breakfast, I ask Mark about Victor, and he holds onto his fork as if someone's trying to take it away. "Don't worry about him," Mark grumbles.

"Tell me what happened that night."

"Which night?"

"The night you 'got rid' of Victor, whatever that's supposed to mean. I remember coming home wasted from Lilly's house. I remember stumbling into the house and finding Mom sitting alone in the dark, glaring at a sitcom. There was all this broken glass . . . obviously from a fight. I tried to sneak by. All I wanted to do was sleep, but she caught me and said, 'Mark got rid of Victor. He's gone.' She never talked about it again."

Mark's jaw tightens, but he doesn't respond.

"Victor never returned. I've always hoped it meant you capped the scumbag and dumped him into the nearest body of water. But that's not your style." I rest my knife on my plate. "I need to know what happened."

He stares at a fly on the wall. I stare at it, too, my upper lip curling in rebuke of the vile insect.

"Your mother'd had enough," he says. His cheeks redden and he plays with some leftover bacon. "We were discussing a plan for her to leave when Victor came home. There was some yelling. There was a scuffle. Then he went after your mother and I stopped him."

Several seconds of dead silence passes.

"You *stopped* him? That's all you're going to tell me?"

"That's all I care to say."

I add ghost pepper hot sauce to my eggs, slam the bottle onto the table, and look Mark directly in the eye. "Is he still alive?"

"Last time I saw him, he was. Barely. Don't worry, though. He's never coming back."

"How can you be sure?"

"Because he knows if he comes within ten miles of here, I'll kill him." Mark grabs his cane and limps to the counter. He tosses a business card next to my plate. "Nina Graham is a friend of mine, a fellow teacher. She needs her bathroom redone. Call her." Then he limps outside to tend to his garden.

A job? My *first client.*

The landline rings. It's Agent Hygleson, telling me that Legion and Delila have agreed to come in for questioning.

So why hasn't Delila returned my message? It's only been a couple of days. I'll give her a couple more, but that's it.

Hygleson's still talking. He's more open about the investigation, telling me he's followed every plausible lead in the case and he's found nothing regarding the woman who wore red lipstick. No one remembers such a woman from that night at the pub. Not the bartender, barmaids, customers, no one. That explains why hypnosis results are inadmissible in court. Under hypnosis, the brain just makes stuff up.

Hygleson hasn't found any witnesses who remember anyone fitting Victor's description, either. Of course not. How could he? I've already explained that Victor has nothing to do with the case. But Hygleson and

Sharman put their agent skills to work and they *found* Victor. The beast is alive and well and living in Nevada, recently booted off a city council board for excessive absences, and presently employed at a water and sewer plant in Reno.

"But get this." Hygleson lowers his voice. "An engineer from Reno's Department of Water and Sewer was reported missing the same night you were attacked at the pub."

My jaw drops, my lips still burning from the hot sauce.

"I compared photos and dental records, and confirmed that Rocko is actually Jimmy Valentine, a maintenance employee who worked with Victor Dragon. Kristen, your ex-stepfather is now our number one suspect in this murder case."

In the dead of night, my eyes pop open and I see Harley jump off the bed and saunter out of the room. I follow him into the living room, only it's the living room from my past.

A shadow stands near an open window. It's thick, lurking, and Victor-shaped. A sound like a violent wind rushes through the room, affecting nothing. *Nothing* flips, lifts, or moves as the silhouette remains rigid and still.

Then I'm inside another room with glow-in-the-dark moons and stars on the ceiling. My childhood bedroom. The sound of wind rumbles beyond the door, and I dive beneath my bed covers, leaving only my head sticking out as I wait for the shadow to come. Instead, the woman from that night at the pub — or at least, from my hypnosis recollection of that night — stands over me, her red lipstick brighter than ever. She opens her mouth as if trying to speak, but nothing comes out.

I'm back at Mark's house, in my grown-up bed. Another woman appears inside the room. It's my *mother*. She sits on the edge of the bed and leans back on one hand, smiling, all graceful and gorgeous. Then it wafts past me — her lavender hand lotion. It's as if it's really her, sitting next to me here on earth.

She leans in, fiercely calm. "He's coming for you." Her whisper passes through the room like a breeze.

"Who's coming?"

But she's already gone.

"Mom, where'd you go? *Who's* coming?"

No answer. She's vanished into the white mist of my blurry morning vision.

Nights pass and I keep having the same dream. Every morning, I wake up shouting for my mother to respond, but she's already gone.

Chapter 30

Still July

⌒◯

ETHAN STANDS AT my front door with an awkward grin spreading across his face.

I tell Mark I'm leaving, and he raises a wild brow at me.

"What? It's just a ride at the beach."

Not like it's a *date*. It's perfectly normal that Ethan and I are acting like friends, ignoring the fact that we shared a magical kiss one sunrise four months ago. So keep your wiry brow to yourself.

Ethan piles our bikes into the back of his truck. I wince at his hairdo. Way overgrown and swooping in too many directions. Loving the beard, though. He clears poop bags and paperbacks from the seat, and we settle inside.

"Finally," he groans. "We're alone."

We're *just* friends. Did he not hear my thought bubble to Mark? How can I keep my expectations low, when he acts so melodramatic?

Whatever. It's not like I have any other birthday celebration options, especially since Alana left town for work. Or so she said.

Ethan squirms in his seat. "We need to talk."

Seriously? *This* . . . already? We haven't even left the driveway yet.

"But let's get there first," he says as he pulls out onto the street. Then he white-knuckles the wheel and accelerates.

Lunch and essentials crammed into mini backpacks, we hit the strand with our beach cruisers. Seventy-five degree sunshine splashes down on us, while wind whips our hair and waves crash in the distance. The plan is to tackle the South Bay trail from Torrance, through Redondo, Hermosa, and Manhattan Beach — flipping back at Dockweiler, assuming we make it that far. Before we've covered a mile, we've already had to dodge dozens of pedestrians, half of them drunk.

Ethan glances at my brace. "Your ankle going to be okay for the ride?"

"It'll be fine."

"You should let me take a look at that." He keeps his eyes on the path ahead.

All I can manage is a grunt. He's joking, right? No way on earth that's going to happen.

For a minute, we cruise in blissful silence — coconut oil, sweat, and beer invading our senses. Then he clears his throat. "Kristen, I . . . like you."

"I *like* you, too," I reply, sarcasm intended.

He's like a child, so naive and adorable that I want to squish the life out of his cheeks.

"No. I mean, I really, *really* like you."

I laugh devilishly, like a Pheasant. "Then why do you always pull back?"

"I've been going through some stuff, something I've been trying to figure out in my head."

"Oh? Like what?"

"I believe my life has a purpose, a chosen path." His breath is heavy. "And I don't want to waste time following trails that take me off track."

"Okay, now you're confusing me. Can you please explain?"

But I don't really want to hear what he has to say, so I start pedaling as fast as I can. I pedal faster and faster, and I still can't shake him. He passes me and snatches my handle bar. I slam on my brakes and his rear wheel swerves a hundred and eighty degrees, clipping an aging roller-blader. Both of us stop, and Ethan faces me, gripping my bike as if his life depends on it, his cross pendant resting boldly outside his T-shirt.

"What I mean is, when I date it'll be with the woman I intend to marry."

"Excuse me?"

He releases his grip. "I'm trying to explain why I've been acting like a jerk. But it's coming out wrong."

"If you're trying to apologize, then by all means—"

"No." He shakes his head. "It's bigger than that. I want to tell you that I believe we're meant to be together."

Adrenaline jolts through my veins. "What do you mean you *believe*? And why'd you say it like that, like someone would say they *believed* they saw a ghost?"

"It's almost like I did. The summer before we met, I had a vision. Sounds kooky, right? But how else can I describe it? I was crossing a stream, backpacking through the Rockies, and suddenly, I was at a cabin, sitting on a swinging porch bench with an old woman."

He glances around and adjusts his bike, as if our dramatic pause could be less of a boardwalk bottleneck than it already is. "I was old, too," he continues. "I saw it in my arms and hands. I didn't know where I was or who the woman next to me was, but I felt saturated with peace. Then I was back on my hiking trail, crossing the stream."

"Wow. Hallucinate much?"

"It was you, Kristen. The woman was much older than you are now, but it was definitely you. I've known it from the moment we bumped into each other in Mojave and I saw those green eyes."

"Do I sound like that when I tell people about my dreams?"

"I saw what I saw. We were together in old age. We're *meant* to be together."

"That's why you keep calling me? Because you believe you're *supposed* to?"

"No," he chuckles. "But that *is* why I haven't given up."

I prepare to explode, but he throws his hand up like a stop sign "Wait — c'mon, you have to admit that it's not always easy between us. We're drawn to each other, I mean, I keep calling you and you keep answering your phone — but for some reason we also want to wring each other's necks."

If he wasn't right, I'd smack him hard. "So why do you bother? Why should *we* bother? *We like each other, we hate each other* — it sounds dysfunctional. Are we supposed to spend the rest of our lives spinning in circles like this?"

"God keeps bringing us together."

"*You* keep bringing us together."

"We *are* meant to be together. I'm not sure what all this garbage is that keeps causing us to stumble, but I believe my dream. And I don't know . . . maybe the answer is found in love. True, honest love, the kind you and I both crave."

My heart drops into my stomach. *Love.* Like the kind Kierkegaard talks about? Yes, I want that. But wait . . .

"If you believe we're meant to be together, then again, why do you always pull back?"

"Because I was taught that relationships should be equally yoked. And I've been confused by this."

"Say again? In English this time."

"*Unequally yoked* means a difference in faith."

The catch.

"Wow. Are you saying that you and I could really have something here — if only I'd become a *Christian*?"

"That's not what I'm saying at all." His voice is loud and people are staring. How many strand cruisers have passed through our conversation? What shocking glimpses of our display have they caught?

Ethan grips my handlebar. "What I was trying to say was that I've wrestled with two opposing beliefs. I believe I saw you and me together at the tail end of our lives, but I also believe the Bible tells me I shouldn't be with a woman who doesn't share my faith."

"That doesn't seem fair. So exclusionary, don't you think? I mean, what is all this stuff you've been telling me about Jesus, how he's all about love? And didn't you say he reached out to sinners? He must've thought it was worth his time to build relationships with prostitutes and tax collectors."

"Kristen, I couldn't agree with you more. Jesus demonstrated a kind of love that went above and beyond all the laws defined in the Bible. I've spent a lot of time thinking about this, and the more I thought about it, the more confused I got. Then my pastor told me I needed to interpret what's clear over what's vague."

"Oh yeah? So what're you supposed to do when nothing is clear?"

"My pastor insists that Scripture is clear when it advises against pursuing someone who doesn't share your faith. A vision, compared to this, would be considered vague."

I roll my eyes and he rakes back his hair, blowing out his breath.

"Believe me," he says. "I've struggled with this. I've fought and fought with it because the vision was clearer than anything I've known. To me, the vision is what's clear."

People keep streaming past. They're just a blur of varying shades of skin accented with bright, colorful swimwear. I feel the heat of Ethan's stare and I face him again.

"I could spend my whole life trying to figure out what's *right* and what's *wrong*," he says. "But to be honest, I'd rather focus my attention on the moment I'm in. Like right now . . . here we are again, drawn together by whatever force wants us to be together, and yeah, we keep butting heads, but then I look into your eyes and I see something more. It's not something I can explain, but it's like I can see our future together and I can't help myself. I can't walk away from you because I'm falling in love with the person you're meant to be."

"You mean the Christian you *want* me to be."

"No. I mean the Kristen you keep hiding from everyone. The Kristen you won't let anyone else see."

"Who are you to say who I'm supposed to be? That's not a judgment you get to make."

"You're absolutely right. That's not my call. So scratch what I just said. If I'm being honest about how I feel right now, the truth is I'm falling in love with the Kristen sitting in front of me. I love *you*, Kristen, just as you are, right here in this very moment."

I scrape strands of hair away from my face, but it's no use. My fingers keep sticking in the knots. My heart races a thousand miles an hour as Ethan's words jump around in my head, battling my own.

He parks his bike and sits on the low cement wall. I do the same. Traffic flows freely now that we've cleared out from the center. We slump in silence. My eyes roll over an entire flock of beautiful people swooshing past. They all look so perfectly photoshopped, as if they just fell out of a magazine.

Ethan side-glances at me. "You know, I've never been good at sharing God's message. It's a wonder I keep trying. That message changed my life, though, and I guess I want everybody else to have the same opportunity." He crosses his arms. "I've always wanted to fix people. Been doing it since I was a boy. I made it my mission in life. I suppose that's why I chose physical therapy. So I can *fix* people. But people don't always see it as a good thing. Even at work, I run into clients who resist. It's like they don't want to be healed. Either they don't want to put in the work or they don't believe they deserve to be whole. Or maybe it's something else, but it irritates me. It's frustrating when I *know* what will help them and they refuse to give it a try."

"You're talking about me, aren't you? You're such an expert, you're sure you can *fix* me?"

He nods toward the brace. "Regarding your ankle, yeah. If you'd give me half a chance . . . if you'd let me *look* at it, I can reduce your pain. I'm good at what I do." He gazes at the passing crowds. "But with everything else? No. Before I met you, I had all the answers. I'm only now beginning to realize there's so much I don't know." He laughs, mocking himself. "Every relationship should be equally yoked, *and* you and I are meant to be together. I still haven't flushed out the conflict. But I'm done trying to save you simply so we can be together. That's one thing my pastor told me I shouldn't do. Yeah, I still want you to discover Jesus, but that's your decision, not mine. Your faith journey is not something I get to control."

A shiver runs up my spine. "So what're you saying?"

"I want to be with you. I'd like to move forward in our relationship, if that's what you want, too."

My cheeks flush hot. "Um . . . yeah. Yes, that's what I want, too."

Now his cheeks are pink, his smile spreading to his eyes. Then he lifts a brow. "I'm not going to stop talking about God, because that's who I am. But I will stop trying to *save* you." He takes my hand in his. "I'll do my best to listen to you . . . your feelings, your beliefs."

If only I could promise that I'll try to listen to him, too, that I'll try not to be as defensive and hardened and cruel, but all I can do is nod as I squeeze his hand.

Ethan stares at me, his chest heaving as he absorbs my unspoken reply. He leans over, scooping me into his arms. He presses his salty lips against mine and we kiss, traffic streaming past, faded and irrelevant. Our breathing escalates as we both keep pressing harder, neither one of us crying this time. What happened to discernment and good old-fashioned common sense? Have I forgotten that I already have enough to deal with? Ethan says we're supposed to be together, so I jump in? Of course I do, because everything inside my body tingles, telling me this is good and right. Every piece of my soul wants to just sit here and kiss this man forever.

After recovering from the kiss, we picnic in the sand on the other side of the wall. I brought chips, turkey-bacon sandwiches, and Zingers. Ethan brought Corn Nuts and a thermos of strong black coffee. We can't keep our hands off each other. Wiping crumbs off the other's shirt. Tucking hair behind an ear. Leaning on a shoulder, holding and caressing each other's hands. Something's still missing, though. Ethan lives in Colorado, so where are we supposed to go from here? I want to run home, now, and take him into my room. But that would be too forward, yes?

Hang on . . . isn't there a Christian rule about that? Are we going to have to *wait?*

Bright, glimmering silence accompanies our ride back. We never made it past Manhattan Beach, let alone Dockweiler.

"Hey," he blurts, "I keep forgetting to ask if you ever got your old phone back."

"No. Why?"

"So you never read my last text?"

"No. Don't look at me like that. I hated you that night."

"I was an idiot. I'm sorry."

"What makes you think I didn't read it that night?"

"Hygleson told me."

My heart jumps into my throat. "When did you talk to Hygleson?"

"A few days after. He said my message puzzled him."

"Hygleson called you and you never told me?"

He winces. "We've talked several times since."

Great. Ethan and Hygleson are talking behind my back? I pedal faster, but Ethan has no trouble keeping up.

"This sucks, Ethan. You say you want to be in a committed relationship and then *this* comes up. Isn't honesty an important part of a decent relationship?"

"Really?" He laughs.

My pace slows. "Fine. You're right. I haven't always told you everything, either. Not always on purpose, though . . . like the bronze-eyed hobo I keep running into. I haven't told you about him yet, not that I'm trying to keep it secret or anything, it just hasn't come up."

"Huh?"

"Long story. I'll tell you about him later, during the car ride home, 'kay?"

"Sure. But don't you want to know what my last message was about?"

I nod.

"Earlier that day, I had a feeling in my gut that you needed God's protection. My message explained that. I said I'd be praying for you all night."

A chill ripples my skin. Ethan pedals faster, and I follow suit.

I imagine a future with Ethan — bike rides, bonfires, and a lifetime of dog rescues. A soft smile spreads across my face. This dysfunctional relationship might actually work. We're great at kissing, that's for sure.

By the end of our ride, I'm flying so high I almost miss the scowling cloud waiting for us at the parking lot where the day's journey began. Almost.

Dorothy stands next to Ethan's truck — locked, loaded, and ready to fire.

"Slut! What are you doing with my son?"

My adrenaline rush crashes to a screeching halt.

"You don't deserve someone like him, you dirty little whore."

Suddenly, I'm transported to childhood, listening to Victor call me the same names. Then I'm a teenager, breathing fire at the world. And there's Dorothy, her persecution fueling my flames. "Children should obey and respect their parents!" she would scold, and my reply was always the same. "Oh yeah? Well I *should* have had a real mother, not one who was a pathetic drunk for most of my childhood years."

I didn't listen to Dorothy then, so why am I listening to her now? I can't move. The hollering, the red face, the threatening fist. They freeze me, keeping me stuck toggling between the past and now. I barely grasp the image of Ethan restraining his wild, animalistic mother. Everything else melts into an obscure glob.

Ethan remains eerily calm. He tells me to step away and call Wayne, a pastor at his mother's church. He shouts the number over his mother's screams.

As I back away from the scene to make the call, Dorothy screams louder. "That friend of yours, Legion, was on the news today. He's marked by the devil, you know. But the whole thing is your fault. You murdered that man, Kristen. I know you did. You're exactly like that tramp mother of yours. I won't let you near my son."

I struggle to speak over Dorothy's rage, but Wayne catches on quickly. He tells me he and Ethan already have an emergency plan in place, asks for our location, thanks me for calling, and hangs up.

I have to get away from that voice. Away from the sight of Ethan struggling with Dorothy. So I ditch my bike and run toward the water, along the shore, until her wicked shrill fades.

I sit on a ridge of sand and watch children dig an ambitious hole. My shoulders drop at the sound of crashing waves. My pulse slows and I imagine lying inside the mouth of the hole and letting the children cover me up, one scoop of sand at a time.

A young woman wearing a floppy hat and a sheer dress over her bikini pats the head of one of the diggers while scanning me with careful eyes. Ah. The mother, deciding if I'm a friend or foe. I try to smile, but I can't. She nods and then kneels down to dig with her children.

After the hole has doubled in size, Ethan drops down beside me. "Sorry," he mutters, raking his rumpled hair. "My mother's very sick."

I wipe my cheeks on his shoulder and lean on him. Blood droplets seep from scratches on his forearms. Clawed by his *mother*. "Did Wayne take her home?"

"No." Ethan hugs me close. "He came with a medi-van from Clearview Mental Treatment Center. She needs professional help." His face stiffens. "Wayne's riding in the van with Mom, but I've got to go, too, so I can admit her."

"Yeah, okay. I'll be fine. I'll call Mark to pick me up."

"You sure?"

"Yes. Go."

I watch him walk away.

Maybe Dorothy's right. I don't deserve Ethan. He thinks he knows me, but he has no idea what he's getting into. As soon as he's out of sight, I walk up the coastline, leaving my shoes and backpack near the edge of the giant hole. Maybe my stuff will slip in and disappear, and then there will be no trace of me left.

I walk to the nearest empty lifeguard station, about an eighth of a mile away, where I stop and face the water. Urgency wrestles inside my stomach.

The *lure*. My old friend.

In the past, it's been intense. But now, it's consuming. I step forward.

Am I really doing this, in broad daylight, with dozens of witnesses, including children?

Keep moving forward, Kristen.

How can I not?

The lure pulls stronger than ever. It's irresistible.

I step forward until I'm chest deep, slashing each passing wave with my arms, as if the ocean can be subdued. I stare down the horizon and prepare to swim forward. Bring it on, ocean. Bring. It. On.

"Excuse me. Miss?"

It's the mother of the sand-diggers, standing on the shore.

"You left your backpack and shoes. I don't mind watching them for you, except the kids have had it. We need to pack up and head out before someone has a full-blown meltdown."

I can't do it in front of her. And really, not in front of all these people.

It *will* happen, though. Just not today.

I wave and smile at the woman, then exit the water. I grab my stuff, find my bike, and ride.

Calm, empty, and soaking wet, I arrive home and pass the library where Mark's got his head buried in my mother's Bible. *Library's* a stretch. It's little more than a pass-through room fitted with a small sofa and a coffee table. And wall-to-wall shelves packed with anthropology texts, rose and garden books, and a ton of speculative fiction.

"Hey, kiddo." Mark lifts his head, but only for a second before falling back into his reading.

I smile and wave and pass on through, bee-lining to my nightstand drawer where I keep my gun and the pint of jd. I just want to hold the whiskey and cradle it like a newborn child. I crawl into bed with the bottle and stare at the top of the nightstand. The orchid Alana gave me is dead, all the leaves infested with spots. If only I had given the plant more water, or perhaps a little more sunlight. Love? Attention? A stroller ride through the park? What else could it have possibly needed?

I can't fall asleep, so I set the bottle down and grab my laptop. It bleeps the second I log in. Delila replied.

"Sorry I didn't respond sooner. I don't get too many messages from my contact page. All my clients call or text. Anyway, yikes . . . I can understand why you might be freaked out by the envelope, assuming you opened it. Did you? I'm afraid you probably did. I can explain, and I want to, but I need to do it in person. Legion and I will be in Redondo Beach next week. Let's meet for lunch. Just don't do anything with the envelope until we meet, okay? You'll understand once I explain."

Are you kidding me? She *does* know about the envelope. I can no longer deny her involvement, but what *was* her involvement, anyway? And who's the creep who sent it?

It's hard to believe, but I actually want to fall into my recurring dream — anything to get away from reality. And assuming I have the newest one, I'll get to visit my mother, see her face and inhale her lavender-scented lotion.

If only I could visit her outside of my dreams and tell her I'm sorry. For everything. If only we could have a real conversation. I'd tell her about all the craziness with Ethan and Dorothy and Delila. And I'd tell her that if I don't walk into the ocean soon, I will lose my mind.

CHAPTER 31

AUGUST

❧

ETHAN PLANS TO keep working in Colorado for a couple more months; so apparently, we'll be dating from afar. How long can we keep this up?

It's not so bad, I suppose. We talk all the time on the phone, like teenagers, except I'm not as obnoxious as I was back then.

Ethan keeps urging me to discuss my ocean lure with Georgina. I keep insisting the urge has faded since the day I confessed to him. I haven't told him I almost walked in, the day his Mom freaked out on me, and I'll never confess that the urge to walk into the Pacific is more unbearable than ever. And why should I? Talking about it will only make it worse, like when I told him about the bottle of whiskey I keep in my drawer.

"Why would you hold on to that?" he'd asked.

I *don't know*, okay? Maybe I'm trying to prove to myself I can have the JD nearby and still choose not to drink it. Maybe I'm grasping a sense of control, a belief that *I'm* the one who will make the next move. But how can Ethan understand any of that?

I keep trying to recall all the specifics of our traffic-stopping conversation on the strand. Did I agree to let Ethan talk about his faith at will? He finds a way to slip God into *every* conversation now, and he never hangs up before praying. He means well, but can't he see how annoying he is? I get that spiritual journeys are important, but frankly, I can list a hundred other issues I'd rather focus on than my spirituality. Like my business — one solid client and growing. Nina Graham liked my proposal so much that she referred me to a friend. If I need to pour my attention into *anything*, it's work. Faith won't pay my bills.

Ethan never lets up with the Jesus talk, though, and I'm beginning to understand the difficulty with an *unequally yoked* pair. How can two animals, reined at different lengths, be able to move a cart without pinching or choking each other to death? With any luck, this religious campaigning will fade over time. If it doesn't, I might have to sever my end of the yoke.

Today, Ethan dives right in. "Have you opened your Bible lately?"

"To be honest, I haven't felt led in that direction." *Led*, ha. Ethan's spewing out so much Christianese, I'm starting to use it against him.

"What do you mean?" He is undaunted.

"I mean that every time I search for answers, it only leads to more questions."

"Can you give me an example?"

Ugh.

"Take the bulk of media headlines. Earthquakes, war, children sold for profit — things like that. What gives, Ethan?"

"None of this is new," he replies simply.

"Yeah. But why does all this awfulness exist? Why do we have to live like this?"

Ethan and I can go on like this forever. If only he would give up already. My resistance only fuels him. I attack him with questions, and immediately, the sound of flipping pages emanates from the phone.

"Suffering can destroy a person," he says, triumphantly, "or it can build character, perseverance, and hope. Would you rather be a slave to suffering, or a slave to hope?"

"Ethan, I'm a big fan of *hope*, but I don't understand why everything in my life, everything in the world for that matter, is jacked up. I want to reach for hope, but I can hardly see it through all the evil and pain."

"I know," he says softly, his recent zest fizzling. "This is a subject that has haunted me, too. It's hard to imagine there's a God who cares about us when we're surrounded by so much pain. I really wrestled with this after our ride down Mammoth Mountain. One of your comments struck a nerve. I claimed I could see God in the landscape, and you just glared at me and said flat out that you could look directly into the center of beauty and not see God. Then you said, if I remember correctly, 'Beauty happens and ugliness happens, too. And sometimes friends die and innocent children are hurt. It just happens. Nothing can explain it away.'"

He pauses and breathes into the phone for a few seconds.

"That comment wrecked me," he continues. "I couldn't think of anything else, so I approached one of my buddies at the men's retreat that night and told him I was confused. I admitted to him that it was easy for me to see God in beauty, but sometimes impossible to find God when everything is dark.

"And Zack gave me a funny, knowing smile, like he was just waiting for someone to ask him that exact question. Then he asked me, 'Are you looking for God inside affliction?' And he let that question hang in the air for a bit, and then shook his head *no*. 'God's not inside the concave stomach of a starving child,' he said. 'He's at the boy's side, inside the breath that comes from the mother's lips as she prays over her son. God's in the friends, family, and strangers who leave their comfort zones to come to the starving boy's aid. He's in the unexpected turn of events that few would *dare* to call a miracle, even when no other term could apply.'

"Then Zack got real quiet and he stared at me. His face was all red and he was shaking. Zack had just returned from a mission trip to the slums of Kibera, one of the largest and poorest slums of the world, so the reality of suffering was fresh on his mind. He *felt* the words he was saying. I felt them, too, and while we were standing there, I remembered one of God's promises—that *nothing* is irredeemable. And it struck me that God can be found inside the hope of knowing this . . . that our suffering is never for nothing, that Jesus *died* to give us eternal life. And, I mean, that's the whole point of our existence . . ."

And I fade out.

He had me for a minute there, but then he went flying way over my head. He gets so ramped up that there's no stopping him. I just keep letting him yap as I listen in now and then. It's like I'm rubbernecking at a fatal accident and can't look away. That rising inflection, bursting with conviction. Gets me every time. But I still don't remember giving him this much freedom to speak.

Famished, I sit at a table inside the Riviera Grill, hoping Ethan gets here soon.

A week's already passed since Dorothy's meltdown. My, how time flies when you're trying to digest a psycho-freak encounter. But thank you, Dorothy. Because of you, Ethan will be returning for frequent visits, and he'll be here today to help me face Delila and whatever explanation she has for that envelope. So yeah, Dorothy, thanks for losing your mind.

I order a Diet Coke and play with my menu. I keep trying to read the entrees, but I can't sit still long enough to concentrate.

Outside the window, across the street, a homeless man leans forward. His body is bent ninety degrees as he pulls against the weight of his possessions piled high on the wagon behind him. It's not the bronze-eyed hobo, but a different weary soul.

A woman flies across the street, heading for the restaurant. Chick's unfamiliar, so why has my throat gone dry? Hair bleach-blonde, and those lips . . . *she* would never wear lipstick that bright red. But those exotic brows . . .

I break into a cold sweat and hide my face behind the menu. She's early and Ethan's not here yet. Pull yourself together, Kristen. This is your chance to finally get some answers.

The doorbell jingles. She's inside.

"De-li-la."

She spins, a fresh tattoo coiled around her upper arm. A snake, much like the one on the red lipstick woman from the pub, or rather, from the hypnosis and my dreams. But Delila can't be the dream/hypnosis woman who wore red lipstick. This tattoo is on her arm, and the other woman's was on her ankle. And it's *Delila*, for crying out loud. A daytime night-mare, yes; the red lipstick woman, no way.

I force a smile. "Did Legion come, too?"

"Of course." Her sapphire eyes darken. "He was strongly advised to return."

"Right." My cheeks flush. Legion's no longer a primary suspect, but Hygleson still has questions for him. Delila and Legion must be going through hell, but then again, so am I.

Her red lips tighten as she plops into my booth and picks up a menu. "He's parking the car."

The bell jingles again as Legion bursts through the door, strutting taller and more forceful than ever.

Hurry up, and get here, Ethan.

Delila waves him over, her coiled snake flashing in my face. That lip-stick . . . she's never worn that color. And that tattoo, reminding me of the scenes at the end of my dream. *He's coming.* Could Mom have meant Legion? How could that be, and why would Mom be smiling about it?

Legion slides in without a word. He leans against the backrest and places his arm around Delila. "Waitress. A pitcher of brew."

Great. Like I want Ethan to walk in and see me chugging beer in the middle of the day.

The waitress fills three glasses. I let mine sit while the newlyweds drain theirs.

"What, you don't drink now?" asks Legion.

I make up an excuse, that my stomach is too upset to drink, which isn't entirely untrue. I'm not going to sit here and get drunk. Legion and Delila refill their glasses and order a second pitcher. The beer washes away Legion's composure.

"I didn't kill him." He scowls.

"I never said you did."

"You sure didn't tell the cops I'm innocent."

"I told Hygleson I didn't know what happened."

"I saved your *life*." Beer and spit slip through his teeth.

"Like I don't know that? Legion, I was unconscious. How could I have known what happened? Then you guys took off. You *never* called me."

"*You* never called us."

"Your phone numbers don't work. And by the way, I only reported what I saw. What was I supposed to say?"

"How about that you know me, and you're sure I would never kill somebody."

Jingle. Ethan, thank God. Dang, he cleans up good, fresh cut, high-lights, and all. He strides over and takes Legion's hand in a firm shake. "How are you, man? We've been worried."

They embrace, short and strong. Legion's eyes moisten. Delila and I wipe our eyes, too. Why didn't *I* embrace these two? Oh yeah, because I'm still trying to figure out whether or not Delila's trying to kill me.

Ethan slides in next to me and I inhale that fresh, clean scent of his. If only we could be anywhere else but here.

The four of us place our order to share piles of crispy tacos and spicy shrimp fajitas, and Ethan asks for coffee. We agree on the tolerable weather and then dive head first into a concrete wall in the conversation. Ethan stares at the full glass of beer sitting in front of me until mercifully, Legion downs it whole.

I try to read the scowls on Legion and Delila's faces. Ethan gazes out the window. Everybody's got something to say, and nobody wants to say it. We're all killing time — Legion pounding beer, Delila rubbing the rim of her glass, Ethan tapping a hole through the top of the table. And me, wiping a sweat mustache that will not go away.

"Listen," I blurt. "I should've tried harder to get in touch. I know you saved me, Legion. I can't remember much from that night, but I've always known if it hadn't been for you, I'd be dead right now."

Delila and Legion glance at each other, and in unison their faces soften. I've said the right thing, but now it would be a good time to bring up the envelope. If only I could stop dripping with sweat.

Ethan leans toward Legion. "What *did* happen that night?"

I wring the life out of my hands.

Legion smirks. "Kristen got tanked, and she sorta hooked up with that Rocko guy."

My heart jumps into my throat. I glance at Ethan, whose sight is set dead ahead. He tightens his massive jaw, his neck muscles jutting out in stiff lines.

"Delila and I hung back to let them have some space. When we came back to check on Kristen, that guy was shoving her into the side of the building. I didn't hesitate, man. Just jumped in. Like I told the cops . . . what else could I do? I pounded on him. It was weird, man; I flashed back to my combat days and got a little crazy. He got messed up pretty good, but he was breathing when we left. We called the cops, too, and Hygleson verified all that. He kept asking me if I owned a Bowie. Apparently, that was the murder weapon. I don't own a knife like that." Legion wipes his bald head with a napkin, his hand shaking.

"We freaked out," adds Delila, rubbing her coiled tattoo. "Legion had to start his new job in Vegas the next morning and we didn't want to spend all night dealing with the cops, so we dropped Kristen off at the hospital and took off."

The waitress delivers our food and before anyone can touch their plate, Ethan thanks Legion for saving my life and then he makes us hold hands while he prays over our food. Bizarre can't begin to describe the moment. We must all be famished because for the next several minutes, there's more chomping and choking on Tapatío sauce than conversation.

I adjust my plate, fork, and knife. Then I clear my throat to break the silence. "Legion. I want to apologize again. I admit there was a time when I wasn't sure whether you killed that guy . . . by accident, self-defense, or whatever. Now I'm sure you didn't do it and I hope we can put that behind us because right now I need to address a different issue. Delila," I face her directly, "I need an explanation for that envelope."

She winces, and then leans in and grabs my hand. "You know I would never do anything to hurt you, right?"

"Actually, no. I don't know that. I mean, you know what's inside that envel—"

"Did you bring it with you?"

"No!"

She leans back and scratches her head as if it were suddenly infested with lice. "I didn't do it, Kristen. I never touched your car. I called him and said he had to do it himself, that I wasn't going to help him anymore."

"Who's *him*? Who sent the envelope?"

Her face goes pale as she shakes her head. "You don't understand. You couldn't possibly understand the control he had over me."

She turns her pleading eyes toward Legion, and he grips his mug handle tight. "It's okay, babe. Just tell her."

Delila crunches up her napkin and stares into her lap. Then her eyes dart frantically around the room and out the window, left, right, and left again. She looks up at me, her eyes wide and wet. "It was Victor. He sent the envelope."

"No," whispers Ethan. He takes my hand in his.

"What do you mean, *Victor* sent it?"

"Your ex-stepdad is dangerous, Kristen. You need to be careful."

My heart skips a beat and my throat clenches around unspoken words. Delila nudges Legion and he slides out, dropping cash on the table.

"Wait, where're you going? I have more questions."

Delila slides out. "I've already said too much." She glances out the window again. "I've got to go."

"But I don't understand. How do you *know* Victor?"

She stares at me, her eyes as dark as night. "I can't explain that right now. I've really got to go." She leans over the table. "I came here to tell you to watch your back. There's so much more to this than you can imagine."

Then she and Legion dash out of the restaurant, leaving me with my jaw on the table. So that's how Delila knew about my awful childhood — she knew Victor. But how? She couldn't possibly have slept with him, right?

I look up at Ethan. "At least now I know I'm not crazy. Someone *has* been watching me. Victor." I laugh, nervously.

Ethan orders another cup of coffee and wraps his arm around me.

I lean into him and he starts to pet my hair

"Alana's going to freak when she finds out she was right about Delila all along. Ethan, Sergeant Hygleson needs to see that envelope."

"Yep. The sooner, the better."

CHAPTER 32

SEPTEMBER

❧

Wow. Alana's finally coming through with her promise to take me to lunch for my birthday. Only two months late.

"Andrue went out to the garden. He wants to pick Mark's brain about roses, I'm sure." Alana throws her hands up. "All of a sudden, Andrue's interested in flowers."

Why did she bring him? Are they a package deal, now that they're married? We've hardly spoken since that weird episode at the hospital when she had a meltdown in front of me. Sure, we've talked, but we haven't really *talked*.

She scans the room and picks up a textbook sitting on the table. "*Anthropology: A comprehensive humanistic scientific study of the origins and cultural studies of man.* Riveting." She tosses the book on the couch, turns to me, and winces as if in pain. "How about we erase everything we said to each other when you were in the hospital and start fresh?"

"Sounds good to me."

"Sorry I've been off, lately. It's just . . ." She brushes her hair out of her face and sighs. "Marriage is more difficult than I imagined." She points her finger at my face. "If you tell anyone I said that, I'll deny it. But I hate Andrue's medications. They turn him into an extra for *The Walking Dead*."

"Wasn't Andrue like this when you first met him — reflective and calm?"

"Yeah, that was before he went off his meds. And I liked that version of him. I did. But I enjoyed the charismatic, off-meds version of him more. He was always entertaining."

Yeah, bipolar's a blast. Especially when the sufferer flies into a rage and traps you in a stairwell.

"So I guess this would be a good time for me to tell you I told you so about Delila?" She smiles devilishly. "I just *knew* it. I'm a pretty good judge of character. But I'd never have guessed that she was partnering with Victor."

I curl my upper lip and shake my head. "I still can't believe it. I mean, Legion saved my life. It doesn't add up."

"Yeah ... but you know for sure that Victor's really after you, right? Aren't you freaked out?"

"Of course, but I'm not going to run and hide. I'm careful when I go out, and you know Mark." I spread my arms out wide. "He's got alarms, sensor lights, and surveillance cameras throughout the house and in the backyard. He's also got electric wiring lining the back fence. I'm not even sure if that's legal, but one thing's for sure. This place is a fortress."

"Any news on the investigation?"

"Yeah. Hygleson tells me everything now that he knows I'm not lying to him anymore. He and Sharman found a box full of props and costumes in Victor's apartment, including a blond wig, and an old lady wig and dress."

"No way ... the hit and runs! It was him, both times, dressed in costume?"

"That's what it looks like. And Legion and Delila are still missing. They never showed up for their meeting with Hygleson, and now they're nowhere."

"Looks like *they* ran and hid."

Mark walks in with a giant, goofy grin on his face, with Andrue following close behind.

"You two done looking at flowers?" Alana slides her arm into Andrue's. "Can we go eat now, before Kristen has one of her food deprivation episodes?"

"Sure," says Andrue, "but first ... uh ..."

Mark glances past Alana and then locks his eyes on mine. "Steve wants to know if we're interested in coming to church with him this weekend."

I can feel my eyes rolling up past my eyebrows. How many times do we have to say no before Steve gives up?

"Andy said he'd like to come, too." Mark slaps Andrue's back. "How 'bout it, the five of us charge the steeple this Sunday?"

"It's *Andrue*." Alana balls her hands into fists. "He hates when people call him Andy."

"Nah, it's all right, babe. What do you say, should we do it?"

Alana's mood flips from light to darkest dark black as she works to control her breathing. What an astounding demonstration of how years of private yoga lessons can prevent someone from blowing fire out of her nostrils.

"Sure. Why not." She clutches her stomach and faces Andrue. "But I'm not feeling great at the moment. Maybe we can postpone lunch until another time?"

"Of course," he says. "Kristen won't mind, right?"

Oh, so all of a sudden, nobody cares if my blood sugar crashes?

Whatever. I need to check on Nina's bathroom, anyway. I can't take my eyes off those tile contractors for a second. Is it even possible to find good help anymore?

Early Sunday morning, we arrive at Seaside Christian Church. The building is modestly dressed in beige stucco and simple stained-glass windows. Not intimidating at all. But we're far from any visible body of water, so *Seaside* is a bit of a stretch.

Steve leads us inside and past row after row until finally he directs our ragtag group into benched seating in the middle section. Hold on. This is *way* too close to the front. What's wrong with that empty bench a few rows back? Is he really going to make us sit *here*, next to these beaming strangers?

Yes. Yes he is.

I settle stiffly into my seat. Everyone's wearing casual attire. A heads-up would've been nice. Even Alana's comfortably dressed in her maxi skirt, flip-flops, and tee. How did she know? My trousers and starched blouse couldn't scream *outsider* any louder if they tried.

A live band spreads across the stage and the lead singer tells us it's time to stand. Then the band comes to life — guitar picks flying, singers belting, and a Plexiglas-encaged drummer banging away. Everyone else is bouncing, clapping, and singing like it's the most natural and ordinary thing to do. They've all done this before. Except for those of us who haven't, like Mark and Andrue, who stand rigid with their arms hanging loose at their sides, and Alana and me, clutching the bench in front of us. I hang on tight as the next two songs pass, the high ceiling creating acoustics I can feel — vibrating in my stomach and thumping in my chest. Then there's a rote greeting ritual, forcing me into clammy handshakes and my best fake smile, as sweat rolls down my back and I try to hide beneath my own skin. Then finally, we're allowed to sit again.

Ahh, phase one complete. I clasp my hands tightly in my lap, bracing myself for whatever brimstone and hellfire might come next.

The pastor struts onto the stage, a chain dangling from his belt loop and a brilliant smile sweeping across his face. "Hello, Seaside Church! Delighted to see you here."

Oh, that's right. Mom's pastor isn't Charlton Heston playing an angry Moses. It's Carl the aging biker, rockin' a short-sleeved button-down and faded blue jeans. Someone needs to talk to him about his wardrobe. Maybe explain how the color wheel works. A bright lime shirt with that red hair? Honey, those tones don't even get along, much less go together.

"If you have a Bible on you," he says. "I'd like to invite you to turn to Hebrews chapter 10. Or you can follow along with the sermon notes in your bulletin."

Sermon notes, sermon notes, sermon notes . . . here it is: *Freedom from the Cycles of Guilt and Shame.*

What the . . . ?

"When I was in Cuba," begins Carl, smoothing out his goatee, "I talked with some of the people who are planting new churches there. They told us they're frequently hassled by officials. Sometimes they're imprisoned. It's a bad scene, man. *Cray-zee* stuff is happening there. But I want you to know that these friends of ours are hardcore. They're faithful and persistent, and the church is alive and well, and it's beginning to thrive in Cuba."

Oh, this is about Cuba. Good. I can relax.

Carl glances at his notes, and then stares into the audience. "I spent a lot of time listening to the stories of these church planting friends. They told me about how they're going from town to town and sharing the love of Jesus. And they told me about miracles that are happening as they do this, like this one story. Now just try to go with me on this and let your mind wrap around it, if you can.

"They told me about a schizophrenic woman who came to faith, and when she was baptized, the people around her witnessed a *demon* coming out of her. I'm talking *cray-zee* stuff happening in Cuba!"

Yeah, cray-zee.

"During this trip, I also met a man named Javier, and I asked him to share his story with me. He choked up as he told me he was ashamed and embarrassed. Through a translator, and with tears streaming down his face, Javier told me he was in prison for fifteen years for murdering his own mother. Then Javier stood there and cried."

Carl pauses for a sip of water, allowing us time to chew on how it could be possible for Javier to go on living after killing his own mother, I suppose.

A woman approaches our row and scans it up and down. A latecomer. There's plenty of room on our bench, if only someone would move their purse to the floor. Fine. I'll move mine. She can sit next to me and help me blend in since she's dressed oppressively, too. Of course, *she's* probably eighty-five. The woman smiles and sidesteps over.

Carl clears his throat. "It wasn't until after Javier got out of prison, that he found Jesus. But he didn't just find Jesus. He found a God who loves him and pursues him. A God who could redeem and restore him, a God who . . ."

Oh my holy perfume tornado. What is this lady wearing . . . some kind of musk oil she found in an old trunk? I cover my nose as discretely as I can as Carl's inked arms come to life, his voice rising as his arms move faster.

"And when this happened, Javier was overwhelmed, and he was like, 'Other people need to know and experience this.' And so he told other people, and a church sprang up. And he kept telling more and more people, and now Javier is in the middle of planting his third church.

"As he told me all this, he wept. And I looked at him and said, 'Bro, you are the Apostle Paul. Paul was a murderer who came to Christ and began starting churches.' And Javier, still choked up, whispered, 'Gracias. Gracias.'"

Wait — who's Paul?

Carl steps away from the podium and sets his eyes on me. Right on *me!* Suddenly, the wooden bench feels like cement. I try to shift in my seat, but there's really no room left for adjustment.

"I wonder . . ." Carl says, and then pauses, his brows furrowing softly. "How many of us here today are walking around with guilt and shame from decisions we've made and the consequences that have happened in our lives?"

Wait — what? When did this become about *us*? I thought we were talking about Cuba. And Cubans, like Javier. Let's talk some more about Javier. Or Paul. Tell me more about that guy.

Carl grins. "I see a lot of wide eyes out there and if I were still a gambling man, I'd bet many of you are thinking I'm talking directly to YOU."

What the—?

"You bet I am!" He holds his elbows wide and thrusts his chest out, mocking macho anger as he scans the audience. Laughter erupts and he raises his hand to settle it. "Yes, I am talking to you — you who are walking around with guilt and shame strapped to your back. But don't freak out, because you're not alone. We've all been there." He takes a moment to smooth his goatee. "You might find this hard to believe, but even *I* have felt guilt and shame."

Someone laughs out loud and he looks right at her. "It's true!"

More laughter. He lets this eruption run its course as he flips through pages in his Bible. Then he continues. "If you have a Bible, please turn with me to Hebrews . . ."

He's coming.

What? Who said that?

No one else heard it. Everybody's captivated by soft-spoken but sometimes excitable Carl, the man in the lime green shirt who goes on and on as if those words weren't spoken.

Were they?

Mom, was that you? Are you here?

No, no, no. You can't be. I'm going crazy, that's all. *Cray-zee.* Like the stuff happening in Cuba. Too crazy to be true. Miracles happening as people come to faith? Pfsht! Mom believed in Jesus, and she *died* from cancer. I'm happy for all the Cubans who saw miracles after they accepted Jesus, but Jenna and Danielle converted, too, and the next thing you know, they were killed by a texting driver. And I mean c'mon, did people *really* see a demon coming out of that schizophrenic woman?

Ack! What's touching my neck? Oh, just sticky little fingers. Whew, it's only an energetic toddler behind me.

Alana side-sneers at me for fidgeting. What. Ever. I fan my face with my sermon notes. The heat and musk are killing me. I need to eat. How long do these things run?

". . . So the problem with trying to sacrifice over and over again, is that the sacrifice is not complete. Something is still missing."

Uh oh, what am I missing? *Ugh.* Something about sin, sacrifice, offerings, guilty conscience . . . blah, blah, blah. Yes, it's a treacherous cycle and we can't seem to get ourselves out of it. Okay, got it. Let's move on.

Sticky fingers again. On my collar this time.

"Sorry," whispers an anxious voice from behind. "I'm out of wipes."

I dig into Alana's clutch. She's always got wipes. Her nose flares and her posture stiffens. Ha! She wants to admonish me for squirming, but Carl's locked in on her and she doesn't want to be caught looking away. Probably not even listening, but she won't turn her head. I could dump the entire contents of her purse on the floor and she wouldn't budge. I reach a wipe sheet behind me and it's taken with a whispered, "Thank you."

" . . . what happens often," continues Carl, "is that when we sin, we feel like a turn-off to God. We think, I did this thing, I made this choice, I was rebellious toward God. I pushed away from holiness, and as a result, God has turned his back on me . . ."

Man, I really need to eat. Do I have anything in my handbag? A power bar, some gum. Almonds, that'll do.

"This is exactly what happened with the first man and woman, when they were rebellious and chose to go against the good that God had established for them. Adam and Eve essentially said . . ."

Hmm. I think I'd rather hear stories about real people, like Javier and Paul. Wait — was Paul a real person? I can't believe the guy two seats down is scrambling to take notes. There's practically no white space left on his handout. Is that really necessary?

" . . . But did God turn from them? No. God pursued them . . ."

I wonder if Mom took notes when she listened to Carl. Or did she just sit and stare at him with a goofy smile plastered on her face like the musky old lady sitting next to me? But it's really not that awful here. I love the high, arched ceilings, and the long stained-glass windows are gorgeous in their simplicity. I wouldn't mind having that warm, colorful light pouring into my bedroom.

Carl stops for water. He hooks his thumbs into his jeans pockets and saunters across the stage, rubs his forehead, and saunters back. Did he forget what he was going to say next?

"But what Hebrews says," he blurts with surprising volume, "is that when Jesus offered the ultimate sacrifice, he offered one sacrifice for all time and for all sin, and he sat down — HE SAT DOWN. He clocked out his timecard, shed his greasy work clothes, and put on his relaxed evening wear . . . you know, those shredded jeans that are a size too big and that shirt that looks like you've worn it every day since your mid-twenties because you have?"

Carl pauses thoughtfully. "If you're here today and you feel like you just keep riding that nasty cycle of guilt and shame, I want you to know that you can find your center of gravity in Jesus. You can stop all that tail-spinning today. And I don't know about you, but I want to flee from that old scene. I want to stop living like I have to strive to get it together. Stop living like I'm not enough. Because *he sat down*. You don't have to let guilt and shame push you away . . ."

I'm going to need a nap after this. He seems to be repeating himself. If Carl has even the slightest grasp of common decency, he'll wrap this up soon . . . wait, everyone's bowing their heads.

Carl finishes his prayer and walks off stage. I try to clear my head while the band plays another unfamiliar song. Ushers pass around collection bags. Put some money into a bag. Easy-peasy. We're on a downhill slide, now.

A woman in shorts and a tee walks up to the front. "Now we've come to the time of communion. Ushers will pass around some trays, and together, we'll take the crackers and the juice while we pray. This is for anyone who has a personal relationship with Jesus."

I sneak a quick look around. I've got a sickening feeling I'm going to be the only one refusing the crackers and juice. Sweat rolls down my back. Curse my impractical clothing. The trays filter through the rows and my heart races. *Everyone* takes the stuff. Seriously? You *all* have a relationship with Jesus? Wait, I'm not alone. Mark might take it. He's been reading the Bible a lot, so I wouldn't be surprised if he did. But Alana and Andrue?

No way. For sure, Alana will stick by my side. And if it happens that the cups are spiked with cyanide, we'll be the only ones able to walk away.

Steve takes a cracker bit and some juice and passes the trays to Mark, who passes them to Andrue without taking anything. Fascinating. Andrue hands them directly to Alana and she takes her time to select the largest serving of each. Andrue's jaw drops. I sweep the trays over to the smelly old woman like they're made of hot burning metal and keep my head turned away from Alana. I can't even look at her. What a *liar!*

Several excruciating minutes later, and it's done. Finally over. I can't escape the suffocating building fast enough. When I reach outdoors, my breath escapes from my lungs as if watchful eyes are pressing against me. But no one's looking at me. No one's acting suspicious. Blue skies sparkle above, as a surging mass of strangers spills into the lot ahead.

CHAPTER 33

OCTOBER

T HE EVENING ROLLS in warm, but I slip on my new winter pajamas, anyway. Did Mother Nature not get the memo about October's arrival? Enough with the skimpy sundress weather — bring on the freeze.

Who am I kidding? It's never cold in California. But it's torture to have to watch all my warm clothing sit in the dresser, rotting from lack of use. So I put the thick pajamas on, then I beg Mark to crank up the air conditioner.

"Sorry, kiddo. Bad for the environment. Bad for the wallet."

I shuffle back to my bedroom and open the door to the garden, allowing the cool night air inside. Hygleson keeps warning me to be careful, but Mark insists that Victor would be dead before he got within fifty feet of our house. "So go ahead and open your door," he says. "Even if Victor does come here, no way he's getting in. The house and backyard are secure."

It sure is. Cameras, lights, alarms, and illegal electric wiring. And water, ammunition, and fifty-pound bags of beans, rice, and flour filling the shelves of Mark's pantries. Every room in the house contains a flashlight, a loaded gun, and a first aid kit with a two-man food ration. We're prepared for anything. I've no doubt Mark's little fortress is the most secure quarter-acre in the city.

So I let the stinkin' door hang open and I soak in the cool. Then I plop onto my bed and turn on my laptop. There's no message from Delila, and her website is down again. So I click over to my personal project photo gallery. Thankfully, I have clients to keep me distracted from all the craziness swirling around me.

Nina Graham loves her bathroom. Why wouldn't she? It's gorgeous, with that white penny tile floor, and the rest done in cool, modern blues. But how am I going to get all the final touches done? Baseboard, crown molding, finding another one-of-a-kind mirror to replace the one clumsy Enrique dropped and broke.

Can I really do this? Succeed as an independent contractor? Maybe today I'll just concentrate on my proposal for Nina's friend's patio. Sketching ideas for a new project is way more fun than wrapping up an old one.

Alana calls. "Any news from Hygleson? Has he found Victor or Delila?"

"No word on either of their whereabouts, but he did find something new. Emails Victor deleted but were still sitting in his recycle bin. It looks like Victor hired Valentine to "get" me that night at the pub, but the details are unclear because they were communicating in code."

"You've got to be freaking out."

"I'm trying not to, so can we talk about something else?"

Without missing a beat, she launches into a brag-fest about how much money she's making. I get it. You're successful. Next subject?

"How's married life?" I ask.

"Fine."

"*Fine?*"

"Yeah. Usual stuff. By the way, thanks a *lot* for dragging us to church the other day. It's all Andrue talks about anymore. He picked up a flier for their Celebrate Recovery program. He's convinced he has an alcohol problem, which is ridiculous. I mean, he doesn't drink any more than *I* do . . . whatever. If it makes him happy, I'll roll with it. But if he tries to bring that Jesus nonsense into my house, there's going to be hell to pay."

I glance at my Bible sitting on the dresser top. "Some of it's kind of interesting, don't you think?"

"No. I don't."

I grab the Bible and flip to the Scripture that popped out at me the time I tried to throw the Bible away. "'Yet when I surveyed all that my hands had done and what I had toiled to achieve, everything was meaningless, a chasing after the wind, nothing was gained under the sun.'"

Silence pierces the receiver. I close the book, regretting what I've done.

Alana's voice comes in low and slow. "Are you throwing *Scripture* at me?" Her pitch rises. "You don't know the first thing about the Bible, so don't you dare shove that crap in my face. Kristen, you are naive. So *susceptible.* You hear or read something, and that becomes your new reality. I will *not* buy into it. At my funeral procession, I want you to blast AC/DC's *Highway to Hell*. Let the neighbors' windows rattle for all I care, because once I'm inside that final padded case, nothing else will matter. *Now* matters, and I can handle the present on my own, thank you very much. I know what makes me happy, and while I'm still breathing, I plan on getting as much of it as I can. You can act like a mindless sponge if you want, but don't you *dare* tell me what to do."

"Okay. Sorry. It struck me . . . that's all. Whatever. Can we forget about it?"

She blows into the phone. "Already forgotten. But listen, I've got to go."

And *poof*. Our conversation's over.

No longer in the mood to work on my proposal, I dial Ethan. At least he'll let me express myself. If only he didn't keep finding ways to sneak God into the mix. But the moment I bring up Victor, *wham!* He does it again.

"Yes, Victor's dangerous and it's pretty scary to think about how much he's been involved in everything that's been going on, but don't make Victor your focus. I mean, sure, you need to be careful, but don't let him become a distraction that leads you away from your path toward God."

"Ethan, *everything* can't be about God. And what makes you sure my path leads to Him in the first place? You're pressuring me. Didn't you promise to stop trying to save me?"

"Sorry. I'll stop. So how'd you like your mom's church?"

Can he hear himself? He won't stop, even when he says he's going to stop.

"I've already told you."

"Tell me again."

Wait . . . all the backyard lights just came on. Now the motion sensor alarm.

"Hold on."

I toss the phone on the bed and within seconds, I'm stepping outside with my loaded Ruger in a two-handed grip in front of me, the safety released. Barefoot, I'm squinting against the blasts of lighting as I move ninja-style through the grass. I scan left and right and see nothing. Then a *snap*, and a *crunch*. I twist around, stopping short of pressing the trigger.

Oh, thank goodness. It's only the neighbor's cat.

The Bombay comes out from a bush and leaps over the fence, deftly avoiding the lines of electric wiring. The motion sensors are supposed to be "pet-friendly," ignoring anything weighing less than forty pounds. But this cat likes to climb up the garden trellis and bat at the sensor, which sets it off. Third time she's done it this week.

Mark charges outside, his shotgun aimed. "Hold your fire." I raise my handgun in the air. "It's only Sugar."

"I figured," he says, standing at ease, his cane beneath one armpit and a stack of mail beneath the other. "I didn't see anyone on the monitor." He limps back inside, tosses the mail onto my bed, and re-sets the alarm. Then he's gone.

I scoop the phone off the bed. "I almost shot the neighbor's cat."

"There you are," sings Ethan. "Would you consider going back?"

What the . . . ?

"To church," he says, assuming I didn't understand.

"Didn't you hear the alarm? The shouting?"

"Uh-huh. I figured it was the cat. So what do you think—would you go again?"

"Yeah . . . I don't know. Maybe."

The dam's broken. There's no stopping the flood. I pull away from the conversation, and then drop Ethan like a cold-calling telemarketer.

I shut and lock my door, change into shorts and a tank, and sift through the mail. It's always the same. Bill, bill, ad, bill, bill . . . something different. A crisp white envelope beaming at me from the bottom of the pile. Hand-addressed. My heart drops into my stomach.

After all these years, it's like I just saw that flawless penmanship yesterday. I can still see Victor sitting at the dining table, writing a note to explain my absence from school. *Kristen was absent due to illness.* Lie! The truth was, Victor didn't want anyone to see the mark he'd made on my cheek. And there he sat, calm as anything, a light, eerie smile tacked to his face as he wrote the note and I stood dumfounded at his utter disregard for the truth, his inhumanly meticulous penmanship, and those mysterious scars lined across the backs of his hands.

Should I open the envelope, or set it on fire? No return address. Postmarked in Redondo Beach. He's in my city! I slice my finger tearing it open. Inside, there's the same wicked handwriting:

"It is with great displeasure that I'm writing this letter. But I have a reputation to uphold, so I'm left with no choice. You've been telling lies about me, and that has to stop. I fear I may be wasting my breath, because you've always had trouble grasping even the simplest concepts. Your poor, weak brain is so messed up that you can't tell the difference between your delusions and reality. The truth is that you have a serious psychological disorder, Kristen. It's not your fault. You inherited it from your mother. Nevertheless, I implore you to seek medical attention, before it's too late."

He signed it with a single V.

The next morning, I pace a hole in Georgina's floor. "*Reputation? Implore?* Who does Victor think he is?"

"Are the police looking into it?" she asks, not bothering to write anything down.

"Of course. I gave Hygleson the original this morning. Trust me, I'm taking precautions, but you understand there's a bigger issue here, right? I need my sanity validated."

Georgina's olive-skinned forehead crinkles.

"When someone tells you you're crazy," I explain, "they plant seeds inside of you. Little. Poisonous. Seeds. Later, it takes almost nothing to trigger their growth. A failed relationship, a rude driver, a light wind — whatever — and all of a sudden those seeds sprout and grow and eventually take over your mind, and you start to wonder if it's true that you're mentally impaired."

I pause to catch my breath. Georgina blinks.

"It's easier to convince someone you're a lunatic than it is to convince that same person you're sane."

Today's mug, *I'm a good listener,* sits alone, cooling beneath the shade of Georgina's jasmine plant.

"All through my childhood, Victor kept planting those seeds in my head. He kept trying to convince me I was demented, that I was always making stuff up. I've always tried to ignore him, but he had a way of creeping into my brain and making me wonder if some of what he claims is true.

"For as long as I can remember, I've felt like I'm living on the edge of sanity. Just one small nudge away from lunacy. And now, with this note, those seeds Victor planted are bursting to life like a freaking little shop of horrors. But no . . . *no!* Victor is a liar. He verbally abused me. He pushed me around and hurt me. I'm not making it up. For crying out loud, how many therapy sessions did we bleed through, recounting all of this? But it bothers me that there are no living witnesses, because I'm not sure if it was as bad as I remember. How am I ever going to be sure?"

Georgina's quiet today, her hands resting in her lap. Is she listening? Or running through her to-do list while I blather on? She neither validates nor discredits my concerns. How could she? She wasn't there. I leave her office feeling unsettled and vaguely sure of what I remember. The session was a bust.

Back at home, I still can't shake Victor's words. *You have a serious psychological disorder.* I grab a pair of gloves and meet Mark in the rose garden. We press our knees into the soil next to the orange and white heirlooms. Gingerly, we remove dying petals. If only I could fall into the pruning and let reality melt away. Instead, I toss my gloves to the grass and confront Mark. "Tell me what happened that night."

"Not now."

"I'm not leaving until you tell me why you kicked Victor out of the house."

"Your mother wanted him gone."

"Everybody wanted him gone . . . every minute of every day. What made that night special?"

Mark rubs his forehead, leaving a trail of soil above his brows. "Not a day goes by that I don't regret waiting so long to throw that scumbag out of your lives. I knew that Victor hurt your mother," he says, pulling away from me. "She was stubborn, always insisting I stay out of it, so I did. But when I found out what he was doing to you . . ." His voice cracks. He slips off his gloves, one finger at a time. He opens his mouth, then closes and opens it again, like a fish struggling to absorb oxygen. "So help me, if that beast ever shows his face again, I will *kill* him."

Mark stands and limps away, leaving me to sit alone in the dirt.

So I'm not mentally impaired? I haven't made anything up? Victor *did* hurt me. And the way Mark reacted . . . Victor must've beat me worse than I remember.

CHAPTER 34

STILL OCTOBER

I'M SITTING ON my bed staring at the blank pages in my sketchbook when Ethan calls. He tells me he's having a hard time recovering from another failed attempt to reach his mother. With a strained voice, he explains that the harder he tries to connect with her, the farther away she slips. Then he breathes into my ear for a while. "I just don't know what to do anymore," he finally says.

Oh, this is new. The ball's in my court.

"You've been fighting hard for your mother, you know? It sounds like you're burned out. Have you thought about taking a break? No one would blame you if you did."

"Yeah . . . maybe you're right."

Then silence, just the two of us breathing out loud. Normally, he'd be preaching by now, but it's almost like he's waiting for *me* to say something. I'd love to be able to pull an answer out of my back pocket. If only the weight of Victor's letter wasn't pressing on me so hard. Then maybe I could think.

I reach over to my nightstand and flip through the feathery pages of my Bible, but all this produces is a light puff of air. And it hits me. "You know what I like to do when I'm feeling like this?"

"What's that?" he asks.

"Eat a ton of ice cream." How many nights did Alana, Jenna, Danielle, and I spend doing that?

"Oh yeah?" A hint of amusement lifts his voice. "And how does that usually work out for you?"

"*Very* well."

"You're on. I've got some coffee and chocolate donut ice cream in the freezer, but I'd hate to binge eat alone."

"And I wouldn't let you. Lemme see what I've got."

265

I shuffle down the hall, through the library and living room, and into the kitchen. "Yay, I've got a quart of raspberry gelato. You ready?"

"Let's do this." He laughs.

I curl into the window seat in the dimly lit dining room and start plowing through my quart of gelato while Ethan dives mightily into his half gallon of ice cream. We moan after the first few spoonfuls, and then we start to groan after we've had many more. We laugh and giggle, and try to determine whose stomach is the most full. And for a moment, life is good and sweet, and ever so scrumptious.

In the middle of the night, Harley runs across my bed. I follow him into the living room of my past, the thick-set Victor-silhouette remaining still as the roaring wind rips through the room. And *nothing* moves.

Then I'm diving beneath the bed covers inside my childhood bedroom. The roar of wind reaches my ears as I wait for the menacing shadow to appear. Instead, the red lipstick woman approaches. She opens her mouth like she's trying to say something, and once again, she has no voice.

Then I'm back at Mark's house, in my grown-up bed, and the mystery woman is gone. Mom comes and sits on the edge of the bed, leans back on one hand, and smiles. Her fragrance fills my room, reminding me of our moments spent together, both good and bad. She leans in and whispers, "He's coming for you."

It's only a dream, so why is my heart pounding like this?

"Who's coming, Mom? *Who*?"

I wake up blinded by the sunshine pouring through my window. No trace of my mother.

I force myself out of bed. Why did I tell Steve I'd go to church again? Just so Mark wouldn't have to go alone? At least I kept Alana out of it this time. She would've killed me if I invited her and Andrue.

We arrive early and mingle before the service begins. Steve, Mark, and I stand in the middle of the crowd, huddled in our three-man formation, clinging together like penguins on an unfamiliar patch of ice. Pastor Carl invades our circle. Dude reminds me of the hog-rider who used to live up the street from my mother. There was always a line of Harleys angled in front of that man's house. But Carl's not an ordinary guy. He's a *pastor*. I'm sure he can see right through me. He *knows* I'm different. That's why he's here — to try to save me. Either that or he's planning to cast me out beyond the city limits along with the rest of the lepers.

"Steve has told me so much about you." Carl smiles wide, his teeth gleaming through his red goatee.

Oh please, God, get me out of here. "Would you excuse me? Gotta run to the car and grab my lip gloss. A gal's got to have her gloss for church, right?"

I force my best fake smile and turn on my heel. Who cares if the joke fell flat? At least now I can flee. My feet hit the ground hard, giving the impression I have a purpose that should not be interrupted.

I reach the hallway that spills into the back parking lot, and slow my pace. Why rush? There's still twelve minutes left before the service begins. If I return early, people will only try to start a conversation. I rummage through my handbag for my keys . . . oh, wait. I put my gloss in my back pocket. May as well go through the motions, anyway. Make my ruse legit.

I keep walking while riffling through my bag. Receipts, gum wrappers, random brochures. I really need to clean this thing out. Do I have a power bar in here? If only I could remember to eat breakfast before leaving the house — *bam*! Head smacking against pole. Serves me right for not paying attention.

Man, I'm getting a lump already . . . oh man, something just made me shiver. That familiar chill. I clutch my handbag and scan the lot. My car's open!

My pulse races. Someone is inside. It's *him*, the man with the black windbreaker, reaching beneath the dashboard.

"Hey! What are you doing in my car?"

He lifts his head and faces me, his eyes flashing like a panther locking on its prey. My hand flies to my mouth. *Victor Dragon.* Exactly as I remember him, with that square face and awful grin. Yellowish skin and thick, meticulously trimmed brows. And a fresh cut and shave, as if he left the barber five minutes ago.

The black windbreaker. *He's* the one who slipped out of Mark's room at Ocean View. How did I not recognize that revolting frame? The limp threw me off. Victor never had one before. Did Mark do that to him?

He steps out of the car, slowly, his dress shirt hanging open beneath the jacket. Nauseating.

Oh, *"He's coming."* In my dreams, Mom must've been warning me about Victor. God, please tell me I'm dreaming now. That can't be Victor leaning against my car, smirking like an idiot — can it?

He laughs. There's no mistaking that awful sound. He limps toward me. Definitely not a dream. He keeps approaching, his soulless eyes drawing closer. I feel inside my bag for my pepper spray. Got it. A metal nail file, too. I won't let him touch me. Whatever it takes, Victor will never hurt me again.

Victor stops within inches of my face. He grins, breathing noisily. I raise my chin and sneer back.

He sighs and shakes his head. "What do you think you're doing here? They'll never accept you. These church types might be tolerating you right now, but just wait until they get a glimpse of the real you. Do you really think they're going to let you through those doors once they find out everything you've done?"

"Your words mean *nothing* to me," I whisper, white knuckling the weapons inside my bag.

"I'm just saying this might not be the safest place for you. So many cars. So much traffic. If you're not careful, you could get hit." One corner of his mouth lifts.

No, no, no . . .

"FIRE! SOMEBODY HELP! FIRE!"

I keep screaming as he growls, his face turning dark red.

He lifts his arm to strike, but just as quickly, I drop the bag, shift the nail file to my left hand, and engage the spray with my right, shooting one long stream at him. He turns his head and uses his arm to protect his face, but not before I strike the right eye.

"You're dead!" Mark's voice echoes through the hallway.

Victor's head jerks up, and he turns and runs. Mark and Steve chase after him, but Victor's surprisingly fast for a man with a limp and he turns the corner before they get near it.

"Are you okay?" Carl looks into my face, and then glances at my left hand, the nail file gripped tight. "Did he hurt you?"

"No. I . . . I'm fine."

Carl picks up my purse and tries to hand it to me, but I'm still gripping the nail file and the spray. I'm still trying to figure out if all of this is real. Carl stands patiently in front of me, holding the handbag to his side now, as if it were his own.

"I just . . . I . . . I . . ." I can't talk.

Mark and Steve return. "He got away, kiddo." Breathless, Mark coaxes the nail file and mace out of my hands and takes the purse from Carl.

"Are you hurt?" asks Steve.

"He didn't touch you, did he?" Mark's wiry brows cross, smashing into one another. "So help me God, if he touched one hair—"

"Who was that?" Carl's tone is soft and calm, but his eyes are wide.

"Victor," answers Mark. "Also known as the spawn of Satan."

Steve takes my hand. "But you're okay?"

Steve holding my hand—this is new. Am I okay? I nod *yes*, and then *no*.

Carl glances at his watch. "Bring her to my office. You can all rest there until the police arrive." He looks into my eyes. "I've got to start my message, but I'll get some people on this. We have lots of police and retired military at this church. I'll have someone make the call, and we'll have some of the men scout around. Victor won't be able to get to you again. Not here."

In the office, a tall woman with espresso skin offers me a cup of juice. "I'm Jala, but you can call me Jalala. Everybody else does. It's fun to say, no?"

I squint at the red liquid. "This isn't . . ."

"Plain juice. Nothing more. Can I get you a cold washcloth?"

"No . . . thanks. I fold my arms over my stomach. "This can't be happening. Was he *really* here?"

"From what Steve just told me, it sounds like he was."

Outside the window by the front door stands a Herculean man wearing a black T-shirt with white lettering stretching across his back. *Old Guys Rule.* Inside, Mark paces a hole in the floor. Steve sits, bowing into his lap. Jalala tries to carry on a conversation, but none of us listens.

The police arrive and take our statements. They search the premises and find nothing. But when they search my car, they find a GPS tracker. It looks like Victor was in the middle of installing it when I interrupted him.

Victor's here. He's really here. And no one seems to be able to catch him.

CHAPTER 35

STILL OCTOBER

How many days have passed since Victor showed up in the church parking lot? Six? That's six full days of walking around like a zombie, barely able to concentrate on my jobs in progress. Then comes today. What clicked inside my brain to make my head clear? If only I could get that numbing fog back.

I'm aware of my past. I know what I've done and I'm okay with my mistakes. Or at least I was. So why are all these memories popping up at once? I could handle them if they came one at a time, but my brain won't let one memory digest before the next one comes crashing through. Having them all play back to back like this, piling on top of one another, is a torture I wouldn't wish on my worst enemy.

That night at the pub . . . so many poor decisions. Drinking way too much and flirting with that Neanderthal. And the consequences that led to Mom's early death.

That awful season when I dated Tommy. The way I gave myself to him. But then, I was manipulative, wasn't I? How is this the first time I'm noticing this? Right when everything seemed to be going well, I made myself unlikeable. Was I trying to sabotage the relationship? The Christmas party. How could I forget the way I flirted with Tommy's friends? Tommy wanted to get me away from them, so he asked me to play pool with him in the back room. I told him to go with Barbra instead. Tommy and Barbra never played pool that night. I knew all along they wouldn't. I knew it, and I sent them in.

I pour myself a cup of coffee. *Blech*, liquid dirt. Did I make it wrong, or are my taste buds off?

Another memory hits me like a punch in the gut. A Jack Daniels' night. I drank way too much and made out with Alana's old boyfriend. How *could* I? That's what Alana asked about a million times. I was never more thankful than when she found us before we got all our clothes off. Then I drove home. Plastered. How stupid could I be? Nearly ran over a child.

If only *that* was the worst of what I had to face. Why are all these memories coming? Please, somebody . . . *something*. Make them stop!

Maybe if I walk around. Put my focus on something else. Walk through Mark's backyard and admire his garden . . . no, *no*. They keep coming, a lifetime of pain and regret lined up, impatient to cross through my mind. My horrible, run off the rails, teen years — in living color. The way I lashed out during the years following Victor's disappearance.

My stomach clenches. Oh, the choices I made back then. Hanging out with that awful crowd. Accepting rides from strangers. Taking drags off smokes laced with God only knows what. Getting wasted. Hooking up with men. Waking up on foreign front lawns. So many desperate attempts to self-destruct. How did I ever survive?

And there's more. Somebody help me, there's *more*. My gut twists as this thing prepares to birth.

I walk toward a bush full of crimson roses and the image I found in Mom's box of photos flashes in my head. Victor standing next to Mom, him with that eerie smile and her in that tight black dress, bleached hair, and bright red lipstick. Yes, Victor made Mom dress like that, and yes, it was for a business dinner. But then when they came home, Victor beat her unconscious. I remember now. I recall the night clearly. That was the first time he came into my room.

Victor's words, recently spoken, slice through my mind. "After every-thing *you've* done."

Then torrents of long-forgotten memories flood in and knock me to my knees. I clasp my mouth. My heart pounds and my lungs contract in a sudden loss of breath. I'm only five or six, shaking beneath my bed covers. Crashing sounds echo through the door. Mom and furniture flying through the house.

And then the silence.

I fall to the grass at the memory of the awful deadness that followed the fight. Then the footsteps, each one shooting pain through my chest. He pounds on the door. I'm *small*, my little heart hoping the chair will hold beneath the knob. But he breaks through, standing over me like an enraged bear as I tremble.

Your mother was unable to fill my needs. Now it's your responsibility.

How many times did he come into my room? My chin quivers as I recount each time. The moments are real, like it's happening again. I writhe in the grass, my arms squeezing my waist. And I weep . . . really, truly weep over a life that has become an open wound.

"Oh God, oh God, oh God, help me," I moan, and then . . . a loud crack of thunder.

I shiver and sit upright, my gaze ping-ponging around the sky.

Clear, blue, and cloudless.

The next day, emotionally spent, I call Ethan. "We can't see each other anymore." Dorothy's right. A man like Ethan shouldn't have to waste his time on someone like me.

"Talk to me," he replies. "What's going on?"

"You don't know me, Ethan. I've done things. Horrible, terrible things."

Please, *please* agree and hang up, so I can move on with my life.

"What sort of things? I mean, do you want to talk about it?"

"No, but the things I've done . . . the things that've happened to me. I'm damaged, Ethan. You deserve better. Somebody whole."

"I don't want anyone but *you*, Kristen. Don't you understand that God put you on this earth for me?"

"I'm serious. You don't know anything about me. You have no idea what you're getting into."

"I know you love anything that's raspberry-flavored, and you care about animals and homeless people. I also know that sometimes you smile when you're in pain, and that somehow you were hurt during childhood and you're still trying to get over that."

He waits for me to respond, but I can't.

"Was it Victor? Did he hurt you . . . physically?"

"Yes." Did my voice actually come out, or was my response soundless?

"I'm sorry," says Ethan solemnly. "I wish I knew what else to say. I wish I had the right words, something that would help you feel whole again. All I can think of right now is *I'm sorry*, but I mean it, sincerely."

I nod and breathe into the phone.

"You know," he continues, "the same thing happened to my mother. She was hurt when she was a child. She was molested by her uncle."

Dorothy?

"It devastated her. She's tried to cover it up her entire life, and that denial has nearly destroyed her. Is . . . is that what happened to you? Did Victor molest you?"

"Yes," I whisper, unable to breathe.

"I'm sorry that happened to you." Tears choke his voice. "I'm sorry Victor stole your innocence. But I want you to know that doesn't make me love you any less." Ethan's voice cracks as he tries to hold on to the next few words. "I want you, Kristen. All of you. Every broken piece."

Dorothy went through the same thing? I can hardly believe it.

"Ethan, I want to curl up into a ball and stay like that forever."

"If I could be with you right now, I would wrap my arms around you and hold you. Forever."

Then I just cry into the phone, and Ethan seems to do the same.

I hang up feeling completely emptied, as if a vampire had come and sucked out all my blood.

"God, I don't know if you're real or not . . ."

No, that feels too weird. I'll address the walls, like Ethan suggested.

"Dear walls . . ."

Nope. That doesn't work, either.

"Whomever or whatever can hear me." Yes, that's much better. "I really would like to know if God is really a real thing. So if you're real and it's you who's listening, will you please reveal yourself to me?"

Evening rolls in fast. Bring it, I say. Bring on the dreams. Nothing can take me lower than this, and I'm tired of waiting by the phone for God to return my call.

Orthodox Dogmatic Theology, Volume Three screams at me from my nightstand. I crack it open. Surely, *this* will put me to sleep. I fan the book back and forth, unable to settle on a page and unable to absorb a word. I toss the book and flip off the light. Before long, I'm following Harley into the same dream as before, all the way up to "He's coming for you."

Then Mom's gone, but this time, I'm still in the dream. As if by instinct, I leave my bed and head out the door. Now I'm outside, in an alley, the one that exists behind my childhood home. Something knocks over a trash can lid and I run, and the mist is close behind.

When I reach the city, the sound of gathering people emerges, and I stop running. The mist stops, too, short of the hairs on the back of my neck. What now? Where do I go from here?

There's something new. The sound of 100 mph winds. No, that's not it. I know that beautiful, violent sound. It's crashing waves. I've made it to the shore.

I race through the line of palms, the mist following close. My feet hit the wet sand, and then I'm splashing into the water. And I stop, my giant white nightgown hanging loose. All my muscles relax, the water like a morphine drip coming up through my feet. I stare into the mighty Pacific Ocean, black as coal in the dead of night. Off in the distance, somewhere near the horizon, a giant orb of light bobs.

You must get to the light.

Salty air sticks to my lips. Waves spit and roar, and murmurs intensify, though there's no one around. Except for the mist.

This is the way. Walk into it.

That voice. Like the transient who told me to be careful that one New Year's Eve. But I'm alone. Voice or no voice, the urge is intolerable. I have to go in. I move forward, marching with all my strength. Waves crash at my thighs, my chest, my neck. The water hits hard as I lean firm, forging toward the light.

The mist groans, swells, and pushes forward, a mass of vapors surging past me and diving into the waves ahead. It feeds itself into the water, appearing as a frame of bones from crest to trough. The powerful, skeletal wave strikes me down, and I tumble. I choke on saltwater as I try again, and once again the wave strikes me down. I'm still dreaming, right? So why does this battle feel more real than anything I've ever known?

I can help. You only need to ask.

I scramble to my feet before the next wave hits, and I stretch out my arms and scream, "Help me!"

Another wave passes, moving through me like wind, crashing behind with a racket like thunder colliding with thunder. I stand beyond the waves now, on the edge of the ocean floor, my mouth barely above water. One inch farther out, the ocean floor drops to a depth way beyond my height. The bright, white light pulsates in the distance.

You must step off the ledge in order to be submerged.

Isn't this what I've wanted all along? To be submerged?

I take a step forward, and the ocean floor disappears below my feet. I lift my legs and swim. What choice do I have? The light is ridiculously far out. I'll never reach it, but I can't go back to shore where the mist waits, lurking. Keep moving your arms and legs, Kristen. Move them like your life depends on it. The closer I approach, the farther out it moves. I'll never reach it . . .

Wait — what's happening? How am I moving this fast? Something is pushing me. There it is. The light. I made it. I reach out to touch it, and it sinks. I dive below the surface, but the harder I swim, the deeper it plunges. So I relax and let my body float below the surface. The light ascends, enveloping me like an embryonic sac. Warm, protective, and utterly satiating. No desire to struggle for air. No desire to struggle for anything.

Now I'm lying in bed, dripping with sweat. Definitely awake. A new urge clenches my stomach, grabs hold of it, and refuses to let go. I must be crazy. Am I really considering doing this? Alana's going to freak out, but I mean, what've I got to lose? If it's anything like this last dream, and if it's anything like the type of love Kierkegaard talked about, it'll be worth the risk.

Right?

I get to the church early and dash into the front office. Before Jalala can open her mouth, I tell her about my dream.

"For as long as I can remember," I tell her, "I've been running from my past. And I've been unhappy with my life. After last night, I can't stand remaining separate from God. But I'm afraid, Jalala . . . *terrified* of approaching God. How can I be sure he won't kill me here where I stand? Even worse, God might listen to me."

I drop to my knees and Jalala meets me on the floor.

"How will I be able to stand it if He really forgives and accepts me?" Tears stream down my cheeks. It's like I don't know the person who's speaking. But I do know her. I've known her all along.

"I'm not exactly sure why I'm here. I'm no more worthy of God now than I was last week. I still have a lot of unanswered questions. All I know is that I can't *not* do this."

Jalala pets me as I cry, her soft, espresso hand caressing my white arm. "God loves you, Kristen. You are precious in His eyes."

Precious. The last word I'd ever choose to describe myself.

She squeezes my hand. "Do you want to accept Jesus into your life?"

The last time somebody asked me that question, I wanted to kill him. This time, the question keeps me on my knees. But how am I supposed to swallow the concept that the God-Man would have an interest in *me*?

I imagine Jesus standing before me and he's radiant. If only there wasn't a giant expanse between him and me. How could I ever get across this gap? With one giant leap, I suppose. That's what Jalala's asking me to do, right? Step off the ledge? To be honest, I'd rather run back to solid ground, but the cliff is crumbling before my eyes. So I jump.

"Yes, I do. I want to accept Jesus into my life."

CHAPTER 36

BEGINNING OF NOVEMBER

I PULL INTO the no parking zone and re-read Ethan's last text. "Plane delayed by a feisty old woman who refused to store her poodle. She wouldn't budge. Kept insisting Humbert had to sit on her lap during takeoff or he'd get diarrhea. You should've seen the struggle they had removing them from the aircraft."

And now I'm stuck circling the LAX pick-up loop. Would it be so bad if I rammed another driver? These people have as much common sense as a horde of gnats. No less than three planes circle the airport, hoping for approval to land. Looks like Humbert wasn't the only bottleneck today. How long, though? How long will I have to wait?

I should've told Ethan my big news during our last conversation. But this will be better, right? The pain of constantly sitting on the verge of exploding will be worth the look on Ethan's face when I tell him in person. I can hardly believe it myself . . . Jalala converting me before the first service that Sunday morning.

Ugh, where is that slowpoke? Round and around and around I go, driving the same loop, caking on layer after layer of frosted raspberry lip gloss.

So that's it, then? I'm Christian now? No papers to sign? Wait — there he is.

He tosses his bag into the trunk. Scowling, his hair out of control, he leans into my opened window. "Mind if I drive?"

"Sure." I climb over to the passenger side. "Everything's set?"

"Yes. Captain Jack's at the harbor now, making sure the yacht is seaworthy."

"Yacht, huh? How do you know this guy?"

"Longtime family friend."

"And he's okay with you driving his yacht?"

Ethan tries to smile. This has got to be the hardest I've seen him work to make those lips curve up. "Yeah, Jack trusts me. Will it be the six of us?"

"Yep. Mark, Steve, Alana, Andrue, and us." I reach for my handbag. "Want some gum?"

"No thanks." He glances over. "What's that white envelope?"

I pull it out of the side pocket. "I don't know. Found it on my windshield just before I came here. My guess is it's another nasty note from the old man who lives next door. He thinks he owns the street in front of his house and that I should never park there."

Ethan exits the pick-up loop. "You don't want to open it and see? What if it's from Victor?"

"No way. My name's written on the front, and it's definitely not *his* handwriting. I'm sure it's from Al, and I'm not in the mood to read his crabby letter right now."

Traffic moves like sludge. Beads of sweat pop up all over Ethan's forehead as he grips the wheel. I clear my throat. "By the way, thanks for setting this up. It means a lot to me. Was it expensive?"

"No worries," he says. "I only need to pay for gas and any damage not covered by insurance, which shouldn't be an issue. But we've got to step on it or it won't happen today. Weather's supposed to get nasty by early evening. You have your mother's ashes?"

"Yeah. The permit says we need to be five hundred yards from shore, but I'd like to go out farther into open water."

Ethan joins the line of cars inching their way onto the 105. "We can go out as far as you need, weather permitting." He rakes back his hair, his brow wrinkling. "I need to check NOAA as soon as we board the yacht."

"Noah?"

"National Oceanic and Atmospheric Administration. Weather forecast and sea conditions. Earlier this morning they were listing warnings of inclement weather — increasing winds, waves up to eight feet. The sooner we get there, the better." He white-knuckles the steering wheel and drives in silence until we get to the 405.

"The freeway's stopped up."

"Like a cheap toilet." I laugh out loud, but I'm the only one. Ethan's grouchy today. There's no way I'm telling him my news right now.

Minutes crawl like hours as we worm our way up the freeway.

He points ahead. "There's the problem."

Dear God, if only I could unsee this, but I can't stop looking at the nut job streaking along the side of the highway. "Can you read that sign he's flashing? Freedom . . . is . . . *hear*?

"I think it's an 'n'. *Near*."

The wackadoodle stares at me as we pass.

"That's him! The hobo with the bronze eyes. Same hair, same everything. Minus the clothes."

"You kidding?

I unbuckle my seatbelt so I can twist around to look back and see more clearly. "It's him. I'm sure of it. But how can it be him?"

"Coincidence? Or somebody different?"

Beyond the lunatic, the freeway opens up as if a plague wiped out the greater Los Angeles area. I've never seen the 405 so empty. Ethan presses the pedal to the floor.

"Easy, cowboy."

We speed along, as free as the wind, until we reach the 710, where we stop to play bumper cars once again.

"C'mon!" yells Ethan. "You see my blinker. Let me in."

"What's with the bad attitude? You need some coffee or something?"

He growls, jerking the wheel to shoot into the next lane. Another driver screeches while pressing hard on his horn. Dear God, please help us get there in one piece. Please don't let Ethan irritate the wrong driver and get us involved in a fatal game of road rage.

An eternity later, we reach Rainbow Harbor and hop out of the car. "Let's get to the boat," says Ethan, rushing ahead across the parking lot.

I trail behind, my mother's ashes jostling inside the crook of my arm. "I can't believe we saw the bronze-eyed hobo," I yell while jogging. "Ethan, am I losing my mind? Did that really happen? I'm awake, right?"

Ethan stops, faces me, and takes my hands in his. "You're awake. I saw him, too. And yeah, some crazy stuff's going on. I've had a vague uneasiness all day. Woke up this morning to God telling me you're going to be okay. That he's *got your back,* which of course, made me start to worry."

"You know you sound psycho, right?"

"Mmm-hmm." He laughs awkwardly and rubs his head. "We'd better go."

We rush up the boardwalk and dart around the circular harbor. Dock 7B, Private Yacht Charters.

We scurry down the gangway, my jaw dropping farther with each step. The sleek white yacht stretches in length as we approach, the name *Convergent Boundary* inscribed on its bow.

"Holy cow. Captain Jack must be loaded."

"He does pretty well."

Ethan takes my hand, guides me aboard, and leads me through a tinted sliding glass door. Everything gleams. White couches and table-tops, white carpet, and cherry-wood accents polished to a high shine. Andrue nods from a scalloped sofa. Steve and Mark wave from the sofa's twin across the salon. Alana leans on the wet bar, laughing with a skinny, white-haired dude with leathered skin.

"Captain Jack," greets Ethan, leading me to the galley. "This is my girl-friend Kristen."

The captain faces me, tips an imaginary hat and bows. "Kristen." Then he faces Ethan. "Nice to see you, but you'd better get going. I've already primed the boat. Bilge and fans are running. I just checked NOAA. Looks like you've got three hours of manageable weather left, max. Won't hurt to check again while you're warming the engine and reviewing your charts."

"Will do. Thanks, Jack. She's in good hands."

"I don't doubt it. Bon voyage." He tips his imaginary hat again, and disembarks.

"Settle in wherever's comfortable," says Ethan. "I'm heading to the bridge. I'll call you in when we're near our destination."

As he walks away, Alana catches my arm. "You want some sangria? Captain Jack made a pitcher. *One* pitcher, mind you, so get a glass now before it's gone. There's cheese and crackers, too. I like this guy. Ethan's got impressive connections. This yacht's fifty-eight feet long and more than seventeen feet wide. A couple of bedrooms below. I gotta get me one of these babies. Only bad part is Captain Jack made me take off my boots. Gave me these lame flip-flops to wear instead, and boy, are they killing my outfit—"

"I'll take that glass of sangria. Gonna need it to get through this."

She glances at the can of ashes shaking in my hands, then skirts around the bar to the fridge. "Great, I'll put out the snack trays, too."

While she's working, I turn to hug-greet Mark. Steve, too. Hugs aren't my norm with him, but nothing's normal about this trip, so why not? Alana slips the sangria into my hand and sets the trays onto the coffee table before she settles in next to Andrue. I'm left standing in the center of the salon, gazing at the radiant overhead lighting, the recessed bulbs sparkling like little spotlights anticipating the show of the century. Except this isn't that big of a deal. Dump the ashes, say a few words, and check this task off the to-do list. Mom wouldn't want anything more.

Everyone's staring. "Thanks for coming. Um . . . I'm going to sit at the dinette for a bit and just watch the water."

"Okay." Alana gives me the kindest smile I've ever seen on her face.

"Here we go," calls out Ethan from the pilothouse.

I sit at the table and look out the windows, a near 360-degree view from here. The boat glides out of the slip and we start to turn. Alana and the others keep talking among themselves, laughing about something. I glance out the window as I gulp my drink, finishing it down to the ice cubes. I gaze at the white lighthouse, standing tall and strong as we cruise past. Is the sky darkening, or is that an illusion from the tinted windows?

The yacht glides along, as smooth as silk and moving at a snail's pace. My head still spins from the hobo freak sighting. Everyone chats on, but it's all white noise. Stay in the present, Kristen. Forget about the dreams and the hobo. You have to focus if you want to get through the dumping of the ashes. Dear God . . . please help me through this.

I leave the dinette and step up into the pilothouse. I stand over Ethan, my hands resting on his shoulders. "You sure you know how to handle this thing?"

"I've got a captain's license that says I do."

"How much longer till we're out in wide open water?"

"It won't be long."

I scoot into the L-shaped lounger. What a view. Ethan sits confident at the helm as he guides this massive ship with ease. The view from the panoramic window's not bad, either. So much water. Cold, salty water. Everywhere. Plunging to depths unknown. Oh, *God*. Not now. I can't battle the urge to go in at a time like this.

"You okay?" One of Ethan's brows lifts as he scans my face. "You're pale."

"No, I'm not okay."

He nods, eying the ocean ahead. "I'll pray for—"

"Can you do it silently? I . . . I need to sort some stuff out."

His head tilts, eyes still focused ahead. "Sure."

I massage my temples and stare into my lap, letting the ocean pass unseen. The truth is, I don't want to sort through anything. I don't want to process anything at all. Minutes labor past, excruciatingly slow.

"Dolphins," blurts Ethan. "Starboard; you see them?"

Seven of them glide along the surface, glistening as they swim. Utterly beautiful. God made those, too, I presume. But what about the cancer that swallowed my mother? Did God make that? And has God really forgiven me for my part in her early death?

Ugh. I need to be able to tell Ethan my news soon. I need to be able to ask him about these and the million other questions making my head throb. But now's not the time.

"We're out in the open now. How much farther you want to go?"

"Maybe a little more."

"Okay. Go tell the others to get ready. I'll meet you on the back porch in a few minutes."

Ten minutes later, Alana and I have our hair fastened in ponytails as we peer out over the swim deck, the ocean surface rippling from a wind that's picking up steam. The yacht bobs gently. Mark, Steve, Andrue, and Ethan stand nearby.

"Blech." Alana grabs her stomach.

"You okay?"

"Seasick."

Mark taps her shoulder. "If you think you're going to lose it, lean over the side and feed the fishes. You'll never make it to the head in time."

Alana faces me, her hair frazzled and her face green, red blotches surrounding her eyes. "A mother is a terrible thing to lose. I'm so sad Mary's gone. You know that, right?"

"Yeah."

There will be no ceremony. A short Scripture read by Steve, and then I'm up, holding what's left of my mother over the edge of the boat.

Ethan glances at my hands. The can of ashes is sticking to my palms like super glue. I reach out to him with my eyes. "I can't do it."

He wraps his arm around me and gives me a squeeze as he stares into the water. "Take your time."

Alana and Andrue cling to each other. Steve bows and Mark leans on his cane. Brown pelicans flap past, squawking.

"Uh-oh." Ethan points to the sky. "Looks like that storm's coming earlier than expected."

A gust ruffles our hair and jackets.

"Waves are forming." Ethan turns away, but keeps talking over his back. "I'm going to run and turn on the stabilizers."

Within seconds, he's gone.

As we wait, the waves grow and the sky dims to a dark purple-gray. The moment Ethan returns, I rip the coffee can lid off fast. Fingers of wind try to scoop up my mother, and I slap my hand over the opening. Then I take in several long, heaving breaths. The sky transforms to an eerie bronze. We don't have much time.

I remove my hand from the opening and tilt the can over, letting the wind steal my mother. It whips her around in swirls. *Please* let her fall into the sea. I lose sight of most of the ashes, but some of them make it down. As Mom's remains hit the surface, the water froths and churns, sweeping spray up to the deck.

I shout over the wind. "Is this crazy, or what?"

The boat starts to turn.

"We need to go," hollers Ethan. "I'm heading to the pilothouse."

We follow him inside.

"Everyone finish up your drinks and bring the cups to me." Alana swipes up the snack trays. She dashes into the galley and tucks away anything that can tumble over. But we're not rocking as much as being lifted and set back down, like a toy airplane being played with by a toddler.

"Uuuugh," moans Alana. "I'm definitely going to be sick." She leans over the sink.

I place my hand on her back. "Anything I can do?"

"I'll be fine," she answers, still staring into the sink. "Just . . . can you give me some space?"

"Sure."

Mark and Steve settle into the sofa. I head over to join them, but they're engaged in deep conversation. Alana settles into the other couch and rests her head in her hands. Andrue slides in next to her and rubs her back. And here I stand, feeling like I'm in the way. I could sit in the pilothouse with Ethan, but then I'd be forced to stare at nothing but ocean, wondering how far my mother's ashes have scattered.

I spy my purse. The white envelope sticks out tall and bright. I still haven't read grumpy Al's note. Maybe I'll go downstairs and take a minute to write him a sincere apology. Then I'll lie down and wait for this awkward ride to be over.

I pass the galley and head down the ladder leading to the rooms below, bracing myself as we roll over a wave. I enter the master bedroom, close the door, and plop onto the bed. Slowly, I peel open the envelope and pull out the note. What the—? Two typed pages. Definitely not a swift handwritten rant from grumpy Al. I flip to the back page. It's from Delila.

My heart thumps hard as I read the letter out loud.

"Dear Kristen, I'm sorry I disappeared on you, but I had no choice. Now that I'm not helping Victor anymore, he's after me, too. I've gone underground. I hope you believe me when I say that I'm sorry for ever helping him. I can't believe I let him control me like that. From the moment I was born, all I ever wanted to do was please him. And he knew that and used it against me."

The paper shakes in my hands as I continue reading.

"After my mother died and the abuse got really bad, I still kept trying to get him to like me. He was gone a lot. Those were the times he was with you and your mom. I longed for him to return, so I'd get another chance to win his approval. I did anything he asked me to do because I thought that would make him appreciate me. I'd have ripped my own heart out of my chest if he asked me to. I wanted to be noticed and to know that I mattered. I needed to know that my own father loved me. But all he cared about was you."

I gasp and my hand flies to my chest.

"I used to hate you. That's why it was so easy for me to help him in the beginning. And every time I did, he gave me praise, which made it even easier. That Tiffany's diamond star pendant I used to wear was a gift from him, not from Legion. It was a bribe, really.

"After I ran away from home and was living on the streets off and on for several years, Victor found me and made a deal with me. He'd get me housing and a job if I agreed to help him. He paid someone to falsify my college records and help me get a position at Hamilton Design. That necklace was my reward for agreeing to help make you fail. He called me his 'best girl,' and I ate it up.

"I hate myself for falling for that. I'm embarrassed to admit I was responsible for all of your project disasters. I even sabotaged my own work and got myself fired and then blamed that random group of seven. It was part of the plan to get me living with you, so Victor could have easier access. By then, I knew your weaknesses, and I played you.

"I'm sorry, Kristen. At the time, I thought he loved me, and I hardly cared what happened to you. But then I got to know you, and you were kind to me and you trusted me, and I started to realize how messed up his mind was. So I stopped helping him. I stopped telling him where you were and what you were doing. And I didn't touch your car — that was all him. Kristen, he's dangerous. He's not going to stop until he's conquered you in one way or another. You need to be careful."

He's here.

What? Mom, was that you? No. It was just my imagination.

I flip to the second page.

The bathroom doorknob twists and I jump up. The letter falls to the floor.

The door swings open. It's Victor!

He steps forward. With one hand behind his back, he squats down to pick up the letter. My heart races so fast it might explode. He scans the writing and contempt washes over his face. I can't breathe. It's like there's no oxygen left on earth. I glance at the door, then at him, then back at the door. He drops the pages and stands quickly. "She's a lying whore," he says, still holding one hand behind his back.

I struggle to draw in a deep breath and assess the situation. If I lunge quickly, I might be able to slip past him. But my legs remain weighted to the floor, like two cement pillars, as the boat keeps rocking and my stomach begins to churn.

He assaults me with those soulless eyes and laughs. "She was always trying to get my attention. Her and those small hips. She was worthless, too eager to please. But you . . ." His voice slithers out in a low moan. "You were stubborn. Even when I had you submitting to me, you were never there. I enjoyed the challenge." His eyes sweep across the bed, then up and down my body. "But I'm done playing games. And I *will not* be ignored."

I'm going to be sick. I lean over, and there it goes, all of the sangria spilling out. Victor lurches forward, snatches my ponytail, and jerks me upward, sticking a knife to my throat. A Bowie. Blade's got to be eleven inches or more.

"Kristen? Everything okay down there?"

It's Alana. She's near the ladder.

Victor grips me tighter. "Tell her you're coming up."

"Be right . . . there," I say through a dry, cracked throat.

"Good," she replies. "If I have to climb down these stairs, I'll throw up for sure."

Victor puts his mouth close to my ear and grunts, "Let's go."

He shoves me through the door and toward the ladder. My head spins. I can't even feel my heartbeat anymore. I'm awake, right? This is really happening?

Alana screams and her hands fly to her mouth. "It's Victor — he's got Kristen!"

Victor clenches my hair tighter and keeps the blade pressed against my neck. "Clear the path or she won't make it up the stairs."

My vision fogs over. I'm in my childhood and here at the same time. There's chaos everywhere — screams . . . shouting . . . pain. It's like I'm six again, frozen in horror while the boat continues to be lifted, then set down . . . lifted, then set down. We reach the top of the stairwell and Victor pushes forward, forcing the others to inch back with each step we progress. Now we're pinned in the small space between the stairs, the pilothouse, the dinette, and the salon, and I'm still struggling to breathe.

"You're a monster." Alana's face reddens. Angry tears form in her eyes.

"You're dead," growls Mark. "Dead."

"Back away." Victor's awful wet breath sprays onto my neck. "Everyone back away."

"It's okay. Take it easy. Everyone take it easy. Mark, can you man the wheel—"

Ethan.

"No!" shouts Victor. "Kill the engine."

"We'll get tossed around if I turn the engine off. It's going to be okay. Let's all just rel—"

"*Kill* it." Victor presses the knife, and warm liquid drips down my neck.

Ethan slips back into the pilothouse and the engine goes silent.

"Let her go." Mark steps forward.

"No!" Victor grips me tighter. "Everybody step back and shut up, or I end this now."

I'm shaking uncontrollably. My mind feels numb. The boat drifts, pitching from front to back. Victor keeps shouting, herding the others like a bunch of sheep — to the front of us, now to the side — out of our way until we reach the glass doors. Andrue is strangely calm, zombie-like from his meds. Steve stands still, unflinching. I'm on my own.

Victor orders me to open the door. "Nobody follow us. *Nobody.*"

We step outside, where the storm rages. Victor whips me around the corner and drags me across the starboard walkway, the water below churning and spitting like mad. How's he going to get me across when my legs have turned to rubber and we're fighting against the wind and the swaying boat?

"Come on! Stop dragging your feet!"

Steve and Andrue watch us pass by the tinted windows, and Alana freaks out in the background, hands and arms flapping like crazy. Ethan dashes through the salon and Mark hobbles behind. Victor tightens his grip when they appear at the beginning of the walkway. "Get back inside!"

Ethan reaches out, standing in place. He says something, but the wind swallows his words. A wave climbs high from the other side of the boat, crashing onto the deck. Victor keeps backing up until we're near the tip of the bow. Ethan and Mark creep forward.

"Get back! Get back! She's mine!"

No! My eyes heat up with tears. I'll kill myself before that becomes true. I swear I will. Victor's shorter than Andrue, so why can't I break free?

Mark hangs back, his face sagging with defeat. His guns and ammunition are back home, and he can't do a thing. He leans on his cane, his eyes narrowed and his cheeks burning red.

Ethan moves forward and raises his *stop* hand. "It's okay, it's okay. Relax. It's going to be okay." But his dog whispering techniques aren't working, not here, not now, and not with his teeth so clenched and the boat turning in the angry water.

I might not make it through this . . . and if I don't, Ethan won't know. My eyes widen, trying to reach him, but it's not enough. I *have* to tell him.

"Ethan," I choke through the pain of Victor's grip. "I did it." Victor pulls me in tighter and I try to form a smile with my quivering lips. "I'm saved."

"Hardly," laughs Victor.

"What?" Ethan asks, standing frozen like a deer in the headlights, his eyes suddenly red and wet.

"Step back!" yells Victor.

"I've accepted Jesus." My voice is now a shrill.

Victor yanks on my hair and laughs loudly, the eerie sound slithering up the back of my neck.

My voice was garbled from tears, Victor's grip, and the wind and spitting waves. Did Ethan even hear me? He's quiet, just standing there, digging his fists into his pockets. He nods at me and then I see it — a hint of a smile, like boundless joy trying to break through a mask of grief and pain.

Suddenly, he shouts at Victor. "You *can't* have her!"

Another wave comes. This one's gotta be more than seven feet. It crashes across the deck.

Victor yanks my ponytail. "Don't you get it?" He laughs. "*No one* can have Kristen." My hair wrapped around his fist, he shoves me toward the rail, his knife pressing into my skin.

"You mean nothing to me," I choke, still trembling from head to toe.

"Shut up," he snaps.

Back in the parking lot . . . was Ethan right? Dear God, do you have my back?

Victor presses me hard against the rail.

Forgive him.

That voice. Did I really hear it? Forgive Victor? How am I supposed to do that?

"Hold on," says Ethan. "Let's talk about this."

Victor digs his head into his elbow to wipe his brow. "She's mine." His voice is raspy, and low, as if he's talking only to himself. "I won. I finally won."

I wriggle around, trying to slip away, but his head snaps back up and he tightens his grip. Another wave approaches, this one larger than the last.

"Back off from the rail!" yells Mark, inching closer.

"No!" Victor shouts. "*I'm* the one in control here. *I'm* the one with the power." He laughs insanely. "And the rest of you can meet me in hell."

The wave climbs over the boat. Victor grunts and forces both of us over the rail, along with the crashing water.

Time expands.

Every moment flows past clearly, exaggerated, as if I'm Alice falling down the rabbit hole, as if I have the luxury of being able to absorb everything in sight. The metal rail digging into my ribs. The crashing wave splashing over us. My hands clinging to the wrist that presses the knife to my neck. Both our bodies tipping over, our feet swinging up over our heads. The blade of the knife slicing through skin. Our bodies separating. Splashing into the rumbling cold sea.

I plunge below the surface, Victor's lumpish silhouette landing four feet in front of me. One corner of his mouth lifts. Visibility's poor, but his expression is clear. Bugged out eyes, the whites flashing at me like death. Death of hope. Death of mercy. Death of innocence.

Our bodies surge up toward the crest of a forming wave, and then we're forced back down toward the trough. And we stare at each other, neither of us bothering to move. We drift back up, up, up. And on our way down, Victor glances up as the edge of the boat slams down on his head. He goes limp, and sinks.

My body continues to drop and drift in the murky water. What's all this debris? I can hardly see my own hands hanging from my noodle-like arms. I can't move. Or can I? Maybe I don't want to move. Maybe this is right where I'm supposed to be. Floating below the surface of the ocean.

No sign of Victor. No sign of anything.

The boat . . . I can't see the boat.

Is that blood trailing from my neck, like a ribbon of black smoke billowing through the dark water? Now *there's* a mood board theme.

Black on midnight blue. Funny. I don't have any desire to breathe. So wooozy. How long have I been under? How much blood have I los . . .

A face.

It's Ethan. Right?

Yes. My lids are so heavy . . . sorry, Ethan. Just have to close my . . .

CHAPTER 37

NOVEMBER TO LATE DECEMBER

❧

I POP OUT of my own body, like a cork out of a shaken bottle of champagne. How bizarre. Is that really me lying on the deck? How can I see myself from this vantage point? Am I dreaming?

Everything's vivid and clear. The stark white boat pitching on top of the angry gunmetal sea. Voices from inside the salon. Mark and Steve. And on the deck, Alana and Ethan leaning over me.

"She was in the water for ten minutes!" Alana is yelling as she tapes gauze to my neck, bright red blood seeping through. "Say it took you two and half minutes to find her and that's when you say she passed out. Say she lost her pulse half a minute after that . . . that means she's been without a pulse for seven minutes. No pulse for *seven* minutes, Ethan!"

Ethan doesn't respond. He's working chest compressions and rescue breaths with tears forming in the corners of his eyes. How can I see the corners of his eyes so clearly from here?

Alana cuts her finger trying to snip a strip of medical tape. "Ow. Forget it. The tape's not working. I'm going to have to hold the gauze against her neck."

Seven minutes is too long. She's going to be brain dead.

Wait, that was Alana's voice, but her lips didn't move. Am I hearing her thoughts?

I can't have a vegetable as a best friend. I just can't.

She leaves one hand on top of the gauze on my neck and wipes her eyes, smearing blood across her face.

Ethan pumps and counts. "One, two, three . . ."

I float away, through the boat. Through the salon and right through Andrue, who's coming out of the pilothouse.

"No." Mark is speaking into the radio. "She still doesn't have a pulse. They started CPR about a minute ago. We got the stabilizers back on and the waves aren't as big as they were a few minutes ago, but we're still pitching pretty good."

Steve's hunched over on the L-shaped bench, talking into his cell phone. "How many have you contacted so far?" He waits a moment. "Thanks, Carl. Help is on the way, but she's still not breathing on her own, so keep making calls. We need all the prayer warriors we can get."

I float through the window and away from the boat, where I hover above the water. Then I plunge, fast and deep. The water's crystal clear. Cool. And utterly quenching. More satiating than anything I've ever known. I could float here forever. A tall cognac boot drops in front of me, sinking down, down, down. That was Alana's. She's going to be furious.

The water glows bright, gleaming with phosphorescence. The brightness grows and stretches out, like a tube. I glide into it, as light as a feather through this . . . this . . .

What is this?

I exit the tube and enter a space filled with brilliant white light and overwhelming warmth. Not a drop of water in sight.

My vision pierces the brightness, and I spot a crowd rushing toward me. A sound rolls in from a distance, like a hundred rivers flowing down a nearby mountain. The crowd surrounds me, their approach and their nearness filling the same moment.

A profound sense of the present envelops me, as if here and now is *everything*. Those familiar faces . . . *oh.* The same plastered grins from my recurring dream with Ethan. Only these aren't creepy at all. They are the embodiment of love.

Two women appear up close, their grins stretched wide, and — *it's Jenna and Danielle!* I slap my mouth and fall to the ground, shaking with sobs that I sense more than hear. My friends kneel next to me, Jenna petting my hair and Danielle beaming. They're happy to see me. They say this without words. My jaw drops as my eyes glaze over at the sight of them. Their presence is too real to be a dream.

Harley hops into my lap. *"Oh!"* I bury my face inside his fur. Have I died, and against all odds . . . made it to—

"He's here."

My head bolts upright. *Mom.* Has she ever looked this stunning? I jump up and embrace her.

"Mom, I love you. I love you, I love you, I love you." Somehow, I communicate this without moving my lips.

I sense her response. "I love you, too, Kristen honey."

We hold each other close. How did I get here? I'm *here*, right? This can't be a dream. This super-vivid aliveness cannot be a dream. And I'm me, right? This is still me, except I'm somehow lighter. I have no pain or shame. Guilt and regret have shed away. I am inside the absence of agony.

"He's here," repeats Mom, and we're approaching a large glimmering gate. We move without taking steps. We draw closer and the gate's brilliance intensifies, along with the sounds in the background, like thousands times thousands of flapping wings, growing ever louder. The closer the gate, the more my chest expands, leaving my heart and soul exposed. The resounding flaps escalate, becoming a symphony of music and wings and songs that fill my senses to overflowing, as if I've become one with beauty, perfection, and love.

The brightness at the gate blinds me. I can't see anything but the light and a figure forming within it — a figure of light within the light, coming in, like a camera lens twisting into focus. A man-shaped figure, with a beard and hair flowing to his bright, white shoulders. Same hair as the bronze-eyed hobo's, except brushed out . . . with light.

But this isn't the hobo. *This* is someone else. I'm blindsided with awe. Ecstasy, peace, warmth, and reverence are wrapped into one.

Oh. *Oh.* I drop to my knees and raise my hands, beaming up at him. "It's You. It's really You. Forgive me for how long I doubted, for everything. Forgive me."

"Rise," roars the voice of the figure. "Your sins are forgiven."

The music of wings and songs continue, the rising intensity like hundreds of thousands of songs upon songs, all in perfect harmony.

I squint at the tremendous light, and I rise, lifted above anything and everything I could ever imagine. I'm utterly present, perfectly secure, and totally engulfed in love and peace.

Where I had seen the shape of a face before, something like lightning flashes, and the figure disappears into the brightness.

"I love you, Kristen," roars the voice from deep inside the light. "You are not alone, nor will you ever be. I will never leave you."

Then another bright, white flash, and then nothing . . .

"I get it, Andrue, but we've already been hanging around for three days. If I miss another meeting, I'll lose my job."

Alana.

I'm *alive?* Why won't my eyes open? *Alana. A-la-na!* Why can't I speak?

"Look, she moved. Kristen, can you hear me?"

Yes, Steve, I can.

"Kiddo?"

I hear you, too, Mark. If only I could speak . . .

A hand rests on mine. "Hey."

Ethan. I peel my eyelids open and squint against the fluorescent bulbs. Faces — Steve, Mark, Alana . . .

"She won't wake," says an unfamiliar voice. "She's still sedated."

I close my eyes and drift.

Awake again. Lying in the dark. Cold. Tubes and wires everywhere. A woman sleeping in a nearby lounger, an expensive-looking throw tucked up to her neck. Alana. My eyes close again.

"We still need to monitor her, but so far everything looks good. Surprisingly good."

Staggering daylight.

"You're awake." A skinny doctor smiles. "I was telling your friend how well you're doing. Somebody must be watching over you."

"You got that right." Alana leans over, her hair more disheveled than ever. "That somebody is me. Uh, and Ethan."

The doctor pats my hand. "Yep. You weren't breathing and you had no pulse, but your friends fought for you and were able to pull you from the drain before it was too late. You'll probably want to sleep some more. Sedative's not quite worn off."

I wake again. How long was I out this time? I lift my eyes to Alana, who smiles back.

"You look terrible," I say, my voice coming out cracked.

"I should get you a mirror." She snort-laughs, and then rubs her face and plops onto the bed. "You do realize you almost died."

"For a few minutes, I *was* dead."

She nods, wipes her hair away from her face, and then glances at the side of my neck. "I can refer a plastic surgeon. Guy's a genius. He can erase that scar."

My hand creeps up to my neck. Stitches. Swollen, tender flesh.

"Victor's gone," she says. "No trace of him anywhere."

"I saw him. The boat slammed down on his head when it came down on a wave. He just went limp and sank."

"Good. Serves him right. That man was a psycho."

"Any word on Delila?"

"She's still missing, but the police found her letter. You read it?"

"Only the first page."

"She spilled everything, how Victor went nuts buying all kinds of gear so he could spy on you. He had bugs on everything—your car, your phone, inside Mark's hospital room, all over your old apartment." She leans in close. "He even bugged your mom's place. Victor probably heard Steve talking on the phone about our plans to dump the ashes and that's how he knew where you'd be."

I shake my head slowly as I try to digest what Alana's saying. "But how did he get aboard?"

"Captain Jack said there's very little security at the harbor. Anyone who knows how to pick a lock and doesn't look terribly out of place can get access to nearly any boat. Victor simply snuck aboard before anyone got there and hid in the master bathroom below deck."

She rubs her face. "In her letter, Delila also said Victor admitted he was responsible for both hit and runs, and that Valentine was supposed to kidnap you, but since he failed, Victor killed him. Remember that night at the pub when Delila and Legion left to take that call? That was Victor getting Delila out of the way. He knew she wasn't helping him anymore and he didn't want her nearby. She had no idea what was happening that night.

"That man was a psychopath. I hope scavengers ate every piece of him when he sank into the ocean. I still can't get the image of his knife to your throat out of my head. Kristen, that was the worst thing I've ever been through."

"You should've seen it from my end." I try to smile, but it feels more like a wince.

She twists a clump of hair. "When he had you, I felt helpless. I've never had that feeling before. *Never.* When I saw Ethan dragging you up out of the water, you were as pale as a ghost. I thought you were dead. Ten minutes. That's how long it took Ethan to find you and get you back on the deck. And that was good time, too. It was crazy, with the storm and the boat moving all over the place. Mark and Steve almost knocked each other into the water.

"Ethan was a rock, though. He fought to get you aboard and did the whole look, listen, and feel thing, and dove right into CPR. I already had the first aid kit ready and was slapping gauze on you as well as I could, but the tape wouldn't stick because you were soaking wet. Every time I dried you off, more water came onto the boat. And all that blood! It just kept oozing out."

"You cut your finger."

"What?"

"When you were cutting tape, you sliced your finger."

"Yeah. Wow, you must have heard me talking with Andrue when you were sedated."

"No, I—"

"Kristen, it was awful. I thought I'd never see you alive again. You're my best friend, *chérie.* What would I do without you? But then *bam!* Three minutes into CPR, you coughed up water and started breathing again. Mark and Steve already went to call for help, and like your doctor said, we had you breathing on your own again before the first responders arrived. But even when the Fire Captain came aboard, you were still unconscious and oozing blood. That awful tape still wasn't sticking.

"They moved you to their boat and headed toward land. A bigger rescue boat came, too, and they were going to send divers down to look for Victor, but they decided not to because of the conditions. So they led us back to the harbor where we had to talk to police before coming here to be with you. It was awful. Awful. I don't ever want to go through anything like that again."

Alana plops back down on my bed. "They said you were lucky the cut wasn't deeper. No one could believe you survived that, but I'm not surprised. You're a fighter, and Ethan and I killed ourselves trying to save you.

"When they took you away, we were left standing on the deck, covered in your blood." She shakes her head. "My thousand-dollar designer jacket . . . trashed.

"Captain Jack's insurance won't pay to clean up the boat, something about 'crime scene' not being covered. So Ethan's going to have to pay for that — what? Why the face? My work will pay for the jacket, and hey, you're alive. It's a great day."

Alana smiles devilishly. "And that's not all. I'm pregnant. How cool is that?"

So that's why she's looked so awful lately. I smile, without wincing this time. "Congratulations."

"Thanks, but something's still bothering you. What's up, *chérie*?"

"If I tell you, will you promise not to call me crazy?"

She laughs. "Sure, why not?"

"When I was . . . um, gone . . . I was in heaven."

"Whoa, that's like acid trip crazy."

"I'm serious. I left my body and saw myself from above. I saw you and Ethan working on me."

"You were hallucinating."

"No, I saw it. You had a red and white first aid kit next to you."

"All first aid kits are red and white."

"I heard your thoughts, Alana."

"Right."

"Your biggest fear wasn't that you'd never see me alive again. You were afraid I would end up a vegetable, and you couldn't stand the thought of having a vegetable as a best friend."

"I never said that."

"You thought it."

She averts her gaze. "No, I didn't. Kristen, you were messed up. Your mind was playing tricks on you, that's all. Hey, let me grab my laptop. You've got to see my plans for the nursery."

Two weeks later, I'm back at home, my feet perched atop the whiskey barrel coffee table in Mark's library. I would've been home sooner if I hadn't gotten pneumonia from breathing in seawater, but hey, I have no brain damage to speak of, so yay me.

My sketchbook sits open on my lap, a half-drawn patio design taunting me from the page. *What next? What next? What next?* Why am I bothering to finish this sketch? Nina's friend fired me from the job. She was too impatient to stick around and see how long it would take me to recover.

No one expected I would heal this fast. "You were lucky," everyone keeps saying. "The knife caught your external jugular, which was serious, but not an immediate threat." If the knife had cut my interior jugular, or carotid, or trachea, it would've been a different ballgame.

I was lucky Ethan found me in the murky water, and that he was able to get me back on the deck and begin CPR as soon as he did. I was lucky I didn't have brain damage from lack of oxygen. I was lucky Alana was there to help.

"You're so lucky," Alana keeps saying. "My God, you could've died."

As if luck had anything to do with it. It's only because of *my God* that I survived.

The doorbell rings, sending combat boots trudging across the hardwood floor. Laughter fills the entryway. Footfalls approach.

Mark peeks into the pass-through library, his brows as wild as ever. "Kiddo? You have a visitor." He steps away.

Ethan leans over and hugs me gently. "How're you doing?"

"Really good, thanks. Honestly, I can't stop smiling."

He can't stand still. Seems a little jumpy.

"Have a seat. Stay a while."

He settles next to me on the sofa and stares at me all goofy-eyed.

I set my sketchbook aside. "Really, I'm fine, but I'm glad you came. Something's been bothering me."

"Oh? What's that?"

"It's my near death experience."

His eyes light up. "Yeah? What about it?"

"Most people don't accept my story. They don't believe I ever left my body, much less that I went to heaven." I narrow my eyes. "People act like I'm crazy. I explain everything I saw — I even provide details I couldn't have otherwise known — and still people say it was a hallucination. And worse, some say it was just another one of my dreams. I *hate* that. I know when I'm dreaming. Dreams don't have that level of clarity."

My mind races while I rub a faint water ring left on the table, only visible in a certain light. "My mother stood next to me, not a vision, but *her*. And she was smiling. *Smiling*. Harley was there, too. I touched him and felt him purring. I picked him up and absorbed his weight. He was *real*. Jenna and Danielle . . . they were real, too. And Jesus. Ethan, I stood next to Holiness!" I lift my gaze up to Ethan's face. "I just want people to believe what I know in my heart to be true."

He smiles and nods, slowly, with great exaggeration, like he wants me to get something. My stomach clenches. Oh, I get it. Irony. How many times have *I* refused to consider Ethan's beliefs?

"I believe everything you say is true," says Ethan. "And I love hearing about your time in heaven. But I also know this is the kind of story many will have trouble accepting. It's not something people can easily relate to, you know?"

"Yes, I know, and it's so irritating."

"So does that mean you will stop telling people your story?"

"No way. Knowing what I know about heaven, how could I possibly keep that to myself? I was with *Him*, Ethan. I was really with Him. I felt Him and it was an explosion of light, love, and beauty crashing over me like a wave. Oh my gosh, yeah. That's exactly how it felt. Like a wave, reaching over me and splashing down, drenching every cell in my body. And then I was whole — w-h-o-l-e. He told me I wasn't alone and I never would be, and I *believed* Him. Ethan, I wasn't only in the presence of God, I was saturated with it."

"Yes, I believe you were." He nods and his smile grows larger than life.

And then we just sit and gawk at each other like a couple of idiots.

After a minute, he clears his throat and shifts in his seat. "I quit my job in Colorado," he says. "And I got the job they originally offered me at UCLA."

"That's great. So you'll be staying in California?"

"Yep. Staying. Yep, yep, yep." His face pales, and he starts to squirm.

"Why are you acting weird all of a sudden?"

He smiles awkwardly and his focus shifts upward to my forehead. Without a word, he slides to the floor, one knee perched, the other pinned to the ground. His complexion is as white as rice, and his eyes are locked on mine.

My hand flies to my mouth.

"Kristen." His voice cracks. "I love you . . . Lord help me. This is not how I envisioned this, but I've already waited too long, so here goes."

Oh my G—

"I've always known you were the one for me . . . except when I wasn't sure." He shakes his head and pulls a white jewelry box from his pocket. "I had this ring with me when we were on the boat. I was going to do this when we returned to the harbor. Then you went overboard and I thought I lost you. I've wanted to do this for a long time, and I shouldn't have waited so long."

He opens the lid, and the colossal diamond refracts every available ray of light in the room. "I love you," he says. "I can't imagine my life without you. Kristen, will you marry me?"

My jaw drops, as I'm struck mute. My heart pounds against my chest, and still I can't make any sounds come out of my mouth. Ethan's smile fades with each passing second. *Tick, tick, tick—*

"Yes!" I shout. "Yes, yes, *yes*, I'll marry you."

His smile reappears and he slides the ring on my finger. Then he sits back on the couch and we kiss, tenderly, with tears streaming down our cheeks.

A minute later, I bolt upright. "Your mother is going to totally freak out."

The following Saturday, my stomach knots up as I prepare for my meeting with Dorothy. Ethan insists his mother's getting better, says she met a new friend, another patient named Howard, a sweet old man who encourages Dorothy to cooperate with the doctors. Ethan claims that Dorothy is ready and willing to accept me in her life. I'll have to see it to believe it.

Before entering Clearview, Ethan and I stop and link hands. Beneath a heavy gray sky, Ethan prays that our visit with Dorothy will go well, that the mighty hand of God will fall upon us, cast away all darkness, and reveal His blinding glory. Then I cling to my melodramatic fiancé and hyperventilate the entire length of the corridor.

We enter the lobby, where Dorothy sits rigid against a high-back chair. My, but her eyes are cold. Like frozen pools of black ink, smooth and featureless. She nods at us regally, and then insists on speaking with me alone.

"I'm going to grab some coffee while you two talk." Ethan kisses his mother's cheek and pats the top of my head. "It'll be okay," he whispers into my ear, and then he slips away.

I settle into a once-plush velveteen couch and fold my hands into my lap. Several patients shuffle about the lobby and melt into the background — except for one. The bald woman in the orange DayGlo tee. Her gaze ping-pongs around the room, then she bites her lip and plops down next to me. She smells like handmade soap. Rosemary, coconut oil, and honey. Am I making that up, or are my senses that clear? DayGlo fusses with her leg warmers as I turn to my future mother-in-law.

Dorothy squints at my neck. "I have a friend who makes a cream that could erase that mark."

I mess with my hair, trying in vain to cover the scar.

"It don't look so bad," says DayGlo.

Dorothy shifts in her seat, then sighs and glances out the window. A murder of crows squawks like mad, descending upon something below. "That ring on your finger is obnoxious," she says, still facing the window.

"It's a little embarrassing." Why did I say that? I love this ring.

"I've seen bigger," says DayGlo.

Dorothy grimaces at me. "My son can be overzealous."

"Uhhh . . ." I scan her face, but her expression reveals nothing.

DayGlo opens her mouth to speak, but Dorothy stands abruptly and cuts her off. "The sun came out. Let's move to the terrace."

I tag behind like a whipped dog.

We cross a hallway and move toward the door leading outside. A winding path lined with thyme-fringed pavers guides us to the north terrace. Potted orchids smother the patio. The flowers spill from their pots, pouring out in astonishing yellows, whites, and reddish-browns, and in the midst of these blooms sits Dorothy, cold and pale. She brushes her creased polyester slacks, and I do the same with my faded jeans. She glances over. Did I catch a hint of a smile? If I did, it's already gone.

Her eyes frost over. "Tell me what happened to you."

I brace myself. At any minute, her words might shred me into a thousand pieces. But there's something else behind the deep blackness of her eyes. Sadness. A childlike sorrow that tugs on my heart. Like an automated machine having been fed a quarter, I perform. I pin my eyes on Dorothy as I speak. For the first time in my life, I tell another conscious, non-therapist soul what happened to me when I was a little girl. I speak with vivid, excruciating detail, while Dorothy sits and listens without flinching. When I'm finished, I notice I've been crying.

A brief silence passes. Then Dorothy starts to talk. How astonishing, the way she describes what happened to her when she was young, wringing her hands as she spares no detail. I nod with perfect understanding. Dorothy and I have suffered the same sort of hell.

I sneak over to her bench to . . . what? Pet her? My hesitant palm hangs in the air, and she reaches over and wraps her big-boned arms around me, squeezing hard.

How surreal this must appear from above. Dorothy and I, the unlikeliest allies, embracing — weeping together — as my low-cut tee presses against her high-collared blouse. Two wretched human beings, clawing our way through this dry earth. In the midst of blooming orchids, for crying out loud.

Ethan finds us still entangled and grins like a psychopath. I grab him and pin him next to me, and we three chat for more than an hour as if it's the most normal thing in the world.

"Your mother has changed," I say to Ethan on our way out of the hospital. "She wasn't super friendly, but I could tell she tried to be civil. And Ethan, we shared our stories with each other." I clutch my chest and try to catch my breath. "I can't believe I shared that with her before I got the chance to share it with you."

He lifts my chin and wipes the tears from my cheeks. "Everything is happening the way it's supposed to happen."

I smirk at him. "I'm glad you've got this all figured out. Now would you please drive me to the Riviera Village? I've got an emergency session scheduled with Georgina, and if I don't talk to her soon, my head will explode."

CHAPTER 38

NEW YEAR'S EVE

⌒✺〇

A QUARTER MOON BREAKS through the cobalt sky, shining a spotlight from the horizon to the shore. It's like a landing strip, for something beautiful and grand. I cinch up my skirt and let my toes settle into the wet sand, then open my eyes wide and soak it in.

"Careful, kiddo. You'll ruin your wedding gown." Mark offers his hand, imploring me to step back from the water.

"It's cotton, Dad. Besides, the ceremony's over."

A smile spreads across his face as if he can't contain his joy. He glances at the scar on the side of my neck, and then at my collarbone.

"Your mother's cross necklace looks nice on you."

"Thanks." I slip my arm around his waist and rest my head on his shoulder. "A cross would look good on you, too."

"Maybe someday, kiddo. Right now, I'm content with reading your mother's Bible. I find it interesting enough, but I'm not ready to go deeper than that."

I give him a squeeze. "I love you, Mark. I'm glad I didn't lose you."

"I'm glad I didn't lose you, too." He clears his throat. "Alana's talking about you at the bonfire. You might want to go over there and defend yourself."

"Let her dominate circle time. She loves it. How many people are left?"

"About a dozen. Steve and all the other diehards refuse to leave before midnight. Are you coming back soon?"

"Yeah. I'm waiting for Ethan. He said he would watch the water with me."

"He had to take a call. Headed to the parking lot with it."

"You're not planning to walk in, are you?" shouts Alana.

"Guess she got tired of dominating." Mark kisses my cheek and limps away.

"No, Alana. I have no desire to walk in. None."

She lifts her skirt to reveal her garter, the same one she wore on her wedding day—with LHC sewn on the silk heart. "You still have your Lonely Hearts Club garter on?"

I lift my skirt to reveal mine. "Of course."

At Alana's wedding, the garter made my heart ache over Jenna and Danielle. I still miss them like crazy, but now I look at these three pretty letters and it makes me smile a little bit.

I admire the lighted path along the water. So defined. It's like I can see every shadow of every ripple.

"Where do you suppose my mother's ashes are now? Spread across the Pacific? Or maybe even washed up on some distant shore? Of course, she's not really *in* the ashes."

"Ugh, *heaven* again. Are you going to keep bringing that up forever?"

"Yes. You might as well get used to it."

"I'm glad you got to have such a vivid, lovely dream with your mother and Jenna and Danielle, but do you really believe you left your body and went to heaven?"

"How do you explain the fact that I saw your boot?"

"You already knew I lost my boot. Your mind is playing tricks on you. Look, I respect your spiritual beliefs . . . and so you *think* you went to heaven. Great. Keep believing it. But don't try to shove that down my throat. I'm not trying to be mean on your wedding day, but I want you to understand my position.

"And by the way, thanks a lot for getting Andrue sucked into the whole church thing. He never stops talking about it, and now he's joined that Celebrate Recovery group from the church near our house."

She shakes her head. "Maybe it's from his medications or maybe it's all that church nonsense, but he's different now. I had to drag him to the dance circle tonight. I don't know, I guess I like the new Andrue. He's more compassionate and less flighty. I mean, I can handle the bipolar disorder, but if he turns into a Jesus freak, so help me God."

She glances at the scar on my neck, and then turns to the water. "The wedding was nice. A little plain for my taste, but it was perfect for you and Ethan."

I shove her shoulder.

"You know what I mean. A ceremony on the beach, an ocean sunset backdrop, Zingers and Corn Nuts for everyone . . . you love that party-in-a-can-of-cheese style. Having both Steve and Mark walk you up the aisle . . . that was spectacular. Pastor Carl did a good job, too, giving you a Christian service without making it too annoying for the rest of us. If I'm not careful, I might start liking that red-headed nutball."

She glances at my scar again. "So have you gotten any news about your stepsister's whereabouts?"

"*Ex*-stepsister, and no. Hygleson got a letter from her saying she and Legion are planning on coming in, but they aren't ready yet. The letter was long and went on about how Victor was the only father she knew and she understands that he was messed up, but she doesn't think he should be blamed for everything he did. She said Victor's dad was a control freak and would beat Victor for messy penmanship or for grades lower than an A . . ."

"So his childhood was screwed up, too? Well, get in line and join the party. I mean, that didn't give him the right to—"

"Hey, I'm with you. He was messed up, and Delila is, too. But I'm afraid she might blame me for his death."

"Victor has only himself to blame. He was on a suicide mission on that boat, and Delila knows it. So if she blames you, it's *her* problem, not yours. *Ugh*, here comes your husband. Don't look at me like that, I didn't mean it in a bad way. I just wanted to talk longer. Catch you later, 'kay?"

She jogs away and Ethan approaches, his confident stride increasing my heart rate.

"You're breathless," I say. "That must've been some call."

He takes my face in his hands and plants one, holding back nothing. Moments later, he comes up for air. "I'm still pinching myself."

"Me too."

He kisses me again and pulls away. "It's a rescue—three shih tzus wandering around Ewa Beach, not far from where we'll be staying."

"You know people over there?"

"My rescue friends do. The Oahu rescue folks have been trying to catch these dogs for two weeks already. Anyway, we don't have to say yes. It *will be* our honeymoon."

"Are you kidding? It'll only add to the adventure. I'm in."

He wraps his arm around me and we watch the ocean surface as it glistens like wet coal. Then he squeezes my shoulder. "How're you doing?"

I draw in a deep breath and blow it out. "Most of the time, I can't stop smiling. Ever since the boat thing, everything seems clearer. More vibrant and alive. It reminds me of when I got laser eye surgery back in college and it was like, man, I could see each individual leaf on every tree. But I also see my past more clearly than ever before, and sometimes it hits me like a ton of bricks falling onto my chest."

I point ahead. "That black horizon is like my past. I can look right into it, but it hurts. And then something like that moonlight catches my attention, and it's like a flickering, shimmering path leading back from the horizon to here." I wipe the corner of my eye. "It's like . . . like God's love, lifting those bricks off me.

"The dreams are gone. Georgina was right. Once I reached the finish line — once I took the plunge — the dreams disappeared. The urge to walk into the ocean vanished, too, like they were related. Georgina also said she believes the woman who wore red lipstick was symbolic of my mother when she was powerless to protect me from Victor, and the hypnosis is what triggered the re-emergence of my repressed memories."

He nods in agreement.

"So I feel like I've gotten some resolution, but I still have a lot to work through. I know God wants me to forgive Victor, but I can't do that right now, and I wish I could find Delila so I could talk to her face to face. I don't know if I'll ever stop mourning the little girl who had her innocence stolen. And I still have a lot of questions about God. So yeah, I'll still be seeing Georgina regularly, but I'm good, Ethan. I'm really, really good."

Ethan nods and we watch the crashing waves.

"I'm thinking of getting a tattoo," I blurt. "Sometimes I wonder if that woman in the bar was also symbolic of me, of how I felt tainted and powerless. I mean, the snake tattoo on her ankle . . . that's like a reminder of the mistake that ruined my running career, which is a reminder of all the times I've failed."

Ethan glances down. "So does that mean you're thinking of getting a snake tattoo on your ankle?"

I smile wide. "No. I'm thinking of getting a spiral in the shape of a heart, only the spiraled line is jointed, rather than smooth.

"Last week, I was standing behind a woman at the checkout line. There were so many plastic spoons and paper cups in her basket I asked her if she was having a party. She said no, it was for a soup kitchen she just opened, and immediately, I was fascinated by this woman and her giant smile. I wanted to know her and help her, but for some reason I froze. I just stood there while she loaded everything onto the belt. Then I noticed the tattoo on the nape of her neck. It was a dark pink, jointed spiral heart, and when I saw it, I lost my breath. It reminded me of love. Not contrived, cookie-cutter love, but intricate, natural love that follows a broken path until it finds the center."

"That would look great on you."

I smile at Ethan and he smiles back, and we gawk at each other for a few silent seconds. Then Ethan leans in and scoops me into his arms and we kiss again. The blasts of the New Year sound off, and we keep kissing, holding onto each other as if neither one of us wants to let go.

Am I really Mrs. Adams now, clinging to Mr. Adams, as if true love really exists?

If I rise on the wings of the dawn,
If I settle on the far side of the sea,
Even there your hand will guide me,
Your right hand will hold me fast.
Psalm 139:9-10

A Note From Theresa

I CAN'T TELL YOU how many people have asked if Kristen Craemer is actually me. Sure, we both reside in Southern California, we both love to wear flip-flops, and yes, I admit that I can be a little snarky at times — but we are not the same person. My childhood wasn't dark at all. It was light, bright, and warm. I had two mentally-balanced parents who loved me, and even though I did struggle through some sorrow and darkness during my teen and young adult years, I never had to face childhood abuse. I did have a high-pressure career back in my twenties, but I've been a stay-at-home mom far longer than I've worked. Besides that, I hate whiskey and am incapable of wearing high heels.

So if Kristen isn't me, who is she?

In December of 2009, I told a friend that I felt compelled to write a story.

"Then write it," she replied.

So I took a pen to paper and simply made up a character named Kristen — a struggling young professional who had survived a horrifying childhood. *Bam*! Kristen was born, conceived out of thin air.

"Great," said my friend. "Now continue the story. Maybe you can write it online, as a blog . . ."

In January of 2010, without knowing anything else about Kristen, I launched her story as a blog fiction. I set up the site as if *Kristen* were the blogger. Nerdy? Yes, and also a lot of fun.

Every week, I wrote two to three blog posts from Kristen. The posts were inspired by whatever random thing struck me. For example, I once stood behind a tall woman with a high, stiff collar at the grocery store. Everything about this woman — her posture, her thick makeup, her judgmental tone — sent a chill into the air. My writing senses tingled, and Dorothy came to life.

Inspiration came from songs, newsworthy events, the weather, or standout lines from something I read. Every time I wrote a post, I asked myself, "How would Kristen react to this song, event, or whatever . . . and why? I came to know Kristen more and more, and I soon realized that she was a deeply suffering soul. I wanted her to find God, but I was afraid to lead her to him.

Blog fiction is a fringe literary niche, mostly comprised of genres like fantasy, horror, sci-fi, and erotica. There were exactly zero Christian blog fiction stories running online at the time. I resisted the idea of becoming the only writer in the world to do this stranger-than-strange thing. Not only was I a new writer, but I was also a very new and timid believer back then. The mere thought of mentioning "God" online terrified me.

It might offend someone!

Then another writer contacted me to say she was working on a story and was interested in starting her own blog fiction. This woman quickly became a dear friend as she inspired me to write freely about God online. Even though I knew my reach was isolated, I became more and more confident about including God in my writing.

After two years of writing this blog fiction, I'd brought Kristen's story to a reasonable conclusion, so I closed the blog and reworked the story offline. I knew I had a story in my hands, but I also knew it needed a lot of work. I eliminated dead-end plotlines. I cut out scenes that did not move the story forward, even if they were my favorite ones, and I removed more than a dozen unnecessary characters.

Fun Facts: Originally, Kristen had a younger sister, Mark was supposed to die, and Jenna and Danielle were alive and well, each with their own dysfunctional plotlines.

The more I cut out, the more clearly my true story arc appeared. It blew me away. It was like I had blindly created this giant, misshapen mud sculpture, and once I carefully scraped off the dried outer edges, something beautiful appeared.

Then in 2013, I entered the FaithWriters Page Turner Contest, hoping to at least finish in the top ten. My jaw dropped to the floor when I learned that I'd won. That prize awarded me the opportunity to work with some extremely talented women who have helped me to fine-tune this thing that was once just a clump of mud.

Kristen is not me, but there is one area where Kristen and I are the same. Once, we were both lost, and then we were found. That is our common thread. Although I will always insist that Kristen is not me, I will concede that this novel is a tribute to my own faith journey. It is a testament to what it might look like for someone to consider the possibility of God after having spent most of her life fumbling in the dark, living apart from Him.

Many hands, many hours, and many talents have been poured into this manuscript. I feel blessed to even be a part of the process. I'm grateful Kristen's story gets to be told.

Theresa Santy
www.theresasanty.com

CPSIA information can be obtained
at www.ICGtesting.com
Printed in the USA
FSOW02n0244220917
38751FS